HOUSE
of
GOLD

HOUSE
of
GOLD

✦

Natasha Solomons

G. P. Putnam's Sons
New York

G. P. Putnam's Sons
Publishers Since 1838
An imprint of Penguin Random House LLC
375 Hudson Street
New York, New York 10014

Library of Congress Cataloging-in-Publication Data
Names: Solomons, Natasha, author.
Title: House of gold / Natasha Solomons.
Description: New York : G.P. Putnam's Sons, [2018]
Identifiers: LCCN 2018002308| ISBN 9780735212978 (hardback) |
ISBN 9780735212992 (ebook)
Subjects: LCSH: Domestic fiction. | BISAC: FICTION / Historical. |
FICTION / Sagas. | FICTION / Jewish.
Classification: LCC PR6119.O455 H68 2018 | DDC 823/.92—dc23
LC record available at https://lccn.loc.gov/2018002308
p.   cm.

Printed in the United States of America
1   3   5   7   9   10   8   6   4   2

BOOK DESIGN BY LUCIA BERNARD

For my family—David, Luke and Lara

The Emperor was an old man. He was the oldest Emperor in the world. All around him, Death was drawing his circles, mowing and mowing. Already the whole field was bare, and only the Emperor, like a forgotten silver stalk, still stood and waited.

Joseph Roth, *The Radetzky March*

HOUSE
of
GOLD

1911

A man's status can be judged by
the number of his bedding plants—
ten thousand for a squire, twenty thousand for a baronet,
thirty thousand for an earl and fifty thousand for a duke,
but sixty thousand for a Goldbaum.

Often-quoted saying

Vienna, April

—◈—

The Goldbaum Palace was made of stone, not gold. Children walking along the Heugasse, buttoned smartly into their coats and hand in hand with Nanny or Mutti, were invariably disappointed. They'd been promised a palace belonging to the prince of the Jews, spun out of ivory and gold and presumably studded with jewels, and here instead was simply a vast house built of ordinary white stone. Though it was the very finest limestone in the whole of Austria, and had been transported from the Alps to Vienna along a railway line constructed thanks to a loan from the Goldbaum Bank, and hauled by an engine and train owned by the Goldbaum Railway Company, painted resplendently in the family colors of blue and gold and adorned with the family crest: five goldfinches alighting on a sycamore branch. (Wits liked to refer to the coat of arms as "the birds in the money tree.") Inside, the great hall was gilded from the wainscot to the highest point of the domed roof, so that even on gloomy days the light it reflected brimmed with sunshine. Such was the power and wealth of the Goldbaums that on dull days, it was said, they hired the sun, just for themselves.

At night every window was lit with electric light and the house shone out like a great ocean liner buoyed along the Vienna streets. Sometimes at the grandest parties they released hundreds of goldfinches into the hall, so that they warbled and fluttered above the guests. (The birds were accompanied by an extra two dozen maids whose sole task for the evening was to wipe up the tiny spatters of bird shit the moment they appeared on the marble floor; there were limits, it appeared, even to the power of the Goldbaums.) All the same, little happened in the capital and beyond without their say-so, and even less without their knowing it. The emperor himself despised and endured the Goldbaums like inclement weather. There was nothing that could be done. They owned his debt.

The palace on Heugasse was merely the expression of their influence. The real source of their wealth was a small, unobtrusive building on the Ringstrasse. Behind the black door lay the House of Gold: the Austrian branch of the family bank. The Goldbaum men were bankers, while the Goldbaum women married Goldbaum men and produced Goldbaum children. Yet the family didn't consider themselves solely a dynasty of bankers, but also a dynasty of collectors.

The Goldbaums liked to collect beautiful things: exquisite Louis XIV furniture; paintings by Rembrandt, da Vinci and Vermeer; and then the great manors, châteaux and castles to put them in. They collected jewelry, Fabergé eggs, automobiles, racehorses—and the obligations of prime ministers. Greta Goldbaum followed in the family tradition. She collected trouble. This was the trait that Otto Goldbaum most valued in his sister. Before her arrival, his mother had visited the nursery, wallowing in state on a chair reserved especially for this purpose, and, with the assistance of his favorite nanny, explained that in a few weeks' time he would be joined by a little brother or sister. They sipped hot chocolate from a miniature china tea service adorned with the family crest in twenty-four-karat gold, and nibbled tiny slices of *Sachertorte* dabbed with swirls of blue and pink, ordered especially from the grand hotel. Otto listened in silence, watching with considerable suspicion the rise and fall of the baroness's vast belly. And yet when, four weeks later, Greta appeared in the nursery with her own fleet of starched nursemaids, he was not put out in the least. For the first time in his three years Otto had an ally. Greta certainly seemed to belong more fully to him than to the parents who lived downstairs.

The baroness was considered an extremely dedicated mother by visiting the new baby almost every day, while Otto was still summoned to luncheon with the baron and baroness at least twice each week. He listened to the cries and gurgles of his sister through the walls and, when the nurses slept, crept in to lie on the floor of her night nursery. He did this so often that the nurses gave up either berating him or carrying him back to his own bed and set up a little cot for Otto beside her crib.

Greta was not a favorite with the nurses. They could never make her look smart for Mama during her visits. Her hair would not lie flat, like Otto's, but popped up around her head in disordered curls. The rubbed patch at the back, like a monk's round tonsure, did not grow back until she was nearly two. She usually had a cold. As she grew older the maids delighted in telling her, "If you weren't a Goldbaum, you'd be given a proper hiding." Greta told Otto in that case she was frightfully glad she was a Goldbaum, but she felt terribly sorry for all the children who weren't, as it seemed that they must spend much of their time being beaten for petty crimes (melting soap on the nursery fire to make modeling clay; hiding unwanted food at the back of the toy cupboard until it was found weeks later, festering; removing the saddle from the rocking horse and fixing it to Papa's favorite bloodhound and riding the dog around the tulip beds). Greta was frequently sent to bed with nothing to eat but bread and milk. None of this mattered. She had Otto.

His character ran counter to his sister's. Where Greta was impulsive, Otto was careful. She talked and he listened. His hair was perfectly smooth, his part immaculately combed. Where Greta was in constant motion, Otto possessed a stillness that often unsettled his contemporaries, although he did not consider himself quiet, since his thoughts were so loud, his mind always restless and busy. It took Otto time to reach a decision, but once he had done so, he acted decisively. He was of average height and slim, but he fenced and boxed with skill, taking pleasure in the exercise and in anticipating his opponent's game. He considered both pursuits to contain the perfect blend of brutality and elegance.

As Greta grew, so did the trouble. She borrowed Otto's clothes and disappeared for a picnic beside the river, where she was discovered sharing a cigarillo with a pair of lieutenants. She persuaded Otto to take her to the university so that she could listen to one of the astronomy lectures he attended. Otto decided that she looked like a bird of paradise roosting among the thrushes, in her bright blue coat and hat, sitting amid a hundred men in brown and gray suits. He asked her if she liked the lecture. "Adored it. Didn't understand a word." Greta went every day for a week, saying it helped her sleep magnificently. She secured clandestine lessons on the trumpet and became rather good, before the baroness discovered her and put a stop to it. Piano, harp or, at a push, the violin was deemed sufficiently demure. Wind instruments were far too louche; all that work with the *embouchure*. The very word made the baroness blush. Otto developed a spontaneous interest in the trumpet. Another tutor was procured. Otto surreptitiously shared his lessons with his sister and pretended the practice was his. Greta, however, lost interest. Trumpet voluntaries were only fun when they were illicit. Otto accepted that one of his tasks in life was to help his sister out of mischief. For twenty years this had been a source of pride and pleasure to him, and of only occasional exasperation.

If anyone had asked Greta if she wanted to marry Albert Goldbaum, she would have said no, certainly not. But no one did ask. Not even her mother. They asked her all sorts of other things. Which blooms would she like in her bouquet? Roses or lilies? Did she want ten bridesmaids or twelve? Greta replied that she was quite indifferent to the number of bridesmaids. Her only stipulation was an assortment of footmen carrying white umbrellas. Her mother paused for a moment.

"Supposing it doesn't rain?" "Of course it will rain," Greta replied, "I'm going to England."

Greta knew that Baroness Emmeline was tormented by the prospect of appearing inappropriately attired. Three cloaks were to be made to match Greta's wedding dress: one of Arctic fur, one of the finest lamb's wool and another of silk and lace. The baroness insisted that a lady must always have a choice and be prepared for the unexpected, in matters pertaining to the wardrobe at the very least. She invariably traveled with at least three pairs of spare shoes in the trunk of the automobile: a pair of stout leather boots, should the weather turn; a pair of elegant shoes to change into afterward; and a pair of satin slippers, just in case. In case of what, Greta never could ascertain.

She offered no further opinion on the wedding preparations. She acquiesced to every suggestion with such pointed apathy that the baroness ceased to consult her. This suited Greta perfectly. She visited her friends and drank coffee, and changed the subject if any of them were tactless enough to raise the topic of her looming nuptials. The wedding was an unpleasantness to be endured, and for a while it was sufficiently far away that she could pretend it was not happening at all. It stalked her, though, through her dreams. Her fear was indistinct and sinister, something nameless to be dreaded. Only it did have a name. Albert.

"He probably doesn't want to marry you, either," said Johanna Schwartzschild one morning as they sat in the orangery, taking coffee and sweets, some weeks before the wedding. "Perhaps he's in love with someone else. Either way, he might just not fancy it."

Greta set down her cup of coffee in surprise and stared at Johanna, who started to color, perhaps wondering if she'd pushed it a little far and this was why she was not one of the twelve bridesmaids. But Greta was not offended, simply intrigued. Up until then she'd considered only her feelings on the matter, and had taken all the reluctance and resentment as her own. Of course it wasn't pleasant to think that someone else was considering the prospect of marrying you with horror and revulsion, but, she reasoned, it wasn't personal. Albert didn't dislike *her*; he couldn't. He didn't know her. But poor Albert probably didn't think much of marrying some stranger simply because she was his first cousin twice removed and had the right surname. Now he became, in her mind, "Poor Albert" and she began to think of him almost fondly. She rang the bell. A maidservant appeared.

"More coffee, Fräulein?"

"No, thank you, Helga. Tell my mother that I've changed my mind. I don't want roses or lilies. I would like gardenias for my bouquet."

For the first time since her mother had summoned her to her dressing room and informed her that she was to marry Albert and move to England, Greta began to read English novels once again. Her English conversation lessons had still taken place for three hours each morning with the apologetic and sweaty-palmed Mr. Neville-Jones, but in a silent and futile gesture of displeasure she'd set aside English literature for French and Italian. Now, softening toward Poor Albert, she penned herself a firm reading list. Dickens she enjoyed immensely. The hustle and stink of London sounded enchanting, compared to the museum hush and desiccated formality of Vienna. On the other hand, Jane Austen she couldn't get along with at all. There were far too many young ladies far too eager to get married. Mr. Darcy sounded like a bore, and Mr. Bingley worse. She hoped that Poor Albert was nothing like either of them.

Then she discovered *Jane Eyre*. Oh, the thrill of being a governess and being entirely dependent on oneself. The danger and wonder of being alone in the world. Jane Eyre might have been a governess dreaming of becoming a bride, but Greta Goldbaum was the bride dreaming of becoming a governess.

. . .

As Greta walked through the park arm in arm with Otto she saw that the crocuses were erupting beneath the aspen trees, regiments of purple and shining yellow in imperial shades, like thousands of miniature soldiers. There were only tiny patches of snow remaining, shoveled into wet heaps the color of sodden newspapers.

A fluttering notice pinned to a tree caught her eye and she paused to read it. Greta liked these notes. The trees in the park were full of them, like a species of white bird. They were messages from another world—the ordinary one, where people struggled and drank schnapps straight from the bottle, and ate schnitzel and sausage for supper, and owned an ordinary number of trousers. (Greta estimated this number to be something between three and fifty pairs.) The notices on the trees were for lost dogs, rooms to rent, or ladies of low regard advertising their services. The most desperate were the most intriguing: a violinist offering lessons in exchange for a decent meal and a bucket of coal.

To Greta, it was the ordinary and mundane that contained the sheen of glamour. The aura of her name followed her everywhere like a gleaming shadow; she could never escape from its glow. People who were not kind in general were invariably kind to her, or so she was frequently informed by her friends. She suspected that her view of the world was distorted, as if everything she consumed was sprinkled liberally with sugar. She longed to taste life unsweetened.

It was better for Otto, she thought, a little resentfully. His misadventures weren't merely tolerated but encouraged. He'd been permitted to spend six entire months at the Imperial Observatory on the border with Russia, where the winds gusting through the great forests were chilled with the enemy's breath. He'd seen not only stars and comet tails, but Cossacks riding through the plains separating the two great empires, the handkerchiefs covering their faces red and blue in the moonlight. Or so she presumed; Otto had been disappointingly vague on the details in his letters home. There had been far too much about the mathematics of observational stars, and far too little about bandits and Cossacks, or the legendary eastern Jews who thrived in the border swamps and had long red beards, flaming out like Moses's burning bush.

Everything had become imbued with sudden meaning: the silver coffeepot and pats of butter stamped with tiny birds were no longer merely objects, but ciphers. Earlier Greta had remained as the maid arranged the baroness's hair—something she'd not done since she was a child, watching the maid brush and brush the long silvering hair, sleek as the tail of a weasel. Then it was wound round and round, pinned neatly into a smooth wheel. The ivory brush sat on the dressing table and Greta looked at it, knowing that the days of such intimacy were nearly over. When she left the baroness to her coffee, she felt a pang of unexpected tenderness.

"Leaving Vienna feels a little like death," Greta declared to Otto when she joined him at the breakfast table a few minutes later. He glanced at her over his newspaper and, seeing that she was perfectly serious, laughed.

"What do you know about death?" he asked, setting the paper aside.

"As much or as little as anyone," she answered primly while buttering her toast.

Newspapers in four languages were laid out on the sideboard in the breakfast room. Only those in German and French were today's. The Italian and English editions were sent from Milan and Paris, but this always took a day, so they bore yesterday's date, as though those nations were always racing to catch up with the present. Greta supposed that in England this would be reversed and she'd be forever reading the news from home a day late.

A bowl of oranges rested on the table like glossy midday suns. They'd been plucked from the greenhouse early that morning. The fruit was cosseted like a dowager duchess, the glasshouses heated and moistened by solicitous gardeners. Greta liked to disappear into the greenhouses with a novel, pick oranges herself, and peel them with her fingers, slurping them untidily, wiping the juice on her blouse. Once she'd been caught, and the offense reported to the baroness. Her punishment had been to sit in the morning room for several hours while learning to peel an orange with a knife and fork, without soiling her white cotton gloves with a single drop of juice. While she was practicing, the baroness instructed her to sit with an orange between her shoulder blades. She needed to become more like a proper lady, with suitable deportment and decorum, the baroness insisted. Apparently, it started with oranges, the most civilizing of fruits.

"Would you like me to peel you one?" she asked Otto.

"Yes, all right."

He sat back, smiling while she skillfully dispatched the orange with a tiny silver knife and matching fork.

"Now, who will do that for you next week?"

"Who indeed?"

He ate in silence as she watched, both of them aware of this awful list of last times—last breakfast, last day at home, last orange. Otto realized that Greta was right and that her leaving, if not quite a death, certainly marked the end of something.

Under the Goldbaum Palace, Karl was sieving for bones in the dark. He reached into the black water with his net and, raising it, poked among the debris for the sharp point of a bird's wishbone, the round nub of a larger animal's shin. He rested his lamp on the ground, relit it, and replaced his matches in his backpack, trying not to breathe in the oily fumes. Some of the other *Kanaltrotters* had nicknamed Karl "Kanalrat," since he was as at ease in the tunnels and pipes as the fat black rats that scuttled about them, their feet scratching in the dark, rivals in their hunt for bones.

Karl squatted barefoot on the edge of an underground canal and rapidly sifted, again and again. An hour passed, or perhaps four or five. He had no clock and it was always midnight down here. When he was asked where he lived, by the condescending but well-meaning secretaries of the children's shelters he periodically visited, he always liked to say, "The Goldbaum Palace. Just beneath."

It was a fair spot. Porters from the Goldbaum kitchens distributed leftovers every night at the entrances leading to the sewer tunnels, and there was usually something, if you were quick about it. Mostly Karl preferred to sieve in the dark. He'd found all sorts of treasures over the years, the most precious of which he hoarded in his backpack. There was a blue glass button, round and smooth as a washed pebble; a twisted metal spoon engraved with five tiny birds. Every so often he found a coin. Those were silver days, when he stopped fishing at once, packed his belongings neatly away and bought his own supper of stew, bread and beer—and once, when he found a whole ten kronen, a fat roll of apple strudel sprinkled with almonds. He hadn't known what almonds were until he licked them, and at first he'd thought them little slivers of bone.

Mud. Mud. A twig. A dead sparrow, its bones too light to be worthwhile. He raked and sieved. Ribs from a pig roast. Some of the others preferred to sieve beneath the restaurants, where the pickings were richer, but the competition was fierce. There was a hierarchy even down here. At the top came those who hunted for scrap metal, while the bone seekers were at the very bottom. The bigger men took the best spots near the abattoirs or the beer halls, while the boys like Karl were left to sieve wherever they could. He didn't mind. He preferred the quiet of the deeper, narrow channels, where even seasoned *Kanaltrotters* were seized with choking panic. He measured time only by the filling of his bucket. A piece of leather. Sludge. Teeth. Animal or human, he didn't know. Half a sheep's skull with the jaw still attached. The bucket was full.

His lamp had stuttered out, but he could find his way in the dark. He raced back through the channel, splashing through the freezing water, his feet numb. He tried to guess the weight of his bucket: two kilos, three? Five kronen perhaps, if he was lucky. The bones were sopping wet, and he would have to dry them carefully before he could take them to Atzgersdorf to sell to the soap boilers.

The evening of the ball Greta soaked in the bath. She unwrapped a fresh bar of mimosa soap from its scarlet-and-gold paper and washed her hands and face. She did not consider who had made the soap or where it had come from. Once she had dried herself, she sat in her new white dress, in a chair beside the fire; tucked her knees beneath her chin; and surveyed her girlhood bedroom. It was already devoid of many of her most precious things. Anna had packed a dozen crates to be sent ahead to England and her new home. They had been filled, at the baroness's direction, with wedding jewelry, dresses from Paris, an eighteenth-century Persian rug, a porcelain dish for earrings that once belonged to the Empress Josephine. Greta had little interest in these objects. They were merely to remind her soon-to-be in-laws that the new bride might not have had quite the wealth of the London family, but she was still a Goldbaum. With Anna's assistance, Greta had stowed her own valuables, which were of a different order than her mother's selections. There was a painted book on hummingbirds that Otto had given her on her eighteenth birthday. The illustrations were hand tipped, but to her shame there was a fat fingerprint of chocolate on the cover. The pictures had gone from her bedroom walls. Already it wasn't hers, she decided. It was bereft of those things that had made it home.

"Sit," commanded Anna, bustling into the room and pointing to the chair before the dressing table. "I've brought Helga to try again with your hair."

Greta sighed and moved over to sit before the mirror, and fiddled with a box of hairpins as the two maids squabbled and pulled at her hair, trying to cajole it into obedience.

"I don't know why you're bothering. It won't work."

"The baroness insisted. She's asking for you."

"Leave my hair, then. I'll go and see her now. I'll tell her you fought valiantly. The enemy could not be defeated."

Greta stood and allowed the two girls to smooth and pat the folds of white silk and adjust the beadwork around her shoulders.

"It's a shame Mr. Albert Goldbaum can't see you. You're a picture," said Anna, admiring her handiwork.

"Yes, poor Albert," agreed Greta without conviction. He had caught a bad cold in London and was unable to travel. Tonight's wedding party lacked a groom, which Greta acknowledged was inauspicious. Who knew what Albert would make of her? She was taller than was considered fashionable, her hair thick and untidy, her hands large, or "expensive," according to the jeweler who had measured her fingers for the engagement and wedding bands. Her mouth, however, was perfectly shaped. Not that people were ever given much of a chance to notice because, as the baroness complained, it was usually talking.

Greta's photograph had already been dispatched to England, no doubt to reassure Albert that his mysterious bride had sufficient charms. No one had thought to send her a picture of him. He was young. He was a Goldbaum. What possible objection could she have?

She turned to leave, but Anna cried out, "Your shoes! You're wearing the wrong shoes. You can't wear the green ones. The white silk are for tonight."

"They're a half size too small. I swear Mother does it on purpose."

Anna nodded sympathetically. "All the same. The baroness—"

"For goodness' sake."

Resignedly Greta wedged her feet into a new pair of low-heeled dancing shoes.

She walked along the east wing to her mother's suite of rooms, a fleet of Gretas dressed in identical white flanking her in the vast mirrors. From below she could hear the strains of the orchestra, strands of Strauss drifting up, warm and sweet as patisserie baking in the cafés along Herrengasse. Footmen in their finest livery stood regimentally on either side, their sideburns groomed and waxed. To the consternation of the recruiting sergeants, her father always hired the tallest, most handsome men lining up outside the recruitment offices of the cavalry of His Apostolic Majesty. Baron Goldbaum sent along representatives of the household staff, who always offered generously more than a soldier's pay. The livery, in splendid blue and gold, was a uniform of sorts for those who hankered after military tailoring; but, the under-butler liked to joke, unlike joining the army, in the Goldbaums' service there was no risk of death. The recruits smiled at this little joke: apart from an all-too-brief skirmish with Serbia, there hadn't been a decent war for years. What use is a soldier in peacetime?

Greta passed two footmen, poised on stepladders, starting to light the five hundred candles on the Montgolfier chandelier at the head of the great staircase. The baron had declined to convert it to electricity, preferring the effect of candlelight as it diffracted through the soda glass. It was not he who had to balance on a ladder at the top of the staircase with a burning taper. After one of the footmen had set fire to his hat while lighting the candles, permission was granted to remove hat and wig in order to light the chandelier—a progression toward informality that was considered by the baroness almost as dangerous as the risk of immolation. Otto, however, more sympathetic and intrigued by mathematical problems, had spent an afternoon devising a system that denoted the order in which the candles ought to be lit, with the least risk. The baron stipulated that this regimen must be followed, and Greta noticed a third footman carefully holding Otto's diagram out of reach of the flames.

She knocked and was admitted to her mother's dressing room. The baroness reclined on a daybed, sipping black tea with lemon, her usual ritual before a party. The cream walls had turned yellow in the gloom, while the red roses on the dresser appeared black. A pair of fat cherubs played shuttlecock with a dove on the frescoed ceiling. The curtains were tightly shut, a coal fire flickering, and Greta grimaced at the stuffiness. She turned on a light and asked the maid to open a window, then she leaned out and breathed in damp spring air. Oil lamps were being lit across the gardens, and through the darkness she could just discern steam rising from the greenhouses. She glanced back to her mother, sitting stiffly in gray lace, a cobweb of diamonds around her throat.

"Did you love Father?"

The baroness looked up at Greta in surprise. They did not have these kinds of conversations.

"Well, not at first, of course. I knew him a little before we were married. I didn't dislike him."

"And now?"

"I've grown very fond of your father."

Fond as a pond, thought Greta. It was a soggy, limp sort of affection. At that moment she was overcome with pity for her mother, and to the astonishment of both of them, she sat down on the couch beside the baroness and threw her arms around her. She wanted to cry, but did not, knowing that the baroness wouldn't like that at all.

"I shall miss you. Really I will," said Greta.

"Then I hope you will write. You're usually a dreadful correspondent," said the baroness.

Greta sat back and looked at her mother, at the familiar blue eyes, not sapphire-bright, but a watery, over-washed sort of blue. In this light she couldn't see a single line or crease on her skin. When she smiled, the baroness was beautiful, only she didn't smile very often. Greta noticed that on the tray beside the glass of tea was another glass, empty, which smelled rather strongly of schnapps.

The baroness took Greta's hand in her gloved one.

"My dear girl, do you know everything you need to about the 'unfortunate side of marriage'?"

"You mean coitus?" asked Greta.

"Oh God," said Baroness Emmeline, rolling her eyes. "Always such language from you." Clearly one glass of schnapps had been insufficient.

Greta toyed for a moment with asking her mother to furnish her with spectacular detail, and then she relented.

"Oh, I know all about it. Otto is a scientist, after all. He never could keep a discovery from me. Years ago at the lake house he found a fascinating book on cattle husbandry—"

"Enough!" said Baroness Emmeline, mostly in relief. "Just remember that, regrettable as it is, that unfortunate part of the business is your duty. Never refuse Albert more than one time in three. But"— she warmed to her topic, a little flush of schnapps in her cheek—"do not accept him every time. A man must be kept on his toes, uncertain as to whether he shall succeed."

"One time in three? Not one in four, now and then? Because if *every* third time I refuse him, then he'll know I'm about to say no, and he won't be on his toes at all."

The baroness fixed her with a cool glare.

"One in three. No more, no less."

They sat in silence for a few moments, Greta's bravado dissipating like popping champagne bubbles as she tried not to think about going to bed with a stranger, in less than a week. She was tired, her feet chafed in her too-small shoes and she felt anger with her mother, pooling in the pit of her stomach like undigested food from a too-rich dinner. She glanced up to meet her mother's eye and spoke slowly.

"When I'm a mother, I shan't be like you. I shall see my children every day. And I shall kiss them and hug them and let them leave little traces of snot on my shoulder like the trail of a snail. And they will know that I love them."

Greta kissed her mother on the forehead and left her alone in the darkening room. Baroness Emmeline reached for her glass of schnapps, to find it already empty.

"Don't you know?" she said, but Greta did not hear.

. . .

There had been much discussion as to how to open the ball. It ought to have been Greta dancing with Albert, but Albert was not there. In the end Greta danced with her father. Baron Peter was a good dancer. It was one of the things about him that his wife was quite fond of. He looked elegant as he stepped out with Greta, the superb tailoring discreetly concealing his growing paunch (a part of her husband of which the baroness was notably less fond). His mustache was waxed, his sideburns combed par excellence, and he looked every inch the proud papa. He steered Greta along the room in a slow and imperial waltz, with five hundred pairs of eyes watching. The room was so long, and the beat so slow, it took them two whole minutes to reach the far end. Hundreds of fans fluttered like a flotilla of tropical butterflies, concealing the whispering mouths of the watching women. The room smelled of powdered bodies and gardenias. Ten thousand stems filled the ballroom in hundreds of vases, perfuming it with an overpowering sweetness. Greta and Baron Peter spoke softly, trying to ignore the onlookers.

"Just laugh at Albert's jokes," said the baron.

"What if they're not funny?" asked Greta.

"Laugh at them anyway."

"Did Mama laugh at your jokes, then?"

"Well, no. But I always thought it might be nice."

He sagged and Greta squeezed his hand. "Mama doesn't laugh at anyone's jokes. I wouldn't take it personally."

"No, you're quite right," agreed the baron, cheering up a bit.

"On the other hand, I'm not sure if I ever heard you tell one," said Greta slowly. Then perhaps he'd always wanted to try, and she'd been too afraid of him to listen, and now she was leaving and it would soon be too late. "Why don't you tell me one now, and I promise to laugh."

The baron frowned and was quiet for a few moments, considering. "I can't think of a single joke," he said at last, his voice full of such disappointment and regret that Greta couldn't help throwing back her head and laughing with such fulsome enthusiasm that the baron began to laugh too, a full-bodied chuckle that threatened to release the carefully concealed paunch from its restraint. The whisperers stationed around the ballroom all commented to one another how agreeable it was to see such a happy bride (despite the lack of a groom), and how charmingly close the baron was to his daughter.

At eleven o'clock the dancers were summoned to supper by a silver swan. The automaton had been made by a jeweler and watchmaker in Paris, who was eager to demonstrate a skill so remarkable that it lingered on the boundary between mechanics and magic. A footman donned a hat with matching silver brocade and turned the handle; then, as the guests gathered to watch, the full-sized swan swam to life. The thousands of silver feathers in its plumage ruffled; the muscular neck stretched and turned to gaze at Greta with cool black eyes. A tune tinkled and the swan struck out into the mirrored water for a tiny, wriggling fish. It swallowed and was still. The music faltered and stopped. The guests laughed and applauded, the gentle thud of clapping gloved hands like distant horses on soft ground.

The baron and baroness led the guests into the dining room. Most followed, but some slid into a side chamber set up for games of baccarat, whist, and tarock, being hungrier for cards than anything else. In the dining room a battalion of footmen and maids in the family shades of blue and gold flanked the walls. Glossy candles ringed with pleats of gardenias sat on long banqueting tables. There might have been no pork loin or lobster or oysters or plump Austrian sausage, but there was a vast and bloody chateaubriand with a jug of Béarnaise, while a special table commissioned by Baron Peter and inlaid with a marble map of Europe was set aside for cheese. Emmenthal and a large slab of Gruyère roosted on the Swiss Alps, while a snowy wheel of Camembert rested in northern France, a cliff of Parmesan sat on Italy, and a forest of smoked cheeses were sprinkled across the Austrian Empire. Only one table was set apart from the rest, where the more religious and observant members of the family and their friends gathered, a little furtively, conscious that fewer and fewer of the city's Jews kept kosher nowadays, yet unwilling to dispense with the laws themselves. The baron and baroness were excellent hosts and even if, in private, the baron may have partaken of a sample of ordinary pork schnitzel, they ensured that all their guests were meticulously cared for. At the end of the meal, if there was any chance that a kosher meat plate had been accidentally sullied with a stray slice of Roquefort, it was broken and discarded. Several dinner services were dispensed with in this manner every year.

Greta found it was too hot and too loud, the chatter and shouts of laughter pushing against the notes of the orchestra, which played louder and faster to compete with the noise. She noticed Johanna in a pink silk dress sitting with a few of their friends, picking at plates of cold chicken and plum dumplings. They waved at her to join them, but it seemed to her as if she'd already left and their voices were floating to her across the sea.

"I'm going to get some air," she said, rising and hurrying from the dining room before any of them could follow.

She slipped into the crowded chamber behind the ballroom and then through a door into the gardens. She could see a scattering of dancers in the ballroom through the great arched windows, silently turning and turning. It was cool outside and a feathering of frost edged the lawn. She sat down on a stone step, took off her shoes, and, with considerable relish, flung them into a rosebush.

"Not your best plan," said a voice behind her.

Greta turned and saw Otto. She smiled and shrugged. "On the contrary. If I can't find them, I can't possibly put them back on."

She rubbed her toes and prodded a round blister on her heel. She did not ask Otto why he was out there alone. He'd always loathed parties. He didn't object to dinners with friends (fellow scientists), but dances with endless acquaintances bored him. Otto, unlike Greta, was rarely compelled to partake in things he did not enjoy. He produced a hip flask from his pocket and handed it to her. She took a swig, spilling cognac down her chin.

"You will come and see me, won't you?" she asked, trying to keep the trill of desperation from her voice.

"Well, I'm terribly busy and you're terribly tiresome, but yes. I might even be in Cambridge before the end of the year."

"And that's in England?" asked Greta, teasing.

Otto flicked a leaf at her.

She grabbed his hand and half-cajoled, half-dragged him to the lowest part of the garden, running barefoot across the gravel, the stones cold and sharp beneath her feet. The night was yellow and full, and Greta imagined she could hear the hum of the stars. Somewhere to the east was the Danube, and breathing deeply, she could almost smell it, a spool of black coiling and uncoiling in the dark. At the stone edge of a pond they paused, observing a tiny moon tremble on the surface. A white statue of Venus watched them mournfully, clasping her sopping dress to her marble bosom. Greta let go of Otto's hand, hitched up her skirts and climbed in. The water was deeper than she remembered, reaching almost to her knees.

"Oh, come in, don't be a sissy," she cried.

Otto sighed and unfastened his shoes and socks, attempted to roll up his trousers and stepped in. He gave a shout at the cold.

"Isn't this better than the party?" Greta asked happily.

Otto reached into his jacket for the cognac. "I'm standing in a freezing pond in wet trousers. And, yes, it is infinitely better."

Above them they heard the scuffle of doors opening and the sound of voices on the terrace. Johanna's voice hissed across the garden, "Greta? Where are you?"

Greta waited for a moment before calling out, "Down here!"

A minute later Johanna appeared with a footman bearing a lantern. His face did not falter as he observed Greta and Otto in the pond.

"Baroness Emmeline is asking for you," said Johanna breathlessly. "You've missed the whole kerfuffle. There was nearly an international incident. The wife of the British ambassador was dancing with the foreign minister, and then the Russian ambassador cut in and started to dance with her and the foreign minister was furious!"

"So there's going to be a duel?" asked Greta, suddenly interested.

"No such luck," said Johanna. "The British ambassador stepped in and smoothed things over. Oh yes, and now you're supposed to dance with him. The British ambassador. Not any of the others."

"God forbid," said Otto drily.

Greta sighed. "Well, I suppose it is a little cold out here."

She climbed out of the water and let go of her skirts, unpeeling them as they stuck to her wet legs. She trailed after Johanna back to the house. Otto, as he followed a few minutes later, noticed the line of wet footprints straggling across the hall. As he walked into the ballroom and watched Greta dance a two-step with a slight, elderly English gentleman, he wondered whether anyone else would notice that beneath her floor-length gown she danced barefoot, with dirty feet.

Behind the Goldbaum Palace a seemingly endless stream of *Kanaltrotters* emerged from a round tunnel entrance near the river's edge and joined an orderly queue, as if waiting patiently for the morning tram to bear them to offices along the Ringstrasse on a Monday morning. Karl was among the last of them. He was in no hurry. The stars were unfathomably bright, after the darkness underground. Somewhere music played. The Goldbaums always distributed leftovers after a party. Seasoned *Kanaltrotters* watched for the orchestra arriving at the palace: the more numerous the musicians, the grander the party and the more plentiful the leftovers. Today someone had counted twenty violin cases and a vast bell-shaped instrument in a case like a coffin, dragged along the pavement on a set of wheels. Karl had high hopes. He slunk forward, keeping his backpack close. Men slipped past, hands and mouths full, pockets bulging as they scattered into the dark, some vanishing down the tunnels and others sliding away into the city streets, as smooth as shadows.

A row of half a dozen servants from the Goldbaum Palace stood behind a long table. One of the serving women was young and pretty. As he shuffled closer he saw that the dark hair pinned above her neck was as smooth and polished as the surface of a nut. He wanted to reach out and touch it with his finger. She handed out large hunks of bread as the stout woman beside her ladled food into the outstretched mugs and bowls of the men. Karl rummaged among the treasures in his backpack for his tin mug. Tonight he would sleep with a full belly. He must be careful and make himself eat it slowly or the cramps might make him sick, and that would be a waste. He watched the woman with the lovely hair. She glanced down at her basket of bread and, seeing it was nearly empty, muttered something to the large woman beside her and hurried back to the palace, basket on her hip. Another servant took her place and handed out chunks of black bread from a different basket.

Karl reached the front, but lingered, letting others shove their way in. He wanted his bread from the pretty girl.

A pair of older men pushed past him. One smiled toothlessly at him. "Kanalrat," he said, with a nod. Karl grunted in reply.

The large woman at the front noticed Karl hanging back.

"You—you're not hungry?" she called.

Karl shrugged. He was no hungrier than usual.

"Let the little one through," she said to the older men in front.

Karl shook his head. "I'm waiting for the pretty one. The one with the nice hair. I want my supper from her."

The woman laughed, so that her significant bosom shook. "Beggars with requests. Would you like to see a menu while you're at it?"

Karl ignored her. The smell of the food made his belly grumble and churn. He began to regret his decision. What did it matter if he was handed his bread from a girl with shining hair? Men shuffled in front of him. He began to feel dizzy, his legs spongy. She was coming back, basket perched on her hip, heavy now.

"Anna, you've an admirer here," called the woman with the bosom. "Won't have his bread from anyone but you."

Karl elbowed his way to the front.

Anna had a snow-dust of flour on her cheek from the bread. She didn't smile and did not meet his eye, only held out the bread, passing him his portion.

"Thank you, Anna," he said.

She made no reply, but as Karl walked away, his mug full of food, he saw that she'd pressed two pieces of bread into his palm.

Goldbaum Trans-Europe Express, Jura, May

Up till now Otto had relished journeys on the family train. The Gold-baum Trans-Europe Express had borne them to summers at their villa on Lake Geneva every July, to the opera in Paris and to visit cousins in Frankfurt or Berlin. Otto had even ridden the train to the Russian border with his colleagues from university (at the baroness's insistence—she wouldn't hear of his traveling on an ordinary passenger train, even in a private saloon carriage). He never slept so well as in his bedroom on the train, picturing himself shrunk very small and fitting into a toy train speeding across an open atlas of Europe. He always instructed his valet to leave the blinds undrawn, so that he could lie in bed looking out at the stars through the mist of steam and watch the moon rise and sink, a bubble in the dark. This trip was different. He wanted it to be slower, but it seemed faster.

Greta's melancholy was catching. It spread through the few passengers like the measles. Otto understood that she was uneasy about her forthcoming marriage, and he was sympathetic, but her predicament also served to remind him of his own fate. For the present he was left to pursue his own course, a degree in physics and astronomy at the university in Vienna, a semester at the department in Berlin and a heavenly summer of research at the observatory on the easternmost reaches of the empire. But he knew that this respite from his fate was temporary. Sooner or later—and Otto had a sense of foreboding that it would be sooner—he would have to leave his love and enter the bank.

He hated it; he hated the smell of the cedar paneling and the whispering of the clerks, the scratching of their pens and the yellow electric light, and the stultifying luncheons with all fifteen partners. Yet he knew it must come. He couldn't exactly plead that he didn't have a head for numbers.

He wondered what it would be like to be a regular man. He did not fool himself that he wanted to be poor, merely ordinarily wealthy. He would step off the train at the next station and become simple Herr Schmitt and live in a pleasant hotel. He rebuked himself: the thought was absurd.

The only passenger who appeared unaffected by the general air of dejection was the British ambassador. Sir Fairfax Leighton Cartwright was traveling as the Goldbaums' guest to Paris, and Otto found himself seeking out the older man's company. Sir Fairfax was a gentleman, author and diplomat in late middle age, with a splendid mustache and fabulous tales of the East. Otto considered there was something terribly English about appointing a novelist as ambassador. But then part of his role was to promote better relations between nations, and perhaps his imagination was so powerful that, by thinking it, he could make it so. Sir Fairfax marveled over everything with boyish pleasure: the specially adapted chandeliers, with rubber plugs separating the crystals so that they rang out only when the train traveled at the very highest speeds; the Lalique glass panels in the saloon showing sylvan ladies dancing with tropical birds. Most of all, the ambassador was transfixed by the vast panorama painting that depicted the route of the Goldbaum Trans-Europe Express—all twelve hundred miles of it compressed into a painting half a mile in length. The painting was displayed in a wooden case with a large glass panel and was kept inside the observation car, with only three or four yards of it being visible at a time. Every hour one of the attendants would fit a handle into a mechanism at the side of the box and wind the painting on another few yards, so that it always reflected scenes through which the train was about to pass: the lights of the royal palace in Budapest, wheat fields pricked by bloody poppies or steamers on blue lakes. On the hour the ambassador would be standing beside the cabinet, gleeful as a schoolboy, waiting to see the panorama unfold.

In the evening they all sat together in the dining saloon, a miniature version of the exquisite dining room of the château at Saint-Pierre. The dining chairs were upholstered in Moroccan leather and the table was polished walnut, although it was only able to seat twelve, being narrower and smaller than the original at the château, which could seat forty-five. At first it was a subdued party. They drank burgundy from the family vineyard and spooned up veal consommé, as clear as glass, swimming with tiny white noodles. The galley was cramped and, despite all the modern conveniences, oppressively hot. The knives on the rack rattled like an army of sabers around every bend. The family knew none of this, though. It wouldn't have occurred to any of them—even the liberal-minded Otto—to consider something like a kitchen. Food appeared magically, perfectly hot, perfectly prepared, and the attendants were so skilled that not a drop of consommé sullied the perfectly starched tablecloth while they served the diners, even as the train roared along at its incredible top speed of 82 miles an hour. The baroness roused herself to inquire after the ambassador's wife and children. Otto knew that she wasn't the least bit interested but liked to ensure that standards, even of conversation, were strictly observed.

Greta ate little and barely stirred herself, even to annoy her mother. As they finished the final course—plates of Bohemian apricot *liwanzen* pancakes—the ladies withdrew to the parlor to take coffee, while the men remained to drink port and Madeira. Sir Fairfax declined a cigar, leaning forward with an unhappy sigh.

"Perhaps now is the time to discuss a little business, Baron?"

"With pleasure."

"The empire wishes to modernize its army. It desires once and for all to heave itself into the twentieth century. On this matter, at least, the emperor and the crown prince are in agreement." Sir Fairfax spoke carefully, his boyish demeanor suddenly serious, the sixth-former promoted to head prefect.

The baron nodded. "Yes, so I understand. There was some discussion as to whether the navy needed dreadnoughts. Both cannot be financed."

"The army is to have its way."

Otto glanced at the ambassador in surprise. The Goldbaums prided themselves on always having the best information. Knowledge was as valuable a commodity as money, and the Goldbaums' trade depended upon it. Information was the seed planted across Europe so that the money trees could grow and bear fruit. Presenting the baron with intelligence that he had not already discovered for himself was unusual. Otto wondered whether his father merely feigned ignorance. In either case, he did not seem put out, and demurred to the ambassador.

"It is a very large sum of money that is required. I'm not willing to provide all the capital. The loan is also being discussed in Prussia. But"—he paused with a smile—"you, Ambassador, do not want Germany to lend money to Austria. You wish me to talk to my French cousins."

"I do. This loan should not come from Germany, but from France. I want to further the good relations between France and your magnificent nation."

The baron laughed at the flattery. "You do not want Austria-Hungary indebted to Germany. It is better for you if we are beholden to France. But why stop at France? You should see if the British government will lend the funds. Then your nation and ours will be firm friends. We cannot do what the Germans tell us if you have paid for our army."

Sir Fairfax shook his head. "I regret they will not. However, the French government will consider the loan, if it is shared with the House of Goldbaum."

"I shall discuss the matter with the Paris House," agreed the baron. "But we are perfectly autonomous. Baron Jacques and Henri will make their own decisions."

"I would ask you to urge it in the most positive terms. In Britain we have stopped considering the French as our natural enemy. It's German ambition that keeps me up at night. The English and the Austrians, the king and the emperor and the archduke, all want the same thing: peace. War is grotesquely expensive, in every sense."

"No one is talking about war, Ambassador."

"Let us all do our bit to keep it that way."

The baron then made a remark about the vintage of the dessert wine, and Sir Fairfax, the ideal diplomat, immediately recollected the terrific late-August hail of 1890 and its regrettable effect upon Burgundian vineyards. They spoke no more of politics, money or war.

The train paused long enough on the Swiss border for passports to be stamped and then continued on its way, hurtling through the mottled foothills of the Jura. Here and there the higher peaks had their tops sliced off by clouds, like boiled eggs. Greta did not join the others for breakfast. She asked Anna to prepare her a bath. She waited as the maid filled the large enamel tub with hot water, ladled in perfumed bath salts, set out armfuls of linen towels pressed with lavender and then left her alone. But instead of climbing in, Greta opened the lace curtains, strictly against the baroness's orders, and stood naked at the window and watched France stream past: the empty fields, the raked soil drenched in the pink glow of morning, shoots of vivid green pricking the surface. Here and there dark pine forests or a silver river trailed the railway companionably for a while, before veering away. They roared past a farmer at a level crossing, trying to mend the wheel on his wagon, his small son perched on a hay bale, staring open-mouthed in wonder at the train. Greta doubted he'd even noticed the naked girl standing at the window.

Later, she slipped into the observation car and sat alone with a hot chocolate that she did not drink and a magazine she did not read. She stared out of the window so lost in thought that she didn't hear Sir

Fairfax enter the carriage and speak to her. He cleared his throat and spoke again.

"Where are we traveling through now, Fräulein Goldbaum?"

She started and then smiled at him. "Near Dijon. We should arrive in Paris before lunchtime. I expect you'll be relieved to be free of us."

"Not in the least. And I hope we shall see one another again in England. I'm an old friend of your fiancé. Well, of his father's, I should say. I have known Albert since he was a boy."

Greta turned eagerly to look at the ambassador, like a sunflower swiveling to face the sun.

"Really you have? What is he like?"

Sir Fairfax sat down on a low sofa opposite her and frowned, considering.

"He's not a talker. He doesn't rattle away, like some young men. I suppose he's what we English call 'reserved.' He's a naturalist. Always collecting things. Traipsing off through the countryside with his butterfly net. He makes remarkable drawings. And of course he has cabinet upon cabinet of the things."

"Butterflies?"

"And moths. Beetles. Silkworms. Quite remarkable."

Greta tried to appear intrigued rather than repulsed. She imagined herself mounted and pinned in his collection among the butterflies.

"Is he handsome?"

The ambassador chuckled. "I'm afraid you're asking an old man these questions. I'm not entirely qualified to answer."

Greta sighed and the ambassador relented.

"I understand ladies consider his person attractive. He's a little taller than average and usually—this dratted cold aside—in excellent health from all his—"

"Striding about with butterfly nets."

"Yes. That's the ticket."

Greta lounged back in her chair and stared out of the window, trying to concentrate on the combed vineyards and the shoals of cloud shadows trawling the low hills.

"His mother is a wonderful woman. Lady Goldbaum is an excellent hostess and a talented gardener."

"A gardener?"

"Yes, the gardens at Temple Court are something to behold. She's established the largest collection of rhododendrons in Europe and the . . ."

At this point Greta stopped listening. It struck her that she'd spent a good deal of time considering Albert, and she'd created an affectionate, if fictional, portrait of him in her mind, while having barely considered the other members of her new family at all. They were to live for the first year with Albert's parents at Temple Court, before moving into their own house on the estate. Lady Goldbaum had written a very obliging letter to Greta, suggesting that she would wish to furnish and oversee the rebuilding of the house herself, in her own and Albert's taste (as though they already shared a harmonious matrimonial view, despite not having met), and until it was ready they would be most welcome—no, joyfully embraced—in the family home. Greta shifted uneasily, unwilling to acknowledge that her initial happiness was as dependent on her relationship with her mother-in-law as on that with her husband. After all, when the honeymoon was over, Albert would spend the week in London and would return to Temple Court with his father only on weekends. There would be long days to while away with Lady Goldbaum and her remarkable rhododendrons. Greta began to dread that they would be very long days indeed.

"What is Albert's brother like?" she asked, interrupting and then coloring at her own rudeness.

"Clement?" asked Sir Fairfax hesitantly.

Greta nodded. Albert was the younger brother and it was unusual among the Goldbaums for the younger son to be married first. No suitable Goldbaum bride had yet been found for Clement.

"I like him," said Sir Fairfax carefully.

"But some do not?"

"No, no. If Albert is somewhat reserved, I'm afraid that Clement is desperately shy."

And fat, thought Greta. This was the only thing she knew with any certainty about the future Lord Goldbaum. When the baroness had first told her she was to marry an English Goldbaum, she'd presumed her mother was speaking of Clement, famed throughout the family for his astonishing girth. When she'd realized it was to be the younger brother, she'd been so relieved that she'd had to sit down on the baroness's dressing room floor with her head between her knees.

"Clement plays chess," said Sir Fairfax after a pause. He whispered it as though confiding some great deviancy.

"Chess?" said Greta in the same low tone. "That is not so very bad, is it?"

It was an unusually inexpensive pursuit for a Goldbaum.

"Anything done to the exclusion of all else is not healthy," said Sir Fairfax, choosing his words with such delicacy that Greta remained unable to grasp the problem. She considered the prospect of her new family with little relish: one a lover of plants, one a lover of insects and another with an apparently unhealthy passion for chess. She wondered whether she could disappear in Paris.

Paris, May

—⋅⟩⋅⟨⋅—

The French and Austrian branches of the family sat together on the southwest terrace of the Esther Château, the ladies wrapped in blankets with hot-water bottles at their feet, the men warmed by Bordeaux, discussing old friends and foes with equal affection and pleasure, and all the while Henri's laughter mingled with the fluted notes of a blackbird. Greta had always liked Henri; as a boy he'd possessed a sharper nose for trouble than Greta herself.

Early summer had snuck into the parterre below. The planting was rigorous and absolute. Beds of white begonias alternated with marigolds planted in precise rows, like spots in a children's dot-to-dot book—looking at them gave Greta the same feeling as when Anna combed her hair back so tightly that it stretched her skin and made her head ache. To her delight, she noted a single stray red begonia sailing amid a flotilla of white ones. She smiled at its solitary rebellion. It made her think of Henri.

He sat between Greta and Otto and, on hearing of Albert's absence from the bridal ball, and Greta's subsequent midnight walk in the pond, was seized with such glee that he had a coughing fit and she had to give him a sip of water from her glass.

"Why didn't Albert come?" he asked.

"He had a cold."

"Oh dear. Poor fellow. To be kept in London by a sniffle."

Greta silently agreed. It was a tremendous pity that she wasn't here to marry Henri. Marriage to him, she imagined, might be rather fun. She wondered why their parents had never considered it. After all, she'd known Henri all her life, and she *liked* him. Every July the Goldbaum Trans-European Express had taken Baroness Emmeline and her children first to Paris and then, after a week or more at the château, had carried them—along with Henri—to summer on Lake Geneva. Even the baroness's severity had been punctured by Henri's charm. She'd been known to sip Madeira wine in the evenings with a sprig of jasmine tucked behind her ear. In recent years Henri and Otto had only joined them for the last fortnight in August. Those two weeks were heavenly days, and the only ones when Greta remembered laughing. She was not in love with Henri, but, as she remembered her father's advice, she knew she would never have had to pretend to laugh at Henri's jokes.

"Have you met Albert? What's he like?" she asked him.

Henri looked at his cousin with surprise. "How extraordinary! You've really never met. How delightfully medieval."

"For you, perhaps," said Greta quietly.

"I have met him," he continued. "Only a few times, but we have conducted a good deal of business together. He is honest and polite and punctual."

Greta reached for her wineglass. She knew Henri well. These were not compliments.

"And I hear congratulations are in order, Otto," said Henri, turning to his other cousin and slapping him roundly on the shoulders.

"Whatever for?" asked Greta, looking at her brother in some surprise.

"He's been elected to the Berlin Academy of Science."

"Oh, *mazel tov*, Otto, but why didn't you tell us?" asked Greta, her pride muted by hurt.

Otto shifted uneasily and set down his spoon. "I can't take it up. I expect this year shall be my last at the observatory."

He sounded so miserable that Greta and Henri fell silent for a moment. "Well, which particular triumph made them decide to elect you?" asked Greta, trying to tease him back into good humor.

"No triumph. They simply liked a paper I wrote."

"A paper?"

"Concerning the use of coarse grating in front of a telescope lens."

Greta smiled encouragingly and without comprehension. Otto gave a tiny sigh. "The grating enables one to measure star color."

"Oh really? I thought all stars were the same color. Twinkly," said Greta, daring him not to smile.

"You may find that you take to the business more than you think," said Henri kindly. "There is a satisfaction to be found in it."

He said this while scraping the last morsel of soufflé from his dish with a tiny spoon and licking it with relish.

"Yes, but you're good at it. You like the risk of it all."

Henri snorted. "Well, it's as close to danger as we get nowadays. Risking a little here or there. Unless, of course, I take up steeplechasing."

"*Non.* Absolutely *non,*" called Baron Jacques from across the table.

Henri laughed, but Greta had the impression this was not the first time Henri's father had heard this joke.

"And," continued Baron Jacques, "it is not about taking risk. It is about risk mitigation. It is harder by far to hold on to a fortune than—"

"—it is to make one," chimed Henri and Otto.

Baron Jacques cleared his throat with doleful disapproval. "Ah, you young men, you think you know everything. That you are the first to discover the world. The first to taste wine, and the first to smell the morning. The first to make a franc. But it is more than words. All of this could be gone in a moment." At this Baron Jacques clicked his fingers and a footman appeared instantly at his elbow, which rather spoiled his point.

Greta surreptitiously slid off her shoes under the table and tucked up her feet under her blanket, suspecting that a parable in family history was about to begin. Sure enough, as the maids set down at each place a plate with a parcel of river trout poached in almonds and champagne, Barons Jacques and Peter grew loquacious in their nostalgia.

"I remember the old house in the Frankfurt ghetto," said Baron Jacques. "Great-Grandmother Esther Hannah Babette never left it. She wouldn't live anywhere else. Her sons, your grandfathers, tried to make the house beautiful around her, but apart from a portrait of her grandchildren, she sent away all the furniture and paintings. She died in the same bed that Great-Grandfather Moses had bought her for their marriage more than seventy years before, and where she'd birthed all ten children. And all living into adulthood. Now, that was something. Esther Hannah Babette was a proud woman, and rightly so—it was no small thing that she did. Moses might have made us rich, but Esther knew that without his five sons he couldn't have managed it. And those sons were all because of her. The Goldbaums weren't even allowed to own their house on Jew Street, but had to rent it. You can't understand what it was like, never to be permitted to own the home where you had lived for eighty years, even though your sons and grandsons could have bought it for you a thousand times over!"

Here Baron Peter interjected. "And in France you don't know how pleasant it is. The easy times you've had. Your grandfather was able to build himself this mansion in the heart of the city. In Vienna my parents were still not allowed to purchase the house where I was born. Can you believe it? The Viennese House of Goldbaum bought more government bonds than all the other banks in Austria put together, yet still they were forbidden to own property. The outrage! We may do business with princes, chancellors and kings, but to them we are only Jews. Rich Jews. Powerful Jews perhaps, but they do not quite trust us. And *we* know that only family can be trusted. And understanding that is a great gift. We did not succeed despite being Jews, despite being Goldbaums. We succeeded because we are Goldbaums and because we are Jews."

Baron Peter reached for his napkin to wipe a stray fleck of spittle from his beard. Greta sat quietly, watching her brother and cousin. These family stories had taken the place of the Brothers Grimm and Aesop in their nurseries. The only fables that had any bearing for them as children were ones featuring Goldbaums: how Great-Grandfather spun his four antique coins into a sea of gold at the court of a benevolent prince; how Gerta Goldbaum disobeyed her father and married for love a poor stockbroker and was cast off. How old Moses Goldbaum had sent out the five brothers—Dov, Moses, Robert, Jakob and Salomon—to the financial capitals of Europe to found Goldbaum banks. Each brother was given a sycamore seedpod cast in silver (chosen for its symbolic resilience and its ability to prosper on the hardest of ground), a letter of introduction from his father's prince and the promise to draw on his father's line of credit. Greta had always thought this story would have been more satisfying if the brothers had been presented with a bag of gold rather than a mere letter of credit, but Baron Peter had patiently explained that lengthy credit is more valuable than any weight of gold. It cannot be stolen by thieves or lost in transit, and it can be used in a hundred ways at the same time, while a piece of gold may be spent or loaned only once. Five Goldbaum brothers: five goldfinches on the branch of the sycamore tree on the family coat of arms.

Greta remembered that, as a boy, Otto's favorite story had always been the one about the horsemen. Every day a courier arrived at each of the banks carrying sealed documents from the other banks. He did not wear blue-and-gold livery—that would have made him too conspicuous. The Goldbaum couriers were discernible only by the swiftness of their horses and the taciturn disposition of their riders, who, it was rumored, were themselves often third or fourth cousins of the Goldbaums. Six days a week these couriers rushed across Europe, crisscrossing between the houses, bringing the family the most current news. The Goldbaums liked to learn everything first, and in private. The letters between partners at the bank were, by tradition, written in Yiddish. It kept missives safe from prying eyes and served as a reminder of their humble roots—something to be celebrated, for they were proud to have risen so high from such a beginning.

"You see," said Greta quietly, with a smile, "it's not all bad, Otto. When you start at the bank you will be able to send the couriers out across Europe. The horsemen will arrive at your offices every day."

Otto sighed. "I'm afraid their appeal lessens with age. Also, I can't understand why the Houses can't simply use the telephone, or at least send a damn wire."

"You're a scientist. Always dazzled by the newest thing. But it's our traditions that have made us what we are," his father reminded him.

"Stuck in the 1890s," murmured Otto.

"Excuse me, Otto? If you wish to speak, say it for us all to hear," said Baron Peter sharply.

"I said, sir, that the telephone is hardly new."

"And we have one installed in the outer office."

"And you use it once a day to telephone my mother and inform her that you will be home in approximately eight minutes."

"A call she is very grateful to receive."

"And was there a garden in Jew Street?" Greta asked, abruptly changing the subject.

Everyone turned to her in some relief. Otto scrutinized his wineglass. These excursions through family history were always the same; they rose and fell like the four questions at Passover. Until all the stories were told, it was unfinished, the ritual incomplete.

"There was no garden in Jew Street. None of the houses had gardens, there simply wasn't room," said Baron Jacques. "And the Jewish children were forbidden from playing in the city parks. The Goldbaum children played on the ghetto street with the others. Your great-great-grandmother Esther dreamed of a garden with lawns and linden trees and pools of golden irises. We thought we could tempt her away from the ghetto with the promise of a garden, but no. She tended pots of herbs and flowers on the balcony and in the small courtyard, and called those her garden. She wouldn't stay away too long when visiting any of her thirty-seven grandchildren, as she always insisted that she must return home to water her garden."

"Lady Adelheid has a famous garden at Temple Court," said Greta, half to herself. "She grows triumphant rhododendrons."

Her family stared at her in puzzlement. The servants cleared away the fish course.

O ver the following days the baroness took Greta to final fittings with the couturiers for her wedding dress and trousseau. The baroness liked to be driven along the wide-open boulevards in Paris. She declared it to be the most civilized of cities with its rows of fastidiously pollarded trees, silhouettes as neat as any of the ladies emerging from the dressmakers along the Champs-Élysées. The new city was marvelously hygienic, explained the baroness, who could still remember the stink of the old. But it was neither the civility nor hygiene of Paris that appealed to Greta. Paris had a glint in its eye that Vienna did not. If Vienna was the aged aunt in her crinoline chaperoning the empire, then Paris was the cousin slipping a glass of champagne into her hand. She escaped from her mother the moment she could and fled back to Otto and to Henri, who, it seemed, preferred not to work in the afternoons.

"You should see me in the mornings. I'm a whirlwind of authority and decisions. So in the afternoons I rest," Henri declared while stretched out on a vast sofa, a cigarette dangling unlit between his fingers.

"Oh," declared Greta, disappointed, perching herself on an armchair opposite. Watching Henri snooze in the Blue Salon had not been her plan at all.

"Darling girl, I don't mean rest here. We must go out! Celebrate."

"Celebrate what?"

"Your wedding, if you like. Otherwise, simply life."

Greta was thrilled. An afternoon in Paris with Henri and Otto: the thought of it was electric. She noticed, to her displeasure, that Otto was shaking his head.

"We can't, Henri. Not with Greta. Don't be ridiculous."

"As long as she's with us, I don't see the harm."

"But with us precisely where, Henri?"

The two men exchanged a look.

"For God's sake, Otto, you're worse than Mother," said Greta, an angry pink circle appearing on each cheek. "You're like one of the old nursery maids. 'Don't this. Don't that.' Don't accidentally take pleasure in anything at all!"

Otto looked away, hurt, and Greta was instantly filled with remorse.

"Don't squabble, my darlings," said Henri, sitting up. "You're going to give me a headache, and I fully intend to give myself one later anyway. Otto's quite right. It's inevitable that I should take you to somewhere perfectly disreputable and plunge us all into tedious parental recriminations."

"But, Henri . . . ," Greta started to say. Henri made it sound so magnificently despicable that she wanted to go at once, but he held up his hand for silence.

"Do not fret, little one. If we can't go to the party, the party simply must come to us."

Henri was as good as his word. After a tedious family dinner in the great dining room, Greta and Otto slipped into Henri's apartments in the east wing of the Esther Château. The dining room, ballroom, bedrooms and all twelve of the salons in the body of the château had been decorated by Baron Jacques's father in the most modern taste, just after the February Revolution of 1848. After inheriting the château, the new Baron Jacques hadn't felt able to change a thing. It remained an immaculate museum.

Henri had no such qualms. On his twenty-first birthday he had requested his own suite of rooms and promptly hired Elsie de Wolfe to redecorate. He'd heard how she'd transformed the mahogany-and-velvet apartments of Manhattan into citadels of light and air, and he wanted the same in the heart of Paris.

Greta had never seen anything like it. She felt as if she had opened the door straight from midnight into morning. Electric light and candle-light pooled; antique mirrors reflected a constellation of tiny flames and the large rooms appeared infinite. The heavy crimson carpets—eighteenth-century Persian or not—had been removed and the floor-boards stripped and rubbed with scented almond oil. The shutters had been thrown back, and gauze curtains fluttered. She felt vaguely that she had set sail on a ship, cruising the skies above Paris.

Henri appeared at her elbow, pressing a glass of champagne into her hand. He'd changed into white tie and tails, a corsage of snowy freesias pinned to his lapel.

"You like it?"

"Of course I do."

"I wish I could take the credit. It was all Claire. Claire makes wonderful suggestions and all I have to do is accept them."

"And pay for them," said a woman, appearing at Henri's side and placing her hand on his arm.

His face ripened into a smile and he bent to kiss her on the lips. She accepted it, brushing her fingertips along his cheek.

"Greta, Claire Bouchard. Claire, this is Greta Goldbaum, my absolutely favorite cousin."

Claire was the most striking woman Greta had ever seen. She wore a white dress gathered into an impossibly small waist, and her black hair was cut short at her jaw to reveal a smooth neck, resplendent with a diamond necklace. Greta was used to jewelry and it did not interest her, but even she was enthralled at how the stones caught the light like pendants on a chandelier spinning in candlelight.

Claire reached out and took Greta's hand. Shockingly, she did not wear gloves and her fingers were warm.

"It's wonderful to meet you at last. Henri has done nothing but talk about you for weeks. I hope your marriage is filled with children and joy."

She spoke French with a slight Spanish accent. Her eyes were dark brown and heavily ringed with kohl, but otherwise she had not made up her face. Greta could not tell how old she was. Her figure was girlish, her skin pale and soft, but something in her voice made Greta guess that she was older than she appeared.

"I feel as if we've met," said Greta, feeling uncharacteristically shy.

Claire laughed. "I'm an actress. Perhaps you've seen my photograph."

"Oh yes, of course," said Greta, suddenly feeling clumsy and awkward, a child beside a debutante.

"Claire's in one of the new motion pictures," said Henri proudly. "We're going to watch it tonight."

Claire turned to him, her enormous eyes larger still. "We are?"

"Yes. I've borrowed the print and the projectionist. And the pianist," he added, gesturing toward a concert grand at the edge of the room. A pianist dressed entirely in white sat at the piano stool, rigid as a toy soldier.

"Darling boy," said Claire, kissing him again.

Henri clasped Claire's hand and, his eyes drunk with love, chattered on to Greta about Claire's remarkable talents: her beauty was indisputable and famous, but now the world would glimpse her talents. Greta was amused and, for the first time in Henri's company, a little bored. After a few minutes she made her excuses and slid away.

Otto found her beside the window. He had declined to wear white and stood out darkly among the other guests. Small talk irked him, and while he acknowledged Claire's beauty, it did not appeal to him.

"This is why no one suggested that I marry Henri," said Greta, following his gaze.

"Yes. Until his fervor subsides, he shan't be offered a Goldbaum bride."

"I shouldn't think he wants one. He might simply marry Claire."

Otto shook his head. "He won't. Make no mistake. She's an actress and she's not a Jew. Even Henri won't marry a Catholic."

Greta glanced back at the lovers, colluding together, oblivious to everyone else. For the first time she felt something she had never expected to feel for Henri: pity.

She danced and sipped champagne, but she remained disappointingly sober and detached, no matter how many glasses she drank. The solitary red begonia in the flower bed wasn't Henri, she decided; it was her. The evening was quite spoiled. She was disconcerted by the prospect of Henri's unhappiness. Greta did not love Albert, but at least she'd never loved anyone else. She tried to imagine what it must be like to be an ordinary person and not a Goldbaum, and to be able to choose: a woman free to select her own husband; a man free to decide his own vocation. The guests whooped and the piano climbed to a rousing crescendo, as a life-sized Claire was projected onto a vast, freshly painted cream wall. Greta observed Otto standing amid the crowd, laughing so hard that his shoulders shook and he had to push his spectacles back up his nose. Otto loved motion pictures: they were a miracle of light, he explained. "See—see what we can do," he'd said to Greta, exhilarated. "Never say that mathematics isn't beautiful. These pictures rushing across the screen are possible because fifty years ago Mr. Foucault made some exquisite calculations measuring the time it took for light to travel between two mirrors. You need mathematics to create art."

Greta slipped out onto the balcony. To her disappointment, she was not alone. Someone else had sought escape.

"Cigarette?" asked a woman.

"No, thank you," replied Greta, intrigued. Most women she knew did not smoke.

"Fräulein Goldbaum?"

"Yes. Excuse me, do we know one another?"

"Not yet. Emilie Flöge." The woman spoke with a Viennese accent and offered Greta the hand that was not clasping a cigarette. She shook it.

"You don't like the motion pictures?" asked Greta.

"Not particularly. I like color. The film matches Henri's apartment."

"You don't like that, either?"

"No."

Greta was not sure what to say to that, and so she remained silent, studying Emilie. She was wearing a remarkable dress. Unlike the attire of the rest of the guests, it was not white. It was red and black, with geometric patterns woven across in silver. The sleeves were loose and free, making Emilie's arms appear slender and smooth. Most striking of all, the waist was only slightly tapered. Emilie turned to Greta and the dress moved like water, catching the light.

"Do you like it?" she asked. She spoke seriously, watching Greta carefully.

"Yes. It's like a living painting. You look as if you're wearing a Klimt."

"No, it is the other way around. He paints my dresses. He is my lover."

Greta stared at her.

"I always hoped I'd see you in Vienna. And then, when Claire told me you'd be here tonight, I decided it was fate," said Emilie.

Disconcerted, Greta said nothing. She peered inside for Otto, but knew it was futile; he would be watching the picture, transfixed until the end. But she was used to these periodic outpourings from admirers. After all, a Goldbaum was as close to a prince as most people came.

"Let me make your wedding dress."

Greta laughed, unable to stop herself. The idea of her wearing such a garment, on such an occasion—the thought was wonderfully absurd.

"My dress is made, along with my whole trousseau."

"I'm sure it is. But let me tell you this," said Emilie, her voice dropping low, to just above a whisper. "I'm not wearing a corset."

Greta considered her in wonder. Emilie smiled.

"None of my dresses need them. I'm simply"—she shrugged—"comfortable."

"No corset?" Greta tried to imagine it: a day as comfortable as a night.

"Be my *mannequin de ville*. I won't charge you. Let me show you half a dozen outfits. If you like them, take them. Let people see you wearing them."

To her astonishment, Greta found herself agreeing to visit Emilie's Paris showroom with Claire the following afternoon.

T he building was on the rue Cambon, smart but tired, its stone-work smeared with soot like a stained blouse. There was no lift and they had to climb the stairs. Claire did not apologize to Greta for the inconvenience or the drabness of the building. She did not ask whether she needed to rest, or required refreshment as they reached the top. So often Greta's acquaintances fawned over her, drowning her in their obsequious concern for her well-being, as though her name had turned her into some brittle, fragile thing.

"Hold this," said Claire, shoving the wet umbrella at her, a tur-quoise ring on her finger as fat and blue as a robin's egg. The Gold-baums were infamous for their expensive pursuits, and not marrying Claire was Henri's, decided Greta.

Claire rang the bell and Emilie opened the door herself and greeted her with effusion, kissing her soundly. She said nothing to Greta, only smiled and waved her inside, a cigarette between her yellowed fingers.

The apartment was tiny, or it appeared so—fabric was draped over every surface. It rippled in waves from picture frames, hung from the curtain poles in waterfalls of crimson and willow green and was spread over chairs, while the table was heaped with boxes of pat-terns, scissors and a pair of gleaming sewing machines. Two girls sat at one end of the table embroidering peonies onto the sleeves of a dress made from glossy glacier-blue silk. The room was chaos in color, and Greta gazed around enraptured. Emilie waved vaguely at the disarray.

"This is only my little Paris pied-à-terre. It's a pity you couldn't come to see me in Vienna. There I have eighty seamstresses." She paused, considering. "It is no tidier. But then, for me, color is joy."

She turned to Greta, offering up in her arms a dress, its fabric embroidered with dozens of shimmering geometric shapes in blue and gold.

"Try this one."

Greta took it from Emilie with reverence, surprised by its lightness and the softness of the silk. Emilie ushered her behind a Chinese screen at the far end of the room. Greta hesitated before unfastening her corset and then, resolute, began to loosen the ribbons.

"Here. Let me."

Claire slipped behind the screen and unbuttoned the hooks, as competent and unself-conscious as any maid.

"Perhaps I will ask Emilie to make me a little something," said Claire. "Henri is taking me to Russia for Christmas. I have always wanted to see the Winter Palace."

Greta looked at Claire in surprise. Goldbaums did not travel to Russia, or holiday with their mistresses. After helping Greta into the dress, Claire left her alone. Greta swayed from side to side. The dress was so comfortable and weightless it felt like being undressed. She could stretch and move. Resolutely she stepped forward and faced herself in the mirror. Her hair had worked loose from its chignon and hung in curling strands around her shoulders. The dress was extraordinary. The profusion of embroidered geometrical shapes rippled and dazzled against the softness of the pale silk. This was some other woman. Greta felt shy of herself. She had been metamorphosed. Then she laughed. This is who I want to be, she decided. I shall be the woman brave enough to wear this dress.

. . .

I'm not sure which is worse. The monstrosities themselves or the fact that you did not pay for them."

The baroness lay back on a sofa in the morning room, her corsets too tightly laced to allow her to sit. Her eyes closed against the hideous glare of Emilie Flöge's creations. Greta stood before her, receiving her admonishment like an unrepentant general after a disastrous battle.

"A Goldbaum always pays his own way," said the baroness.

"They were a gift," said Greta.

"There are no gifts—only obligations that must be repaid."

"Mama, there is no obligation. I am simply to wear them."

"Out? Where someone can see you?"

"Yes," replied Greta steadfastly.

"Dear God!" said the baroness, and rang the bell for tea.

The two women remained in churning silence while a maid brought tea and lemon for the baroness. She poured herself a cup, sipped and, thus fortified, looked up at her daughter.

"You will send them back. Explain that Goldbaums do not accept gifts. What would Albert think if he saw you in such a concoction? That you were some bohemian or New Woman?"

The baroness shuddered and took another sip of tea. Her horror was such that the tea was unable to restore her. Greta wondered if she ought to ring the bell for something stronger, but decided it was a little early and that she was quite content for her mother to suffer. And yet the baroness had asked an interesting question: What, indeed, would Albert think?

Greta found Otto reading beside a fountain in the parterre garden. It was warm and he wore a broad-brimmed hat. He was so lost in his papers that she had to speak twice before he noticed her.

"Did you know that Henri is taking Claire on holiday to Russia?"

Otto set down his paper. "Russia? Are you sure?"

"Quite sure. She wants to see the Winter Palace."

Otto frowned, considering. "It must be business. Henri will have some plan or another."

"Have you bought me a wedding present?"

"Not yet."

"Good. I need money. Rather a lot, I'm afraid."

Otto winced. "Oh dear. What have you done?"

"If you don't want to give it to me, I shall ask Henri," said Greta, wounded.

"I don't mind the money in the least. I'm simply concerned as to why you need it."

"I wish to buy something."

"Are you going to tell me what?"

"Something Mother doesn't like." She smiled.

The following afternoon Henri received an unpleasant visit from the Russian ambassador. Claire Bouchard would be welcome as a guest of Nicholas, by the Grace of God, Emperor and Ruler of All Russia. Henri Louis David Goldbaum would not be. Jews, however rich, were not permitted to enter Russia.

"We have Jews enough of our own, Monsieur Goldbaum, we do not need more," said the ambassador with a little bow, revealing a polished circle of bald skin on the crown of his head.

Henri stared at him in mute rage, waiting for an apology, a hint of regret. There was none. The Russian ambassador was unembarrassed. He seemed to expect Henri to acknowledge the great concession he displayed by coming himself to inform Henri that his entry visa was denied. Henri dismissed the ambassador without offering him refreshment or a tour of the fabled château gardens.

The Goldbaums knew that the tsar needed money, and a sojourn at the Winter Palace had seemed to Henri an ideal occasion to discuss a little business with Nicholas's advisers. But now he accepted that the Russian hatred of the Jews was a poison pumping outward from the court into the furthest reaches of Russia's empire. He summoned a courier. A young man in a flannel jacket took notes. Henri rolled and crushed a ball of paper in his hand.

"I need the answer to two questions. First, how much money is the tsar seeking to borrow, and from which banks? And second, how exactly are the Russian Jews faring? Not the official position—a true picture. Find out through our networks."

"Of course, monsieur."

Alone in his study, it occurred to Henri that he must confess his failure to Claire. There was to be no holiday at the Winter Palace, no fireworks above the Hermitage or court balls. He was unused to such humiliation and he did not like it.

It was the Viennese Goldbaums' last night in Paris. In the morning they would begin their journey to London. In the end, Greta asked both Otto and Henri for money to purchase the dresses, embarrassed to request the full cost from either. Henri gave Greta a check with a kiss and, knowing from Claire what it was for, asked only that he could see Greta wear one of the dresses before she left.

After a dinner that was lavish and tedious in equal parts, the younger generation of Goldbaums withdrew to prepare for a small party in one of Henri's favorite places: the roof of the Esther Château. A dismal air had descended over all three; these days in Paris had been a brief interlude and they were now reminded of what must come, each preoccupied with his or her own lot.

All the discussion about weddings was making Henri feel guilty. Claire had accepted with equanimity the disappointment about the journey to Russia. Henri understood that his name and its obligations liberated him from a decision, just as much as they trapped him.

Claire never asked about marriage or requested any kind of commitment. She knew it was impossible. He was a Goldbaum. A prince and a Jew. But if he had been free to make his own decision, then he would have had to choose. To his immense shame, Henri knew that he was relieved to be released from such a quandary. Of course he told Claire how he would marry her, if he could. They consoled one another with this late at night as they lay in one another's arms in Claire's bed. But he knew it was an easy promise that he gave: it was one he would never be asked to fulfill. Disconcerted by such uncharacteristic introspection, he quickly thought of other things. Claire was a magnificent woman who deserved a magnificent gift. He would buy her a truly splendid bracelet. Diamonds perhaps. No, emeralds. The biggest and greenest that Cartier could find. He felt much better.

Henri and Otto sat on the roof, waiting for Greta. Chairs had been carried up for them, along with a sofa, a low coffee table and a small sideboard laid with a drinks tray. They did not talk, each lost in uneasy thought that was not driven away by an excellent bottle of Bordeaux from the family vineyard.

For once, Otto considered, it might be pleasant to drink something that was not stamped with the Goldbaum crest. They ate beef, duck, chicken or venison sent twice each day from their estate outside Paris; they peeled fruit nurtured in their own greenhouses, pollinated by their own bees; and they drank their own champagne, all because it was the very best. But perhaps it would be enjoyable to have something second-rate, just for a change.

"If you'd married Greta, then at least she could have stayed in Paris," Otto said now, startling Henri from his reverie.

"Are you scolding me?" asked Henri, surprised.

"Perhaps I am," answered Otto.

Henri fell silent, considering.

"I didn't mean to fall in love with Claire," he said at last.

"You make it sound like an unfortunate accident."

Henri shrugged. "Love isn't something one does on purpose. One doesn't choose."

"On the contrary. I think you can. I think if you'd been a little less selfish, you could have chosen to love Greta. She's a good sort. She would have loved you back in the end, just to be decent. Everyone would have been much happier."

"For goodness' sake, Otto. What's the point of this?"

Otto sighed and then nodded. "You're right, of course."

Henri reached inside his jacket and produced a letter from his pocket and handed it to Otto.

"From our courier. The Russian Jews live in daily fear of a new wave of pogroms."

Otto read in unhappy silence. "What can be done?"

Henri sighed. "Very little by us in Paris, I'm afraid. Our government is happily in bed with the Russians and the new *entente cordiale*. They will say nothing to disrupt the honeymoon. You must speak with Lord Goldbaum when you reach England. Perhaps he will have more luck with the British government."

"Is this newfound concern with Russian Jewry born out of sympathy for your coreligionists, or a desire for retribution, after the tsar agreed to entertain your mistress but not you?"

"Can't it be both?"

With a roll of his eyes, Otto placed the letter inside his pocket. "I'll do my best with Lord Goldbaum." He reached for his glass. "Did your father speak to the British ambassador?"

"We spoke to him together," said Henri. "The ambassador wants France to form an alliance with Vienna; to lend Vienna the money for a new army. The British government is all hot and bothered about German imperial ambitions. The ambassador wants to insert a wedge between Vienna and Berlin. He'd like it if that wedge was France shaped."

Otto huffed in irritation. "The only nation permitted to have an empire is the British themselves."

"Quite so. They have had a century or more to learn to tolerate

French interests in Africa, but they are not willing to put up with German aspirations."

"And you are?"

Henri winced. "I grant you, the German saber-rattling is wearisome. But it is noise, nothing more."

"Well? Are you going to lend the Austrian government money for our army? Cement a Franco-Austrian bond?"

Henri took a sip of wine and shifted on his chair. "It's not good business. Vienna wants the loan far too cheaply—I expect because the German government has offered them extremely favorable terms. We must speak to Cousin Edgar in Berlin. He will know." Henri smiled. "Whether the loan comes from Paris or Frankfurt or even London, it will be one of our Houses that floats the bonds to make it possible."

He stretched out, resting a foot on the low table.

"All the same, I shall expect a disagreeable letter from Lord Goldbaum any day. He's a stalwart champion of His Majesty's Government and will doubtless urge us to reconsider."

"He is a British peer," said Otto. "You can hardly blame him."

"Oh, I don't," replied Henri with a smile. "He presses for his nation's interests, and I press for mine."

Yet family interests join us all, thought Otto, silently voicing the unofficial family motto. The balance between nation and family always had to be minutely negotiated. The key to assimilation was to become a citizen of one's nation, fully absorbed and committed to its affairs, and yet underneath it all one could never forget that one was also a Goldbaum. During the Franco-Prussian War, when diplomats withdrew from Paris and Berlin, couriers still traveled between the Houses, quietly sharing information with their respective governments. Politics and power irked Otto. The perpetual scuffles over empire and gilts. He knew it all fascinated Henri, who savored a negotiation over interest rates with the same relish as he did a game of backgammon or an argument over the best vintage of Château Goldbaum. Otto looked up at the stars, pale pricks of white above the yellow lights of Paris. The heavens at least remained undisputed, belonging to no one.

Greta was exhilarated by her mother's wrath. The baroness's anger was so absolute that she felt liberated by it. She insisted that Greta had deliberately circumvented her authority with sly insolence, and she was ashamed of her. A Goldbaum daughter obeys her parents in all things. Greta protested; she had obeyed her mother. She'd followed her command to the letter, but with imagination and vim. The baroness looked coldly on Greta's humor. This was simply further proof of her daughter's defiant nature. Thank God she was soon to be someone else's concern. The baroness withdrew from the Blue Salon after dinner, in ghastly silence, and would not look at her. Greta knew she ought to feel remorse for upsetting her mother, but after years of igniting either rage or irritable silence, she was inured to both. She wondered whether during her twenty years she had ever made her mother happy. It didn't seem likely.

Wearing the black-and-white dress, she hurried into the narrow passageway leading to the roof. Two servants stood silently at the top and bottom of the stairwell, holding lanterns. The lamplight illuminated her dress, making the white squares appear to glow, the long, loose sleeves fluttering like the wings of a moth.

The parterre was stretched out below, its symmetry most remarkable when glimpsed from above in the moonlight. Grudgingly she admired the resolve and tenacity required to create such rigorous, defined beauty—the sharp triangles of box hedge, the rectangular flower beds. It was a garden for Pythagoras and for lovers of angles, she decided. Presumably Otto adored it.

"Greta?" called Henri. "Come here, so we can see you."

Shy and vexed to have been discovered before she was quite ready,

Greta turned and walked toward the others. The wind caught and lifted the hem of her dress so that it tickled her calves.

"I love it!" cried Henri. "You look like you're floating. Emilie Flöge is the Canaletto of cloth, and you are her Venice."

Greta smiled.

"It's certainly different," said Otto, unconvinced and clearly trying to find words that were both tactful and true. "For goodness' sake, Greta, your feet are black."

Once again she was not wearing shoes.

"Nothing goes with the dress," she said with a shrug. "Only feet."

"It's perfect," said Henri. "But you should paint each toe to match." He poured her a glass of champagne. "Let's toast."

They raised their glasses.

"To Greta and an unsuspecting London," declared Henri, and they all drank. "It's a pity you've left Vienna," he added, setting down his glass. "Gustav Klimt ought to have painted you otherwise."

Otto continued to stare at her, half-fascinated, half-appalled.

"I can see why Mother wasn't quite convinced."

"Oh no, she was. She was convinced she didn't like it."

Otto laughed, but his face suggested that, in this instance at least, he had some sympathy for the baroness.

"The question still to be answered is what poor Albert thinks," said Greta.

"Ah yes, what indeed will poor Albert think?" echoed Otto.

"Think about what?" asked a voice.

A tall man lingered at the top of the stairs. He wore a top hat that made him look taller still. He held on to it with considerable resolve, clearly afraid that if he let go for a second, it would be snatched off by the wind. Greta wished he'd surrender. She thought one of the cherubs in the garden below would be much improved by the addition of an insouciant top hat.

"*Bonsoir,*" called Greta. "Or good evening, if you prefer. Who are you?"

"Poor Albert, apparently," replied the man.

. . .

They all sat in the Blue Salon, drinking an excellent vintage of champagne and desperately reaching for something to say. All Greta's ebullience had burst along with the drawing of the champagne cork, and she perched on the edge of the sofa in her white-and-black creation, feeling as if she'd been caught playing make-believe in one of her mother's evening gowns. She stared resolutely at her bare feet. The baroness had been roused from her bedtime toilette and reappeared, fully dressed. Baron Peter smiled and nodded at his soon-to-be son-in-law, overwhelmed by the significance of the occasion.

It fell to Otto and Henri to inquire after Albert's journey: "Perfectly pleasant"; his cold, "Much improved"; and whether he was tired, "Not particularly."

Greta steeled herself to study him. His suit was beautifully cut and he wore it well. No tailor's skill was needed to flatter him. He appeared pristine, spotless from his journey, as if he'd just been taken out of the wardrobe, pressed and aired. His hair was dark, nearly black, and his mouth was neither big nor small. He wasn't unattractive, but he reminded her of the parterre, all hard lines and orderliness.

"I hear you like butterflies," she said at last.

He started, taken aback that these were her first words to him since the roof.

"Yes. Moths and beetles, too. I've amassed nearly ten thousand specimens. Two thousand of which I've caught myself."

"Goodness, that's quite a collection," said Greta, trying not to shudder.

"Indeed," said Albert. "Perhaps one day I may have the privilege of showing you?"

He met her eye, blinked and quickly looked away.

Greta pictured a suite of rooms at Temple Court packed with display cases, each one brimful of insects, all the cabinets dusted and polished, every insect meticulously identified. Labeling things was simply another form of tidiness, decided Greta. Somehow she couldn't imagine his striding through the long grass with his net and jars; she could only see him sitting at his desk, writing out the labels in his precise hand for scores of unfortunate creatures in bottles.

"I have a gift for you," said Albert, reaching into his jacket pocket and producing a large leather wallet. "I had them reset."

Greta watched as Albert unfastened the wallet and carefully withdrew a necklace. He placed it on her lap.

"This is the yellow Goldbaum diamond. Mined in the Transvaal in 1852. It's twenty-six carats. Flawless. My mother says that it now belongs to you."

Greta looked down at the necklace. A vast teardrop diamond, yellow as sunshine, formed a butterfly's forewing, the hindwing fashioned from smaller yellow diamonds joined together by white-gold filigree, delicate as spider silk. The veins were similarly traced in white gold, and the antennae and thorax were picked out in rubies. The jewel butterfly appeared as if it were midflight, about to settle on a leaf, wings folded. For a moment Greta felt it flutter in her lap.

"It's the perfect replica in diamonds of one I discovered in a wheat field on the Temple Court estate. It hadn't been identified before. So I've named it *Greta aurum*. The jewels were yours anyway. The name is my wedding gift."

He reached out and, with cool fingers, fastened the necklace around Greta's throat. It was too tight and for a moment she felt as if she could not breathe.

She looked up at him. "Thank you," she said.

The butterfly pressed against the pulse in her neck. A tiny beat of blood like a wing. She wasn't sure if she liked the necklace or not. It, like Albert, unsettled her.

London, June

————◆◆◆————

Albert did not approve of the dresses. He did not say so. In fact he pressed both Otto and Henri to permit him to repay Greta's debt—she was to be his wife, her bill by rights belonged to him—but they demurred, insisting that it was not a loan, but a gift. Albert was too polite to press the issue. Greta knew that he did not like them when she appeared at breakfast in a fashionable narrow-waisted blue skirt and one of the new Parisian blouses that the baroness had selected. His compliments on the pinstripe were elegant and protracted. Greta thanked him, feeling a ball of disappointment burn in her chest like indigestion. She wanted him to be the kind of man who smiled at his wife's daring.

Albert was as solicitous as he was neat. He inquired as to which brand of paint she preferred for making watercolors, and whether she liked to embroider with silk or lamb's wool. He wished everything to be shaped to her comfort on her arrival at Temple Court. Greta did not paint, and she had not made a sampler since her last governess had given in her notice more than five years earlier and the baroness, tired of recruiting capable women who were, it seemed, incapable of managing her daughter, decided that Greta's education—while inadequate—was complete.

She feigned seasickness during the journey on the packet from Ostend to Kent and, declining Albert's offer of a doctor, requested only privacy and fresh air. His presence oppressed her like a swaddle of blankets on a too-hot night. He withdrew, leaving her in a deck chair to the tactful ministrations of Anna.

To her profound relief, they did not stay at the house at Number One Park Lane with Albert and Lord and Lady Goldbaum. Baroness Emmeline insisted that, until after the wedding, the two branches of Goldbaums ought to remain divided. Greta was both thankful and bewildered, since the house was large enough to lose the entire family tree, and not merely a branch or two. In the end she concluded that the baroness wished to have the pleasure of complaining about the hotel. They had taken a floor of the Savoy, but to her gloomy triumph, the baroness discovered that the shortcomings in English plumbing extended even to the finest of establishments. On showing them the royal suite, the unfeeling concierge had even briefly implied that the baron and baroness might share a bathroom.

Greta, on the other hand, liked the hotel immensely. There were a bar and restaurant downstairs that were filled with people she did not know. The relief of anonymity was even more refreshing than the cool, cucumber-scented martinis that they shook at the bar. She had visited London only once before and had found it grimy and damp. This time it was grimy and hot. The pavements softened like caramel and stuck to her shoes when she ventured outside; the milk soured before it was delivered, and coffee was served black. The leaves on the trees in the Royal Parks curled and shriveled. Yet, to her surprise, Greta found that she liked the city. Everyone constantly marveled at the heat—and she discovered that she could initiate an enthusiastic conversation with anyone at all simply by saying, "Goodness me, what weather!"

The afternoon of their arrival they were invited to the house on Park Lane for tea. Albert and Lady Goldbaum and two ranks of servants received them in the great hall with military decorum. Ten thousand blue cornflowers and golden marigolds had been woven into a vast living tapestry displaying the family crest, the bright hue of the cornflowers bringing out the Canaletto blue on the series of vast paintings of the Grand Canal hanging along the staircase. The family's private orchestra had been sent up from Hampshire and played a dutiful arrangement of Viennese waltzes alternating with English chamber music. A photographer snapped uneasy portraits of Greta and Albert, who, as they posed hand in hand at the foot of the stairs, contrived to look like strangers appalled at one another's proximity. Toasts were issued and congratulations proclaimed. Yet, to Otto's astonishment, Lord Goldbaum was absent: he sent his profound apologies, but he was much taken up with matters in the House of Lords.

The Goldbaums were famous for their scrupulous civility, and not greeting one's future daughter-in-law and her parents was perilously close to a slight. Otto knew that the London Goldbaums quietly understood the baroness's anxiety over the smaller fortune held by the Vienna House, and were usually fastidious in paying them every possible respect to allay any hint of condescension. The unity between the Houses was tantamount in family lore. What on earth was so important as to keep him away? Otto felt uneasy. The moment he was able, he quietly drew Albert aside.

"Where is your father? I had hoped to speak with him about Russia. See if the British government can't exert pressure on the Duma to stop the pogroms."

"My father will raise the matter with the foreign secretary, but I don't have high hopes. He's battling against the government himself at present."

"This business with the budget?"

Albert sighed. "According to my father, it isn't a budget but a revolution."

Otto raised an eyebrow. "Surely it can't be quite as bad as all that?"

Albert shook his head. "I worry that it will be the end of England as we know it, one way or another. The government is taking down the constitution, brick by brick. My father led the charge in the House of Lords to block the budget and now they want revenge. This is a war against us and our class, make no mistake."

Otto was silent. He was less sure than Albert as to which class he belonged. In Vienna the moneyed, privileged Jew was in a class parallel to that of the privileged Christian. They were never quite grafted onto the establishment's tree. Otto was unhappy to hear that Lord Goldbaum was at the forefront of a political dispute, for he'd been taught to understand that Goldbaums must labor unobtrusively behind the seat of power, instrumental but overlooked. He was troubled at the thought of Greta's father-in-law as the figurehead of a hopeless and much-vilified campaign.

Albert set down his glass without having raised it to his lips. "Everyone here is fretting about German naval ambitions. Ought we to match them and have four dreadnoughts, or eight or twelve? We are arguing about naval deterrents when England is already at war with herself."

"At least you can distract yourself with something other than wedding preparations," said Otto, attempting to lighten the tone. "That is a silver lining."

Albert did not laugh. In fact, if it was possible, he looked more apprehensive still.

After tea, Albert led Greta in to view the wedding presents. Two saloons had been set aside for this purpose, and yet still they were not large enough. Clients of the Goldbaums from all over Europe had sent tokens expressing felicity and gratitude, in the silent hope of generous terms in future negotiations. Tables heaved with silver dinner services from President Fallières, and Persian rugs from Emperor Franz Joseph himself. The British empire was expressed in miniature: hand-painted wallpaper from China, a carved chest from the maharajas of Rajasthan filled with finely colored rugs, an ivory jewelry box from Ceylon. The butler had recorded the names of the givers in a black bound book and displayed each name on a little card before each gift. A string quartet played while the invited guests inspected the assembled treasures.

Greta escaped the minute she could, wishing that so many strangers had not been quite so generous, requiring so many hundreds of thank-you letters. If she had remained a moment longer she might have overheard Albert remark that he found the habit of ingratiating gift-giving obsequious and excessive. If he had wanted a set of eighteenth-century porcelain finger bowls adorned with dancing bears, then he would have purchased them himself.

The wedding was to take place at half past two the following afternoon, and to Greta it felt like an execution—if not of her life, then of part of herself. She might remain a Goldbaum, but she would lose her name: Fräulein Greta Margot Esther Goldbaum would become absorbed into Mrs. Albert Goldbaum like blood into rust. Unfortunately, it was quite clear to Greta that Albert required a proper Englishwoman as a spouse: someone who not only knew who to seat beside whom at dinner, but who fretted with quiet gravity over the consequences; someone who could both recite the names of the hothouse flowers and embroider them onto a cushion with élan. Greta did not want to be a good wife. She did not wish to check the quarterly wage bill of the servants or ensure that sufficient lavender was gathered during July to scent a year's worth of laundry. She had been a dutiful daughter for twenty years and the prospect of a lifetime playing the role of compliant wife, charitable patroness and dedicated hostess was too awful. She pushed aside the uneasy question as to what it was that she did want.

Instead, she resolved upon action. It was her moral duty to warn Albert of her own inadequacies. It was an act of conscience, she reasoned. She might not have wanted him as a husband, but he certainly would not want her as a wife.

After retiring for the night, she sat at the desk in the window in her nightdress and set out her faults at length, adding a few more to be on the safe side. The baroness would have marveled at her contrition:

I'm afraid that I do not believe our marriage will be a happy one. Of course I do not love you. But I'm afraid that, after a year or two, we shan't even like one another very much. And why should we agree to live in the murky un-happiness of our parents? For once let us be brave. Let us refuse to do this thing that is expected of us. Say you won't marry me. Tell them that you won't do it. Let this be the one act that we perform together: tell them no. Then we might have a chance at happiness. And after all, that's all anyone can ask for—a little chance.

She rang the bell and pressed the letter into Anna's hand, speaking to her in rapid German.

"Give this to a porter and tell him to take it to Park Lane. He's to wait for a reply."

Anna blinked at her, eyes thick with sleep. "It's nearly two. Mr. Goldbaum will be asleep."

"Then wake him up. Hurry! *Bitte schön.*"

Greta paced the room. On the dressing table rested her jewelry box. The butterfly choker had been taken out of the hotel safe, ready for the morning. She unwrapped it and set it on the table. In the darkness the jewels looked black, simply the ordinary fragments of carbon that Otto delighted in telling her were all diamonds really were.

Anna returned. The porter had been dispatched. Should she sit with her and wait? No. Greta wished to be alone. The maid withdrew. Greta opened the window and listened to the growl and rattle of the city outside her window. She tried to imagine what she would do if Albert agreed. She would have to leave London, but she couldn't go back to Vienna. Her mother would not bear the shame of returning with her unmarried. She'd become a parable in the family story box, a warning to other wayward girls. But mingled with fear was a thrill-ing sense of possibility. Her father would have to grant her an allowance—enough for her to live on. A small house on Lake Geneva perhaps; she had been happy there. Otto would visit. Maybe he would follow her example and decline a Goldbaum bride. They could share a household in cheerful companionship. One day, she might take a lover. Someone who read novels and laughed a good deal, and asked very little of her.

It was nearly four o'clock. Where was Albert's reply? A simple yes or no would suffice. She felt sick. Her nightdress stuck wetly to her back. It was unbearably hot. She rang for some ice. The door opened. It wasn't ice; it was a letter. She read it, standing in the middle of the room.

"What does he say?" asked Anna.

Greta looked up, her face shining with tears.

"No. He says no."

The letter was brief and elegant. The hand that wrote it had not trembled. Albert expressed his sorrow that she felt such anxiety, but suggested that all brides, Goldbaum or not, were renowned for experiencing last-minute doubts. Her knowledge of her own faults—not that he accepted she possessed them—revealed a remarkable self-awareness and a humbleness of character of which he had been previously unaware. Indeed—he did not wish her to worry about it—he liked her more rather than less because of her outpouring. He wished her a good night's rest.

Greta dried her eyes. She was angry. "Piffle! He doesn't mean a word. He's just a coward."

"My cousin Ursula ran away the night before her wedding," said Anna.

"Even I can't bring that much shame upon my family. I'm many things, Anna, but I am not a coward."

Greta allowed the baroness to supervise the battle over her treacherous curls. She hardly spoke, but everyone else chattered and argued so much that they did not notice the taciturn bride. They adjusted her veil and sewed fresh roses onto the toes of her silk shoes. Greta allowed herself to be preened and prodded without complaint. They pinned lily of the valley in her hair and she noticed a bouquet of the same resting in a vase. Greta roused herself.

"I asked for gardenias."

"Lily of the valley is traditional in England. For society brides," explained the baroness.

Greta laughed. Gardenias had been her only request.

It was over one hundred degrees by twelve o'clock, and the baroness selected the very lightest of lace shrugs for Greta to wear. Heat or not, a bride's suggestive wrists had to be covered in the synagogue.

"You look tired," complained the baroness.

"I didn't sleep," said Greta.

"No, of course not, too much excitement," said the baroness, almost tenderly. She kissed her daughter on the cheek. Greta started at the affection. She could not think of the last time her mother had touched her spontaneously.

"You might decide in time that you like him," said the baroness.

"I might. But do you not find it miserable that no one even pretends love is a possibility?"

"Of course it's possible," said the baroness.

"Just unlikely."

"Love isn't always desirable. It can be . . ."—she hesitated, fumbling for the appropriate word—"messy. A sensible, restrained affection that never gets the better of one has much to recommend it."

She plucked a stray petal from Greta's shoulder and handed it to the maid to place in the wastepaper basket. She made no further remark about the possibility of love.

Greta and Baron Peter were conveyed to the synagogue along Piccadilly in the coach used by Lord Goldbaum on state occasions. It gleamed with gilt, the family crest emblazoned in blue and gold, the eyes of the five goldfinches picked out in lapis lazuli, the sycamore pods in glossy pearls. Inside the coach the cushions had been restuffed with new horsehair, and pinned below the windows were tiny crystal vases filled with yet more lily of the valley. Yet beneath it all Greta could smell the musty scent of decay. The coach being pulled along by four silver-tailed horses was a relic, moldering at the back of the Goldbaums' coach house underneath a tarpaulin, while the Rolls-Royce and the Daimler and the Wolseley motored in and out.

Inside it was as humid as a greenhouse, and Greta felt herself wilting. Each time she tried to open a window, her father put out a restraining hand.

"I promised your mother we'd keep them shut. She doesn't want your dress to get spoiled."

A film of grime coated everything like a second skin, and curls of smut floated on currents of warm air like flecks of black snow. The movement of the horses was rough, jolting Greta to and fro.

"I feel sick," she said. "I need some air, or you'll be carrying me swooning into the temple, and that will make Mother crosser still. You know she can't abide women who faint—it reveals a wanton lack of self-control."

The baron considered the two evils for a moment and then acquiesced, opening the window. As they reached the Great Synagogue on Duke Street, Greta noticed a sizable crowd had gathered on the pavement. Some of them waved Union Flags, while others had banners in blue and gold.

"Oh dear," said the baron. "Some are clerks from the London House, but I believe the others are hoping for a glimpse of His Majesty. He'd planned to attend, but is taken up with matters preparing for his coronation."

"Thank goodness for that. I hadn't known there was a danger of his coming. Let us brave the disappointment of the crowd."

The baron handed Greta down and together they walked into the synagogue, through the cheers and the flags. The baroness waited for them with two rabbis in the entrance, both sweltering in their black tailcoats.

"Rabbi Reuben," said Greta, smiling on seeing a familiar face from Vienna, and for once wishing the law didn't forbid her from planting a kiss on his bearded cheek.

He chuckled. "I don't think you've ever been quite so happy to see me."

"No, I don't think I have," agreed Greta.

"Well, your enthusiasm for your wedding is wonderful. God will be pleased."

"Oh dear," said Greta. "I'm going to disappoint Him again. But He's probably used to it by now."

The baroness cleared her throat in irritation.

Rabbi Reuben gestured to a side room. "Shall we?"

They followed him into a flower-decked room where, to Greta's relief, Otto was waiting. He poured her a glass of water and she gulped it quickly, her nausea subsiding. A high-backed chair had been garlanded with roses and white freesias, like Titania's bower. Greta wished she felt more like a fairy queen and less like a rude mechanical. Rabbi Reuben motioned for her to sit upon the bridal throne.

"Shall I summon the groom for the bedecking?" he asked.

Greta nodded. Her forehead itched with perspiration and she could see the baroness grimace, longing to order one of the maids to dab at her. The door opened and a procession of Goldbaums entered: Lord and Lady Goldbaum; Albert's brother, Clement, round and soft as a marshmallow and pink with heat. He winked at her, and she smiled before she realized that he too was blinking away the drops of sweat that rolled in a waterfall down his forehead. They murmured their felicitations of joy, and Lady Goldbaum—tall and elegant as a tulip, in a purple suit—leaned in close as though she was about to confide something and then withdrew, squeezing Greta's hand instead. Where was Albert? It had taken Greta a moment to realize that he wasn't there. The door opened again with a crack, and Albert stood in the doorway, looking paler and less tidy than Greta had ever seen him. His *tallit* was not on straight, and his yarmulke slid off his head.

"I'd like a moment with the bride," he announced.

Every face swiveled to look at him in surprise.

"A moment, if you please," he said. His voice was snappish, and the others looked at him in alarm.

"Is everything all right?" asked his mother with concern.

"Perfectly, thank you. But I would like a moment's privacy." He spoke firmly, in a voice expecting to be obeyed.

Lady Goldbaum glanced at her husband. He frowned, but gave a tiny nod, and Greta watched in astonishment as the assorted Goldbaums filed out again. Under other circumstances she would have laughed. Albert took her hand and helped her step down from her throne of flowers. It was a perfectly ordinary room. Chairs had been laid out for the family, each one set with a blue-and-gold cushion, and the walls had been freshly whitewashed. But the parquet floor was worn and the only decorations were a series of dreary oil paintings of the last incumbent rabbis, with a full bushel of beards. Albert took a moment before speaking, and Greta looked around in silence without prompting him. When at last he spoke, it burst out of him in a rush.

"I'll do it. If that's what you want. Hang the consequences!"

Greta stared at him.

"I'll call it off. You seem . . . well, pleasant. And I don't like the thought of making someone miserable. And if you really think that I will, then, well, I shan't marry you."

For the first time in weeks Greta felt calm. The noise fell away. There was only Albert and the scent of a hundred freesias. At that moment she had a choice. She could disappear to her house of air on Lake Geneva or she could marry Albert, but it was up to her. His momentary act of bravery and rebellion made her wonder for a moment if, perhaps, she could find something to like in Albert after all. She hoped she wasn't mistaken.

"I'll marry you," she said slowly.

The relief on his face was palpable.

"Here." She poured him a glass of water. He swallowed it in a gulp, spilling some down his chin. She poured him another and he drank that, too.

"Shall we ask the others to come back?" she said after the third glass.

As Albert ushered them back inside, all of them scrutinizing bride and groom with wary curiosity, Greta smiled. None of the others knew that she had freely chosen to marry Albert Goldbaum. It might have been a good decision or it might have been a bad one, but it had been hers.

Temple Court, Hampshire, June

At night Greta dreamed she was lost. She found herself in some unfamiliar part of the house and couldn't find her way back to her bedroom; the darkness grew tongues and hissed at her on every side. She was always falling. Sometimes she dreamed she was on the roof, unable to find her way to safety, and she would slip and plunge over the edge. Or else she was at the top of one of the dozen staircases and missed her footing, and then she was tumbling over and over into nothing. She never landed. She would claw herself out of the fall, out of sleep, and find herself in bed, her nightdress and her hair sticking slickly to her skin. She'd ring the bell, summoning Anna to bring her a glass of water (there was already a jug on the nightstand) or a clean nightdress (beneath her pillow). Really she clung to the maid as the only familiar person, the sole remnant of home.

Greta felt a stranger to herself: perpetually off-kilter. She might have been fluent in English, but the nuances still tripped her. She wasn't witty in the language, or else she simply had no friends to amuse. She was treated with respect by the family, with deference by the servants, but with fondness only by Clement. Albert was polite. Solicitous. His manners were as meticulous as his person, but Greta never penetrated beyond the armor of his careful social self. She felt a perpetual guest.

The house was too big. It was the last calendar house to be built in Britain: it had three hundred and sixty-five windows, fifty-two principal rooms, twelve staircases, seven towers and four wings. In the fortnight that she had been a resident, Greta had not visited all the rooms. She'd been lost twice and had to be rescued by a housemaid who, she was fascinated to discover, kept a map in her apron pocket, despite having worked there for nearly half a dozen years. There was a floor for the family bedrooms; a wing for visiting bachelors, with bedrooms, bathrooms, a smoking room and a library; another for married guests of various social status. Queen Alexandra's state bedroom was carefully dusted and set aside for the most important visitors, the blinds always drawn to save the fragile silks on the priceless wall hangings from rotting in the light. To Greta, it appeared like a mausoleum, and she could imagine nothing worse than spending a night in such a chamber. A separate wing constructed around a courtyard housed the dining room and a city of kitchens: the bakery, the patisserie kitchens, the still room and stores for jams and preserves, meat lockers and the cavernous wine cellar, a cool subterranean tunnel nearly a quarter mile in length.

The plans had been drawn up by the same architect who had designed other Goldbaum residences, and it was as if the excesses and whims he'd been asked to curb in his other commissions had finally been indulged here. The house was inspired by the palaces of the Valois kings—it was a vast French château nestling in the Hampshire countryside. It sat poised on a ridge, the trees and valley falling away below. It was built from Portland stone, with a façade of arched windows over three floors crowned by a steeply pitched gable roof in gray slate, with several conical towers rising to sharp spires. At the front the great house stood alone in a semicircular moat of driveway, large enough for fifty cars.

It was more like a hotel than a home. Every comfort and luxury had been imagined and the servants anticipated each whim, sensing when privacy was required and immediately withdrawing. Even the baroness would have been satisfied with the plumbing. There was an abundance of bathrooms, and the water was always hot. Anna never needed to run up and down stairs to fill a basin or bath with jugs from the kitchen. And there was a telephone on every floor.

As well as modern luxuries, the house was stuffed with other kinds of treasures: paintings, porcelain, tapestries, carpets, furniture and clocks. At midday and midnight the place shrilled with the chiming of nearly a hundred clocks along the West and East Galleries. It was the sole task of one of the footmen to tend to these clocks, to wind and oil them—as attentive to their caprice as the gardeners in the greenhouses to the orchids and out-of-season fruits. Despite his best ministrations, they could never all be kept precisely to time, and they rang out continuously for nearly five minutes on the hour and half hour. Time itself was marked with more panache by the Goldbaums than by other people.

The house's collections were truly remarkable, greater than those of nearly all the public museums. Yet despite the lavishness of the treasures, it seemed to Greta a house without a history. Before the construction of the present mansion in the 1890s there had stood on the site a small Elizabethan manor. Only a single fireplace remained. Everything else was newly built or bought in. The exquisite paneling in the breakfast room was taken from a château in the Loire, dating back to the reigns of the Louis kings. That in the Gray Salon came from a town house in Paris built for an immensely rich financier and rival of the Goldbaums. They defeated him in business and, if that was not enough, purchased the interior of his dining room when his house was sold. In the same room hung three portraits of George IV's mistress, the actress, poet and beauty "Perdita" Robinson, as painted by Gainsborough, Romney and Reynolds. These dazzling eighteenth-century portraits had nothing to do with the Goldbaums, except that they thought them beautiful and could afford to buy them. The house was bursting with paintings of lovely strangers—like paid guests invited to a party to make it more scintillating. They owned the best of other, more ancient families' histories, sold off a duchess at a time by nobility who were unable to pay the interest on their land debts. A quartet of countesses smiled wanly from each wall in the Yellow Drawing Room. The Goldbaum family history was too recent to have its own such display. The Goldbaums had been painted by Whistler and Singer Sargent and Renoir, but since their fortune went back only a generation or two, so did their family portraits. The most treasured possession was a tiny painting of old Moses Salomon and Esther Hannah Babette Goldbaum, seated in their modest parlor in the Frankfurt ghetto, by an unknown artist. It was the least expensive of all the collection and the most valued.

Greta could have borne the house. She would have wandered among the towering indoor palms, the Riesener desks and gilded wall lights commissioned by Marie Antoinette and converted to electricity by Lord Goldbaum, and could have learned to appreciate their splendor, if only she could have liked Albert more. That moment of generosity before the wedding remained the only happiness, like a balloon in an otherwise empty sky. She returned to it again and again, insisting to herself that a man who was usually bound by convention, but who had found courage in that one moment to offer her freedom in the face of social and familial condemnation, must be a good man. In fact he was a better man than one for whom the social niceties meant nothing. She tried very hard not to regret her decision to marry him.

They had not gone to bed together the night of the wedding. Or, rather, they had lain side by side, exhausted, terrified, too tired to sleep and too nervous to touch one another. Greta had considered reaching out and brushing his hand, but it seemed so absolute that the first touch must come from the bridegroom that she did not. At last Albert had announced, to the relief of both of them, "Let us commence the business of marital relations once we're established at home."

Yet the business had not commenced. An entire week of nights passed without Albert's appearing in her bedroom. Greta felt increasingly anxious. Anna dressed her each night in a silken nightdress, combed her hair and scented behind her ears. Each morning the maid would enter, an eyebrow raised, and Greta would shake her head, humiliation burning in her cheeks. She had some fears about the marital act, but the absence of it worried her more. The notion of going to bed with a stranger was discomforting, but she was reconciled to her duty, and at least Albert's person was not repellent. And if they took the time to spend some days together, then perhaps they could go to bed for the first time, if not as ardent lovers, then at least as affectionate acquaintances. Albert, however, avoided her. Greta began to dread that she would still be a virgin at the end of her honeymoon.

By the time she appeared downstairs after breakfast (married ladies breakfasted in bed, recovering from the supposed trials of the night), Albert had invariably gone. He left profound apologies that he'd had to go up to town; he was out on an expedition to seek a rare species of moth glimpsed in the barley fields. They met at dinner, where they exchanged pleasantries and retired to bed, alone.

After more than a fortnight had passed, Greta decided that something had to be done. She was prepared to refuse him one time in three, as was her instruction, but the baroness had offered her no advice on how to manage this difficulty. Albert's passions had to be inflamed, but how did one go about such a thing?

At first she'd tried to arouse his interest by asking him about the Boucher paintings of young mistresses with blouses undone to reveal a hint of décolletage as they flirted with older men, hoping that their eroticism might encourage Albert, but he described their history and acquisition without so much as a flicker. She supposed that, considering the number of exquisite Watteau nudes in the dining room—during one particularly dreary dinner she'd counted thirteen nipples—he was inured to artistic suggestiveness. She decided to try again, this time by engaging him in his own passion. If she could not awaken his desire, then she could at least gain his attention. She asked Albert to show her his insect collection.

He turned to her in surprise, his initial dismay on seeing her at breakfast vanishing in an instant.

"Certainly. Certainly. I have matters to attend to this morning, but after luncheon perhaps, if you are not busy?"

Greta was not.

He found her after luncheon on the loggia, sipping tea among the pots of blue hydrangeas.

"Shall we?"

He offered her his arm, for once in perfect equanimity. If Greta was pressed, she might even have said that he hummed a tune. As they entered the house, it seemed to her, as always, that they exchanged day for night. She blinked against the gloom, her eyes taking a few moments to adjust. Clement had told her that when the family was up in town, the entire house was shuttered to preserve the collections, and the maids had to clean by torchlight.

Albert led her up the stairs to a suite of rooms on the second floor. Bookshelves lined the walls and a large mahogany table stood in the center of the largest room, empty except for several Tiffany desk lamps especially commissioned in clear glass. Vast cabinets stood beneath the bookshelves, taking up every inch of wall space—there was not a single painting or adornment. Even the ceiling lights were simple and scientific, rather than decorative. It smelled of lavender and camphor, faintly medicinal. The blinds and curtains were open and the room was filled with summer sunshine, and as she looked out onto the gardens below, Greta realized she could glimpse the shimmer of the sea in the distance.

"What a glorious view," she declared.

"Yes?" answered Albert, as though he'd never really noticed. "If you could just step back, I need to shut the blinds before I can open the display cases. The specimens are damaged by the light."

My God, thought Greta, everything in this house is precious and fragile and damaged by light. I couldn't love anything that had to be swaddled in darkness. I can't bear it. If I had a passion, it must thrive in sunlight. Grow fat in it, not wither.

"This red light is gentle and doesn't harm the specimens while we're choosing. I'll put the white light on, once we've decided what to examine, so we can see them properly." Albert's voice was filled with an excitement Greta had not heard before. It was endearing, and she wished she'd asked him to show her the collection earlier.

He pulled open a drawer and lifted out a glass display box, stuffed with butterflies, and placed it on the table. He stood and switched the red light to an ordinary white one.

"These are all English butterflies. Mostly ones I've collected from around the estate. They are not the most spectacular, or at least not at first. They're not like the swallowtails or giant monarchs, but I like them the best. Those who think they're ordinary or drab simply don't know how to look."

He pulled out a chair for Greta and they sat side by side. Their knees touched and Albert, either not noticing or not minding, did not move away.

"Look," he said, "look," and it was an imploration.

Greta leaned down over the case, taking his magnifying glass, and tried to see what he saw. A dozen butterflies lay before her, white and yellow and brown and sapphire blue, their bodies softly furred.

"This is a brown hairstreak. A female. Look at the black-and-white stripes on her antennae—aren't they marvelous?"

Greta agreed, not wanting to disappoint him.

He smiled at her. "I'm so glad you like her. So glad."

He showed her case after case of butterflies and other insects: trays of beetles, from tiny crimson ladybirds to glossy stag beetles, their fearsome horns echoing those of the antelope and deer antlers mounted in the corridors below; vast orange-and-black monarch butterflies from California, the size of birds and more extravagantly colored than any of the paintings in the Goldbaum collection.

"I think they're more beautiful than anything else in the house," said Greta, truthfully.

"I quite agree," said Albert, with some emotion.

"Will you show me the *Greta aurum*?" she asked.

"Yes, of course. What a good idea."

He slid out another drawer, placing it reverently on the table.

"This is she."

He pointed to a small gold butterfly, its thorax coated in soft gray fur, a tiny black mark like a mole on the upper part of its wing. He reached out and brushed above Greta's lip with his fingertip, where she had a little brown freckle.

"See, it is you."

Greta parted her lips and kissed the top of his finger. Albert hesitated, staring at her, and then, seeming to have come to some sort of decision, leaned forward and kissed her on the mouth, gently at first and then with more force. Their teeth touched, and Greta felt his tongue pushing into her mouth, warm and intrusive as a caterpillar. He stroked her hair and then tugged it loose, pulling it and forcing her head back. He started to kiss her neck and then nimbly unfastened the buttons around her throat and then lower still, until her corset and the tops of her breasts were exposed. With one hand and without stopping kissing her, he unbuttoned her stays. Albert, Greta realized, was definitely not a virgin.

He paused, but only to reposition the trays of insects laid out on the table, moving them further away. The safety of his specimens could not be endangered by passions of the flesh. He tugged her to her feet and lifted her onto the table, nudging her legs apart with his knee. Greta was torn between relief—the act, it seemed, was happening at last—and discomfort. The library table was solid oak. She was also puzzled; considering his enthusiasm for the task at hand, why had he waited this long? Yet, as he continued his attentions, Greta found herself quite unable to ask herself any more questions and discovered that, despite the uncomfortable library table, she was starting to enjoy herself. This was not something the baroness had warned her about.

Albert laid her back carefully on the table, finding a cushion to place beneath her head, and began to fumble with his trousers. For once Greta was grateful for the gloom, not feeling up to the close examination of yet another unfamiliar specimen. Her bosom was now exposed and Albert kissed each nipple in turn, murmuring endearments. Greta found herself arching toward him, not in the least reluctant, and helped him to slide up her skirts and find her stocking tops. Albert, she observed with considerable satisfaction, was no longer tidy. He'd lost a button on his shirt, his tie was askew and his trousers hovered around his knees. He paused for a moment to remove them altogether, flinging them aside. He kissed her again and reached down, trying to guide himself inside her. Greta flinched in surprise at the intrusion, flinging her arm back so that she caught it on one of the stacks of glass insect trays, which tumbled and broke as it fell, cascading glass and beetles and huge brown moths all over her. They rained on her hair and across her face. Greta screamed.

Albert recoiled in horror, thinking for a moment it was he who had caused her to call out. She struggled to sit up, crying out and clawing at her hair, catching wings in her fingertips.

"Are you hurt?"

"No. Get them off me. Get these god-awful things off me!" cried Greta, yanking at her hair and pulling insects from her skin.

"Please be careful, they're very fragile," said Albert.

Greta looked at him askance, unwilling to believe that in such a moment his first concern was his specimens and not his wife, and hurled a fat black beetle at him. It missed and broke against the wall. She straightened her dress as best she could, removing a large moth from her bosom and placing it on the table. Albert plucked the last few insects from her hair and deftly set them aside, making no remark. She looked at him, her shock subsiding, and waited for him to laugh. It would be all right if only he laughed.

He did not.

"You're definitely not hurt? Did the glass cut you?" he inquired, polite and unsmiling.

"No."

He was already dressing, adjusting his tie. She sat on the table in disarray, trying to button her blouse and doing them up all wrong, in her confusion.

"I'm all right. It was just a shock. That's all."

He looked at her coldly. "I understand. The 'god-awful things' revolt you. I'd thought that, despite everything—miracle of miracles—we might share some common interest. But tell me honestly: are you interested in entomology in the least? Or was this all some trick?"

"Trick?" Greta was angry now. "A trick to persuade my husband to spend five minutes in my company? Or to persuade him to make love to me? Forgive me, but I hadn't known that tricks were necessary. Do you find my person so repulsive? Or is it my character?"

Albert stared at her. "'Of course I do not love you. But I'm afraid that . . . we shan't even like one another very much.' You wrote that, didn't you?"

Greta could only nod.

"You made your feelings toward me very clear. That I was a man you didn't even like. How could I come to your bed? I'm many things, Greta, but I'm not a man who wants to force himself upon a woman, even if she's my wife. Pardon me for trying to spare you something that was clearly so abhorrent to you."

Greta felt damp with shame. She wanted to explain that, because he'd given her a choice, she did not dislike him. That the act of love, even without love itself, was intriguing to her—even though ladies were not supposed to admit such a thing. That the insects on her skin repulsed her, not Albert himself. She tried to find the words in her mind, wishing that for once in her confusion she could simply express herself in German.

"I think that one day I could like you, Albert," she said at last.

He gave a little snort of irritation. "Well, if you do, let me know. But do make quite certain. You change your mind a good deal." He stared at her, his face set with disappointment. "You are very young. Father said it would be better to wait a year or two."

He turned to leave. Greta called to him, desperate to salvage something, wanting to tell him something that was absolutely true. "I did like the butterflies. Really I did."

He hesitated, his hand on the doorknob.

"Everyone likes butterflies," he said, and left the room.

Greta sat on the library table, hugged her knees to her chin and cried. This was how Anna found her some ten minutes later, having been sent by Albert to attend her mistress. That evening Greta shook Anna off as the maid attempted to scent behind her ears, and the next morning she breakfasted meekly in bed. Greta and Albert did not speak of the event again. In fact, unless they could help it, they hardly spoke at all.

T he only cool day was that of the coronation on June 22. It was proof, everyone declared, that God was indeed an Englishman. A breeze fluttered the leaves on the lime walk in Temple Court's park and sprayed the water rising from Neptune's fountain into a fine mist. Clement was relieved at the respite. He was a fat man and he disliked the heat immensely. He would have preferred to be slimmer, but he liked food more than he liked the idea of being thin. The only pleasure he savored more than eating was playing chess, although a half-pound bowl of chocolate-coated Brazil nuts or candied orange peel often helped him concentrate on the game before him.

Yet despite his girth, his movements were quick and light. Had a woman been tempted to dance with him, she would have discovered him to be quick footed and musical. Perhaps, as a legacy of the horrors of the Jew hunts that he and Albert had been subjected to at school at Harrow, he'd learned to conceal himself in small spaces, unnoticed. Imagining others' disgust, he avoided company whenever possible, and when forced into it, he said little, until it was universally acknowledged that Clement Goldbaum was extremely fat and extremely shy. He did not wish to subject others to either of these weaknesses (and his father made it abundantly clear that they were both failings of character), so he politely declined all suggestions of marriage. When his mother had suggested he might consider Greta Goldbaum, of the Vienna Goldbaums, as a wife, he had intimated that his younger brother, Albert, would be a much more suitable match.

That morning Clement sat opposite Greta in the Rolls-Royce Silver Ghost specially commissioned in gold, ready to join the parade through Temple village. It was everything that he loathed: to be displayed before the public in a festooned open-topped car, the grotesque son and heir. He heard their hisses of mirth, whether or not they voiced them. As church bells rang out in celebration, Clement began to regret his decision, though was amused by Greta's rapture at the decorations and carnival atmosphere.

"Look, look," she said, pointing to the multitude of Union Flags fluttering above each shop and clutched in countless small hands, weaving in the wind like shoals of tropical fish.

Greta sat beside Albert, their knees carefully not touching. She looked fetching in a yellow summer dress and white cotton gloves, clasping to her side a furled umbrella, which would reveal a vast and resplendent Union Flag when opened. She'd demonstrated it to them after breakfast, sending flying a coffeepot and three rounds of toast and marmalade.

"Isn't it marvelous? I had it specially made. I should have liked a petticoat to match," she'd announced.

Albert had not remarked on the umbrella, merely venturing drily that he was glad she had restrained herself regarding the petticoat.

"I'm an Englishwoman now, you see," Greta declared, polishing the ivory handle. "And this fabulous umbrella declares me so."

Albert muttered to Clement, seated beside him in the motorcar, that in fact it did quite the opposite. No English lady—Goldbaum or not—would sport such a garish item.

Greta apparently decided not to hear her husband's remark, and in any case the crowd adored the umbrella. The drizzle began, and as Greta unfurled it, displaying its bold silken stripes, the crowd

pointed and hollered and cheered. She smiled and waved back, twirl-
ing the brolly round and round between her hands, and Clement
decided she looked the happiest he'd seen her since her arrival at
Temple Court. As a man who'd spent most of his life dueling loneliness with games of chess, he recognized the symptoms in others. He
also knew that Albert, for all his good looks and the way that smiling
women rushed at him during the season, was not good at noticing
unhappiness in others. Yet despite his rigidity, Albert was not entirely unfeeling. Clement, hopelessly bullied at school, would often
find a small beetle or moth inside his pillowcase tucked in tissue paper, and he would understand that this was not a further act of cruelty
from his tormentors, but a piece of tenderness from his brother,
who knew that he himself would have been infinitely comforted
by sleeping on a rufous-minor moth or a rhinoceros beetle. Clement
could only hope that one day Greta would find beetles tucked beneath
her pillow.

After the parade Greta, Albert and Clement lingered on the loggia
sipping champagne, toasting His Majesty and looking out across
the gardens, the low hedges like emerald beads in a necklace around
the throat of the château. The leaves glistened now from the recent
rain, a haze of steam rising from the ground so that it appeared unreal, otherworldly in its perfection.

Servants hastily dried the terrace and furniture, bringing out
cushions and rounds of cucumber sandwiches. Clement ate while Albert and Greta talked at him with such animation and focus that they
did not need to address one another.

"So colorful! Such a crowd, didn't you think, Clement?" enthused
Greta. "It's wonderful to have a young king. It breathes vitality into a
nation. Our emperor," she corrected herself. "The *Austrian* emperor is
so very old."

His mouth full of sandwich, Clement nodded. "Yes, it all went off jolly well. All we have to endure now is luncheon and the sporting afternoon."

"And the meat tea," added Albert without relish.

"A meat tea?" asked Greta, turning not to her husband but to Clement.

Clement smiled. "In England events of great significance, like funerals, christenings and coronations, are marked by a ham tea. I believe," said Clement, warming to his explanation, an expert on all matters food related, "that traditionally the ham is served so pink and finely sliced that a newspaper could be read through the meat. Not that I've tried," he added, a shade disappointed.

"How funny," said Greta. "And you serve a ham tea here?" she asked, intrigued.

"No. Here on the Temple estate, the ham is quietly replaced with rather more thickly sliced roast beef. No one has ever objected. The 'ham tea' has simply been renamed the 'meat tea.' We might not attend the church service to celebrate His Majesty, but since we're funding the celebratory tea for the entire village as well as those on the estate—nearly twelve hundred people in all—our absence has been overlooked," he added with a wry smile.

"Who knows how long we shall be able to continue?" Albert commented. "Within a generation we'll be taxed beyond such acts of generosity. It's the charities that'll suffer, the hospitals and free schools and the widows, no matter what they say."

Clement sighed. "Albert, Father isn't here. There's no need to pontificate and echo his opinions. He can't hear you."

Albert turned to his brother, his expression furious. "My views are my own."

"In that case, let me reassure you, there will still be money for sandwiches."

They remained in an irritable silence for some minutes. A robin landed beside Clement and began to peck at the crumbs on his plate. They sat perfectly still and watched the jerking dance of the tiny bird.

"Little *schnorrer*," muttered Greta with a smile. "That's what Otto used to call the sparrows that thieved at breakfast."

"At Temple Court we try to avoid speaking Yiddish," said Albert coldly.

Greta bit her lip and looked out over the parterre, her expression blank and unseeing, despite the glories of the garden. Albert cleared his throat.

"It's nearly twelve. We ought to ready ourselves to greet our guests."

With Lady Goldbaum absent, this was Greta's first occasion as hostess of Temple Court. A dozen of the country's second best were to join them for luncheon, the younger sons and lesser baronets whose titles weren't sufficient to allow them to attend the coronation at Westminster Abbey.

"It will all go off splendidly," Clement said softly, trying to reassure her.

"I'm not worried," answered Greta with a smile. "Everyone is kind to a bride. They only want to look at her and say how well she appears. I have at least a year in which I may say and do anything."

Albert, catching this last remark, turned and contemplated his wife with some anxiety.

"Within reason, my dear," he admonished.

He seemed to exist in a state of permanent embarrassment, waiting for her to say or do something unbecoming. His expectations lay before her like snares ready to snap, whenever she disappointed him.

After a hot and dismal luncheon, they were driven out into Temple Court's park. The sea was close, but not visible, instead lending a temperate climate that enabled delicate and exotic plants to thrive. For the most part, nature was not allowed to intrude unless it was imported from elsewhere: the tropical birds in the aviary with their extravagant fascinators, and the family of flamingos that fished forlornly in the river, as though they'd missed their train home from their holiday and were now marooned.

They motored along the driveway that snaked for three miles, edged with rhododendrons and camellias, alighting at the edge of the park, ready for the culmination of the day's celebration: the village races. They walked in pairs, the ladies sheltering under white parasols. Greta walked beside her husband, her gloved hand resting on his arm. Clement could not help observing that they did not exchange a single word with each other during the entire ten-minute stroll.

The party ambled to where a vast white tent had been constructed at the far end of the park, large enough to seat all twelve hundred guests invited for the meat tea.

"It's quite a spread," remarked one of the gentlemen.

"The Goldbaums look after their tenants," replied Clement.

"Is it true you bring coffee and rolls to the farm workers at eleven o'clock each morning?"

"Don't you like coffee and something sweet at eleven?" inquired Albert.

"Well, yes . . ."

"There you are then," replied Albert. "Wait, look!"

He pointed to where a brilliant blue butterfly rested on the side of the tent, its wings iridescent against the white canvas.

"A male Adonis blue," murmured Albert, reaching into his pocket. "Isn't it beautiful? I've never seen one here. It must have flown across the Solent, all the way from the Isle of Wight."

"Or perhaps it caught a lift on a skiff," said Greta. "It's here for the party."

Albert produced a small collecting jar, opening the lid like glass jaws.

"What are you doing?" asked Greta.

"I don't have a male Adonis blue. Only a female," said Albert.

He reached out, but before he could catch it, Greta snatched the butterfly, cupping it in her palms, and released it out of the side of the tent.

"For goodness' sake, Greta," said Albert, profoundly annoyed.

"It's a visitor. We must be hospitable to our guests."

Albert turned away, muttering in irritation about the whimsy of children and women.

The games were about to commence. White lines had been painted on the flattest part of the grass, and the vicar stood in sun hat and dog collar clutching a notepad, calling out the title of the latest race: "Men under forty, seventy-yard sprint." The gamekeeper fired the starting gun and they were off. The villagers cheered and whooped; the ladies clapped in their white cotton gloves. Half a dozen races went off in the same manner: "Men over forty, half-mile dash"; "Egg-and-spoon race"; "Boys under fourteen"; "Single ladies' sprint, one hundred yards"; "Married women's race, seventy yards."

"Oh, I should like to join in that one! Wouldn't that be fun?" said Greta, scrambling up from her chair and removing her shoes. Any moment she would be hitching up her skirts above her ankles.

Albert, who had barely looked at his wife, now strode over and whispered something in her ear. She shook him off.

"You don't know everything," she said, loud enough that everyone could hear. "They liked the umbrella, even though you didn't approve. I might even win. And they will like it, if I run."

"But I will not."

Albert seized her arm and pulled her toward the back of the awning. Greta had only succeeded in removing one of her shoes and she stumbled, off balance. Albert held her up, his fingers tight around her arm.

"I forbid it. You will sit and you will watch."

The guests all chattered loudly, remarking to one another upon the weather with forced interest. Greta sat in her chair with one shoe on and one shoe off, and removed her shawl so that the red marks from Albert's grip were clearly visible along the white flesh of her arm. She did not cry, simply stared ahead, furious, unseeing and unhappy. Albert crouched beside her, pressing a glass of water into her hand, murmuring apologies. He hadn't meant to hurt or embarrass her. He simply didn't wish her to make a spectacle of herself. Things were different here. He was terribly sorry. Greta pushed the water away, and Albert, not ready to take it, fumbled the glass so that the contents spilled all over his trousers. He stood, infuriated. Greta did not apologize. Albert stalked away and made conversation with his guests.

Clement had never seen his brother being angry or unkind. Up until now he'd been puzzled by the cool antipathy that existed between Albert and Greta. From that moment on, he was worried.

Clement sought out his mother the evening she returned from London after the coronation festivities. Lady Goldbaum's private sitting room looked out beyond the parterre to the green shadow of her rhododendron walks. She declined to have her suite furnished with the same quality of carpets and paintings as the rest of the house, preferring the curtains and shutters to be left open to see her shrubs. Those were her treasures. Clement found her seated at her dressing table, supposedly attending her toilette, but actually reading a letter.

"Julian Stein has sent me some seeds from his expedition to China. Look at that color."

It was a cerise rhododendron blossom that looked to him like any of the countless bushes she'd planted, but he also knew that, from the outside, one game of chess looks very much like another.

She kept up an enormous correspondence with dozens of adventurers across the globe, assisting financially with their expeditions, asking only for seeds, cuttings and voluminous descriptions in return.

"Well, darling," said his mother, reaching for his hand, "it's always a pleasure, but did you need something?"

Clement smiled. After being in Greta's company, he was aware for the first time in years of his mother's slight German accent. Once upon a time she too had been a young Goldbaum bride sent from the Continent to marry an unknown Englishman. His parents were resolutely unalike, yet after more than a quarter of a century together they shared a bemused affection for one another, even if they shared nothing else.

"I don't believe Greta is happy," said Clement.

"And Albert?"

Clement shook his head.

Lady Goldbaum sighed and set down her letter, rhododendrons for once forgotten. "I'm sorry to hear it. But I'm not terribly sure what I can do, my darling."

Clement took his mother's hand and kissed it affectionately. "I know you'll think of something, you always do."

"Oh dear," replied his mother. "Do I?"

Lady Goldbaum took Greta for a walk before dinner. It had been another hot day and the air hummed with insects. They walked briskly through the arboretum, the damp air full of unfamiliar smells.

"These are mostly plants from the Himalaya," said Lady Goldbaum. "I might never see the mountains myself, but I like to think I've visited them in my own way. Wait until next spring. A camellia and rhododendron garden sleeps for most of the year, but in April and May"—she stopped walking for a moment and clapped her hands in joy—"*wunderbar!* It's like nothing you've ever seen."

Greta noted that Lady Goldbaum wore stout leather boots, sensible rather than elegant. She was sure-footed and walked fast, so that soon Greta was trotting to keep up. Lady Goldbaum was attractive, her skin lightly weathered from hours spent outdoors. She was of average height with mousy brown hair, turning to gray at the temples, and bright, intelligent eyes. She listened rather than spoke. Her tastes, except in plants, were frugal for a Goldbaum, and during the day Greta had never seen her wear any jewelry other than her wedding ring.

Swallows surfed the skies, while faint streaks of white clouds blemished the bold summer blue. They reached the edge of the park, where the huddles of trees and managed wilderness gave way to farmland in the west, and the Fontmell River and eventually the Solent to the southeast. Greta had ventured this far only once before, when Albert took her to show her what was to be their new house, and again she felt the closeness of the Solent before she saw it: gulls screamed overhead and the air began to smell different.

Lady Goldbaum held back ivy and more prickled ropes of brambles and blackthorn so that Greta could pass. Greta stung her ankles on a bed of nettles, feeling a blister bloom on her toe. Glancing at her mother-in-law, she noticed a fine sheen above her lip, which she did not bother to mop with her handkerchief. Albert had not inherited his fastidiousness from his mother.

They emerged from the huddle of trees like swimmers into the open air. They stood at the edge of a vast field of grass, bluish in the late-afternoon light and dotted here and there with scarlet poppies like spatters of crimson paint. A knot of cornflowers wobbled in the breeze, while great streaks of bright yellow buttercups striped the field in broad, loose strokes. Somewhere a curlew called. At the far edge of the grass snaked a black river, wide and smooth.

"As far as the river, all this is yours," said Lady Goldbaum. "Your wedding present."

"Mine?"

"Yes. There's a hundred acres. You can have more, if you come to need it, but I think a hundred is a good beginning for a garden."

"I don't know anything about gardens."

"Well then, you'd better learn."

Greta looked around the spot, taking in the sea of grass, the damp meadows beside the river and the dark huddles of trees.

"Fontmell Abbey is behind that copse. The house is for you and Albert to rebuild together. But the garden is yours alone."

They pushed their way through the scrub, and Greta saw nestled in the bend of the dark river the small honey-colored manor of local stone.

"Of course you'll need to knock it down and build something quite new, to your own and Albert's taste. But the views are charming."

Greta blinked, as the sun sheering off the water dazzled her. Her skin felt tight and a little burned. Lady Goldbaum turned to her.

"Don't think about Albert. Don't think about marriage. Think only of your garden. I didn't like it here at first. My English wasn't half so good as yours. I didn't like the food or the climate, and I wasn't so sure about my husband, either. But my English improved, we hired a better chef and I discovered the climate is excellent for rhododendrons."

Greta did not ask whether she was similarly reconciled to her husband.

Lady Goldbaum glanced at her watch. "Blast! It's after six. We'd better hurry."

They returned to Temple Court, walking quickly and in silence. As they reached the driveway, Greta realized she hadn't thanked her.

"No need. And for goodness' sake, call me Adelheid."

"Thank you, Adelheid," said Greta, unsure if she was thankful or daunted.

Lady Goldbaum waved aside her gratitude.

"Don't pursue happiness. Don't pursue anything except your garden."

Hampshire, August

—⟶•⟵—

Everyone agreed that the season had been a disaster. The hostilities between the House of Lords and House of Commons, suspended for the coronation, had resumed the day afterward with renewed vigor, as though the baronets, lords and dukes, on donning their robes, found that their wrath had been warmed by the ermine. Each weekend the Shadow Cabinet gathered at Temple Court and raged at the treachery of the government, the despicable conduct of Herbert Henry Asquith, Winston Churchill and David Lloyd George, the cobbler's son. It was Churchill they most despised. He, who was supposed to be Blenheim minded, was the greatest traitor to his class. The ladies withdrew after dinner with some considerable relief and left the men to their cigars, brandy and outrage, which continued well into the night.

When Lord Goldbaum spoke, his voice cracked with anger. "David Lloyd George is a demagogue. He promises the workingman the impossible, simply to gain power. And he will use that power to destroy England and all she stands for. He holds nothing dear. England has had two houses of Parliament since the fourteenth century. How dare he seek to change that?"

"They are not seeking to abolish the House of Lords, merely curtail its power," said Albert softly. "You would no longer be able to block money bills."

The others turned to look at him in profound distaste, while the Marquis of Salisbury, several brandies to the good, scrambled to his feet. "The Lords is all that is saving the nation from that man and his band of duplicitous cranks. He doesn't want reform and improvement for the workingman. He wants bloody revolution. And we, my friends, are the last bastion against that revolution."

"I do not like revolution," said Lord Goldbaum grimly. "My family survived two in France. I would not like to take my chances on a third."

Albert surveyed the flushed and gloomy faces of his father and his acquaintance. They wore the expressions of generals who knew that the war had long been lost but sat plotting the next battle with dreary inevitability in the shadow of the grave. The warmth of the dining room was insufferable; for once the curtains had not been drawn, and even though the windows were open, there was no fresh air to be had. The only cool faces were those of the bare-bosomed Watteau beauties, whose nakedness seemed sensible rather than erotic.

Albert continued, "We can't be seen as the party who are happy to pay for armaments, but not pensions for the poor."

"It's not that bloody simple, Albert," objected his father. His younger son was starting to form his own opinions, a habit both admirable and irritating.

"No, of course it isn't, but they make it out to be so in the press."

Lord Goldbaum watched his son in silence for a few moments, apparently taken aback by his candor.

"This wave of strikes will only get worse," continued Albert. "Perhaps, gentlemen, you ought to give an inch. If you think that revolution is indeed possible, then accept a modest reform to the upper house as the lesser of two evils."

His father grunted, and signaled for the butler to send the port and Madeira round again. Albert took this as permission to press his point.

"You are making enemies in government, Father. You asked Lord Gray to speak to the Russian ambassador about the pogroms. Has he done so?"

"He wrote a letter."

"A good one?"

"Feeble."

"Well, there you have it. This fight is costing us dearly."

Albert glanced between his father and his brother. Despite Lord Goldbaum's rank, they remained outsiders, with more to lose than the other grand men in the room. The Goldbaums were invited to donate to high society's charities and attend their balls, but not to marry their daughters. And the joining of great families, Albert understood, was how power among the top five hundred was maintained. The Goldbaum family's strength and vulnerability lay in their separateness.

In all the years of the Goldbaum Bank, the partners had worked with the government and dined quietly with the opposition. When His Majesty's Government inevitably became His Majesty's Opposition, the Goldbaums made little adjustments, but the principle did not alter. Enemies are expensive and bad for business. Yet ever since his ennoblement, Lord Goldbaum had become partisan. He liked Arthur Balfour and he made an enemy of the prime minister, and baited Lloyd George in the press. He would not dine with him. Albert had confessed to Clement that it appeared to him as if, after a lifetime of knocking on the door of the country's most exclusive club and gaining admittance, the club was suddenly facing closure and their father couldn't bear to surrender his membership so soon.

He also understood something that his father and Arthur Balfour utterly failed to convey in public: that they did not oppose reform because it was in their interest to do so; rightly or wrongly, they believed that the House of Lords existed to protect England from party interest, from the selfishness of politicians and the sinister influence of socialism. The great estates leaked money like vast and holey Wellington boots. Albert knew that the farm laborers, as well as the servants, gardeners and village schools, were subsidized by funds from the Goldbaum financial interests, and Lord Goldbaum believed it his moral duty to do so. His father considered that a man must support

those less fortunate through charity and philanthropy. He complained
vociferously that it was not the role of government to compel an
Englishman to do the right thing through taxation. Lord Goldbaum
was proud of Temple Court and her park and model estate of fifty
well-maintained farms, as it proclaimed him to be something greater
than even a peer of the realm and a man of money or influence; it revealed him to be a gentleman. To threaten the system of the English
squire and its ideals of benevolent responsibility was to risk the honor
of England herself.

Sometimes his father's conviction gave Albert pause: was the country lurching toward revolution? When he ambled among the seas of
wheat studded with poppies as the skylarks trilled above, it all seemed
terribly unlikely. The only pitchforks here were busy with the harvest.
Yet a little further west the army had been called in to keep the peace.
Mines were closing. Tempers were short and dangerous.

Lord Goldbaum heaved himself to his feet. "I'm going to bed."

Most of the gentlemen followed him upstairs, attended by a dozen
valets who'd been waiting below for the footman's signal; only Albert,
Clement and Arthur Balfour ventured into the Chinese Salon, where
a chess table had been prepared. Albert liked to watch his brother play.
Upon the checkered board he was as nimble as a March hare. Clement
gave an easy smile. He offered Arthur the first move.

"Accept, Arthur. You need all the help you can get," said Albert
with a low laugh.

"Very well. I accept."

Albert watched with satisfaction as, in twenty minutes, Clement
took Arthur's bishop and knights and shot Albert a look, as if to inquire whether it was impolite to place the former prime minister and
leader of their party in check so soon. Albert wished that the game
could go on a little longer, and the moment when he would have to
ascend the staircase to his and his wife's suite of rooms could be delayed. He resolved that, as he passed her closed door, he would not give
it a glance. He would not think of the woman lying behind it and

wonder whether she slept or tossed restlessly in the dark. A familiar sensation of anger and dread rose through his veins like heat.

They breakfasted late. Trays of beef sausage, eggs (fried, poached, scrambled, baked and deviled), rows of fat smoked kippers, kedgeree, kidneys and roasted tomatoes had been set out on the sideboard in the morning room, alongside silver dishes of strawberries picked from the garden, still damp with dew. All the newspapers—half a dozen copies of each—had been ironed and laid out ready. Coffee and tea waited in flasks beside jugs of milk and cream (labeled "Jersey," "Guernsey" or "Red Poll," according to which championship herd on the estate the milk had been sourced from). Albert sat quietly before a plate of kedgeree, made with smoked trout as he preferred, and hid behind a copy of the *Times*, which he did not read, but used as a buffer so that the other fellows at the table would not attempt conversation. Although, he acknowledged with relief, for the most part his father's friends viewed discussions over breakfast—especially ones regarding politics—as horribly gauche. A gentleman serves himself at breakfast, in silence.

There was a shout of dismay. Albert, Clement and a handful of the others lowered their newspapers in alarm. Lord Goldbaum was staring aghast at the paper in his own hands. Albert gently took it from him and saw a piece reporting Lloyd George's latest speech:

> Now, really, I should like to know, is Lord Goldbaum the dictator of this country? Are we really to have all ways of reform, financial and social, blocked simply because of a notice board? "No thoroughfare. By order of Lord Goldbaum"? This country won't have its policies dictated by great financiers.

He noticed some of those around the table quietly avoiding his gaze. If not at present, he was sure that one or two of them had harbored such an opinion in the past.

"The man is odious and offensive," said Arthur Balfour softly from the other end of the table. "But I'm afraid Mr. Lloyd George is also effective. There is nothing more to be done. He has cast us as hypocrites. We must vote for reform."

Lord Goldbaum surveyed his friend, aghast.

The Marquis of Salisbury shook his head and thumped his hand on the table, making his scrambled eggs jump. "Never, Arthur. You are the leader of my party, but I will resist this until the last bloody ditch."

Arthur poured himself another cup of coffee. "As you wish." He turned to Lord Goldbaum. "Robert? Will you vote with us or are you in the ditch?"

"Father, please don't vote in anger and haste," said Albert quietly. "You are the only Jewish peer. More eyes look to you."

Albert watched his father. Lord Goldbaum sighed and rubbed his eyes, which were faintly bloodshot, the skin beneath heavily pouched. For the first time Albert realized that his father was starting to look old.

Greta's sitting room was piled high with gardening books, none of which she had read. She felt instinctively that her garden must complement the new house, but this was rather difficult, as the design of the house was supposed to be agreed upon with Albert, and it was impossible to agree anything with someone who would not speak to her. On the other hand, Greta wondered whether she could turn this to her advantage. She would quietly resolve upon what she wished to do, and she suspected that when she presented her plans to Albert, he would agree quickly and without complaint, to escape conversation.

She'd thought Albert humorless, but then she'd discovered that he did laugh, just not with her. Walking in the kitchen gardens with Stokes, who had been commissioned by Lady Goldbaum to educate her, she discovered Albert in the arboretum glasshouse balancing on a stepladder held aloft by two under-gardeners, wielding a butterfly net. He craned forward to catch a small white butterfly on the edge of a palm leaf and, leaning an inch too far, tipped off the stepladder and landed on his backside on a pile of compost. On his descent, he deposited the net over the head of the younger of the two gardeners, a spotty-necked youth of about seventeen, who stood there openmouthed, the net perched on his head like a frilly bathing cap. Albert saw the dismayed face of the young man, threw his head back and laughed.

"Well, I don't have a greater-spotted Bernard Jones in my collection."

For a second, young Bernard looked anxious and then grinned, until he too began to laugh. Albert's amusement swelled, until he was laughing too hard to be helped up, so he remained sitting in the compost, shoulders shaking.

Then he caught sight of Greta, and his smile was instantly replaced by his customary expression of fixed seriousness. He stood and brushed himself down.

"Good morning," he said, the last of his humor shriveling.

"Good morning," said Greta.

Albert had a yellow leaf sticking up jauntily in his hair. She longed to pluck it away, but knew he would flinch at such intimacy. The last time she had seen him this unkempt was when they had almost . . . well. Greta steered her thoughts away. Albert retrieved his net from Bernard and, with a nod to her, quitted the arboretum. She was as disregarded as the white butterfly, which now rested on a glass pane, high out of reach.

Stokes turned back to Greta. "Is there anything else that I can tell you about the arboretum, madam?"

Greta sighed and wished she had something sensible to ask. She was to spend an entire week with the inscrutable Stokes.

The arboretum glasshouse was a wonder: it was a nursery for trees and a miniature map of the world and of the interests of the Goldbaums. Greta observed that the problems of Europe were reflected here in the glasshouses and shrubbery. Stokes explained the dilemma: ought they to group specimens according to the country where they were to be found, or according to species? It made Greta think of the empires of Europe, those loosely arranged collectives of countries and peoples that threatened to break down, as their subjects asserted a desire for devolution and new nations re-formed along ethnic and religious lines. Stokes and Lady Goldbaum experienced the same difficulty with plant groupings within the arboretum and beyond. But at least the plants were unlikely to express revolutionary intent.

Like all the glasshouses, the indoor arboretum had its own stove to keep the tropical specimens warm in winter, while water was sloshed onto coals to preserve the humidity. The boiler was meticulously concealed in a cavernous underground cellar, so as not to despoil the beauty of the glasshouse. The exhaust pipes had been tunneled beneath the lawns for three hundred feet to be properly concealed.

A library had been built beside the glasshouse to house relevant books, as well as Lady Goldbaum's correspondence with the various explorers, in order that the gardeners could readily avail themselves of all the information while tending to their charges. Whenever a plant failed, an inquest was held. Lady Goldbaum was informed, and the correspondence and notes relating to the specimen were refiled in the library in a special envelope with black edges. When Stokes called on Lady Goldbaum during those ill-fated weeks, he was not offered his customary glass of Scotch.

There were forty greenhouses in all. Greta tried to sketch a map in her head. Fifteen were required for the continuous cycle of bedding plants that were replaced at least twice each season: pansies, daisies, begonias, marigolds, geraniums, violas and asters for summer in a hundred different shades; while cyclamen, ivy and purple heather were planted out in the cooler months. Apparently, Stokes confided, Lady Goldbaum had wanted to try white-and-mauve ornamental cabbages, but to this her husband had objected. There could not be such a thing as an ornamental cabbage—it was too whimsical for a Goldbaum parterre. Greta made a note to herself to plant an entire bed with decorative mauve cabbages. She might even put them in a vase on the dinner table or send them in a bouquet to her mother-in-law.

The remainder of the greenhouses were dedicated to the kitchen gardens. These were an industry within themselves, and if the arboretum and tropical glasshouses revealed the geographical influence of the Goldbaums, the kitchen glasshouses displayed their triumph over nature on a domestic scale. Two gardeners in brown leather aprons knelt on monogrammed cushions, trimming runners from strawberry plants.

"Lord Goldbaum requires a continuous season of fruit for his table," explained Stokes. His forehead creased into a well-worn frown, like a piece of paper folded and refolded. "It was a struggle, I'll be quite honest with you, madam," he confided. "It took a good few years and a good many headaches until we managed it. The glasshouses must be kept warm, but at different temperatures, or else all the raspberries would be ready in March. And every glasshouse has its own hive of bees. It's all very well to make the cherry trees flower in December, but if there aren't any bees to pollinate them . . . well."

Greta glanced around her. Plumes of moisture licked the windowpanes, and steam buffeted the roof like smoke. She could hear the hum of the hothouse bees and, as she looked, saw that the air was thick with insects.

"We produce more honey than even we can use," said Stokes. "The fruit trees don't last long, being forced. All the kindling in the house is cherry and apple and pear. Apparently it lights better and smells delicious." He pointed to another glasshouse. "After the smaller plants are forced in the heat, we move them to the coolhouse and pass them through ether fumes to curb the rise of sap."

"Are you a gardener or an alchemist, Stokes?" asked Greta with a smile.

He gave a little bow, but Greta was not quite sure that she meant it as a compliment. She was used to excess, but there was something about the ambition of the gardens here that disconcerted her. It proclaimed the power of the Goldbaums over nature herself, on a scale even she had not glimpsed before. She appreciated that her own view of nature had been guided by the poets, but nonetheless she preferred the idea of a garden working with nature rather than against it. There was something uncanny about pear trees being tricked into blossoming at Christmastime.

That afternoon Greta, Lady Goldbaum and Stokes conducted interviews for the position of Greta's head gardener. After the last candidate had departed, they stayed behind in the small library in the west wing, the afternoon light sneaking beneath the half-drawn blinds. The two ladies sat on sofas opposite one another, cups of orange-infused tea resting on the ivory-and-ebony-inlaid tables beside them. Arthur Stokes sat on an upright chair, his gardening boots meticulously cleaned, but his feet resting upon a neat square of brown paper nonetheless. A dish of almond sugar cookies beside him remained untouched.

Lady Goldbaum turned to Greta. "Well, what do you think, my dear? Shall we engage Mr. Grinstead?"

Greta swallowed. She did not like to displease her mother-in-law, not when she had shown her such attention and kindness, but she was resolved. "No, Adelheid. I'm sorry, but no to Mr. Grinstead."

Lady Goldbaum set down her teacup. "Very well. It's your garden. Who did you prefer? Mr. Perkins? Mr. Butler-Jones? They are all splendid choices."

Her garden project was starting to feel like a ruse, whereby she was coaxed into creating yet another precisely portioned Goldbaum garden and, in the process, became shaped herself into the ideal Goldbaum wife. Greta did not want to be trimmed like a piece of topiary, shaved and cropped until she fitted the correct mold. She had done her duty and married Albert. She would endeavor to fulfill the role of wife as far as she was able. But she needed a place where she could be free of all constraint. If she was to create a garden, she would make it her own.

"There was no one you liked? They are all eminently qualified." In her irritation, Lady Goldbaum's German accent rose to the surface with a little hiss, like steam.

Greta leaned forward with a frown. "I know they are all excellent gardeners and are all infinitely experienced and knowledgeable. But I need to find someone myself. Someone who wants to create the same sort of garden as I do."

"And what sort of garden do you wish to create, Greta?" asked Lady Goldbaum, intrigued.

"I have absolutely no idea," she replied.

That night Greta was unable to sleep. Temple Court teemed with people and yet she was lonely. Throughout her childhood she'd frequently spent weeks or even months away from Vienna, on holiday with Otto and the nanny at the house on Lake Geneva, or in Italy or Paris with cousins, and never once had she missed home. Now the homesickness kept her awake like hunger pangs. She longed for her old bedroom, the familiar smell of patisserie and horse in the Vienna streets, the sound of the Danube rushing in the dark; she yearned for a taste of *Sachertorte* and for mornings spent teasing Johanna Schwartzschild about her boyfriends. Most of all she missed Otto. She wanted to sip coffee and discuss her garden with him. She remembered traipsing through the park at the château at Saint-Pierre with him the previous autumn. The men had been off shooting partridge, and Greta had huffed that it was only men who had the pleasure of sport. The following morning Otto had roused her at dawn and snuck her out into the woods, where a beater waited with a shotgun. They spent a joyful hour gamely missing bird after bird. Greta returned to the house breathless, mud dashed and happy. Later, when rumors of the escapade reached the baroness's ears over caviar and *blinis*, and

Otto was summoned, he denied Greta's presence. They were quite mistaken. He had been alone.

I am alone now, Greta realized. She had not understood what it really meant before. There was no Otto to pull her back from trouble or unhappiness. She had to find her own way to survive and not surrender to self-pity and bitterness. She wondered briefly whether Albert was as miserable as her—but, she thought, anger prickling her like gooseflesh, he had rejected her, punished her for admitting her doubts.

She turned on the light and slid out of bed and into her sitting room. Piles of gardening books reproached her from the surface of every table. With a sigh, she picked them up one after the other, discarding them. She flicked one open and this time the title caught her eye: *The Wild Garden, by William Robinson*. She read a sentence at random:

> How these early frosts accentuate the essential difference
> between one style of gardening and another. The . . . bedded-
> out plants are "all dead men," and in a few hours . . . a
> pappy mess of corruption. Look now at the slimy putridity
> of plants which cannot compare in beauty or perfume with
> Rose, Anemone . . .

That was exactly it, decided Greta. The hothouses filled with flowers to be bedded out were really charnel houses. At the first frost the gaudy reds and oranges and purples of the begonias and marigolds and pansies would end in a soggy death. The pleasure of a garden ought to be in waiting for a treasure hoard of golden crocuses or pale narcissi to erupt from the soil, and when they die, it is only to bloom again next year. Why would anyone forgo such cyclical magic in a garden? She read the rest of the book in her nightdress, agreeing wholeheartedly. Inside the front cover of the book she noticed an inscription: *"To dearest Doris, wishing you all the luck in the world at*

Miss Hathaway's Gardening and Finishing School for Girls, Buck-thorne, Hampshire, 1908."

Greta rang the bell.

A few minutes later Anna appeared, still in her nightdress, eyes red rimmed and blurred with sleep.

"Yes, madam?"

Anna had become used to these nighttime intrusions. The other servants considered them beyond the pale. The Goldbaums might have had dominion over every waking hour, but one's sleep was surely sovereign. Anna dared not grumble, but showed her displeasure by speaking in German, contrary to her mistress's instructions. Greta did not appear to notice, replying unthinkingly in German herself.

"There is a finishing school for young ladies near here specializing in gardening, run by a Miss Hathaway. I'd like you to telephone, Anna, and tell them that I'm coming to visit today."

Anna rubbed her eyes and stared at her mistress. She was very tired. She hadn't climbed into her own bed before midnight any day this whole week, and she needed to be up by six o'clock to press Greta's clothes, prepare her breakfast tray and arrange her room, which, she thought as she glanced around at the disorder of books and papers and the discarded dressing gown, might take some time.

"It's half past four in the morning, madam. I doubt very much that anyone will be answering the telephone."

"Oh. You're quite right. Well, you can call in the morning, then. Perhaps at half past eight?"

"Yes, madam. Anything else?"

Greta shook her head. She stood in the middle of the room, her face almost as pale as her nightgown. She looked very young and almost as tired as Anna herself. Anna found her irritation sinking to pity. She had discovered friends below stairs. Lady Goldbaum had two Swiss maids, with whom she shared a passion for Ludo and proper chocolate, while Mr. Albert Goldbaum's valet was a charming devil who had promised to take all of them out punting on their Sunday afternoon.

Her mistress, on the other hand, was lost. Anyone could see that—all this bloody fretting about plants. And Anna was privy to the worst secret of all, a secret she would never tell: her mistress was still a virgin.

Miss Winifred Hathaway received Mrs. Goldbaum herself. Aware that they needed always to be on the lookout for employment opportunities for their girls, Miss Hathaway and Miss Ursula Ogden were doing their very best to make a good impression on Mrs. Goldbaum. They made Greta tea; offered her one of the good cookies out of the Queen Victoria jubilee tin, kept only for guests (and consequently its contents always slightly soft); and then walked her around the grounds.

"They do look charming in their outfits," said Greta.

The girls, like Miss Hathaway, wore brown breeches tapered at the knee, wide at the thigh, with loose cotton smocks, crowned by straw sun hats. Despite these, they all sported deep tans. Greta thought how refreshing it would be to exchange her own large picture hat with its vast brim (however becoming) for a simple straw boater, and her own white lace gloves for a pair of thick leather gardening ones. She was intrigued by the two older ladies, who were spinsters in ruddy-cheeked middle age, quite at ease with one another and constantly finishing each other's sentences.

"I understand that you teach the girls according to the principles of Miss Gertrude Jekyll and Mr. William Robinson?"

"Indeed. The girls learn right away that nature is their ally. Their role is to enhance her and to work alongside her. They must complement what is already there—whether it's an old stone wall with honeysuckle and climbing roses or irises planted beside a pool."

"They paint with flowers," said Ursula. "But we insist on perennials. The only annuals we permit are wildflower seeds."

"The girls come from respectable backgrounds. Some might make good marriages, but some of the others . . . ," said Miss Hathaway.

". . . Not everyone wishes to be a governess. All that time indoors," finished Ursula.

"With children," added Miss Hathaway, with some distaste.

"Ours is a mission," said Miss Hathaway sternly, pushing her spectacles up her nose. "We fervently believe in our vision of the garden. We train our girls and then send them out into the world to glorify the gardens of England, large and small, according to our principles."

"I'm quite certain that I've come to the right place," said Greta, with a smile. "My garden is in definite need of glorification."

"Ours is a very different style from that of a Goldbaum garden," warned Miss Hathaway, addressing Greta with a frown. "We're less 'Parks Department.'"

"You're quite right," Greta replied. "The Temple Court garden is exactly like a park. Formal and orderly. Everything about it tells you to act with decency and decorum: low hedges and straight paths, where all one can do is pace to and fro and admire the beds stuffed with stubby marigolds and pansies. But a garden!" Greta clapped her hands and laughed at the astonished faces of the two women. "Now, that ought to be different. A garden is there to help you misbehave. God was expecting far too much. Eve had exactly the right idea, if you ask me. I mean, why have an apple tree in a garden that one can't eat from? It doesn't make any sense."

"So, Mrs. Goldbaum, you are looking for a girl to assist Mr. Stokes? You wish to try something new?"

"This has nothing in the least to do with Mr. Stokes. It is me who needs help. I'm afraid I'm a horticultural novice. But I'm going to create a little garden all the same."

"A little garden?"

"Yes. In about a hundred acres."

"A little garden of about a hundred acres?" For once, amazement confounded Miss Hathaway.

"Yes, that's right. A hundred to start with. We may have more land, if we require it, later on."

Miss Hathaway leaned against a convenient yew hedge. Miss Ogden found her hand.

"What's there at present, Mrs. Goldbaum?"

"Nothing."

"Nothing?"

"There's a cornfield. But I don't suppose that will help much."

"No."

Miss Hathaway and Miss Ogden, who were, it seemed, struck quite dumb by the scale of the task proposed, stood hand in hand leaning against the hedge and gazing at Greta.

"I believe you may need several gardeners, Mrs. Goldbaum," said Miss Hathaway at last.

"Yes, of course. But first I must have plans drawn up. And I was hoping that one of your girls—"

"I'm afraid such a task is far beyond them. They are rather new, you see."

"But so am I," answered Greta, with a smile. "And I'm not in the least afraid of mistakes. Or not in the garden, in any case."

Regaining their composure, Miss Hathaway and Miss Ogden led Greta to inspect the individual plots, small lines of terra-cotta flowerpots or broken pieces of china marking the divisions between the girls' patches.

"I like that one," she said, pointing to the section at the end. Hollyhocks in creamy white with buttery crowns leaned casually against the brickwork, while candy-floss-colored sweet peas grew in a tangle around a knot of willow, scenting the air with summer. It was a charmingly curated wilderness.

"Whose is this?"

"Mine," said a voice. A vigorous young woman of about the same age as Greta stepped forward. She had sandy-colored hair, cropped short, and small green eyes, and her skin was sprinkled with a constellation of freckles. "Enid Witherick," she said, and stuck out a hand that was rough and lined with dirt.

"Greta Goldbaum," said Greta, shaking the hand, which clasped hers with surprising strength. "I should like to engage your services."

Miss Hathaway and Miss Ogden sat in the parlor, perched side by side on a hard Victorian sofa. While they would have noticed instantly if a garden rose had died from blight and would have had it dug up the same afternoon, neither Ursula nor Winifred observed that the rose fabric on the armrests was torn beyond repair.

Greta was seated on the only good chair, an Arts and Crafts armchair carved in oak with ivy engraved across the back, and gifted to Miss Hathaway by Mr. William Morris himself. It was immensely beautiful and immensely uncomfortable.

Enid Witherick appeared mesmerized by the bobbing of the ostrich plume on Greta's picture hat, which moved as though it were trying to conduct the room each time she turned her head. A portrait of Queen Victoria surveyed them lopsidedly from above the fireplace.

"While engaging Enid is an excellent choice, she is far too inexperienced to be a head gardener. The task is gargantuan." Ursula raised her hands above her head and then let them flop for emphasis.

"I can manage," said Enid quietly, thrusting her hands in her pockets. "If you and Miss Hathaway will advise us."

"Wonderful," said Greta, clapping for joy. For the first time in months she felt a surge of something like happiness. "Fontmell was a priory before the Reformation. It began as a nuns' garden, and it is exactly right that it shall be a women's garden once again."

"And after all, we believe that the first-ever gardener was a woman," said Enid softly, looking around. "And I'm quite sure that after she'd finished picking apples, Eve pruned the tree."

Number One Park Lane, London, August

⟡

Lord Goldbaum was displeased. He complained in no uncertain terms to his younger son. Not only had his daughter-in-law hired a woman as a gardener, but the woman in question wore breeches.

"You've not been married three months, and they're already making fun of her in *Punch*."

He slid a copy of the magazine across the breakfast table and tapped at a sketch on page 4. "Girton Gals dig for Gold-baum," read the line, while in the picture three bosomy women in breeches dug in a garden, as a caricatured Greta in a feathered hat egged them on, wielding a silver spoon as a trowel.

"You must bring your wife to heel," he said to Albert. "We have standards to maintain. As a Goldbaum, she ought to understand. I will not have her in this ghastly publication again."

Clement saw his brother wince. His sister-in-law was quite capable of acting as the ideal hostess, holding on to Albert's arm—family diamonds glinting at her throat—and she could make even the most austere of statesmen laugh. At the dreariest of gatherings she exuded just the right amount of mischief, puffing life into the assembled company as a bellows hurries flames from the embers. Arthur Balfour always made a point of asking that Greta be seated beside him at dinner. In the evenings, if the party was becoming stolid, Lady Goldbaum would ask her to entertain the guests, and Greta would sit at the piano and sing German *lieder*, the archness of the meaning clear from her expression. She was kind and attentive to all the guests, no matter how unimportant, and remembered everyone's children's names and ages like a brilliant schoolboy effortlessly recalling his Latin verbs. In fact, Clement concluded, she charmed everyone except her husband.

Yet there were also moments when Greta seemed to forget what was required of her. She was late for luncheon with the American ambassador, Mr. Reid, and, sent out to look for her, Clement discovered her beside Poseidon's fountain, using her stockings as a fishing net to rescue a drowning toad. After formal dinners excellently prepared by Monsieur Arnold, which she barely touched, she ordered bread and cheese and sat beside the fire in the Gray Salon with a toasting fork, while the others consumed coffee and petits fours and polite conversation. One evening the Swedish emissary had joined Greta for what she termed a "carpet picnic" and they sat on silk cushions on the floor, eating melted cheese and singed toast, which he declared was his favorite of the nine courses served to him.

Since the afternoon of the coronation when he had lost his temper, Albert had never uttered a word of reproach. He simply pretended not to see when Greta folded her table napkin into a fishing boat or a chicken (using a silver pepper pot as its egg) for the entertainment of her neighbor.

In the matter of the lady gardeners, however, Lord Goldbaum had reached his limit. A line had to be drawn. The girl had to be made to recall that she was a Goldbaum.

"I shall speak to Greta when I return to Temple Court," said Albert at long last, with great reluctance. He pushed away the magazine with displeasure, turning it over so that he did not have to see the grotesque of his wife.

Lord Goldbaum grunted. "She's a good girl. Just a little more . . ."—he searched for the right word—"Continental than I expected." He frowned, evidently unhappy that he felt compelled to have this conversation with his son. "You understood your duty when you married her, Albert. Sometimes your mother and I worry that you have forgotten it since. Our House has always been strengthened by marriage. I won't have yours undermine it. If your wife is misbehaving because she is unhappy, then make her happy, Albert. Increase her allowance."

"She does not want for money."

"Then find out what she does bloody want. Ask your mother. This marriage isn't a simple union between you and Greta. It's a union of Houses. You will fix this."

Albert sat silent and miserable. Clement surveyed him with sympathy, knowing perfectly well that his brother hadn't the least idea how to address the difficulties in his marriage.

"When the time comes, I want you to run for the seat at Fontmell West. And if you're to be a member of Parliament, your wife needs to be an asset and not a liability," said Lord Goldbaum.

Clement noted that his father did not suggest that he should run, something he observed with both sadness and relief. He was entirely unsuited to politics, and yet the quickness with which his father dismissed him wounded him all the same. He dared not object. Everyone's tempers were short. The breakfast room of Number One Park Lane looked straight out onto the yellowed grass of Hyde Park. The Thames was at the lowest level anyone could remember, and it stank of human filth and rotting fish. The capital was motionless. Strikes at the docks had stopped supplies of coal, so that the great railway stations were silent, the trains still. A shortage of motor oil meant that omnibus services were suspended, and motorized taxis hiked up their prices to levels that even a Goldbaum considered obscene, while the heat had led to an outbreak of mange among the horses, and with most of them quarantined, even hansoms were hard to come by. Anyone without a motorcar was forced to walk, and, Clement thought unhappily, at present that entailed running the gauntlet through buzzing crowds of angry men demanding jobs.

In the immediate vicinity of the city and Park Lane the family were well-known for their generosity; all spare birds from shoots were brought up to town, and no hungry man or woman was ever turned away from the back door of the Goldbaum kitchens. Consequently their motorcar was usually greeted with good humor by passersby, but yesterday Albert and Lord Goldbaum had found themselves set upon in Piccadilly. Young men had drummed on the roof of the car and pummeled it with rotting eggs. Lord Goldbaum proclaimed himself unshaken, merely relieved that the ladies were in the country. Clement was not convinced. The cartoon of Greta was one of the least offensive in that week's papers. Albert and Clement tried uselessly to conceal from their father those lampooning him. He was painted variously as the Guy Fawkes of greed, a villain against the people and the rapacious financier. Clement knew how this wounded him. The headaches that had plagued Lord Goldbaum as a young man had returned, and in the evening as he sat beside the fire, Clement noticed a tic in his left eye. Soon his tailor would have to be summoned to take in his suits.

Lord Goldbaum reached out and clasped his sons' hands.

"Today I shall vote for a reform I do not believe in, because the consequence of not agreeing to it would be disastrous. Our family arrived here with nothing but a piece of paper and a foreign name. Within three generations, we are peers of the realm. It was my duty to protect England, and I have failed."

His sons started to voice their objections, but he held up his hand.

"This is the end. Of precisely what, only time will tell. I hope that when you inherit this title, Clement, it will still mean something. You have a responsibility, even if those you seek to protect abhor you."

"You have done all that a man could," said Albert, his tone measured, implying that in his view his father had done more than he ought.

"We may have to extend our Argentine loans," said Albert, trying to change the subject to other business. The concerns of the House of Goldbaum Bank were always the greatest salve to their father. Considering the relative profit and risk of a loan, or the organization of an issue of gilts on behalf of His Majesty's Government, consoled and relaxed their father more thoroughly than a good night's sleep. His loyalty was to his family and his country, and while he considered himself to be laboring for the good of both, he was soothed and comforted.

Albert shifted on his chair, stretching out his long legs beneath the table. "A hundred thousand pounds' worth of Argentine beef is turning green in Bermondsey harbor, with no one to unload the container ships. They want to sell it to the government for the army, but Churchill won't have it."

"Of course the government won't have it. There is never a good moment to poison the army," said his father with a grunt.

"We shall take a loss."

"Then we take a loss. This is not a financial decision, it is a moral one." Lord Goldbaum sighed and closed his eyes for a moment, perhaps relieved at the opportunity to demonstrate that he was, after all, a good man.

Albert made a note. "Ought we to insure the passenger ship, then, Father? I'm being pressed for an answer. I rather think we should. It's unsinkable. We'd make more than six percent."

Lord Goldbaum shook his head. "I don't like it. I don't care what they say. The thing is too big to float."

Albert and Clement exchanged a look, both exasperated and amused by their father. There was no use in reasoning with him once he'd resolved upon a course of action, however illogical.

"Coutts will make the profit instead," said Albert, in one last attempt to change his mind with a reminder of their rival.

"Let them," said Lord Goldbaum.

L ord Goldbaum returned from the vote at the House of Lords at two forty-five in the morning and woke up both his sons, instructing them to join him shortly in the library. It occurred to Lord

Goldbaum that in his determination to do his best for his country, he had neglected his own people. The letter from Henri describing the pogroms in Russia weighed heavily in his breast pocket. Distracted by events in the upper house, he had not given it the attention he ought. Shame prickled across his flesh like a rash. He sighed and swallowed a yawn. It was his duty to show his sons that they had responsibilities beyond England's shores. They had to do better than he. Yet he was so tired, and the hours spent standing for the vote in the House had irritated his piles, so that they itched his backside like a scourge of mosquito bites. Patting the letter in his breast pocket, he decided that he deserved such petty discomforts.

Albert and Clement entered the library, bleary-eyed and wearing their dressing gowns. Their father pressed glasses of brandy upon them, poured from a bottle dating from the days before the French Revolution and reserved for the most significant of occasions.

Lord Goldbaum raised his glass. "We must mark our defeats as well as our victories."

Albert and Clement toasted. Albert stifled a shudder. The brandy might have been priceless, but it was also unpleasant.

"A great loss is as invigorating as a win. It reminds one of what is at stake," said Lord Goldbaum.

Albert observed that his father's cheeks were flushed and he suspected that this was not the first brandy of the night.

"What is at stake, Father?" asked Albert.

"The name of Goldbaum. We shall show them a defeat in the Lords has not dimmed our influence. We shall not be ignored. I've asked the foreign secretary half a dozen times to voice objections to the pogroms, and Lord Gray prevaricates or sends a letter so feeble that the Russian ambassador couldn't possibly discern whether he's being admonished or invited to tea."

"Is there anything more to be done?" asked Albert.

"There's always something more to be done," snapped his father. "These wretches in Russia look to us. If we can't defend the Jews there, no soul on earth will. The British government won't risk displeasing the tsar by interfering. But we can always make the tsar listen. After all, we have what he wants."

"Money."

"And he shan't have it, not until the violence against the Jews stops."

Lord Goldbaum sat down awkwardly at the library table and scribbled a note, then rang the bell. Stanton, the butler, appeared moments later, fully dressed as though it weren't nearly three in the morning.

"Send this to the editor of the *Times*. And send a bottle of the Château Gold sixty-three to Asquith, Lloyd George and Churchill."

Stanton withdrew.

Later that morning, when Asquith, Lloyd George and Churchill gathered for a cabinet meeting in Downing Street, none of them mentioned the gift they had received from Lord Goldbaum. Each understood it to be not so much a magnanimous gesture upon defeat as a reminder.

Hampshire, August

———◆≻◆≺◆———

On seeing the paper the following morning, Lady Goldbaum telephoned her husband to register her disapproval. She read aloud his
letter to the editor of the *Times*: "'Terror from the tsar and those above
may stave off revolution, but it will be at the cost of national bankruptcy.' It sounds rather like a threat, dearest."

Lord Goldbaum muttered something inaudible.

"Why can't you lie low and lick your wounds after a defeat?" continued his wife, profoundly irritated. "As if national strikes weren't
enough, now you have to pick an argument with the tsar of Russia."

"I ought to have done it before, Adelheid. It's to my own shame that
I didn't."

"Wonderful! I shall expect Cossacks in the rose garden by luncheon."

"I had to do it. The boys need to understand their duty. We are the
voice of European Jewry. It's time we shouted our objections to pogroms and slaughter."

"So that one day your sons can learn to pick their own fights with
emperors?"

Lord Goldbaum apparently thought it best not to reply.

"You must make things better for the poor souls in Russia, not
worse."

"That I promise you," said Lord Goldbaum.

Lady Goldbaum paused, aware of the operators listening in on the call.

"Good. Remember, a promise witnessed is an oath, dearest."

Lord Goldbaum grunted.

"Are you taking the pills for your gout? And how is your digestion?"

Lord Goldbaum hung up.

A little later Greta accompanied her mother-in-law to the kitchen gardens. Observing Adelheid's crossness, she wisely made no remark on Lord Goldbaum's letter in the morning's *Times*. Lady Goldbaum stopped to deadhead a rose, taking out her frustration on the shrub. She always kept a pair of secateurs on her person, holstered to a leather belt like a cowboy's gun. The two-hundred-yard walk to the kitchen gardens took considerable time, as Lady Goldbaum paused at every bush. Arthur Stokes had the gardening boys snipping from dawn in preparation for her inevitable inspection. Each time Lady Goldbaum found a desiccating flower or—outrage!—a scarlet hip, she snipped it and retained it in her pocket to present to Arthur in cheerful triumph.

At last they reached the wooden buildings beside the six acres of kitchen garden, and as they entered, Greta stared at the vegetable cornucopia: every surface was covered with produce—stacks of striped marrows like fat skittle sets, baskets of tomatoes as shiny as Yuletide baubles, veined cabbages, potatoes and rows of brown onions, their white roots dangling off the tables like dirty, uncut hair. Forty gardeners in white cotton gloves diligently packed them into lined crates and sealed them up. Lady Goldbaum took charge.

"It must be packed properly with straw and ice. I won't have it going bad before it reaches the strikers' families."

"Yes, m'lady."

"Greta, you are to oversee the delivery for the East End and the Synagogue Relief Fund."

"Yes, Adelheid," said Greta, surveying the mountain of boxes.

Lady Goldbaum was kept as busy by her charities as by her rhododendrons, and if she was not as passionate about good works as good leaf color, she remained diligent and committed. The heat inside the packing shed was immense and Greta peeled back her sleeves and doused her neck and wrists with iced water, melted from the vast blocks of miniature icebergs that floated in tin baths on the floor. The plans for her own garden had been paused, her newly engaged gardeners all commandeered to assist with the general effort of picking, packing and resowing food.

Greta experienced unease at the pleasure she felt at the task at hand. It was jolly to be part of the gang, and she was relieved to be occupied with something useful. The lurid newspaper descriptions of the squalor in the slums and the misery of the strikers' children were simply too awful. And yet Greta also harbored the unpleasant feeling that the good she was achieving was mostly to ease her own conscience, and that even if the Goldbaums dispatched every lettuce and each strawberry from their own beds to strikers' children in Southampton or London or Liverpool, it would make no difference at all. Nothing she could do would secure them the extra three shillings a week they demanded. In the evenings when the men were at home, she heard Lord Goldbaum fret about the new trade unions, lamenting that they were the thin edge of socialism, as Albert attempted to reassure him. All the while, as Greta listened, she knew that the corset rubbing her skin to blisters and forcing her to sit at the edge of her chair like a canary on its perch had cost far more than the seventeen shillings with which a workingman presently had to feed his family each week.

There had been power cuts all morning and the house was without electricity, so instead of eating in the darkened grandeur of the dining room, they took lunch on the terrace. Even beneath the shade of the parasols it was sweltering and the scarlet geraniums flopped in their pots, fainting like schoolgirls. They were served spatchcock poussins roosting on a virulent puree of broad beans dotted with little chanterelles foraged from the estate woods, but all Greta wanted was a glass of lemonade and a cool washcloth.

"Are you feeling quite well, dearest? You're looking terribly flushed," said Lady Goldbaum.

"I'm only a little warm."

"Not unwell? Feeling sick?"

"No," answered Greta firmly. She knew that they were all watching her for any signs of pregnancy. Well, all of them except Albert.

"Why don't you go inside and lie down this afternoon? The boxes are packed, and we've given orders for the rest."

"Yes, all right, Adelheid. Thank you."

Greta set down her napkin and ambled back to the house. Even when they were alone, out of hearing of the servants, Greta and Adelheid never spoke German. Sometimes Greta longed to speak and hear it, like a marooned seaman longs for fresh water. Perhaps it was for the best. She liked Adelheid more than her own mother; she was endlessly kind toward her, and yet to her surprise Greta found that she missed the baroness and all her foibles. The baroness penned letters that were tenderer in Greta's absence than she'd ever been in person. Occasionally she was even amusing and self-aware, and Greta puzzled over how it was that she'd had to travel so far away to discover this other side to her mother.

She hurried through the darkened East Gallery, past three hundred ticking clocks starting to proclaim the hour in a clashing Schoenberg of bells, but instead of going upstairs to her rooms, she walked straight out through the furthest doors and back into the gardens, far from Lady Goldbaum on the south terrace. She carried with her a small parcel that had arrived from Otto via the family courier that morning.

The sun was at its hottest as she reached the edge of the park and the boundary between the Temple Court estate and that of Fontmell Abbey. The managed wilderness of the park turned into scrub and overgrown hedges. Greta shouldered her way along a path lined waist-high with ferocious stinging nettles and brambles, studded here and there with early blackberries. She picked them as she passed, discovering that she was hungry after all. In a few minutes her lips and fingers were stained purple with juice, her skin bleeding from the thorns. The scent of wild honeysuckle mingled with the salt smell of the river.

Her white blouse was stained with blackberries and she'd torn her sleeve. Her stays chafed against her ribs. She longed to pause and rest, but then, at last, peeking out from above a dark knot of yew, she saw the soot-stained chimney stacks of Fontmell Abbey. Unconsciously she began to hurry, as though the place were already home. The unmade road leading there had been newly paved in preparation for the planned building works, but the hedges remained towering and uncut, the twisted iron gates rusted and broken.

Opening a small door in the garden wall, she found herself on the south lawn—if it could be called a lawn—the grass long and flowering and filled with cowslips and meadow vetch and fat thistles. The grass swayed with rabbits. A white rambling rose had climbed all the way up a catalpa tree, filling its branches with cascading flowers. She'd visited Fontmell a month earlier with Albert and Lord and Lady Goldbaum to discuss the new house with the family's preferred architect, a whiskered gentleman who designed new châteaux in high French style. His proposal was to demolish the old manor and the remnants of the ancient abbey and build a modern house, comfortable and exquisite. She'd not voiced any objection; in fact, she hadn't spoken at all.

Now she looked at the place as if for the first time. She gazed through the wilderness up toward the old house, crouching on a gentle rise above the gardens, its sandstone façade almost entirely covered by a vast and ancient wisteria. Swinging tresses of *Clematis montana* climbed upward to the roof. The glass was missing from several of the windows and birds flew in and out unheeded; part of the lead guttering had swung down and dangled dangerously above the door. The manor looked as if it had grown there, as if somehow it had always existed in this fertile bend in the river, with the bindweed and forest of dandelions sprouting up around it. There was little left of the abbey. Most of it had collapsed centuries ago and the stone had been reused in the newer parts of the manor, but to the west of the house survived archways from the cloisters. There was a peace and serenity to the place. It blew through her, catching her off guard. Perhaps it ought to have felt odd, a Jew contemplating an abbey with a sense of equanimity and pleasure, but God existed in the landscape, she decided.

"I shall not let them knock you down," she declared.

She would dismiss the learned architect and his elaborate plans for three electric lifts, and hire a man who could restore the manor and see it as part of the gardens. The abbey ruins had to be allowed to remain in their state of quixotic decay. Nature needed to be pruned, but Greta was determined to preserve the feeling of the meadows spilling in waves up to the house. She wanted to wake to the rattle of sparrows cracking snails for breakfast, not the mechanical whir of a lift.

Leaning against the wall, she opened the package from Otto, discarding her gloves and using her nail. Inside were a note and a small pistol, its grip covered in shining mother-of-pearl:

> In case you ever want to miss some partridge again. And, after all I've been reading in the papers, in case the furious hordes descend on you at Temple Court, so that you can miss them, too. Vienna is quiet without you. And dull. Your loving brother, etc.

Greta smiled, wrapping the pistol back up and slipping it into her pocket. Only Otto would send her a gun as a joke. It was something else to conceal from Albert, who would certainly not approve. With an intake of breath, she wondered whether there was anything about her that he valued.

Feeling deflated, she walked slowly back toward the house—*her* house, she reminded herself—and realized that she was becoming light-headed from the heat and that a dull throb thrummed behind her eye. She cast about for a tempting shady spot. In the center of one of the lawns stood a towering cedar tree, higher than the roof, its branches reaching out across the garden wall. She stretched out in relief, kicked off her shoes and then her stockings and, with a surge of exhilaration, unfastened her skirt and wriggled out of it. Discarding her blouse and folding it into a makeshift pillow, she lay down in her underwear and slip. But the temptation was too great. She could not resist. She unclasped her stays and discarded her petticoat and knickers and lay back on her bed of moss, perfectly naked. The velveteen moss cooled her hot skin and smelled deliciously of fresh earth and leaf mold. A miniature forest of green ferns flourished at the base of the cedar tree, and she could taste their metallic odor on her tongue. A wood louse embarked upon an expedition across her stomach, and she watched as it tickled its way along the fine down leading to her navel, before flicking it away. Through half-closed lids she observed an iridescent dragonfly investigate a clump of daylilies. For a heavenly moment she did not think about Albert and the failure of her marriage, the heaviness of the treasure-stuffed house or her life as a clockwork doll instead of a person, trundled out to make visitors smile. There was only the sound of the leaves, the heat and the pleasure of her own skin on the damp ground. Then she was asleep.

In her dream she was in the garden still, but the one that she imagined. The lawns were speckled with a confetti of white daisies. The old brick wall formed the back of a large herbaceous border filled with tree peonies in yellow and white, and sculpted peaks of ice-cream-pink hydrangeas. A host of golden butterflies alighted on honey-scented buddleia, each thorax shaped from a single glittering diamond.

The house had been restored, and blue pools of heather and lavender flourished beneath the ground-floor windows, which had been thrown open. Curtains of roses, clematis and wisteria covered the entire front with a galaxy of flowers. Glancing upward, she saw that the roof was thatched. She'd never seen a thatched manor before, only cottages, and the result was original and enchanting. She watched the path, certain that someone was about to walk toward her.

"For Christ's sake, Greta! Put some bloody clothes on."

She woke to find Albert standing over her. Instinctively she covered herself with her hands, and then, decisively, took them away again, deliberately placing her arms behind her head, so that her breasts were exposed. They had been married for several months and it was high time he saw her naked. She stretched out to the tips of her toes and gazed up at Albert.

"Lovely weather," she said.

"Anyone could see you," he hissed, trying valiantly not to look.

"And yet no one did. Only you. And, after all, we are married."

"Put your clothes back on," repeated Albert.

"Why? I'm the most comfortable I've been all day. You should join me."

He coughed in irritation. Color rose around the back of his neck.

"It's very kind of you to come and find me."

Greta knew that she was teasing him, but she felt a little drunk on the scent of the garden, the sleepy heat of the afternoon and the unexpected power she presently wielded over Albert.

"I can't talk to you, Greta, until you're dressed."

"In that case . . . ," she said, closing her eyes and pretending to go back to sleep. Through the slits of her lids, she saw Albert eyeing her. He looked deeply irritated, but Greta perceived the outline of a large erection in the confines of his trousers. The thought of his discomfort made her want to laugh. And perhaps even have him kiss her, which was interesting, since she disliked him.

"Will you at least sit up?" asked Albert, defeated.

Greta sighed and raised herself on her elbows, removing a twig and an earwig from her hair.

"The women gardeners you've engaged," said Albert, "they're not to wear breeches while they're working here. It simply isn't nice."

Greta laughed. "Oh dear. I'm causing nothing but trouble. My gardeners are wearing the wrong thing, and I'm wearing nothing at all."

"Well, do you agree?" demanded Albert, trying desperately to preserve his dignity. He shifted from foot to foot, profoundly uncomfortable. "You will arrange for an alternate uniform. If you must hire women, they shall at least be properly attired."

Greta couldn't help laughing again. "Oh, do sit down, Albert."

Beaten, he sat beside her on the moss. She reached out with a bare leg and stroked along his trouser leg, venturing beneath to flick the garter of his sock with her toe. He let out a little gasp. There were small beads of perspiration around his throat. She edged closer and, pulling his face toward hers, kissed him, slowly at first, more out of curiosity than desire, then longer and with interest. He made no move to touch her, his hands rigid at his sides as she curled around him, sliding into his lap. She loosened his cravat, feeling the bump of his Adam's apple with her tongue.

"I could make love to you now, Albert. But I think I'd like it better if I liked you more. And you did say that you were willing to wait until I was absolutely certain of my feelings."

He groaned and swore softly under his breath, but made no other objection.

She moved off his lap and stretched out beside him. She had absolutely no desire to put on her clothes. This sway she held over Albert was delightful.

"Your father seems to be intent on starting a fight with the Russians."

Albert stared at her for a moment, unable to focus.

"We are going to discuss this now, with you . . . ?" He gestured at her nakedness.

"We are," said Greta firmly. "For once, I seem to have your attention."

Albert sighed before answering. "The Goldbaums are trying to persuade the Russian government that protecting the Jews is in their financial interest. The tsar wants a loan. A very large one. Unless he vows to protect the Jewish population, he's going to find it very hard to raise the money. Every Goldbaum House will refuse him."

"Won't he simply try somewhere else?"

"Yes. But no Jewish bank will lend to him. We have written to them all. He'll get his money eventually, but it will be difficult and extremely expensive. There's a chance the Russian government will go bankrupt while waiting."

"If that happens, won't they blame it on the Russian Jews?"

Albert was silent for a moment, considering. "That is a risk. But we are hoping that the tsar will take our loan at a low rate, in exchange for stopping the pogroms. That is in everyone's best interest."

"I'm glad we're using our money to buy something useful."

Reluctantly she stood and began to dress herself as Albert watched, pulling on her slip and then her stockings, muttering as she found a tear in the silk.

"Blast! Will you pass me my shoe?"

He stared at her for a moment as if unable to hear and then, blinking heavily, reached for the stray shoe. Handing it to her, he turned away in silence and resolutely did not look at her. He waited until she was completely clothed, and when he finally turned back to her and resumed the conversation, it was as if he had merely stumbled upon her fully dressed and inspecting the begonias.

"Greta, I didn't come here to discuss Russia. Will your gardeners be appropriately attired? Or are you going to defy me?"

Greta glanced at her wristwatch. "Oh dear, it's later than I thought. We'd better hurry back or we'll be late dressing for dinner."

Albert stood and looked at her, unsmiling. They started back to Temple Court together as Greta cleared her throat.

"The women who work for me may wear what they like. Breeches are simply more practical for outside work," she said slowly.

"It is not kind, Greta. I have asked very little of you."

In irritation, he picked up his pace and she had to hurry to keep up.

"I shall defy you, Albert, but only in my garden. In all other ways I'll try my best to be a useful sort of wife. But in my garden I shall do as I please."

Her life had been carefully planned on her behalf: she felt detached from it all, as though she was not so much living as watching herself in a play, one where she already knew the plot and it appalled and bored her. Yet she was starting to realize that she could endure it all, so long as she had freedom in this one place. Here, she would obey only herself. This, Greta resolved, was to be a garden of defiance.

1912

As long as you work with your brothers,
not a House in the world will be able to
compete with you or cause you harm, for together
you can undertake more than any House in the world.

Moses Salomon Goldbaum to his sons, 1867

Goldbaum Bank, the Ringstrasse, Vienna, March

Otto waited in the partners' room for the Goldbaum courier to arrive with the mail. The most important and private of correspondence was always delivered in this way. It was the method trusted not only by the Goldbaums, but by all of Europe's monarchs and ministers. The emperor himself, when he had something vital or of a personal nature to communicate, sent for the Goldbaum courier. The clock struck nine, and a minute later there was a knock on the door. Otto opened it, took his package from the courier and settled back at his desk to read.

So, the tsar had finally managed to raise one hundred million rubles through Barings Bank. Stearns and Lehman Brothers had joined with the Goldbaums in their refusal to underwrite the loan. They had forgone nearly three million pounds in profit, but a note from Henri suggested it had been worthwhile. The tsar had issued an edict to the districts that if there were further pogroms, budgets would be cut. He wanted the next set of loans faster and cheaper. On the other hand, Henri wrote, the Russian finance minister had been forced to resign, not because of the loan debacle, but because his wife was a Jew. Otto harbored doubts as to how long the truce would last.

He opened another letter, this time from Clement. Greta and Albert's marriage was not a success, Clement confided. The entire household was disturbed by the tremors of unhappiness that emanated from the couple. Albert had turned to work, and he was in real danger of becoming a success. He spent some weekends in town, which wasn't the thing at all. There were rumors of a mistress. Clement, knowing his brother, was quite certain they were only malicious whisperings, but still, if the marriage were in order, no one could spread such gossip. And Greta . . . well, Greta was lost in her garden. It was going to be a thing of magnificence, but her dedication to it was dogged and excluded almost all else. Goodness knows, Clement appreciated that Albert was not an easy man, but he worried that Greta had rather given up. She complained that she was simply too busy to pretend to be interested in bonds, or bugs or butterflies. Clement confessed to Otto that he was worried. About Greta. About his brother. About the family. There were only whispers at present, but what if the whispers grew into shouts? His father could not bear a scandal.

Otto set the letter down. The strength of the family lay in its unity. The Houses across Europe were folded into one another again and again through marriage, kneaded together like dough. If a marriage should break apart, the effect it would have on the family would be devastating. The trust and concord between the Houses would be shaken. The shock would be felt in the money markets; the price of gold would falter. Otto cared little about this in itself, but he knew that his sister would be forced to suffer the consequences. He was concerned with her happiness, rather than with a scandal, but he understood in a way he feared she did not that she would not be allowed to be happy if her marriage failed. Otto tried to remember if anyone in the family had ever divorced. If they had, they had been so efficiently removed from history that he had never even heard their name.

He wondered if he ought to go to England. He knew nothing about marriage, but he did know Greta. He needed to understand why she was so set against Albert. Only then could he consider what was to be done.

Having begun his trade at the home bank, it was now time to venture out to one of the other House of Goldbaum banks, before returning to Vienna as a full partner. Though he took no pleasure in it, Otto possessed the same shrewd judgment as his father. The baron strongly favored Berlin. The bullish young kaiser, with his penchant for spending on the military and his consequent thirst for capital, provided great opportunities for Otto to learn the balance between business and political expediency. He wondered how he could make the case to his father for London instead.

"You should leave at once," Baroness Emmeline told Otto, when he informed her of his plan.

He looked at her in astonishment.

"I don't want you to leave Vienna. I shall miss you, and you must write with every post. But you will be able to see your sister."

The baroness's affection for her son was uncomplicated. He, unlike his sister, did not give her trouble. Although he had hobbies that did not fit with the family interest, as a good son, he repressed them. The fact that he considerately kept his discontent to himself was something the baroness admired, while not being fooled by it.

She remembered the night she had given birth to Otto; too excited to sleep, she had lain awake all night gazing at the little wrapped figure in the cradle with his bruised blue eyes. When they had taken him away to give him to the wet nurse, she had sobbed at the theft, knowing he would never truly be returned to her. Greta had stolen him further away, monopolizing Otto the moment she joined him in the nursery. Try as she might, the baroness could not penetrate the sealed unity of their twosome.

She appreciated how, even as a boy, Otto sensed she was left out and, on spying her in the garden, would break away from pursuit of his ball and present her with a wild strawberry, like a secret. He always pressed Greta to include her in their games of charades ("Too silly for Mama," she'd say) or picnics beside the river with Nurse ("No, Mama won't sit on grass"). Greta always won. But the baroness never pushed—she did not know how to play charades and, indeed, did not wish to sit on wet grass, and would have needed great encouragement to try. Instead, Greta would fix her with a look of contempt and bewildered disappointment, and the baroness would concede that she was not up to the task and withdraw. At six years old, in white knee socks and pigtails, Greta had the power to devastate her mother, who felt herself wither under her disdain. She loved her daughter with exasperation and without understanding.

And so missing Greta had come as a great surprise. She tried to inquire in her letters minutely after Greta's health, anxious to know if she was pregnant. She fretted endlessly about English doctors—she'd heard of their reluctance to sanction chloroform during childbirth. The baroness was outraged; how could a man understand the savagery of such pain? Greta answered her letters warmly, but never intimated that she was expecting. The baroness herself had fallen pregnant by the end of her honeymoon. Greta did not invite her to visit, and the baroness could not bring herself to ask. She consoled herself with the thought that, aware of her mother's infamous dislike of travel, Greta did not wish to inconvenience her.

"I've spent years complaining about your sister's noise and untidiness, and now I spend each evening wishing there was a pile of novels on the floor and a trail of cookie crumbs across the Louis XIV sofa."

Otto laughed.

"I know something is wrong," said the baroness softly, "but she won't tell me what it is."

"How do you know?"

"She is polite and solicitous and kind in her letters. Not once has she set out to provoke me. Something must be wrong."

Otto smiled, but the baroness did not. "I'll go to England, Mother. I'll make sure Greta is all right."

The baroness poured him coffee, adding a dash of plum liqueur and whisking in a little cream. Otto drank obediently. This had been their ritual for years, and he couldn't bear to tell her that he disliked the sickly drink immensely. The baroness smiled at her son with such frank love and admiration that Otto was forced to look away, embarrassed. She reached out and clasped his hand.

"Every post you will write to me, yes?"

"Yes, Mother. Every post."

Jewish Poor Boys' Home, Vienna, March

———◦>•<◦———

Karl was no longer living in the canal beneath the Goldbaum Palace, but he was living under Goldbaum largesse. For three months he'd been in a school for poor boys provided for by one of the baroness's charities. He'd sickened from typhoid, and during his stay at one of the hospitals for the poor, a nurse had noticed his circumcision and whispered to the matron that the child in bed number twelve was a Jew. This being a Goldbaum hospital, penniless Jewish boys were cared for with special interest. Karl accepted his diagnosis of Jew with the same weary resignation with which he'd accepted that of typhoid fever. Both seemed to come with disabilities and advantages. Typhoid: agony and sweated fever, but regular meals during a generous convalescence; Jew: Karl knew that no one in Vienna much liked the Jews, but on the other hand he discovered they took good care of their own. After he was well enough to be released, instead of finding himself back on the streets, or indeed beneath them, he had been found a place in a home for unfortunate boys and, for the first time in his life, was learning to read. Karl decided to acquiesce to his fate, at least for the present. If they said he was a Jew, then he'd be a Jew.

He experienced his first Passover, eating the matzo only after he was assured that it did not contain the blood of Christians.

The only book they had to peruse in the hostel was the Torah, helpfully provided in both Hebrew and German, and out of boredom rather than interest, Karl began to read. He discovered that he liked the Song of Songs. It had the fewest mentions of God—a definite advantage—and while he hadn't the least idea what it was about, he enjoyed the descriptions. Other boys of fifteen or sixteen, tired of the rules, slipped off in the dead of night, planning on joining the army or hoping to find work in the factories, but Karl was in no rush to leave the boys' home. Food and a real bed, in exchange for chores and a dash of God, was an excellent arrangement, and Karl was stubbornly small, hardly growing from year to year, so he was in no present danger of being pushed out to find work.

London, April

—⸙—

For the first time since he was a boy, Clement was losing chess games. He'd discovered the joy of playing grandmasters. These newly crowned champions were rare, and Clement found to his delight that he could not win against them. This was novel and thrilling. Then, unexpectedly, he played against a truly remarkable player summoned from Hungary to his club on Pall Mall explicitly for the purpose, and after four hours and twenty-three minutes, Clement beat him. He lost the next game and won the one after that, and then lost again. Losing wouldn't have mattered, except to his pride, save for the fact that Clement had started betting on himself to win. He found that it heightened his enjoyment of the game to a tremendous, exhilarating degree. But soon he had embarked upon an unhappy losing streak against a series of truly brilliant players. The amount he lost was becoming uncomfortable, even for a Goldbaum. Everyone was being terribly patient and polite in recovering their debts—after all, there was no question that Clement could not pay—but soon the matter would have to be addressed.

He was anticipating tonight's game with relish and anxiety. He was almost too nervous for supper, managing only a quail stuffed with pear and blue cheese, a chocolate-and-almond soufflé and a very small dish of set peach custard. As the car drove him to the club, he experienced a thrill of anticipation, a fierce joy threaded through with fear. Tonight he would win and recover all his other losses and there would be no need for Papa to discover his debts. He could quietly pay them off himself and there would be no disgrace or unpleasant scene.

The Rolls-Royce drew up on Pall Mall and Clement slipped inside the Royal Automobile Club, of which he was a founding member. The porters all tipped their hats, assisting him with his coat and hat, while his friend Dr. Matthews hovered in the entrance hall, waiting. The men greeted one another warmly.

"Is Slivinski here?" asked Clement.

Dr. Matthews had been arranging all the matches as per Clement's precise instructions. He hesitated.

"Yes, but—"

Clement frowned, holding up his hand. He did not wish to listen to provocations, he wished to play chess. "Then let us go. I am ready."

Dr. Matthews led him up the stairs and then opened a door to the left.

"I ordered the game to be set up in the library," complained Clement.

"Yes, but there was a problem," said Matthews. "We must play in here."

Quietly outraged, Clement entered a small sitting room decorated with delicate blue paper, and a trio of sofas in the same summer blue. A lamp burned. In the middle of the room two chairs had been set up on either side of a small table, a wooden chess set placed carefully in the center. Clement did not see his opponent immediately, and then he noticed a petite dark-haired woman seated with her back toward him. She stood and gave a little bow.

"Irena Slivinski."

"Clement Goldbaum."

Clement took her hand, kissed it and then stood, awkward and uncertain. Now he understood why they had been placed in the ladies' drawing room, the one room in the gentlemen's club where women were tolerated, if not actually encouraged. He was not entirely certain

how he felt about playing a woman. He wondered whether it was ungallant to play, or ungallant to object.

"Do you speak Russian?" she asked.

"I'm afraid not," said Clement.

"German?"

"Yes, a little. My mother was from Frankfurt," replied Clement in
perfect German. "I did not know that . . ." He faltered, frowning.

"You are cross. Is it because you do not like to play against a woman,
or rather that you do not like to lose to a woman?" she asked with an
arch smile.

Clement stuttered, quite unable to reply. She was extremely pretty,
with pale skin and large brown eyes, the same dark mahogany as the
black chess pieces.

"I should have let them tell you, but I prefer to surprise my opponent. It is my little game before the game. We must take all the advantages we can, yes?"

Clement found himself agreeing aloud, although privately he
thought it most unsportsmanlike to deliberately unsettle a chap before a game.

"Don't worry. From now on, there will be no more surprises. Or
only ones upon the board. My apology to you; you may be white."

Clement demurred. Ladies surely should go first.

"No. In this game, if nowhere else, we play as equals."

Clement felt that to press the point would be an insult, and accepted.
He opened play, moved his knight. She smiled, slid across a pawn. She
played with a dexterity and fearlessness that took him by surprise; she
was unafraid to sacrifice pieces, and decided her next move with a
quickness that both irked and harried him. He was used to a sumptuous pause while his opponent considered his play at length, and invariably had long enough to suck the coating off three or four chocolate
Brazil nuts before his turn. He'd scarcely popped a nut in his mouth
before Miss Slivinski swooped. The money riding on the outcome distracted and unsettled him. He wanted to recapture the sensation he'd

had during previous games of exhilaration—that, win or lose, he was flying, his blood buzzing hot in his veins. He dabbed at the perspiration seeping from beneath his cravat. He signaled for water. He took her bishop. Immediately she castled her king and rook so fast that Clement had to close his eyes to remember where they had been before. He dithered in almost all things except chess, but prided himself on his decisiveness upon the board. His speed and purpose were often all that was needed to derail lesser players. He felt a nudge of sympathy toward those he had beaten.

When it was over, it was almost a relief. They poured him a brandy. He drank and signaled for another. He could speak to his mother; she would pay the debt with only slight reproach, but she would also tell his father. Lost in such unhappy thoughts, it took Clement a minute to realize that Miss Slivinski was addressing him.

"You are very good," she said.

"But you are better."

She shrugged. "Yes. Than almost everyone. With a little coaching, perhaps you could—"

"Beat you?"

"No. Improve," she said, with polite regret.

Clement laughed, despite his predicament.

To his great surprise, later that night he found himself in Irena Slivinski's hotel room and then in her bed. He did not regret everything he lost that night.

Hampshire, April

———◆>◆<◆———

It was raining when Otto arrived in London, and it was still raining when the motorcar drew up at Temple Court. There was something about English rain that defeated him. It seeped inside one, cold and insidious. He dashed from the Wolseley to the house, the chauffeur trotting beside him to hold the umbrella over his head. Greta rushed down the steps to meet him, apparently oblivious to the weather, and hurled herself into his arms, almost knocking him off balance.

"I'm so happy you're here. Was your journey awful? Come and have tea. That's what we do here. Drink endless tea. Don't worry, one gets used to it in the end."

Able at last to get a word in, Otto suggested they go inside and get out of the rain. Greta led him inside and Otto found himself in a hot and dim hall, surrounded by a jungle of palms. A footman took his hat and coat.

"You're here. You're really here," said Greta, staring at him in bemused wonder.

"I am, I really am," said Otto, pleased. "Where are Lord and Lady Goldbaum? Your husband?"

"In the Chinese Salon. They're all being terribly tactful and allowing us a few minutes."

They smiled at one another, awkward for a moment. There was too much to say, too many questions to be asked.

"You look well," he said at last, knowing it was the remark of a maiden aunt.

Greta rolled her eyes. "Come on then," she said, taking his hand.

Lord Goldbaum offered a gruff welcome, while Lady Goldbaum was all unaffected charm, finding Otto the pleasantest spot beside the fire and ringing for a whiskey to warm his insides. Albert shook his hand with affection, while keeping a careful distance from Greta. Clement intrigued Otto. The months of letter writing had forged a confidence, and Otto had imagined himself to know Clement rather well. Yet on seeing one another in person, each man realized the intimacy was one that existed on the page rather than in the flesh. Clement remained mostly silent on the sofa, studying his highly polished shoes with determined interest. During their correspondence, Otto had redrawn his image of Clement and, on seeing him again, found himself shocked at the size of the man. His waistcoat was enormous, and his cravat with its pink pearl tie pin struggled to hide his swell of chins.

"Well," said Lord Goldbaum, "I daresay you shall restore us all to good order, Otto, won't you now?"

Otto laughed, but realized that every one of them was looking at him, their faces bright with expectation. He gulped his whiskey in relief.

After luncheon it was still too wet for Greta to show him the works being undertaken on the house and garden at Fontmell.

Instead she reluctantly agreed to show him the Temple Court collections. She gestured vaguely to an exquisite piece of Sèvres porcelain in Pompadour pink on a side table, festooned with flowers and shepherdesses.

"That's a vase," she said.

"Anything else you know about it?" said Otto, peering at it closely.

"You could put flowers in it. But you probably shouldn't."

"Ah," said Albert, appearing in the doorway. "Is my wife giving you the tour?"

"I'm not sure I'd quite call it that," said Otto.

"My information was minimal, but correct," said Greta.

Albert strode over. "This is one of the first pieces of Sèvres that my great-aunt Agatha ever purchased. The pink is very rare, as it is so difficult to produce. The figures are painted by Dodin in the style of Boucher. It is actually for potpourri rather than fresh flowers."

Otto turned to Greta. "Your information was minimal and incorrect. Albert, would you join us? I would very much like to hear about the collections."

"I'd be delighted," said Albert.

As he drew Otto's attention to another piece of Sèvres porcelain, this time a green candelabrum vase with three elephant heads, Otto felt Greta direct a sharp kick at his heel. He ignored her.

To Greta's relief, the following day dawned brighter and the rain cleared, leaving only smears of mist across the low ground. She would be able to escape the confines of Temple Court and the humiliation of Otto scrutinizing her and Albert. She saw her husband and herself afresh through his eyes—distant and uneasy—and a wave of shame and despondency washed through her. This was not a part of Otto's being here that she had anticipated. Glancing out of her bedroom window, she saw that the barrage of freezing rain had turned the bedding plants to sludge, and the cerise begonias that had formed a smash of colors in the parterre were browning and disintegrating, quite spoiled. Already a fleet of gardeners was busy replacing entire beds with gold-streaked busy Lizzies and speckled tobacco plants from the glasshouses. The garden would be restored to scrupulous loveliness before the rest of the family woke.

Greta breakfasted hurriedly and then ordered the car to take her to Fontmell. When she arrived, Enid Witherick was already waiting to open the car door and hand her out, to the irritation of the chauffeur, now gloomily resigned to such unorthodoxy. Greta hailed her with her customary greeting, "Well, Withers, what is new in the garden?"

She declined to call Enid Witherick by her surname, the conventional form of address for a head gardener, complaining that it was a mouthful. "Enid" was a gross overfamiliarity that did not occur to either woman. Instead, Greta had settled upon "Withers." Enid held her employer in far too high regard to point out that referring to a gardener as "withers" was perhaps not the most auspicious or tactful of names. Only Greta's soft Austrian accent, which blurred "Withers" into "Vithers," made it more acceptable.

"The daffodils are starting. They've not been too damaged by the rain," said Enid.

There, beneath the green shade of the willows, lay a brilliant shock of yellow daffodils, their fierce brightness almost unreal in the muted morning light. These were the very first bulbs she'd ordered to be planted in the new garden, and she regarded them like a ship's captain surveying a treasure hoard.

"I want more bulbs planted under every window in the autumn. I want to look out at the view down to the river through a wash of gold."

Each woman knew all that was necessary about the other. Why would they ask each other personal questions, when they could spend the time discussing the garden? Like proud parents of an infant glimpsing genius in every grimace, the women only perceived the garden as it was supposed to be, rather than as it was. The lawns had been resown, but it was early in the year and the seed that had sprouted was as sparse and tender as a newborn's scalp.

Greta looked up toward the house. It was obscured by scaffolding, and sections of the roof had been removed entirely and covered with waxy tarpaulins. In an hour the air would ring with hammers and shouts. This was why she liked to visit so early, for only now could she enjoy Fontmell in peace.

"I shall plant the first geranium myself," said Greta.

"Of course."

Enid carried a spade, a kneeling cushion and a pair of thick leather gloves. She passed them to Greta, who unpeeled her cotton ones and replaced them with the stout gardening ones, and then took the spade from Enid, who disappeared to fetch the geraniums.

Greta had discovered, in Mrs. Loudon's *Instructions in Gardening for Ladies*, the importance of digging the soil oneself—even if only on occasion. By wielding a spade herself, she felt she was marking herself out as a different sort of Goldbaum (even though she did not yet dare to appear at dinner with dirt beneath her nails). She did not know that Withers had three men rigorously turn the soil before her mistress appeared with her spade, ensuring that every lump and sod was broken up, the earth soft and loose, in preparation for the entry of the shining silver spade. As long as she dug, Greta could not think. Her arms ached, her lungs burned and her mind was released from weary and well-worn trails. She attempted to bury her spoiled hopes for herself and Albert in the damp soil.

"I should have worn my boots," said Otto, interrupting her thoughts.

Greta turned to him, smiling as she set down her spade. "I'm so glad you came," she said.

"I have to catch the train to London with the others," he said. "But I knew you wouldn't forgive me if I didn't see Fontmell first."

Otto allowed himself to be taken around the gardens, every possible beauty being pointed out. The yew hedge would grow here; this was to be a hidden rose garden, but underplanted with moss and snow-in-summer; stone benches here, painted with yogurt to encourage lichen. This was to be a series of large pools, not a pond—but informal and natural, the edges softened with reeds and yellow irises, and planted with giant water lilies, as at Giverny. Otto listened with affection rather than interest, wondering, as his thoughts trailed off in their own direction, whether this was how Greta felt when he attempted to explain to her about mathematics or stars.

Deflated, she stared at him, realizing he wasn't listening. "I suppose it's all too hard to picture. I only see how it's going to look, not how it is now."

"That's quite a skill," agreed Otto, surveying the sloshing mud with distaste. "And the house?"

"As soon as the weather settles, they're going to thatch the roof."

"Thatch it? Whatever for?"

"Beauty," said Greta firmly. "I saw it in a dream. I prefer charming to grand, even if that is not the usual family style."

"And what does Albert make of it all?" asked Otto.

"Oh, you know," said Greta, looking away.

"I don't know," said Otto gently. "Tell me."

Greta studied her muddy boots. "We don't discuss it very often."

"There aren't many husbands, Greta, who will agree to the thatching of a large house because his wife glimpsed it in a dream."

"He doesn't agree, Otto. He merely goes along with everything because he prefers that to speaking to me. We've learned to ignore one another with great panache."

"Stop it. Cynicism doesn't suit you."

Greta sat down on a bench, looking out toward where Enid was directing half a dozen men as they prepared the groundworks for a series of stone steps leading into the lowest part of the garden, which sloped down to the river.

"In a year or two, or five, I'm sure all this will be wonderful, Greta. But you're playing make-believe. You will live here with Albert. When it is finished, you'll live unhappily in the paradise that you've created. You need to mend things with him or there is no point to any of this."

Greta kicked stubbornly at a pebble with her boot.

"We are not suited to one another. He disapproves of me. And being disapproved of isn't as much fun as you might think."

"It seems to me that you've given up."

A small red circle appeared on each cheek, signifiers of her fury.

Steeling himself, Otto continued. "While I'm away, I urge you to consider how you can make things right with Albert. I know you, Greta. You're polite to him and deferential in company, and you might persuade everyone else. But I don't imagine that you're very kind to him when no one else is listening."

"You have no idea about any of it. Don't you dare tell me this is make-believe, Otto. The garden is the only thing that is real. I'm only real when I'm here. In the rest of it I'm an automaton, a woman version of the clockwork swan at home, wound up when guests appear. I play at being a wife, a daughter-in-law, a Goldbaum."

Otto felt the force of her unhappiness and had no solace to offer. He put a hand on Greta's shoulder, but she pushed him away.

London, April

—◆⟫•⟪◆—

Otto visited the London Stock Exchange and was introduced to three dozen whiskered gentlemen whose names he could not remember, before returning to the partners' room for luncheon. Lord Goldbaum sat at the head of the table, his sons and Otto on either side. A large game pie was brought in along with a jug of water. Lord Goldbaum never drank wine at lunchtime.

"The foreign secretary wants to persuade the kaiser to call off the arms race," announced Lord Goldbaum, wiping gravy from his chin. "He'd like our assistance in arranging a conference. Otto, I need you to write to our cousins in Berlin."

Otto smiled, thinking at first that his lordship was making a joke. "But the kaiser intends to win the arms race. He thinks it's his only way of gaining an empire."

Lord Goldbaum waggled a finger at Otto. "Quite right. And the British will never let him."

"So any conference will be a failure."

"It will, inevitably. But our assistance has been requested by His Majesty's Government and we must oblige. They are turning to us once again. And"—here Lord Goldbaum paused and studied the faces of the younger men—"remember that failure can be useful."

He smiled and rang the bell for the car to take him to the House of Lords.

Otto watched him leave, certain that the old fox had a plan, but unable for the life of him to fathom what it might be.

That evening Lord Goldbaum did not return for dinner. Clement dined in his club, leaving Albert and Otto alone, in what might have been an awkward tête-à-tête. Otto had worried that he might discover Albert's character to be flawed, that he was guilty of some hideous failing, to justify Greta's aversion. But as far as he could tell, there was none. From the time when he and Greta were very young, he had discovered that to persuade Greta to like something, he only had to show interest in it himself. As children, this included midnight stargazing, train sets and visits downstairs to luncheon with their parents (until Otto convinced her of his pleasure at the excursions, Greta hid in the nursery closet). When they were older, Greta's basic ability in arithmetic was entirely due to Otto's own devoted acumen, and she invariably liked his friends, paying rapt attention even to those scientists whom Otto suspected held little appeal, save to their colleagues. He was not sure that the principle would still hold concerning husbands, but he felt that he was duty-bound to pretend to find Albert an engaging and interesting fellow, in the hope that Greta might be persuaded to soften her avowed dislike of him. In the end, no pretense was necessary.

He found Albert taciturn and serious, but also interested and interesting, quizzing Otto closely on matters of astronomy. Albert, like Otto, was a gifted but reluctant financier whose real talents lay elsewhere. Over brandy, Albert explained how some moths hatched only during certain phases of the moon. He wanted to hear all about Otto's adventures in the Imperial Observatory, and his experiences on the Russian border.

"Did you see the Cossacks? And the eastern Jews?"

Otto laughed. "Do you know, your wife wanted to know the same thing."

Albert refilled their brandies, but made no remark.

"We did indeed see the Cossacks," continued Otto. "They would gallop their horses right along the border, racing our imperial dragoons. It was all bravado and display, shouts and kicking up dust and smashing bottles, but quite a thing to see all the same. Where we were stationed at the observatory, we heard the odd report of a pogrom, but they were always much further east."

"Such misery and violence."

"Less at present. Your father stopping loans to Russia has made them more cautious."

"You don't sound as if you believe it will last."

"I don't. I think funds ought to be made available for those Jews who wish to emigrate to America."

"While my father wants a permanent resolution in Russia," said Albert, leaning back in his chair, "you can see his point, Otto. Five million Jews can't emigrate."

Otto considered his cousin. "In England, you always seem to be surprised by hostility toward Jews. In Austria, we expect hostility and are only surprised when we find goodwill."

"So is your way better?"

"It is only that, with lower expectations, we are less often disappointed." He was silent for a moment before asking, "Albert, what is your father's plan regarding the kaiser? We know the Germans won't stop building dreadnoughts. Any peace conference is pointless."

"I don't know. And there is no use in asking. Father likes us to work it out ourselves."

"Us?"

"Me and Clement."

Otto repressed a smile. "Has Clement ever unraveled one of your father's financial schemes?"

It was Albert's turn to smile. "No."

"Perhaps Lord Goldbaum feels that your government needs reminding of the kaiser's intractable character."

"Perhaps," said Albert, unconvinced.

"The kaiser is an odd fellow. I mean, I think all emperors have delusions of holiness—it does rather go with the territory. But the kaiser is a special case. You know he has a withered arm?"

Albert shrugged. "What of it?"

"When he was a small boy, his parents used to make him bathe it in the entrails of freshly killed lambs, in the hope it would grow."

"How perfectly revolting."

"Yes. I don't think it helped him in the development of a pleasant disposition. He's known for tormenting his ministers. He made one of his courtiers dress up as a poodle and howl. Apparently the man's crime was to be fat. According to Edgar Goldbaum, who claims he was there, the kaiser spanked the king of Bulgaria on the behind. You should make sure that you read everything the couriers bring from the German cousins, for it is always interesting, if disturbing."

"Our king seems almost dull in comparison."

"And safer. I think we would all sleep a little easier if the monarchs of Europe were modeled upon King George."

The two men lapsed into thoughtful silence. It was much easier to discuss politics than women—particularly the one woman with whom they were both so closely allied. Otto shifted, acutely embarrassed, but determined to raise the subject.

"I would never presume to know what has happened between you and my sister." Otto saw Albert stiffen with displeasure, but pushed on regardless. "I know she is irritable, stubborn and displays a wanton disregard for convention. But she is also tremendously loyal and she's fun."

Albert frowned. "And is that a valuable quality in a wife?"

Otto held up his hands in surrender. "Never having had one, I wouldn't know. But it's a valuable quality in a friend. Makes life a bit more bearable."

Albert coughed and was silent for a moment. "The thing is, Otto, everyone else seems acutely aware of my wife's virtues. It only serves to remind me of my own failure to appreciate them."

Otto was considered, reflecting.

"I suspect that you think her frivolous. She isn't. She has a sense of mischief and takes delight in the absurd. It's only when an argument is started that she has to win, no matter the consequence."

Albert sighed and looked at Otto, his face full of frank unhappiness. "There are no winners here. What would you have me do?" he asked, exasperated.

Otto had little advice to offer. "Talk to her," he said at last. "And while you do, pretend to yourself that you don't dislike her."

O tto resolved to return to the matter the next day, however difficult it might be. But the following morning he awoke to discover that the *Titanic* had struck an iceberg in the Atlantic, and no one could speak of anything else.

To the nation's relief, there was thought to be no loss of life. The only loss was to shipping and national pride. To the family's profound distaste, Lord Goldbaum was complimented on his uncanny prescience in declining to insure the vessel. Editorials wondered slyly whether it was a Semitic skill. The day after the sinking, it was revealed that the initial reports were mistaken, and the loss of life was catastrophic. The Goldbaum men convened in the morning room after breakfast. Stanton brought Lord Goldbaum and Albert a stream of telegrams, while Clement studied the first-class passenger lists to see whether there was anyone of their acquaintance on board. Otto felt at a loss, with nothing useful to contribute.

"The Astors were sailing," said Clement.

"Then the richest man in the world is drowned," said Lord Goldbaum. "We are all equal in the end. Even gold sinks."

No one spoke for a moment or two.

"At least something good came of the strikes," said Albert at last. "The coal shortage meant that hundreds canceled their passage. The ship was half-empty."

"That's little comfort to the drowned," said Clement.

A footman appeared with another telegram on a silver tray. Lord Goldbaum waved him away.

"Enough. It might not be the usual thing, but under the circumstances, I would like to say kaddish. Then we must go at once to the stock exchange. See if we can't calm the markets."

They stood, heads bowed, with Lord Goldbaum reciting the familiar words. Otto looked out of the window—it was still raining. The golden Rolls-Royce Silver Ghost idled outside in Park Lane, waiting to convey the Goldbaums into the City.

Hampshire, April

———❖———

"Perhaps we ought to cancel tonight's dinner," said Lady Goldbaum for the third time on Friday afternoon. They sat in the Blue Sitting Room, lists of guests, menus and table orders spread out before them on Marie Antoinette's former desk and spilling onto the floor. A maid silently picked up the fallen papers and set them back upon the bureau.

"We don't know anyone on board. We're not in mourning," said Greta, knowing it was what her mother-in-law wished to hear.

"The entire nation's in mourning."

Greta sighed. She could say nothing right. "Well then, perhaps you'd better cancel."

"No. I don't think that would do at all. We shall say a few words for the departed. A prayer perhaps."

"Yes, Adelheid."

"And after all, if I delay the dinner until next week, the titan arum won't still be in flower, and everyone is simply desperate to see it."

Greta knew this was the real reason tonight's dinner could not be called off. Lady Goldbaum usually adhered to social codes with absolute rigidity—as Jews, they had to behave with particular sensitivity. But social convention paled next to matters of horticultural significance. The pride of Lady Goldbaum's exotic plant collection was a giant titan arum, and a specimen had unexpectedly, after twenty years of failure, erupted into flower. And, as Lady Goldbaum had announced with some awe after breakfast, it was the first time the species had ever been known to bloom in England. Greta believed that if she were ever to carry the heir to the British Goldbaums in her belly, his arrival could not be anticipated with more eagerness than the flowering of this bizarre and exotic plant.

Until now, Greta had barely noticed the shrub. It merely looked like a vast and ungainly leek, sprouting several feet high and protruding unremarkably from its enormous terra-cotta pot. It was vaguely, unobtrusively ugly. Then yesterday, when one of the under-gardeners was feeding potash to the exotic species, he noticed that the greenhouse was filled with the rotting smell of death. On searching the glasshouse for the dead creature decaying surreptitiously in some corner, he discovered instead that the titan arum had unfurled, the pale green leaf springing open to form a single red petal, the color of fresh meat. It bloomed enormously and revoltingly. Exhilarated by her latest conquest of nature, Lady Goldbaum could think about little else. Greta found it oddly morbid. It was too close in name to the lost ship, and it had waited until she had sunk to produce a flower.

"Will you check the floral arrangements in the conservatory?" said Lady Goldbaum. "You have my list."

Greta nodded, and Lady Goldbaum bustled out to terrify the poor projectionist. That evening she was to host one of her famous explorers' dinners. An expedition of plant hunters that she had sponsored had recently returned from China and Tibet, including the great Julian Stein. Thank goodness Lady Goldbaum would have someone with whom to share her horticultural bliss. Greta's list of superlatives was quite exhausted. She'd be glad never to look at the titan again. She knew Lady Goldbaum would consider it most irregular, but Greta was finding to her own surprise that her greatest satisfaction was often to be found in the smaller native species. Best of all, she adored wildflowers—cornflowers, meadow vetch and sweet alison; lady's bedstraw, moon carrot and the nocturnal display of night-flowering catchfly.

Drinks were to be held in the conservatory. Lady Goldbaum had naturally wanted them to be served in the glasshouse, but Greta pointed out that the foul smell of the titan tree might turn the stomachs of those with less vigorous constitutions. Greta viewed the conservatory as not so much a room as a jungle. Norfolk Island pine and banana plants provided architectural foliage, while a vast bed of calla lilies and white chrysanthemums, round and fluffed up as snowballs, flourished in indoor beds. Three tiger skins brought back from previous expeditions had been laid in the center of the room so that, when they were glimpsed through the palms and ferns, Greta had the eerie sensation that she was being stalked from the undergrowth.

The head of the largest tiger was stuffed with the ears pricked up and mouth open midroar, haptic orange and black stripes along its back, and she reached down to stroke the pelt, experiencing initially a civilized ripple of regret at the death of such a magnificent wild thing, followed by an uncivilized shudder of fear. The yellow teeth of the open mouth were very large indeed, like polished daggers. Then she noticed a tiny blemish on the tiger's eyebrow, above the amber bead of an eye. Peering closer, she realized it was not a blemish but a butterfly, a high brown fritillary, one of the few butterflies that she remembered, on account of its being so rare. Now, as she studied it, Greta realized that it wasn't brown at all, but the same golden orange as the tiger, and almost perfectly camouflaged. Perhaps that was why it was so rare; it needed a tiger skin to hide, and those were generally hard to find in Hampshire.

Albert would like the butterfly for his collection. Greta knew that to catch the butterfly and set it for him would be a peace offering. But she disliked the habit, despite Albert's insisting that, unlike the killing of the poor tiger, catching butterflies was all in the pursuit of science. There was a swirling tightness in her chest, a sensation so familiar and constant that it took her a minute to recognize it as a symptom of her unhappiness. If relations were better with Albert, was it possible that this feeling could pass? Greta tried to imagine a life without this dizzying numbness. Soon she would have endured an entire year of a marriage lacking intimacy, companionship and sometimes even civility.

She had attempted to distract herself with her garden, but charming as it was, it was not enough. She couldn't bear the prospect of another year of loneliness, of waking in the night, livid with resentment. If she did nothing, that was all she had to expect for the next year, and the one after that. She could not accept that gilded loneliness and disappointment were to be her lot for life. Perhaps Otto was right, she decided with a sigh; she must try harder with Albert, attempt to reach him once more. She rang the bell. A footman appeared.

"Fetch Herzfeld," she said, speaking almost in a whisper. "Tell him to bring tools to catch and set a butterfly."

A few minutes later, a slight and balding man in early middle age appeared with a brown leather bag, rather like that of a doctor. He nodded to Greta and knelt beside her on the tiger skin, as though this was his usual occupation after morning coffee.

"Mrs. Goldbaum."

"Look, a high brown fritillary," she said, and pointed to the butterfly poised upon the tiger skin.

Paul Victor Herzfeld was her husband's most valued member of staff, the curator of his collections while Albert worked away in London, and his collaborator when he was at home. He was always scrupulously polite to Greta, but she viewed him with the same mild revulsion as she did Albert's insect jars. She associated him with beetles and things with too many legs.

"A female," said Herzfeld, looking at it closely. "Once we've pinned her, we must check the leaves in the conservatory to see if she's laid any eggs. It's so warm in here, she must have been tricked into thinking it's summer." He spoke with hushed excitement.

With a smooth movement he brought out a silken butterfly net and slipped it over the insect.

"We don't want her escaping, now, do we?"

"I suppose not."

The butterfly caught, they stopped whispering. Herzfeld passed Greta a glass bottle.

"Here, you do the honors. Slide the butterfly into the killing jar. Careful of her wings, and pinch the thorax between your fingers to stun her, or she might damage her wings hurling herself against the glass as she dies."

"I think I've changed my mind."

Herzfeld shrugged. "She won't know anything about it, I assure you. It's simply instinct. There's a little rubbing alcohol on a piece of cotton wool in the jar. The butterfly will die very quickly. They can't feel a thing. Then we can pin her and mount her on blotting paper so that she dries."

"For science?"

"Of course."

Wondering how it was that she needed to kill a butterfly in order to save her marriage, Greta put her hand inside the net and gently squeezed its thorax, feeling it grow still in her hand, the wings ceasing to flutter. She eased it into the jar and watched as, after half a minute, it became quite still.

Herzfeld passed her a pair of slender forceps. "Shall we take her up to Mr. Goldbaum's library and mount her there?"

Greta had not ventured into Albert's library since her first and only unfortunate visit. She repressed a shudder. "You may do all that, Herzfeld. I think I've reached my limit. I'll stay here and look for butterfly eggs."

"Very good, madam. I shall inform Mr. Goldbaum that you were instrumental. He will be profoundly grateful."

To Greta's great regret, the explorers did not come to dinner in their pith hats but in perfectly ordinary evening dress, with the same dull winged collars as less well-traveled gentlemen. After dinner Julian Stein would present his findings: he promised something revelatory about the reproductive cycle of the rhododendron at high altitude. Lady Goldbaum was pink-cheeked in her enthusiasm at the prospect.

The Goldbaum men were late. The sinking of the *Titanic* continued to cause unease in the money markets. The reassurance of Lord Goldbaum's presence, as well as his capital, was required. They telegraphed their apologies; they would arrive as soon as they could. The two hostesses, Greta and Lady Goldbaum, sipped champagne and made small talk with their guests beneath the ferns, the palms competing with the ladies' elaborate fascinators. For the first time in many months, Greta wore her butterfly necklace. Anna had fastened it around her neck before she could object, and then claimed that the catch was stuck when Greta asked her to remove it. She was dressed in an emerald silk evening gown, extremely fitted around her waist, which she hoped would prevent the other women scrutinizing her figure to see if she was expecting. Sometimes she felt rather as if it were a detailed photograph of her own body projected onto the screen, for the assembled company to dissect and discuss.

Before she'd dressed for dinner, Herzfeld had sent to her rooms the high brown fritillary, pinned and set and beautifully mounted against white blotting paper inside a small glass box, which Anna had in turn carefully wrapped.

A footman glided past with canapés, and Greta speared a quail's egg and dipped it into a well of caviar. She circulated with the regularity of one of the West Gallery clocks, greeting the ladies and receiving their compliments in turn with grace. "Such a pretty dress, Mrs. Goldbaum— may I call you Greta? It brings out the green of your eyes. Oh, it's so kind of you to remember little Harold. Yes, he's quite recovered. And it was so thoughtful of you to send the calf's-foot jelly and the basket of raspberries. Temple Court fruit is the best in all the world! Now, Mrs. Goldbaum, that waist is looking so terribly slim; when is it going to swell? Yes, my dear Greta. I'm afraid darling Hermione is right—we're all waiting. I've heard that eating cucumbers is quite the thing. And there's a wonderful spa in Switzerland that helps us ladies to get in the family way."

Greta could think of nothing but escape. She excused herself and hurried away, lingering beside the French windows and opening them to take a few breaths of cool air. Turning, she noticed Lady Goldbaum at her elbow. Perhaps it was the wash of champagne and the effect of the heat and the arrows of chitter-chatter that made her turn to her mother-in-law and say in German, "Adelheid, how did you bear it?"

Lady Goldbaum considered her for a moment, and Greta wondered if she was about to be rebuked; then Lady Goldbaum unpeeled a black evening glove and placed her bare hand in Greta's, displaying her up-turned palm. Greta glanced down and saw that the skin was riddled with tiny white scars, the shape of fingernail half-moons. Adelheid balled her hands into tight fists, her nails digging deep into the flesh.

"It's an old habit. At dinner, I would smile and ask after their awful children, and beneath the table I'd clench my fists until my nails made my skin bleed," she said.

Greta stared at her, uncertain.

"Now I invite the people I like to my parties, along with those I'm obliged to ask."

A moment later Lady Goldbaum pulled on her jeweled evening glove, hiding the scars. As Greta watched her return and mingle with her guests, laughing at a joke from Julian Stein, she thought of her mother-in-law's marked hands and felt a little less alone.

The Goldbaum gentlemen arrived in time for dinner. Albert nodded at her from the far end of the room, but made no move to come and speak with her, escorting another lady guest into the dining room. The table brimmed with vast arrangements of narcissi, freesias and carnations on the sideboards, all in the softest shades of white, and with rings of miniature daffodils looped around the candlesticks. The scent was sweet but pungent, and one of Julian Stein's fellow explorers began to sneeze volcanically into his handkerchief. Greta wondered how on earth he survived the tropics, when the dining room appeared to be testing him to the limit. She saw with some regret that both Otto and Clement were seated at the far end of the table from her. To her surprise, she found herself being helped into her chair by Albert, who then sat down beside her. She tutted at him.

"We've been married nearly a year. Sitting next to your wife at dinner really isn't the thing. Lady Hermione will not approve."

"Yes, well. Unfortunately, one of Mama's voyagers thoughtlessly succumbed to malaria at the last moment and ruined her table order. This was the least disruptive solution."

"How tactless of him," said Greta, smiling, mostly from astonishment that Albert was attempting humor.

"You look very . . . You're wearing the necklace," said Albert, trying for a compliment and finishing instead with an observation.

"I am."

"It looks . . ."

"And you are as neat as ever," said Greta.

"Good," said Albert, glancing at her sideways to see if she was teasing him.

Greta reached out for her napkin, to discover the neatly wrapped box containing the butterfly concealed beneath. She slid it to Albert.

"I found a high brown fritillary hiding on a tiger in the conservatory. Anna and Herzfeld want me to tell you that I trapped and mounted it for you, so that you'll forgive me all my neglect and impertinence and we can spontaneously make a go of things."

Albert unwrapped the box and surveyed Greta and the butterfly with equal surprise.

"Did you set the butterfly for me?"

"No. I caught it, and then the shudders and Herzfeld did the rest."

"All the same, I'm most obliged." He examined it closely, drawing a magnifying glass out of his pocket. "And I think you're right."

"About what?"

"That Herzfeld wanted me to believe that you set the butterfly. He's set ten thousand of them for me and I've never known him to so much as crush a clubfoot antenna. And, look here, there's a tiny crease on the wing where the paper used to stretch it has snagged. A common amateur mistake."

"The sort of error you would expect me to make?"

"Quite so."

"Goodness! I never knew that a dead butterfly could be made to fib." Greta laughed, and after a moment's hesitation, Albert smiled.

Before the first course was carried in, Greta carefully placed her napkin on her lap and, beneath it, began to remove her gloves, quietly and slowly. Albert had never really paid attention as she did this before, but now found himself watching as the napkin slid to one side, and white evening gloves gave way to soft bare skin.

After dinner, the guests were brought back to the conservatory to listen to Julian Stein recount the story of his expedition and present his slides and findings. He was due to give the same presentation to the Royal Society the following week, but it was a condition of Lady Goldbaum's patronage that she should hear about his discoveries first at Temple Court. Once again, Greta saw that the seat next to Otto was taken. Albert gestured to the empty chair next to him, and she sat next to him among the potted ferns and tried to attend as Stein pounded his fist, describing how he and his fellow travelers were plagued by mosquitoes and natives, poisoned by food and water; but, he insisted, the collection of rare and exotic plants, the discovery of new species and subspecies, made it all worthwhile.

"Hear, hear!" cried Lady Goldbaum, rising from her chair at the front to applaud.

"In general I prefer the softer, native species," said Greta quietly to Albert beside her. "But I would like to grow some of those irises. True blue is so rare in nature."

Unthinkingly, her hand went up to the butterfly choker around her throat and when she touched the diamond, she realized it was not pinching her skin as it had.

Albert watched her. He wondered how she would look wearing the butterfly and nothing else. He recalled her appearance as she had slept naked beneath the cedar tree, and realized that he could picture the prospect with some precision. His wife was willful and impolite, but not unattractive. And, grudgingly, he admitted that he admired her dedication to her garden. Her interest in nature was something that he could understand, and her determination to learn all she could thoroughly and properly was something he would have respected in a man. In her sitting room he sometimes observed lists containing the Latin and common names of plants. He would very much have liked to test her on them. To have made a game of it. Perhaps he might still suggest it.

As Julian began in hushed tones to reveal his grand discoveries about rhododendron reproduction, Albert nudged Greta and, leaning forward, whispered in her ear, "May I confess something truly dreadful?"

"Oh yes, please."

"I abhor rhododendrons. Don't like them. Never have."

Greta laughed aloud and Julian Stein faltered, his flow temporarily interrupted.

"Neither do I," she whispered as the lecture resumed.

"We must never, ever tell Mama," said Albert, low and serious.

"I swear, on the life of the titan arum," said Greta, offering him her hand.

They shook.

After Stein's lecture and the rapturous applause that followed, the rest of the guests were ushered out to pay their respects to the titan tree. Albert nodded to Otto and started to follow him, but Greta held on to his arm. He turned back to her in surprise.

"I've seen it and I've smelled it," said Greta. "I don't wish to do so again."

Albert laughed. Greta realized it was the first time she could recall ever having made her husband laugh. She felt a tiny starburst of exhilaration. In a minute they were quite alone in the conservatory. Greta could think of nothing else to say and searched desperately for topics, unwilling to let this moment of shared good humor pass.

"Did you know that rhododendrons are poisonous to bees?" said Albert, at last finding a topic of conversation. "The nectar is toxic to them. All the outdoor hives at Temple Court have to be kept closed during the flowering season and the bees fed on sugar syrup."

"But the garden is full of such riches in May!" objected Greta. "Poor bees."

"I quite agree," said Albert warmly.

"At Fontmell we shall have our own hives and absolutely no bloody rhododendrons."

"Shall we?" said Albert, watching Greta closely.

"Yes," she said, coloring under his scrutiny. She was silent for a moment, thinking. "You must treasure the high brown fritillary, for I am never catching you another butterfly. I'm too squeamish for killing jars—science or not. But I should like to create a butterfly garden at Fontmell. An entire four or five acres just for bees and butterflies." She hesitated. "Perhaps we can decide on the planting scheme together?"

"Yes," said Albert. "I think we can agree on that. And, Greta—"

She held up a hand. "Albert, don't. At present let's talk of nothing but the garden. Agreed?"

"Agreed."

Greta considered—if they could share a single interest, might that be enough for a beginning? They spoke pleasantly for a quarter of an hour on the plants that bees and butterflies like: buddleia, thistles, asters and globe artichokes; and the ones they didn't: azaleas and oleander. When it was time to join the others for coffee in the Gray Salon, Greta wondered whether Albert might attempt to kiss her. He did not. But for the first time in nearly a year, she rather wished he had.

Hampshire, June

———◆❯◆❮◆———

Clement sat in his dressing gown and looked at the pile of letters on the silver tray with revulsion. Bills. Bills and angry letters demanding money. They'd ceased to politely inquire, and now demanded with loud and furious capital letters and scoring underlines. They threatened to tell his father, or go to the press. Or so Clement presumed. The letters had become so unpleasant that he'd ceased to open them some months ago. He pulled a laundry basket out of the back of his wardrobe and stuffed the latest post inside. There were now three baskets brimming with unopened letters. At night, unable to sleep, Clement thought about the baskets and their ghastly contents. He pictured the laundry maids finding them by mistake and hundreds of letters tumbling into the tubs with the washing, a sludge of ink and socks. He needed to raise some money as a matter of considerable urgency.

And yet, while his quest for greater stakes had brought disaster, it had also brought him Irena. She was his one solace. She comforted him, she cajoled him and, when all else failed, she beat him at chess. To his profound astonishment, losing at chess to his beautiful mistress was a pleasure almost as great as that of the flesh. It was nearly as exhilarating as gambling upon the outcome of a match. Clement discovered the pleasure of playing quite naked. Irena initially demurred, complaining that were she to join him, it would sway the already uneven odds further in her favor. Clement said he was willing to take the risk. The only money she accepted from him was those sums that she won from him. And, even then, she would not allow him to chance more than ten pounds on a game. But soon this could not satisfy Clement and he was forced to play elsewhere for higher stakes. The greater the stake, the greater the thrill. Facing the chessboard at the start of a game, he was never lonely, or a disappointment to his family. He did not tell Irena. She could have borne another mistress with greater equanimity than his playing chess elsewhere. The truth was that occasionally Clement liked to win.

He began to speculate in the stock market. He had no cash, but more loans were taken out. His companies would flourish and the loans be amply repaid! He would, at last, reveal a talent for investment, and his father, far from being ashamed, would be proud. The companies Clement selected were not of the first rank—he chose ones that his father would not hear of, when Clement joined their boards. Few that he invested in were listed on the stock exchange. This did not concern him—the returns would be higher, the glory more heavily gilded. The first company failed. Then a second. Nothing flourished, it seemed, apart from his debts, which grew and grew like one of the abominable tropical plants in his mother's glasshouse.

At eleven o'clock the car took him to Temple Court Lane, where his brother, cousin and father had been at work since ten past nine. Clement mounted the steps to the family bank with ever-increasing dread. His father occasionally inspired a sprinkling of schadenfreude in others, and this was entirely due to Clement: the pathetic and useless eldest son. Everyone knew it would have been better if Albert had been the heir. Yet they all continued with the façade that Clement would become head of the London House. It was perfectly hopeless. As his debt ballooned, he ate to console himself, swallowing eggs a dozen at a time like oysters. He puffed as he climbed the stairs to the partners' room, his palms damp. No one looked up as he came in. Albert was reading through correspondence that had arrived from the family courier. A clerk took notes. The Goldbaum clerks were revered for their moral integrity and neat handwriting. Mistakes in the minutes and ledgers could not be erased, for risk of accusations of fraud.

Clement settled himself at the partners' table and listened to the others. The German and British peace conference in Berlin had ended in failure. The British had refused to agree to total neutrality in the event of a war with France, an event so unlikely and preposterous that the outraged kaiser could not understand why the British would not concede. Now the German House intended to raise further capital for the kaiser. Out of courtesy they invited the London House to participate. It was an offer that the British House promptly declined, and with equal courtesy, as the Germans knew they would. It was unthinkable that the British Goldbaums would participate in a loan raised for the purpose of expanding the German army.

"Family interest must give way to national interest," said Lord Goldbaum, with a definitive thump of his fist upon the table.

And yet it seemed that out of the failure of the Berlin peace conference, something useful had arisen. Outraged at the failure of his ambassador to persuade the British to agree to neutrality, the kaiser had fired him. With a little persuasion from the earnest and good-natured Edgar Goldbaum in Berlin, and a hint of advantageous interest rates on the new loan, the kaiser appointed as his new ambassador to Britain Prince Karl Max von Lichnowsky, a man both intelligent and unafraid to stand up to the kaiser, and a good friend of the Goldbaums.

Otto was quiet for a moment, considering. He turned to Lord Goldbaum. "You knew the kaiser would dismiss the German ambassador after his failure at the conference?"

Lord Goldbaum shrugged. "I only knew that the kaiser would never agree to halt the arms race, and the British would never agree to neutrality." He paused. "The kaiser is intolerant of failure. In this case, failure was useful."

"Knowledge is a currency as powerful as sterling," said Albert, echoing another of his father's favorite maxims.

Lord Goldbaum cleared his throat. "With a little persuasion from our cousins in Berlin and Prince Karl Max, we hope to arrange for the kaiser himself to visit England. That would be the most significant way to improve relations between nations," he said. He glanced at Albert. "Any news from Paris?"

"Henri wishes to buy a painting," said Albert.

"That's all?" asked Otto.

"It's a very expensive painting," said Albert. "He asks us not to try and buy it too as he doesn't want the price driven up."

"What painting is it?" asked Lord Goldbaum.

"He declines to say," answered Albert. "On account of his not wanting us to buy it."

Otto rolled his eyes. "Well, there's not much we can do in that case, is there?"

"I want to see this week's list of insurance policies and the major risks contracted," said Lord Goldbaum, resolutely turning the conversation back to business.

Clement wasn't entirely without hope. His father had given him one last idea about how to raise the money. His family would be appalled by his plan. As he considered the risk, a familiar pleasure buzzed through him, as deep and rich as the finest burgundy in Lord Goldbaum's cellar.

Jewish Poor Boys' Home, Vienna, September

—❧·❧—

Karl liked to read the newspapers. The print on the workingman's edition was only slightly smaller than that in the reading primers, and the stories were more colorful than those in the Torah. Tabloids were banned from the Poor Boys' Home, but the rules were not enforced with any great rigor, and so long as he hid the latest *Reichspost* beneath his mattress, he was safe enough from discovery. As he read, Karl felt the world grow; it lit up and spread out beyond the sewer tunnels and reached above to the busy streets of Vienna, and then on again into the far reaches of the empire. He read about peasants in Hungary who had reared a giant cow nearly six feet tall, and he saw photographs of the crown prince and even, once, a glimpse of his wife, who was usually not mentioned. He read about a ship the size of a palace striking an iceberg, and about men leaping overboard in their tailcoats, brandishing cigars, as it sank. He pictured the vast Goldbaum Palace on Heugasse with lights shining in every window as it tipped onto its side and sank slowly beneath the pavement into the cold black tunnels below.

He studied the adverts in the *Reichspost* as if they were an encyclopedia of the world: there were pills to make your hair grow longer, and to stop it sprouting in unwanted places; powders to aid nervous digestion; mail-order knitting patterns for capes and caps; alongside columns with housekeeping advice for ladies. He had never been inside a real home and could only imagine these battalions of aproned housewives. On the paper packet of a cake that he'd bought for a penny was a picture of a round-cheeked woman with long plaits, rolling out pastry. He tore out the drawing and kept it under his mattress. He had no memories of his real mother, Jewish or not, but he liked to think of her as the woman in the picture, the sort of woman who would have scoured the *Reichspost* for recipes and tips. He liked to think of her baking vast and ringed *Kugelhopf* cakes while fat-kneed children played upon the hearth. In his imaginings, he always had brothers or sisters and was never alone.

The story in the newspapers that captivated him most was the murder of two Catholic girls on the banks of the Nyíregyháza River. They had been found drowned, a month after they had disappeared from the home of their employer, a Jewish carpenter, Moses Samuels. Samuels was swiftly arrested and charged with their ritual murder— the corpses were pale, their blood apparently drained and used for the Passover bread. Samuels's son was also arrested and given iced-water treatment until he confessed to his father's crime. Karl was perplexed by the crime: he had tasted the Passover bread and the ritual did not involve blood. In fact, in his new experience as a Jew, he found those of the faith particularly averse to blood. The kosher meat they were served was bloodless and pale. He found himself considering the other possibility: that the carpenter was innocent and the girls had simply drowned; that the carpenter had been blamed because he was a Jew.

Hampshire, October

———◆❖◆———

At dawn the bees in Fontmell hive number three swarmed again. The gardener's boy told the under-gardener, who knocked on the door to Miss Witherick's cottage at ten to seven and informed her of the bad news. With misgivings, knowing it would spoil her mistress's morning, Withers composed a note for Mrs. Goldbaum and sent it up to Temple Court. Mrs. Goldbaum would have to tell Mr. Goldbaum, who would unquestionably be displeased.

Greta placed the note straight in the wastepaper basket. She wished Withers wasn't always in such a hurry to send her bad news in these little early-morning notes. She suspected Withers disliked imparting anything unfortunate in person. She never sent her notes containing charming snippets—such as the first cyclamen erupting on the eastern lawn, or that an owl had moved into the hatching box. Those pieces of news she happily dispensed as she handed Greta out of the motorcar, words tumbling in her enthusiasm. No, the blasted notes contained only these petty travails—slugs massacring the pansies, a mole tearing up the lawn. Greta was learning to dread the small white envelopes in the now-familiar cursive hand, propped up against the marmalade jar on her breakfast tray. She was particularly cross about the bees. Frankly, they were ungrateful. They'd been provided with every comfort and simply would not stay put. She wished that she did not read an omen into their restless discontent.

However, Greta's ill temper could not survive the splendor of the garden. Withers accompanied her around the copse to the west of the lower walk, hands thrust deep into her breeches, a mackintosh thrown over her sweater, and pointed out a surprise of autumn crocuses lurking under a carpet of beech leaves, petals as white and smooth as polished mushroom caps. Withers, decided Greta, suited autumn. Her freckles were the color of fallen leaves, and as profuse. She slipped a handful of glossy conkers into Greta's coat pocket.

"Ask Anna to put these in your closet, keeps away moths and spiders," said Enid.

"Really?"

Enid shrugged and gave a quick lopsided smile. "Who knows? But aren't they an enchanting color?"

Greta agreed. She had vases of rowan berries and butcher's-broom placed in her rooms instead of hothouse flowers. Withers shared her view on treasures; Greta had once offered to show her the collections at Temple Court, but Withers had fobbed her off with polite regrets: she had too much weeding. Greta's admiration for her increased immeasurably.

Before luncheon, Otto came to find his sister. Flushed from the cold air, Greta walked with him. The wind jostled the green from the willow trees, so the grass was thick with leaves that crackled like balls of paper. Otto was not a man who was comfortable out of doors. No matter how many times she reminded him, he inevitably wore the wrong shoes. Goodness knew how his poor valet managed to get them clean again afterward. Albert, despite his many faults, always seemed more at ease outside. His restraint softened under a big sky. It took Greta a moment to realize that Otto was speaking to her.

"I'm afraid I wasn't listening. You're being summoned to where?" she asked, sitting down on a bench and watching a pair of ducks dabble half-heartedly in the pool among the thin whips of willow fronds.

"Nyíregyháza. It's in the northeast of Hungary. You remember I told you about the trial there of that poor Jewish carpenter accused of murdering two Catholic girls."

"I can't see what any of it has to do with you."

"I put up money for the defense of the carpenter. We can't let a man be found guilty of ritual murder in our own country."

"*Your* country. You must remember I'm an Englishwoman now. The whole thing is so ghastly it almost makes me glad to be Austrian no longer."

"That might be so. But since I am still an Austrian, I'm going to do all I can. I shall fight superstition and prejudice with law and reason. They shan't make me ashamed of my country."

"I applaud your sentiments, Otto. But why on earth are you being called as a witness?"

Otto sighed. "The prosecution is arguing that the case is part of a greater Jewish conspiracy. That old specter of the Goldbaums and Jewish international banking. Or, as the trial lawyer has been saying, 'The Hungarian nation is writhing in the octopus tentacles of the Jewish money kings.' I'm afraid that somehow they discovered that I'm paying for the defense, and that seems to add credence to their idiot fantasy."

"You can't possibly go."

"No, of course I shan't. They almost certainly know that I'm in England and there is no chance of it. I expect they shall use my non-appearance as further evidence of the conspiracy."

"Is the poor man going to hang?"

Otto shook his head. "I don't know. The bodies of the two girls have been exhumed and a pathologist from Budapest concluded that death was from drowning—they appeared pale and bloodless from having been submerged in water for some time. There may have been a slow leakage of blood through cuts in the fingernails. They sliced their fingers on the bank as they tried to climb out of the river before they succumbed."

"How horrid," said Greta with a shudder. Otto never spared her any scientific detail, having more respect for the truth than for the supposed delicacy of ladies. Mostly she was glad. "None of it can help the dead girls. But I suppose we must believe that even a rustic jury will choose science over magic."

"We can hope. But they've listened to two months of the prosecution's lurid accounts of ritual murder and financial conspiracies. They've read twisted phrases from the Talmud. They've even pointed to Lord Goldbaum's refusal to insure the *Titanic* as evidence of his unnatural Semitic prescience."

Greta cast a stone into the green pool, watching the ripples spill outward long after the pebble had sunk. "It's medievalism in the twentieth century. It makes me feel quite sick."

Otto shredded a leaf between his fingers, dirtying his gloves.

"I worry that if the carpenter is convicted, there will be more trials, and not only in Austria-Hungary. There are already whisperings of arrests in Russia. This nonsense must be stopped."

"A little international outrage might help. Perhaps I could write a letter to the *Times*?" suggested Greta.

"What a good idea. Why don't you discuss it with Albert?"

The water from the pools flowed over a small waterfall and down toward the river. Three miles from here the river met the sea and the tidal wash. The Nyíregyháza river, where the girls had drowned, would be sloshing into another sea at the far reaches of another empire, but to Greta, sitting in the shade of the green willows, it seemed unnervingly close.

In the easy light of an autumn afternoon the stonework of Fontmell Abbey was honeyed, softened by the thick wrists of an ancient wisteria and the last pink rosettes of a rambling rose. The crowning thatch glowed bright gold like ripened corn, and it lent the ancient building a sense of newness and gloss. The house was near completion, and Greta found herself worrying more and more as to how she and Albert would manage when they lived there together, alone. They must meet one another at luncheon and dinner without the buffer of the rest of the family. The abbey would slip into a single wing of Temple Court, and their new bedrooms had been situated inconveniently close together by the well-meaning and modern-minded architect. Neither Greta nor Albert had the courage to ask for them to be repositioned.

Albert found her dawdling on the terrace, looking at the newly delivered terra-cotta pots waiting to be filled.

"This is nothing like the other Goldbaum houses," said Greta. "It's exactly what I wanted. But do you think that you shall like it?"

"Do you ever greet a fellow with a simple 'Good afternoon'?" he asked wearily.

"Good afternoon, Albert. Do you think you shall like the house when you live in it? It is all done according to my taste rather than yours."

"I don't know," he answered honestly. "I suppose we shall find out."

Albert and Greta walked side by side along the stone path away from the house and down toward the lower gardens and the wilderness leading to the river. They fell into step, while preserving a small distance between one another. Greta slipped on a sodden beech leaf and Albert reached out to steady her, then hesitated. She regained her balance and he withdrew his arm without touching her. She asked his advice regarding her proposed letter to the *Times* objecting to the blood-libel trial. He listened patiently, before saying slowly, "Why don't you ask one or two of your admirers to lend their names? Arthur Balfour would, I'm sure. And Mr. Bernard Shaw informed me after luncheon that he admired my clever and attractive wife."

"Really? He told me that people in love ought never to marry. I found it oddly reassuring, although I'm not sure that was quite how he intended it. But if you think it might help, I shall write to him."

As they ambled along the riverbank they conversed politely on other matters pertaining to the family interest. Albert informed her that his father had decided the time had come for him to run for Parliament.

"And I must campaign during the election?" she asked.

"A little. Appear at my side here and there. Open the odd bazaar. Clap at my speeches, smile as though they are sensible."

"I'm sure they will be. But, Albert, are you quite sure you want to be an MP?"

"My father believes it is important. The influence of the House of Lords is waning. He wants us to hold a seat in the Commons."

"Yes, I know what Lord Goldbaum thinks. But what do *you* think?"

"It's not too arduous. I shan't need to attend Parliament all that often. Every few weeks ought to suffice. I have no ambition as to government."

Greta frowned. "But they might have ambitions for you. A Goldbaum in the Treasury or the Foreign Office is always useful."

Albert shrugged. "It's my duty."

Greta said nothing else. Sometimes she felt that duty was an excellent excuse for making no decisions regarding one's own life.

Albert pointed to the distance. "The first of the oaks are here."

He had insisted on the transplanting of forty large oaks mature enough for hairstreak butterflies to lay eggs in the bark crevices. Greta squinted into the cool sunshine and saw several vast carthorses hauling a trailer on which lay an oak tree, its roots stretching into the sky like a black, inverse canopy. A caravan of trees followed, some on trailers pulled by lumbering horses and others by steam tractors. The tractors were needed to haul the trees into the waiting holes, which had been carefully prepared so that the field was littered with vast muddy craters. To Greta's eye, it resembled a desolate and pockmarked netherworld. She felt a little like Lady Macbeth watching Birnam Wood walk to Dunsinane, but she had vowed not to squabble with Albert. She dug her nails into her palms to stop herself from complaining.

"By God, it's quite something," said Albert quietly.

She glanced at him; he was mesmerized by the spectacle. This was the moment to impart bad news.

"The bees have swarmed again," she said softly.

"How unfortunate. It's too cold for them. If we don't find them quickly, they will die."

"Yes," agreed Greta, realizing that Albert was not quite as distracted as she had hoped.

They watched as a steam tractor growled forward, clunking over the uneven ground, the tree jostling on the trailer, half-hidden in the manufactured mist, its branches and roots wavering frantically. It paused beside one of the deepest holes and a hydraulic lift was pumped by four men; the tree rose up and was then gently placed the right way up into the ground. A team of gardeners armed with spades moved in to fill up the earth around the tree with fresh soil.

Greta paused and then pointed to a dark clump of earth on the root system of one of the largest oaks. The soil appeared to be writhing and twisting in the air, forming some kind of black and oozing shape.

"What is that?" she asked, before realizing. "It's the bees!" she said with a cry. "You must rescue them, Albert."

Albert glanced at his wife, taken aback at this unexpected display of faith.

"I'll try," he said, and Greta looked at him with frank approval.

All work on the trees was paused to avoid frightening the bees and making them swarm again. A boy was dispatched to Temple Court, and within half an hour Herzfeld arrived in the Wolseley. They unloaded a new hive warmed with hot bricks, as well as Albert's gown, gloves and mask and assorted paraphernalia. Albert took a white sheet and laid it on the ground beneath the bees swarming in the tree roots, then donned his mask and long gloves. He clambered up onto the trailer and scaled the inverted tree, climbing up toward the roots until he was close enough to gently shake the bees from their resting place, so that they dropped onto the sheet below. When the sheet had turned black with bees, he jumped down and began to brush them into the hive with a broom. He moved slowly, quite unafraid as the bees coated his gloves, stroking them off into the hive. However, it was quite clear to Greta that he needed some help, for the hive kept rolling over and most of the bees missed, landing back on the sheet or flying up into the branch, which was once again growing thick with a dark fog of insects.

"Do you have spare gloves and a mask?" she asked Herzfeld.

"Yes, but I'm not terribly good with bees. I'm more of a butterfly man. And bees sense fear."

"I'm not afraid," said Greta.

Suitably attired, she held the hive steady while Albert scooped in the bees. He held out his hand, and she saw that on the end of his gloved fingertip was a bee twice the length of any other and marked with a dab of white paint. Its dark furred stripes made Greta think of the tiger skin in the conservatory.

"The queen," Albert said with reverence. "Once she's in the hive, the others will follow."

Within a quarter of an hour they were finished. Only a few stragglers remained. Albert turned the hive the right way up and signaled to Herzfeld, who, now that the bees were safely contained in the hive, hurried over.

"Feed them with sugar syrup. Have the hive placed near one of the glasshouses for warmth. See if we can stop them swarming again," said Albert, removing his mask and gloves and shaking a stray bee from the carnation in his buttonhole, where it was hunting for pollen.

Greta's heart hammered with exhilaration; she had not been frightened at the time, but now she felt the swoosh of blood in her ears. The sound of three thousand bees had awoken some primitive instinct buried deep within her cultured self. She unfastened her gloves, tipping several bees out of them.

"You've been stung," said Albert.

Glancing down at her hands, she saw that he was right. A few red welts were swelling on her wrists, the stings still protruding from her skin. She was too excited to feel the pain.

"Carry on," he said to the gardeners, signaling to them to continue planting the trees. "Come," he said to Greta, and led her back through the gardens and up to the house.

When they reached Fontmell, it was approaching dusk and the carpenters had gone. The house was empty and swathed in gloom. There were no servants as yet, and Albert opened the door himself into the bare hall. There were no pictures and all the furniture was yet to be delivered. Only a large Jacobean mirror too big to be moved hung over the stone mantelpiece. When the roof had been restored and thatched, Greta had asked the architect to design a cupola made of glass, so that light could spill down onto the galleried landing and the great hall far below. Now, as she looked up in the darkness, Greta could see a wedge of moon and the silver flare of the North Star. The hall echoed emptily, their footsteps clattering noisily on the flags, and yet it smelled pleasantly of polish and lavender and new wood. Albert searched for the light switch. He had insisted on the modernity of electricity in the house—on that point he'd been intractable. He found it, and a converted chandelier illuminated the room with spinning and diffracting light.

"Sit," he said, motioning to a carpenter's bench that had been left there for the night.

Greta sat and Albert moved beside her, taking her wrist in his hand.

"I don't have tweezers," he said, raising her wrist to his mouth. He started to pull out the stings with his teeth. It was painful, but took only a moment.

"I hope this hasn't put you off bees," he said.

"It hasn't."

They sat, suddenly awkward, aware of the absolute stillness of the house and the fact that they were quite alone. Greta could still hear the tick of her heart, the dwindling thrill from her encounter with the bees. Her cheeks were aglow. On the other hand, Albert sat stiffly upright, his hair unruffled from his mask, his waistcoat and jacket perfectly fastened, his mustache neatly combed and symmetrical. Even the white carnation in his buttonhole remained uncrushed. On impulse, Greta reached out and ran her fingers through his hair, rumpling it. Then she tugged his cravat askew. He stared at her for a moment and then reached over and pulled out the pin from her hair. It spilled onto her shoulders. Albert gathered a rope of it and twisted it around his wrist, tugging her uneasily forward so that it almost hurt. He drew her toward him, closer and closer, until his lips were nearly brushing her forehead. She could feel his breath on her skin.

"Thank you for your help with the bees," he said, and released her.

She looked at him, a cool disappointment settling in her belly. She had thought he was going to kiss her. Working together with a common purpose had been unexpectedly satisfying, and now she felt herself sinking back toward the usual caution she maintained with him. He was studying her intently, a small smile at the corner of his mouth.

"Were you hoping for more than a thank-you?" he asked, apparently amused.

Greta looked away, for once shy.

"If you want me to kiss you, I'm afraid you're going to have to ask," he said, yawning and closing his eyes.

"That's not the usual way between a lady and a gentleman," objected Greta, irritated.

"Ah yes," said Albert, stretching out his legs, "but we did agree that you needed to be quite sure. Excuse me for removing any semblance of doubt. But you do keep on changing your mind."

Greta knew that he was teasing her. She supposed she deserved it. She considered walking out and returning to Temple Court, but it was cold outside and the motorcar might not be waiting. And, she realized, she was worn out from loneliness. Now that she'd enjoyed a brief respite she did not want it to end.

"Fine," she said. "You can kiss me, if you like."

He leaned forward and planted a chaste kiss on her cheek, gentle as a butterfly wing.

She opened her eyes and frowned. "That didn't really seem worth the prelude."

Albert laughed, unoffended. "If you want me to kiss you somewhere more interesting, I'm afraid you're going to have to ask."

Greta sighed and rolled her eyes. "For goodness' sake! Kiss me properly, Albert. On the mouth."

He reached behind her head, gathering her hair up again and splitting it into two braids, then used it to tug her toward him and kissed her. He tasted of tobacco and fresh air. Her skin grew warm. Greta wondered if perhaps it was because it was many hours since luncheon, but her head was starting to swim. His fingers tugged interestingly at her coat buttons. When he finally pulled away, Greta noted with satisfaction that he no longer had the same air of self-control.

"Would you like me to kiss you again?" he asked, feigning nonchalance. "If you do, you must tell me where."

Greta stared at him, wondering if she dared. However, once she had started a game, she simply had to win. She wanted desperately to shock him, and to startle them both out of the impasse that had developed between them. She knew he was trying to embarrass her, but she would not let him. He might be older and more experienced in matters of the flesh, but Greta liked to think of herself as intrepid in all new adventures. Slowly she lifted her skirt to reveal an ankle, then leisurely raised it higher to display a well-turned calf, then a soft white thigh. She hesitated and then pulled it up again above her chemise, until she was sitting on the cold bench in her finest cambric knickers. She unfastened the ribbons and stifled a shiver that was partly from cold, partly from something else, then slowly slid them down over her boots.

"I'm afraid I only know the word in Latin, will that do?" she said, with a boldness that she wasn't quite sure she felt.

"Say it in whichever language you prefer, and I promise I'll kiss it," said Albert, meeting her eye.

She leaned forward and whispered it in his ear.

. . .

The following morning Anna bustled into Greta's room at a quarter to eight balancing a breakfast tray, threw open the curtains and turned to her mistress's bed to bid her a good morning, only to be greeted by the sight of Mr. Albert Goldbaum's bare buttocks. She apologized profusely and withdrew, banging the door behind her in her hurry. Greta pulled the sheet up to her chin and laughed.

"Poor Anna, I think she'd rather given up on us."

"I'm sure she'll recover from the shock," said Albert, still not bothering to move.

The night before, Greta had experienced pleasure and joy, all the keener for being unexpected. This morning, she felt mostly relief. At last it was now a marriage in all regards. The fact that it had taken more than a year to consummate was a secret that no one else ever needed know. She understood that most women were expected to be ashamed or revolted after their first experience of marital relations, but for Greta the shame had been in celibacy rather than intimacy. She was euphoric at her sense of release.

She slid out of bed, retrieved the breakfast tray and, placing it down on the blanket, nudged Albert in the ribs.

"Move up. There isn't room."

Grumbling, he heaved himself upright.

"You don't have enough pillows."

"Well, if you're going to become a regular visitor, I shall get some more."

"Am I going to be a regular visitor?" he asked, watching her closely.

"Yes," said Greta. "But we need to agree on some rules."

"Oh?" said Albert with cautious interest.

"First, coffee," said Greta. "I'm afraid we're going to have to share a cup."

She took a sip and passed him the cup; he dutifully sipped and handed it back. "I think you ought to know that in the mornings I'm more of a tea chap."

"Well, I suppose, you are an Englishman."

He leaned against the headboard, eyeing her a trifle warily. "What are your terms, Greta?"

"I don't want children." She held up a hand before he could interrupt. "Not yet. One day, of course. But, Albert, let's be us for a while longer. This thing between us is new and fragile. I'm only just starting to get used to you. Heaven knows how I'd feel about your children."

Albert considered her with some gravity.

"All right," he said at last. "I agree. No children for a while. At least, not on purpose. A man can only do what he is able to, in these matters."

Greta smiled. "Of course. And thank you."

"Anything else?"

"You're going to have to learn to laugh at my jokes."

"I'm not renowned for my sense of humor."

"I know, darling. But it is important. How on earth will we manage when we annoy each other, unless we can laugh? We'll start with a dirty limerick and work our way up."

"Dear God," said Albert, burying himself under the pillows. "I had a choice of at least three Goldbaum women."

"Ah well, it's too late for that now," said Greta cheerfully. "Besides, they might have been worse. Helena is awfully nice, but she's rather fat."

"I'd have taken her."

Greta took the spoon from the marmalade jar and flicked a round glob of sticky orange at him. It landed in the middle of Albert's forehead.

London, December

———◆∘◆∘◆———

The white Portland-stone façades on Park Lane and Regent Street trickled soot-stained tears. The puddles were black with a thin crust of filthy ice. Otto's coat was damp the moment he stepped outside, and although it was carefully dried beside the fire in the airing room, the Goldbaum residence at Number One Park Lane smelled vaguely and permanently of wet wool. He'd had a cold for a fortnight. Lord Goldbaum's was even worse. He honked constantly, his nose swollen and raw from blowing. During partners' meetings, Otto found himself transfixed by the drip on the end of Lord Goldbaum's nose, wondering precisely when it would fall.

It was barely three o'clock, but the fog was thick and yellow—Otto suspected the sun itself was in bed with a streaming cold and had quite given up—and the first of the lamplighters was busy in the street outside the Goldbaum offices on Temple Court Lane. Lord Goldbaum placed a copy of the morning's *Times* on the table and grunted approvingly at Otto and his sons.

"Your wife did well," he said to Albert, before starting to read. "'The question is one of humanity, civilization and truth. The "Blood Accusation" is a relic of the days of Witchcraft and Black Magic, a cruel and baseless libel on Judaism, an insult to Western culture.' And blow me if, as well as H. G. Wells and Mr. Shaw, she didn't get all the archbishops to sign."

Albert smiled. "My wife can be persuasive."

"Reuters news agency is to circulate the letter in the United States," said Otto. "I hope that, with international pressure, the poor fellow will be acquitted."

"We can't allow the man to hang," said Albert. "The prosecutor keeps invoking our name like a profanity. We're in the middle of this abhorrent mess. Blast them for calling you as a witness, Otto."

Lord Goldbaum was silent for a moment. "I shall speak to the Duke of Norfolk—see if, as the country's most prominent Catholic, he can't persuade the Pope to issue a bull denouncing the whole business."

Otto cleared his throat. "There have already been two papal bulls: 'those accusing the Jews of drinking the blood of children are blinded by avarice, and only want to rob their money.' The duke need only ask the Pope to state the authenticity of the earlier bulls."

The others surveyed him with some surprise.

Otto shrugged. "I was called as a witness. I might have chosen to ignore the summons, but I like to be prepared."

While for the others the sorry business of the blood-libel trial was a distant horror at the edge of a foreign empire, for Otto it was an offense at home and he felt it keenly and personally. It made him ashamed of his own countrymen, and reminded him that while he and his coreligionists might have been citizens, the veneer of acceptance was brittle. The sadness lodged in his chest.

Albert began to read the summaries from a variety of companies with which the House of Goldbaum held an interest, and which were seeking to spread significant risks: a cargo shipment of lamb from New Zealand, insured for a hundred and ten thousand pounds. Clement sat rigid in his chair while Lord Goldbaum listened with his eyes half-closed, head resting on his fingertips, snoozing to all outward appearances. They all knew that he was not. Albert read the risk for a new Scottish railway line, at seventy-five thousand pounds, and then he hesitated. Lord Goldbaum looked up, alert, a dragon awakened by a thief.

"Go on," he said.

"I'm quite sure it is a mistake," replied Albert.

"Then we shall have it corrected."

"There's no need for me to read a mistake, Father."

"You're trying my patience, Albert. Read the lists."

Albert sighed and then continued with great reluctance. "First on the Alliance Assurance list is an insurance policy taken out upon the life of Lord Robert George Moses Goldbaum, contracted by Mr. Clement Robert George Goldbaum for two hundred thousand pounds at four percent."

Here Albert stopped and looked desperately at his brother, who sat bolt upright, his eyes wide and terrified.

"It is simply a mistake, isn't it, Clement? Some error."

"Well, Clement?" said Lord Goldbaum, turning calmly to his eldest son. "The clerks are very careful fellows. I don't expect it's a mistake at all, is it?"

"No," said Clement, his voice barely a whisper.

Lord Goldbaum reached across the table, took the list from Albert and read for a minute in silence.

"You didn't receive very good terms, Clement. You ought to have negotiated much better. But figures have never been your strongest suit."

Otto wondered if he could quit the room. Lord Goldbaum sensed his objective and turned to him with cold fury.

"Stay where you are, Otto. This will affect all the Houses and the partnership agreements. I don't want any rumor or innuendo in this matter. From now on, we shall deal only with the truth."

Otto remained where he was. Clement shifted under the gaze of three pairs of eyes: the fury of his father, the bewildered disappointment of his brother and the embarrassment of his cousin.

"How much debt are you in, Clement?" asked Lord Goldbaum. "It must be a very large sum for you to resort to such measures."

Clement began to sweat. He muttered something inaudible.

"I can't hear you—speak up, man," snapped his father.

"I don't know," said Clement.

"How can you not know your own debts? Did you simply pluck a number to put against my life?" Lord Goldbaum regarded his son with amazement and disgust.

"I insured my own life as well," mumbled Clement. "So that if something happened to me, you would not be saddled with my debts. The returns on my investments were not what I'd hoped."

Lord Goldbaum rang a bell. Joseph Caplan, chief clerk, appeared moments later.

"Joseph, it seems that my son has made poor investments. I would like you to go with him and start what, I fear, shall turn out to be a monumental task—to make a thorough inventory of all these ventures, with precise figures."

"Yes, sir." Joseph nodded. "Mr. Goldbaum, sir, shall we go into the meeting room? There is a fire lit," he said, turning to Clement, who rose to his feet without a murmur.

Clement followed Joseph, a figure of utter dejection. He paused by the door and turned back to his father as if to speak and then, changing his mind, quitted the room without another word.

That evening Lord Goldbaum did not return to Number One Park Lane for dinner. Otto and Albert sat in the gilded dining room at seven thirty, wondering whether Clement would join them. The footmen, in blue coats with golden buttons, waited poised behind their chairs.

"Should we start without him?" asked Otto.

"I've never known him to miss a meal," said Albert.

"He won't have done anything . . ."—Otto prevaricated—"*rash*?"

Albert shook his head, but looked deeply troubled. "No. He wouldn't do that. This is shame enough. Damn it. We should eat." He signaled to a footman. "Keep Mr. Clement Goldbaum's dinner warm. You may serve us."

Neither Otto nor Albert was hungry. They were presented with grouse casseroled in sloes and port, but they mostly picked out shot, drinking an excellent 1889 claret rather than eating. Unable to face discussing the afternoon's events, they resorted to silence. Clement arrived during the cheese course. He sat down in his place, offering no explanation or apology for his absence, merely serving himself a right angle of Stilton and most of a Camembert, fondly stroking the downy rind with a large forefinger, before helping himself to a dozen Bath Oliver cookies and a significant helping of port. Otto and Albert regarded him without comment for some time, before Albert finally exploded in a resentment of uncharacteristic fury.

"For pity's sake, man, stop eating and speak. What in God's name were you thinking? What kind of idiocy have you committed?"

Clement wiped his mouth on his napkin and waved at the footmen to leave the dining room.

"I apologize, Albert. I realize my actions will have consequences for you. I think we can all agree that finance is not my forte."

"Yes, Clement, I think we can all agree on that," said Otto.

Clement turned to his brother, eyes wide and beseeching. "Albert, you must help me. Otto, you too."

Clement's lips were stained with port like blood, and his skin was bloated and very pale. Otto wanted to be angry with him—his cousin was guilty of utter stupidity. In the gilded dining room, beneath Van Dyck's portrait of the aging Cardinal Guido Bentivoglio in his crimson robes, Clement stared at Otto and Albert with weary hopelessness.

"Please help me," he said. "I need to tell you about the laundry baskets."

Hampshire, December

———❦———

A list had been drawn up pertaining to Clement's failed investments, but the details of his other creditors remained in the baskets,
along with their correspondence and all Clement's bills from the last
year. It seemed that, once overwhelmed, Clement had turned his
face to the wall and had neglected to pay a single tailor's chit or
settle the rather impressive bill from his club. Otto persuaded Albert
to let Greta help. She was discreet, competent with figures and not
easily shocked. Greta was extremely fond of Clement, and was relieved to be useful. Lord Goldbaum wished to be informed only of
the final figure for the debt and of the names of the creditors. He
did not desire to spend a month trawling through the pathetic affairs of his son and to be constantly confronted with evidence of his
ignominy.

They confided only what was essential to Lady Goldbaum, who
instructed Clement to take a holiday in Switzerland while his affairs
were brought to order. Irena listened with equal dismay and, to his
astonishment, sympathy. She worried that, alone, Clement would be
tempted into further disaster, and declared that she would put aside
her sense of betrayal and accompany him. He quit England in equal
shame and relief.

The others commandeered the library to pore through Clement's
papers, sorting the correspondence into various piles. It was a peculiar task, and although the accumulated sums involved soon became

dizzying, Greta found an odd sort of satisfaction in attempting to pull order from the chaos. The men were frequently enraged at Clement's naivety and pathological inability to confront his troubles—the thing had spiraled into such a labyrinthine mess since he had refused to do so. Yet as she read through the often cruel and mocking correspondence, which here and there skirted awfully close to blackmail, Greta felt herself tracing the journey of another human being's frailty and despondency. She was frustrated by Clement, but she also pitied him. Goodness knew how he had managed to continue for so long with such a burden upon his conscience.

The newspapers sensed a scandal and there were scurrilous mentions in the press, and gleeful descriptions of a large debt. The *Daily Express* suggested a sum of one million pounds, and wondered whether Lord Goldbaum would be forced to offer up for sale a dozen portraits of his beautiful Gentile women.

"Whenever they sense blood, all their natural prejudice comes out," said Albert with revulsion, on reading this latest story.

"It does," agreed Otto. "But when the dust settles and they need a loan, it'll recede again like the tide."

Albert made some last calculations in the ledger. "I make the final account to be three hundred and sixty-eight thousand pounds."

They fell silent, considering the stupendous sum. Greta paid Enid Witherick for her position as head gardener at Fontmell eighty pounds a year, plus a cottage and logs from the estate. She envisioned Clement's debt as a series of Enid Witherick stretched out across the estate, and estimated nearly five thousand of them.

Her reverie was interrupted by a footman announcing the arrival of a courier. The young man stepped forward and murmured something quietly to Albert, who nodded.

"Tell them," he said, gesturing to Otto and Greta.

"Yesterday afternoon the jury in Nyíregyháza District declared Lajos Werkner not guilty of two counts of murder," announced the courier.

Greta clapped her hands, relieved and jubilant.

Albert dismissed the courier and produced a decanter of brandy, pouring glasses for himself and Otto. "It is a victory, nonetheless, of logic and reason over fear and prejudice."

"I beg your pardon," said Greta, pointing to her lack of brandy. "I should like to toast."

With only the smallest show of reluctance, Albert poured her half a glass.

"To reason," declared Otto.

But as they drank, each of them privately wondered whether they should rather be toasting money. It was the family's wealth that had provided them with the influence to persuade philosophers, dukes and popes to intervene on the side of reason. In this instance, reason had the glitter of gold.

Otto sighed. "It's a melancholy triumph. A battle that we should not have had to fight. If a fellow takes against me, I'd like it to be personal rather than on account of my race."

"My dislike of you was entirely personal, darling," said Greta, blowing Albert a kiss.

"Thank you, I'm not entirely reassured," replied Albert, and left Otto and Greta to continue sifting through the contents of Clement's final laundry basket.

"You and Albert seem happier with one another," Otto said to his sister.

"Do we?"

"Yes."

Greta stopped opening envelopes and sat back in her chair. "I find Albert attractive enough and not unintelligent, but he is so serious. In private he can be domineering, and in public he considers me flamboyant. I like him a good deal more than I did, and that, brother dearest, must be sufficient for the present. You may put that in a letter for Mama. I'm sure she is pressing you for details."

Since this was exactly true, Otto said nothing more.

. . .

Albert and Greta moved into Fontmell shortly before Christmas. Greta wondered what the hall would look like with a blue Norway spruce felled from among the specimens in the arboretum, hung with lights and paper angels. Dutifully she placed a silver menorah in the bay window of the drawing room.

Fontmell Abbey was the smallest house in which Greta had ever lived. There were a mere eight bedrooms. Hardly anyone would be able to come and stay, Greta concluded with relief. She had pressed Albert to resist the usual furnishing style of the Goldbaums—the crowded, overheated rooms stuffed with treasures. There were no Persian carpets on the exquisitely restored seventeenth-century oak floors, only rush matting, which softened the echo and in the warmth gave out a sweet, haylike scent so that it smelled perpetually of summer. Most of the walls were plastered and lime-washed with chalk. At the heart of the house was the large skylit hall. Cool winter sunshine poured in from the round glass window cut into the thatch two stories above, spilling onto the blackened Jacobean paneling in the great hall beneath so that it brimmed with light. Leading off the hall were the reception rooms: a cheerful dining room able to seat just twenty; a bright morning room; a billiard room; a small library mostly containing books on entomology and gardening, all the volumes rebound in Goldbaum-yellow vellum; and, lastly, a sunny south-facing drawing room with French windows opening onto a wide terrace with views of the gardens beyond.

On the other side of the hall, through the green baize door, were the kitchen and a servants' hall with a vaulted ceiling fashioned from oak from the Temple Court estate. The under-butler slept on a bed in the gun room, between the store containing all the silver plate and a large china closet holding Greta and Albert's wedding gifts of Sèvres porcelain, crystal and Meissen. The female servants had bedrooms in the attics under the eaves, containing the epitome of luxury: a washbasin with hot and cold running water and a radiator. Below the servants' rooms was the nursery suite, which had been left strictly unfurnished and unpainted.

Greta's own bedroom was situated on the first floor, with large southerly windows framed by a *Clematis montana* and the waxy leaves of an ancient magnolia, which knocked against the glass during high winds as though seeking shelter. The room was decorated with absolute simplicity, the walls lime-washed and the woodwork rubbed with beeswax. There was only a single painting in the room, a large canvas hanging above the fireplace by Dante Gabriel Rossetti, depicting one of his flame-haired women, a green-eyed beauty with pale skin, her plump bosom spilling out of a gauzy dress. The woman's shock of crimson hair was the only flash of color in the room. The painting had been a wedding gift from Henri, and Greta thought it both gaudy and glorious and decided that it, along with the view, was what she wished to wake up to each morning.

Some weeks ago, after inspecting Greta's bedroom, Albert had declared to her surprise that he admired her taste, and she should decorate the rest of the house in the same style. She had accepted the task with pleasure, papering the drawing room in William Morris's "Honeysuckle" design, as it seemed to tone so beautifully with the myrtle, lavender and rosemary growing on the terrace just outside. Greta selected only furniture that was elegant and, equally important, comfortable. She liked Chippendale, but had it mixed with new commissions from local carpenters, all simply upholstered in bold, clashing silks and velvets—cerise, emerald and vermilion. The paintings were an unusual mixture of Pre-Raphaelites and Renaissance masterpieces, the honey-scented and light-filled rooms setting off the lapis blue of the Madonna's robes. Over the main staircase stood a large and empty space. Greta had found no painting both that she loved and that fitted, and she preferred to have nothing than to hang a mistake.

"You asked me whether I should like living here," said Albert to her one evening before they went upstairs to dress for dinner, "and the answer is that I do."

Greta smiled. She sat curled on the new elm window seat in the drawing room and gazed out across the garden at the sun that was sinking in the west, the sky already fading from pink to gray to black. Living closely with Albert was informative. She had learned more about him in the last few weeks than she had during all the previous months of their marriage. His habits were regular: he went to bed late and rose early, shortly after dawn. He had his loose change washed every morning, before it was placed in a wooden dish on his bureau. He dressed himself without the assistance of his valet and even shaved himself. This, she understood, was because Albert did not like to be touched. The one person he did not flinch from was her—but then only during intimate encounters. A casual brush of the hand or knee and he would stiffen, before self-consciously relaxing with a force of will. He liked order and cleanliness in all things. The spare furnishings of the house suited him. Mess and changes to his routine alarmed him. Albert might not have said so, but he became ill-tempered with the servants and at night she could hear him pacing in his rooms.

He was imperfect, full of strange habits, and yet she liked him. He knew a great deal about a great many topics, but he also liked to listen, and he paid quiet attention while she spoke, always interested in her opinion even when he disagreed. Despite the tranquility in their new home, Greta had the odd sensation that she was simply playing house. That none of this was quite real, or else that the serene and pleasant life with Albert was only fleeting. This, she concluded, was because she was happy, or very close to it. And when one feels happiness, one starts to fear its loss.

Finally, after a slow beginning, they had discovered a mutual interest in the bedroom. Albert did his best to make sure that he did not plant a seed in her womb, while reminding her of the difficulty and inaccuracy of the method. To her surprise, Greta discovered that her mother's advice was not entirely wrong. Albert knocked on her bedroom door slightly more frequently than she wished to receive him, and every now and again she locked her door. Whether it was one time in six or once in ten, she could not say. On the odd night, however, she sat up in bed waiting for his knock, straining to hear his footstep outside, and he did not come. She remained alone, unaccountably cross and sleepless. In regard to those occasions, the baroness had furnished her with no advice.

That evening Lord and Lady Goldbaum were dining at Fontmell for the first time. As she checked the arrangements in the dining room once again, Greta found herself cheerfully anticipating their arrival. This was the first occasion on which she would receive guests in her own home. The winter roses in the Fontmell glasshouse had bloomed that morning and Greta had them placed in the center of the table. In the dining room she insisted on the softest of lighting: the electric light was only for the convenience of the servants; the family would dine by candlelight.

Lord and Lady Goldbaum complimented Greta on all her preparations. The menu was simple, comprising four courses: a clear duck consommé; smoked-salmon mousse with melba toast and chives; beef filet with a sauce whisked with lemon, watercress and Parmesan; and pears and walnuts from the estate for dessert. Albert accepted the tributes on his wife's behalf with gratification, and as she sat in the warmth of the dining room, watching the long shadows flit upon the walls, Greta was content.

After they had finished she stood ready to lead her mother-in-law to the drawing room and leave the men to talk over their port, but Lord Goldbaum held out his hand.

"Sit awhile, my dear, Adelheid and I wish to talk to you both."

Taken aback, Greta sat. She glanced across at Albert, who studied his father with some concern. Lord Goldbaum closed his eyes, and when he spoke it was evident that he had been rehearsing his words for some time.

"Clement has been the great disappointment of my life. I had hoped that, given time and patience, he would mature, and even if finance was not his natural inclination, he would prove to be a competent and tactful head of the British Goldbaums and, in time, senior partner in the London House of Goldbaum. It is not to be. This latest debacle, regrettable as it is, has at least served to shake me out of my own delusions. Clement has neither the temperament nor the skill to be trusted with the partnership. He shall inherit the title; there is nothing to be done about that. But on my death, everything else will come to you, Albert. All the properties, the capital, the shares, and the senior partnership of the firm will be yours."

Albert was very quiet. "What is to happen to Clement?"

"Once his debts are cleared, I shall set up a trust for him. He shall be looked after like a child. Paid an allowance. After my death, it will be yours to administer."

Albert nodded once. Greta looked across to Lady Goldbaum, but she was staring into the fire, her face concealed.

"Perhaps this is not the life you would have chosen for yourself, Albert, but I know that you will accept your responsibilities with fortitude," said Lord Goldbaum.

"Yes, Father. I shall endeavor to fulfill your expectations," said Albert.

"Of course you will," said Lady Goldbaum, reaching across the table to squeeze his hand.

"This was not supposed to be your lot," said Lord Goldbaum. "But if your brother had died, it would have been thus. You shall find yourself the leader of the family, the head of the firm, but also something more. You are not a rabbi, or a king or a prince, but you shall be—I'm afraid whether you like it or not—the lay leader of the Jews. They will look to you for charity, for advice and to provide them with a voice. Your position enables you to speak for them to men who will be forced to listen."

As Greta attended to this, she was filled with a sense of ominous solemnity. She glanced across at Albert, who sat silent and serious, as though he were indeed a prince receiving news of his brother's abdication. He swallowed and then looked at his mother, before turning to his father.

"I shall try to be worthy of such responsibility." He spoke softly in a tone of absolute seriousness.

His father smiled gravely. "You have a good wife, and she shall support you in all things, as is her duty."

Lord Goldbaum looked at Greta as he uttered this last part, and she felt the familiar dread seep back into her, like cold fog blowing into a warm room. She glanced at Albert and saw his jaw set with uneasy disquiet. That night she sat up in bed, waiting and hoping for his knock on her bedroom door. It did not come.

1913

I decide who's a Jew.

Karl Lueger, mayor of Vienna

Esther Château, Paris, March

The erasure of Clement from the House of Goldbaum required new partnership agreements to be drawn up between all the Houses. The senior members of the cousinhood were all in favor of a gathering of the family. At the beginning of March, on a cold morning when even the snowdrops seemed to shiver together beneath the plane trees, the Goldbaums gathered in the Blue Salon at the Esther Château. They greeted one another with gusto, the older ladies holding court upon the sofas, the gentlemen paying their respects in English, French, German and here and there a scattering of Yiddish.

An assembly of the Goldbaums in such numbers only occurred once or twice in a generation, and everyone had been rehearsing one another's names for days. The men outnumbered the women by some margin. Wives attended only if they so wished and were not busy with their houses and their children. Sons who had graduated from the nursery were brought along, so they might observe the business that one day would be their lot. Greta considered the usefulness of this custom questionable, noting with amusement two boys no older than seven or eight, playing tiddlywinks in the corner and, on growing bored, firing the counters into unattended coffee cups. Daughters of marriageable age were brought so that they might see, and be seen by, prospective Goldbaum boys. Clement, alone of the men, had not been invited.

Greta was glad to see Edgar from Berlin and his sons David and

Saul, and even more gratified that she remembered their names when she introduced them to Albert, whom they had never met. Edgar was the eldest of her father's cousins and the only one to still wear a yarmulke beneath his bowler hat. He was serious minded, scrupulously fair and one of the few Jews to whom the kaiser himself paid attention.

The gentlemen laughed good-naturedly, and the women made pointed remarks on the trimness of Greta's figure. If Greta had found the ladies of British society to be pushy, they were reticent compared to the Goldbaum women. The one relief was tinged with unexpected disappointment: her mother was unwell and had not come. She would have questioned Greta unflinchingly. Greta was relieved to avoid her mother's inquisition, but found herself sad that the baroness had been too ill to travel. The only recompense was seeing her father. He greeted her with a dry peck on her left cheek, and was taken aback when she pressed herself into his arms. He hesitated for a moment, before embracing her and patting her on the shoulder, pleased and awkward. She was seated beside him at luncheon, and they chattered in German, a treat in itself.

"I hope you are feeding poor Mama tureens of soup."

"We are taking good care of her. If it had only been a little warmer, she would have come. By spring I'm sure she shall be her usual self, complaining happily about everything."

"Give her a hundred kisses from me. Oh, for a spring in Vienna! To see the tulips erupt in the imperial palace gardens. You can smell the spring for a good week before you see it," said Greta, lost in reverie.

"Well then, we must all breathe in deeply," said the baron. "There are no tulips yet."

"And I miss the *Kipferl* served in the Sacher Hotel. Lady Goldbaum had the pastry chef try to make it, but it simply isn't the same."

Charmed as he was by this easy talk of old times, the baron had been commissioned by his wife to find out how his daughter, and the marriage, were faring.

"I must congratulate your husband on his success in the by-election. How does it feel to be the wife of an MP?"

Greta smiled, the stoic and well-practiced smile of a campaign wife. The election had been undramatic, considering the uncertainty of the times. The only sticky moment had come when Albert was dragged off his horse during the hunt by several men from the ranks of the unemployed. He had been shaken, if unhurt.

"Now that he is elected, I am not sure that I really feel the difference. I'm hoping that on some afternoons, when he is supposedly in the House, he can slip away to the Natural History Museum and gaze at moths and African beetles. But he is so terribly conscientious, I doubt that he ever will," she said.

"Very good," said her father. "I am glad that you have Albert, because soon Otto must leave England."

The pleasure of the luncheon drained away. "How soon?"

The baron shook his head, uncertain. "His apprenticeship in London is nearly complete . . ."

"But you have been running our affairs at home for years. You can't need him."

"One always needs the considered opinion of a sensible man. But the cousins are discussing New York."

"Again? I thought it had been decided years ago. We are the bankers of Europe, not America."

The baron nodded. "That is true. But the New World is not so new anymore. The partners are wondering if our decision not to open a House of Goldbaum in New York was a mistake. A wise man can make a mistake, but only a fool fails to correct it."

Greta sighed. Her father had resorted to his old habit of speaking in adages, so that every conversation felt like a lesson from Aesop.

"I like having Otto in England," she said, resisting the impulse to bang her soup spoon.

"And I liked having him—and you—in Austria. But we all do what is best for the family."

Greta turned to her father in exasperation. "But, Father, a family is made up of individuals. What is good for the family as a whole isn't always good for us as people."

The baron raised his glass. "Wise words, Greta. Marriage agrees with you."

She bit her lip in frustration. "I'm not playing proverbs, Father. I don't think Otto should go to New York."

"No. You don't wish for him to go. That is not the same thing. And nothing is decided yet."

Even though they returned to easier topics—the engagement of Johanna Schwartzschild, a new statue in the Stadtpark—for Greta, lunch was spoiled.

A grand ball was held that evening. The Esther Château shone out across Paris, lit up like a second moon. An orchestra played music from the cities of the Goldbaums—Viennese waltzes, Handel, Mozart and Ravel, and, as the hours grew longer and the champagne glasses drained, furious flights of Offenbach. Albert sought Greta's hand for a lugubrious foxtrot.

"You're quiet," he said, concerned.

"Am I? Father says they want to send Otto to New York."

Albert steered her past the banks of great-aunts, lined up on the gilt chairs at the edge of the ballroom, their floral fascinators like entries at a county show.

"They've been talking about New York for years. I'm sure it will come to nothing. Besides, he can't leave yet. The kaiser's visit is arranged for April. My father wants your brother, as one of the Continental Goldbaums, to be present."

"And after the spring? When the kaiser's visit is finished?" Greta looked at him with frank unhappiness.

Albert was quiet for a moment, considering. "I shall need his help on a project in London for at least another couple of months. I'll talk to your father."

"Will you really?" She beamed up at him, suspecting that this project had only just been invented, and experiencing a rush of gratitude toward him.

"Of course," he said. For a moment it seemed like he might kiss her, but they were in company, and Albert disliked such displays.

Just after eleven, Henri led Greta into supper. He was full of cheerful complaints.

"Papa wouldn't let me hire cancan dancers for the party," he said, tucking her arm into his.

"Spoilsport."

"And he barred me from inviting Claire."

"Now, that was to be expected, Henri."

"She sends you her love. She would very much like to see you while you're in town."

"Do send her my best. I should like to see her, too."

Henri stopped walking and turned to Greta. "Would you really?"

Greta blushed, uncertain why this had provoked such a heartfelt response. "Of course."

A line of guests—Goldbaums mingling with the Parisian great and good—had formed behind them, but Henri lingered, oblivious. Greta tugged him into the dining room, where a bacchanalian feast had been laid out. Henri and his father had not concerned themselves with keeping kosher. There were oysters and lobsters, goblets of sorbet in a rainbow of colors, a dozen cheeses, fans of savory crackers, and a baker's shop of fresh bread. A towering *croquembouche* of profiteroles with a chocolate cascade formed the centerpiece of the dessert table, surrounded by a forest of elaborately carved pineapples grown at the Goldbaum estate in Saint-Pierre. Henri broke off two large pieces of bread, instructed the footmen to carve two marbled slices of beef and then placed them inside the bread, busying himself with various sauces and pickles. He seized a napkin with a flourish and then pro-pelled Greta out of the dining room and onto the terrace beyond.

"Here," he said, handing her the bread.

"With all that, you've made me a sandwich," she said.

"A truly excellent sandwich. And look, I've champagne, too."

He produced a bottle from under his arm and two glasses from his pockets. They sat on the top step, picnicking. He draped a shawl around her shoulders.

"I don't know if this is yours."

"It isn't," said Greta, wrapping it tightly.

A low mist wreathed the statuary and Grecian urns like smoke, so that they appeared otherworldly, their strict symmetry distorted.

"You're in love," said Henri.

"Am I?"

"Certainly. You have a buffer of serenity around you that only a woman in love possesses."

"Well, I'm glad you told me," said Greta, annoyed. "'Love' is such a lazy word. I'm afraid it's very overused in England. We currently live in a haze of superlatives. An evening is never pleasant, it is only a magnificent triumph or deathly dull. Society ladies adore or despise. I suppose I'm not permitted to be attached to Albert. To be growing ter-ribly fond of him. I must either love or abhor him."

Henri chuckled. A moment later his face clouded. "Claire's preg-nant. She wants me to marry her."

"You can't."

"I know."

Having no comfort to offer him, Greta reached out and took his hand.

"How far along is she?"

"Five months or so. She's only just starting to show. A neat little bump. She says it's a boy, because she's been craving steak tartare."

His voice glowed with affection, but his brow was creased with anxiety.

"Father doesn't know. That I'm sure of, as he keeps parading all these simpering Goldbaum cousins before me, suggesting that Rachel or Hannah or Sophie would make a charming wife. How can I possibly marry? Have two families. Keep Claire and my son in some apartment in the Eighteenth Arrondissement and see them on Tuesdays and Thursdays, and my legitimate family on Wednesdays and Fridays?"

"And what would you do on Saturdays and Sundays, shoot grouse?" asked Greta.

"Oh, don't make jokes, Greta. It's too awful."

"I know, but there is really nothing for me to say."

"Will you see her?"

Greta hesitated. Albert and the British Goldbaums would not approve. "Of course. Although I'm not sure what I can do."

Henri kissed her hand. "Thank you. It means more than I can say."

The following day the ladies and gentlemen separated, the men departing in a series of motorcars to undertake business at the bank on rue Saint-Antoine and the ladies assembling in the Gray Salon after breakfast. Glancing out of the window, Greta watched several photographers snap pictures of the Goldbaum men as they hurried away—a gathering of Goldbaums on this scale was newsworthy, or so it seemed. Henri had left no instructions for Greta on how to meet Claire, and she vaguely hoped that his request had been a spontaneous whim, forgotten the next morning. The gentlemen returned to the château for luncheon, and Greta found herself pulled aside by Otto before they could step into the dining room.

"Henri has told me that you are to see Claire this afternoon."

"I am? I'm pleased that someone told me."

Otto sighed in relief. "Good. I'm glad you are not going. I'm not without sympathy. But it's Henri's own mess and I don't want you dragged into it."

"I simply meant that I wasn't aware there was any arrangement. I was going to visit the Louvre, but I shall call on Claire instead."

Otto stared at his sister with frank concern. Greta smiled and elbowed him gently.

"Come on, Otto. I'm a married woman visiting an old friend. There's no harm."

"So you'll tell Albert, then?"

Greta frowned. "Of course not. And neither shall you."

Otto coughed in irritation. "Sometimes I get tired of keeping secrets for you, Greta."

"Then tell on me," she said.

They both knew he would not.

After luncheon, when the gentlemen had returned to the bank and the ladies broke up into small groups to visit a museum or to call upon the milliner or furrier, Greta visited Claire. She was living in a sunlit apartment, not in the Eighteenth Arrondissement but in the Fourth, with a charming view of the Seine. She received Greta with genuine pleasure, taking both hands and kissing her warmly on each cheek.

"It is so kind of you. But you are Henri's favorite cousin."

"We are all Henri's favorite when we do what he wants. You look well, Claire."

This wasn't true. Claire's skin was paper white, as though she had not ventured out in weeks, and although she was no longer corseted to create the grotesquely small waist that had been her signature as an actress, she looked thin and ill. Greta could only just discern the smallest bulge beneath her dress. A maid carried in a tray laid with coffee and macaroons.

"Sit, please—eat," said Claire.

"I will if you will," replied Greta.

They sat opposite each other on matching sofas with a silk stripe.

Greta detected the hand of Henri in the decor. It was blue and white and bright, feminine but not blowsy. It was the perfect apartment for a mistress, the sort of place where a man would feel at ease. There was a leather armchair in the choicest spot beside the fire, which Greta knew must be Henri's, for even in his absence it suggested his presence. A vase of scarlet roses rested on the windowsill. Another sat on the piano.

"Henri," said Claire. "He sends me roses twice each week. It used to be every day, but I told him to stop as I had nowhere to put them."

She poured Greta coffee and piled a plate with macaroons.

"You must eat, too, Claire. I hope you are looking after yourself properly."

Claire laughed and patted her belly. "I am, see how fat I have grown."

Greta couldn't see at all, but said nothing. To her relief, at her insistence, Claire did eat—half a dozen macaroons and a jug of creamy milk, which she tipped into her coffee cup. When she had finished, she placed her small hand on Greta's knee, saying, "And you will help us, won't you, Madame Goldbaum? You will talk to your father-in-law and Henri's father and persuade them to let us marry."

Greta set down her cup in dismay.

"Oh, Claire, I can't do that. I mean, even if I speak to them, it wouldn't do any good. No one would listen to me. Is that what Henri said I would do?"

Claire nodded through her tears, racking sobs that shook her whole tiny body.

"Blasted Henri," muttered Greta.

She knelt and attempted to help Claire dry her tears, but the woman remained distraught. Greta rang for the maid, and told her to bring her mistress a hot-water bottle and a blanket. Together they tucked her up on the sofa. Greta held Claire's hand and tried to offer consolatory nothings, while inwardly seething at Henri. At worst, he'd sent her in to break news to Claire that he was too cowardly to confess;

at best, he knew Claire was fooling herself and had dispatched Greta, without warning her of what to expect. Mostly she felt sorry for Claire.

"What am I to do?" said Claire, gazing up at Greta with vast doll-like eyes. "After the baby is born? I can't go back to work as an actress. I was already nearly too old, and now . . ." She lifted her hands help-lessly, letting them fall to her lap.

"Henri will take excellent care of you both. Of that, I have absolutely no doubt at all."

"But he will not live with us. He will visit us like the butcher's boy, twice each week."

Greta thought it best not to reply. For a woman approaching forty, Claire seemed strikingly naive. The entire situation appeared to have caught her utterly by surprise. Greta thought that a baby must surely be considered an occupational hazard, on becoming a gentleman's mistress. She thought of Albert and his insistence that a man can only do his best in such matters.

"I did not think I could have children," said Claire, as if sensing her thoughts. She continued, her voice flat, "And I don't know how to be a mother. My mother was a terrible woman. She sold me when I was twelve years old. The man she sold me to thought I was younger."

Greta felt nauseated by this confession. She wondered if Henri knew.

"I'm terribly, terribly sorry. But of course you will be a good mother, Claire. You will love the baby, and Henri will make sure that you want for nothing. I promise you that."

"What if they take the baby away? Give him to some childless Goldbaum woman like you, or to Henri's wife to raise as her own? Then I shall be all alone."

Claire had turned even whiter than before and she clung to the blanket with thin hands. Greta felt frightened.

"No one will take your baby. And Henri does not have a wife."

"And he promised me he never will," said Claire, lying back down. "If he can't marry me, then he shall marry no one."

. . .

When Greta left, it was nearly half past six and she was terribly late dressing for dinner. There was no time for her to bathe or change her underthings before she was laced into an evening gown, diamonds fastened in her ears. On descending the stairs, already late, she realized that in her haste she had neglected to put on her gloves. She paused in the glittering hall and saw, in a dozen gilded mirrors, her face reflected back at her, anxious and drawn.

All through dinner she was aware of Henri, Otto and Albert watching her. She realized that all three men were concerned for different reasons: Henri wanting to know how she had found Claire; Otto fretting about her involvement; and Albert, aware of nothing, wanting only to know why his wife looked so pale and unhappy. Henri was the first of the men to rejoin the ladies in the drawing room after dinner. He made a beeline for Greta, who waited at the far end of the room ready for him.

"How could you?" she whispered. "You let me go there quite unprepared."

Briefly, in a low voice, she told him what had happened. They stood together before the fire, heads bowed, their backs silently repulsing the efforts of others to join them.

"She isn't well," said Greta. "You need to hire a nurse, someone to take proper care of her until the baby is born. Claire clearly isn't eating, and that isn't helping her or the baby."

"You're absolutely right. That's an excellent idea. It shall be done tomorrow."

Otto joined them. "I don't think you should see her again, Greta."

"That's the least of my concerns," said Greta, irritated. "It's the twentieth century. Whom I call upon is nobody's business but my own."

Otto sighed, resigned. "I suppose everyone will know soon enough. These things never stay secret for long. I'll go and see Claire in your place, tomorrow."

"Do, please. When the family notice her, she's much happier," said Henri.

"Very well. I shan't go tomorrow. But have you spoken to Father?" asked Greta, turning to Otto. "Are you having to leave England?"

Otto smiled. "Not yet. Apparently there is a complicated modernization program that Albert wishes me to collaborate on. We're to try it in London and then see if we can't persuade the other Houses to follow suit."

"What is a modernization program?" asked Greta.

"Typewriters," said Otto. "And telephones."

"It doesn't sound complicated," said Greta.

"It sounds superb," said Henri. "I've absolutely had it with handwritten ledgers, and information arriving by couriers on horseback. It's absurd."

"That may be. But installing a telephone and buying half a dozen typewriters doesn't sound as if it should take long," said Greta, puzzled.

"Well, Albert and I have discussed it, and there are several manufacturers of typewriters to choose from. And the clerks will need persuading, and they do not like to be rushed. So I think I have a reprieve for at least a few months before I must return to Vienna. I like England."

It seemed that her father had not even mentioned New York. Perhaps Albert was right, and the scheme had already been abandoned. For the first time that day, Greta felt some of the heaviness in her soul lift. She glanced around the drawing room and, on spying Albert, smiled at him with absolute gratitude. He acknowledged her with a single nod and returned to his conversation.

L ater that evening there was a gentle knock on her bedroom door, and Albert appeared in his dressing gown. She tapped at the empty space on the bed beside her and he sat down carefully, before lying down, pleased but not at ease.

"I'm glad you came," she said firmly.

He relaxed a little and took her hand, brushing his lips along her knuckles. He hesitated, then said, "Baron Jacques wants me to talk to Henri about the possibility of my cousin Margaret for his wife. Do you think that's a good idea?"

"No. It's a very bad one. Particularly for poor Margaret."

She leaned over and kissed him, forgetting briefly the unpleasantness of her day.

"I don't have to work tomorrow. Spend the afternoon with me," he said as she pulled away.

"In bed?" she asked, teasing.

"No, in Paris."

After Albert returned to his own room, Greta could not sleep. She lay awake thinking of Claire, alone and frantic in her beautiful, lonely apartment with its view of the Seine.

They had a splendid afternoon. The sun shone, and Albert and Greta lunched in a very pleasant restaurant, where they shared an excellent bottle of wine, and then Albert bought her a painting. He steered her into a private gallery on the rue La Boétie, where the proprietor, a slim young man with a high forehead, greeted Albert warmly.

"Monsieur Goldbaum."

"*Bonjour*, Monsieur Rosenberg. Do you have it?"

"*Oui*. I do."

Monsieur Rosenberg led them through to a bright, plainly decorated room, where on one wall hung a Klimt painting of a woman in a rose garden. The woman was a small figure among the profusion of roses and the dark greens of the grass and trees.

"She's wearing your dress," said Albert. "We must have it."

"But you don't like the dress," said Greta.

"I didn't like it."

"Oh, you do now?"

Albert prevaricated. "I like it in the painting. And the painting will fit perfectly on the staircase at Fontmell."

Greta laughed, aware that she was exhilarated by the sunshine and the wine. She went up on tiptoe and kissed him, and even though they were under the earnest gaze of Monsieur Rosenberg, for once Albert did not object.

G reta was glad that she could visit Claire, because otherwise during the long days while the men were busy at the bank she would have been bored. The nurse who came in the mornings was kind and efficient, and Claire seemed to improve under her care. She had more color and seized Greta's hand, pressing it onto her belly and saying, "Feel him kick!" with a little gasp of pleasure. Greta read to her and they played cards, or else she told Claire about when she, Henri and Otto had been children: the afternoons spent lazing on a rowing boat on Lake Geneva during summer holidays, lighting firecrackers in the gardens at the Esther Château, and once setting a potting shed ablaze. Early on Friday afternoon, when Greta was in the midst of such a story, there was a knock, and the maid opened the door to Otto and Henri.

"We were allowed out early, for good behavior," said Henri, striding over and kissing Claire on the forehead.

"What a treat! How delightful," said Claire, sitting up, her cheeks flushed with joy.

The men had brought pastries and cheese and grapes and a bottle of champagne, and they set out a picnic on the low table in the drawing room. Henri sat on the floor at Claire's feet, feeding her morsels with his fingers.

"We need only music," said Greta.

"It is a little hard for me to sing, I don't have much room to breathe, with the baby," said Claire. "But I shall try."

She closed her eyes and sang a lullaby. As she sang, she took gulping breaths, her hand resting on her stomach while Henri gazed at her with such unabashed adoration that Greta began to feel uncomfortable. She glanced at Otto, who was similarly scrutinizing the ceiling with apparent interest; he caught her eye and winked. When Claire finished, they all applauded, and the maid hurried in to close the curtains.

"Leave them," called Claire. She turned to Henri. "I like to see the lights and the stars. They keep me company when you have gone."

"I really am sorry, but we must go," said Greta. "It's dusk and we're already late."

"A few minutes more won't hurt," objected Henri, unwilling to break the spell.

"There is to be a Shabbat dinner," Greta reminded them. "I ought to be there for the lighting of the candles."

Claire sat up and clapped her hands. "I've always wanted to light a candle. To be part of the Shabbat rite, just once."

Her face was bright with longing, and none of them had the heart to refuse. The maid brought candles and matches, and Greta set them on the table, kneeling on the rug. She lit the first candle and then, drawing her hands in circles before her face, recited the Hebrew prayer: *"Barukh atah Adonai, Eloheinu, melekh ha'olam, / asher kidishanu b'mitz'votav v'tzivanu, / l'had'lik neir shel Shabbat."*

"May I light one?" asked Claire.

"Of course," said Greta. "Would you like to say the words after me?"

She repeated the prayer slowly, allowing Claire to echo her. When they had finished, Claire beamed at Henri. "After all, our son is half a Jew."

Unable to stay any longer, the others put on their coats. Claire stood to say good-bye.

"How long does Shabbat last?" she asked.

"Until the first three stars appear in the sky tomorrow night," said Otto. "My first stargazing was looking out of the nursery window for the end of Shabbat."

"I shall look tomorrow at this time and think of you," said Claire, turning to Henri. "Will you think of me?"

"Always," said Henri, and kissed her.

Greta found the constant declarations between the pair a little wearisome. She supposed that Claire had been an actress, and now perhaps expected her own life to conform to the extravagances of a moving picture. She admonished herself for being uncharitable; after all, these interludes were all they had. Perhaps she and Albert did not need roses and passionate avowals since they shared a house, a dining table and Monday mornings.

Otto enjoyed that evening's dinner at the Esther Château immensely. Perhaps it was the relief of being surrounded by noise and children and chatter, after the stillness of Claire's apartment. The new partnership agreements between the Houses had been signed. The House of Goldbaum was ready for a new generation of European collaboration, and there was an air of celebration. He was able to forget Claire's ghostly existence, the way it felt as though she came to life only when Henri appeared, while the rest of the time she waited, suspended. There were no guests, only the family, but even that was nearly fifty people, including the assorted children. Wine was spilled, custard dropped, and the tablecloths were sometimes beyond laundering. Everyone laughed at all the jokes, not caring if they were funny or not. Henri and Lord Goldbaum were engaged in a jovial spat across the table.

"That space behind your head, Lord Goldbaum, was where I was going to hang the Rubens."

"The winsome Rubens *Andromeda* that is now in my study?"

"The very same. I did ask you not to buy it. I wrote you a letter."

"I remember the letter. But, my dear young cousin, you asked me not to buy a painting that you were hoping to purchase. However, and this I'm afraid is key, you declined to give the specifics of the picture."

"Because I knew that then you'd buy it yourself."

"Well, it was an honest mistake. I'm terribly sorry."

"Sorry enough to sell it back to me?"

Lord Goldbaum laughed, his shoulders shaking. "No. Afraid not. It looks splendid in my study. Or, rather, she looks splendid. Andromeda is just the kind of comfortable woman I like to look at while doing my accounts."

Otto chuckled. Lord Goldbaum was making it quite clear to the others that, even after settling his son's debts, he could still add treasures to his collections. The rivalry between the Houses extended beyond business to beautiful things. Each Goldbaum wanted a rarer, more remarkable item in his possession than his cousins. Outsiders believed that the Goldbaums wanted to surpass the legendary collections at Chatsworth or Blenheim, but they were mistaken. The Goldbaum rivalry was an internal affair; they wished only to outdo one another. Otto was not interested in this game; it amused him to watch the others, but he had little interest in objects without function. He was confident that he had the greatest array of telescopes in the family, but he was equally confident that the others would not be interested in besting him. His sister similarly was unconcerned about the smiling family rivalries. She had broken with tradition and built the smallest house among the Goldbaums, but in Otto's view, it was easily the loveliest.

The following day there was a downpour, waterfalls sluicing from the roof and turning the paths into streams. No one left the château; they talked and they ate, and the rabbi hurried over from the synagogue to recite the morning service—there already being a *minyan* among the men. Mostly they sat before one of the fires blazing in every grate and talked of old friends and old times, glad that the rain prevented them from the obligatory postluncheon walk. At dusk the rain lifted to reveal clear skies, and Otto retreated into the smoking room, waving at the maid not to bother with the lamp. He wanted to watch for the first three stars. They appeared one by one, popping shyly into view. He drew a chair to the window and sat watching for some time.

"What are you doing, sitting here in the dark?" asked Henri, joining him and fumbling in his pocket for a cigarette.

"Looking at the stars. The visibility isn't terribly good. But you can still make out the North Star, and that's Venus, the Evening Star."

Henri joined him at the window, squinting. "Yes. Very twinkly. Have you got a light?"

Otto shook his head and Henri started to rummage through drawers for matches. The maid reappeared, and at first, thinking she had returned to light the lamp, Otto waved her away. Then he saw that she was showing in a policeman from the Sûreté Nationale.

A pall fell over the gathering. No one spoke of it except in whispers. Henri did not appear that evening or the following day. Greta found herself moving from room to room, unable to settle for more than a moment or attend to anything that was said to her. Albert was angry; furious that she had gone to see Claire, outraged that Henri and Otto had allowed it, knowing the fragile state the woman was in.

"What if she had shot you, rather than herself?"

"Don't be ridiculous, Albert. She didn't want to harm anyone else."

Except that wasn't true. Claire hadn't killed only herself, but also her baby. For once, Greta wished that Otto hadn't been such a stickler for the whole truth and had spared her a few of the details. She wished that she didn't know that the gun Claire had used was an antique, and it had taken some time for her to die—a full twenty minutes or so, according to the poor maid, who had heard the shot. On rushing into the bedroom, she discovered her mistress bleeding profusely from the temple, a bullet lodged in her brain, her eyes fixed and open, but still alive. Greta wished that Otto had not confided details from the postmortem: the bullet had lodged in her optic nerve and destroyed her speech center, so Claire had died in the dark, mute. Greta felt desperately sorry for the maid. She had not run for help. Deciding it was hopeless, she stayed. "No one should die alone," she'd informed Henri, before she was dispatched with a hundred francs to her mother in Provence, to recover from the shock.

Greta tried not to think about the baby. Did it suffer in the womb, hear the mother's heartbeat fall silent, alone for a minute before it, too, passed out of the world? She was too horrified and revolted to feel pity for Claire. There was a malevolence in the act. Claire's existence was immured in wretchedness, apparently too much for her to bear. Yet, like the ripples from a pebble dropped into a pond, the consequences of her desperate act moved in ever-expanding circles blackly outward.

The rain trapped them all inside under a siege of weather. Greta escaped to her rooms and sat in a chair beside the window, watching the constant deluge. Claire had seemingly waited for the Sabbath to end, and for the first three stars to appear, before she had raised the gun, perhaps in an attempt to prevent a worse sacrilege. Yet, Greta realized, what she had achieved was to create a ghastly memento. At the end of every Sabbath, Henri, Otto and she would think of Claire— the lifting of her hand, the blood and the two deaths, one of them so very small. Was it possible that Claire, a woman so fearful of being overlooked, had done it deliberately, ensuring such a grisly weekly remembrance?

The door opened and Henri stood in the doorway to Greta's bedroom. He lingered for only a moment and then rushed in; hurling himself down at Greta's feet and burying his face in her lap, he began to sob, unrestrained and wretched. Greta stroked his head and cried with him. It was the least she could do. After a few minutes he stopped. He drew himself up and stood beside the window, carefully drying his eyes.

"There," he said. "I have cried for them both. I shall not weep again."

He was silent for a moment, and when he spoke his voice was even and measured.

"I shall never marry, and I shall never have children. The *Maison Gold* stops with me."

The priest of Sacré-Coeur, Claire's favorite church, declined to conduct the funeral service or to bury her in the churchyard. The priests of seven other churches in Paris similarly declined. Finally, after Henri offered to contribute substantially to the repairs on the leadwork on the roof of the Saint-Gervais-et-Saint-Protais church, the priest relented. He was certain, he confided to Henri, that as she lay dying, unable to speak, Claire had repented of her mortal sin. She certainly had not said that she did not repent. The only concession the priest asked for was that the service be held after dusk. The newspapers had been circumspect in their reporting: a beloved actress had died in a tragic accident. Neither her condition nor her "friendship" with the Goldbaum family was mentioned. But still, the priest demurred, there were whispers and he did not want a crowd. Henri agreed. It would be held after dusk on Thursday.

On hearing the news, Greta escaped outside to the rose garden. She couldn't bear the oppressive atmosphere of the house any longer. It was still raining and the bushes were little more than pruned twigs battered by the weather, the earth around them sloppy. The metal railings were hung with raindrops like diamonds on a necklace. Greta stood in the rain, her mackintosh growing heavy and cold, her face slick from the downpour. She felt an odd numbness inside and out. She watched Albert hurrying across the parterre toward her, carrying an umbrella.

"You're wet," he said, holding it over her. "Please don't go to the funeral. I understand that she was a friend of yours, but I really would prefer it if you didn't."

"I don't want to go," said Greta, seeing his eyes widen in surprise. "I don't forgive her. Not yet. This was her choice, but I can't help finding a vindictiveness in it. She killed herself, the baby and any possibility of Henri having a family. She's made quite certain that if she can't marry him, no one shall."

"I know he says that now, but what a man says and feels at such a moment might change over time," said Albert gently.

Greta shook her head. "You're wrong. You don't know Henri like I do. He'll always be Claire's now. What she couldn't manage in life, she has secured in death." She paused, plunging her hands deep into her coat pockets and stifling a shiver. She turned to her husband, saying quietly, "I can't go to her funeral hating her."

She glanced back across the garden. A bedraggled thrush alighted on a statue of Diana and flew away. She could hear the traffic and hum of Paris through the clatter of rain.

"Albert," she said, "can we please go home?"

Hampshire, April

———◆❯◆❮◆———

The household was preparing for the arrival of Kaiser Wilhelm. He had spent a week on a state visit with his cousin King George before embarking on a short tour of England. He had been undecided as to whether to call upon the Goldbaums, for he was not overly fond of Jews. But then, it seemed, curiosity overcame antipathy—presumably with the coaxing of his ambassador Prince Karl Max—and the visit was confirmed. At Temple Court, carpets were rolled up and dusted underneath, and a two-hundred-and-twenty-five-piece Sèvres dinner and dessert service (hand-decorated by Louis-Victor Gerverot) was readied for the evening banquet. A fleet of gondoliers had been imported from Venice so that His Imperial and Royal Majesty could enjoy the vista of Temple Court from the river. Ten thousand flares were hammered into the garden along the paths, and the glasshouses were emptied of roses, lilies and Japanese chrysanthemums. Lady Goldbaum, fearing these were still insufficient, ordered a further five hundred pounds' worth of roses from the Channel Islands. The pair of Gobelins tapestries that had belonged to the French Sun King were carefully rehung in the royal bedchamber, while the toilet in the adjoining water closet was fitted with a new wooden seat (the imperial behind could not sit where a bare bottom had sat before). The preparations below stairs were mirrored by those above, as the servants crammed into shared bedrooms to make way for the kaiser's army of staff.

Greta retreated to Fontmell to dress for dinner, relieved to escape the frenzy. She climbed the stairs, pausing as she always did to admire the Klimt hanging midway. It fitted perfectly, as though the entire staircase had been constructed to accommodate it, the glass window in the thatch specially commissioned so that the light could fall on the woman's face, illuminating it just so. The painting, although closely associated with Paris, did not depress her. Instead, it reminded her of the fleetingness of happiness. How contentment in marriage is a matter of chance, uncertain and inconstant. She did not need every moment with Albert to be blissful; the fact that there were moments, and hours and days, when she enjoyed his company more than that of anyone else was sufficient, and she was glad. Perhaps this was love, perhaps not, but after witnessing the catastrophe between Claire and Henri, it seemed unwise to want anything more.

Greta wrote to Henri, but his replies were full of false bonhomie and accounts of the theater and concerts, with asides of "Alas, poor Claire would have so loved the show" and "If our little one had lived," as though mother and baby had expired during childbirth. Greta could not bear this sudden reimagining of Claire as a Madonna, complaining about it to Otto, who entreated her to have patience with Henri. He argued that Henri had to rewrite it, to forgive Claire and find some peace. Greta felt only indignation at such a lie. Yesterday morning she had risen while it was still dark and, wrapping a woolen shawl around her nightdress, had walked out to the river. In her hand she had held the pistol Otto had given her. In the ruddy dawn light she had cast it into the water. The pistol was no longer a joke, but an obscenity. She was relieved it was no longer in her possession.

Albert had not yet returned to dress and the door to his bedroom was ajar. Greta pushed it open and entered his room. She rarely ventured inside. It was inevitably Albert who knocked on her door at night, unless he chose to sleep alone in his dressing room. It simply was not done for her to come tiptoeing to him.

Albert's closet was as immaculate as his person: rows of perfectly pressed trousers and shelves of brushed hats. It smelled of him—cedarwood and the distinctive sweet odor of the ether that he used in his collecting jars. She pulled down a bowler hat and tried it on, tilting her head in the mirror to inspect herself. The door opened and Albert entered. He leaned against the wall, studying her and registering no surprise on finding her in his dressing room perusing his hats.

"I think it very fetching," said Greta, adjusting the brim.

"It is."

"I want to watch you dress," said Greta, moving to lie on the single bed, propping herself up on her elbow.

Albert made no objection and proceeded to unfasten his cravat and remove the studs from his shirt, quickly and with no hint of self-consciousness. In a minute he was naked, but as she glanced at the black hair that drifted down from his chest to below his navel, Greta felt as if it were she who was at a disadvantage. Even in his bare feet, he was extremely tall. He studied her with amusement.

"If you want marital relations, Greta, you can simply ask. You don't have to wait for me to come to you, as it were. I take it that's why you're here?"

"Yes, I believe it is."

"Are you going to undress?"

She hesitated. "No, I don't think I shall."

"Very well—but the removal of some undergarments might be necessary, for convenience."

Biting her lip with a flush of embarrassment, Greta started to slide out of her knickers.

"Much as I enjoy your discomfort, it isn't necessary," said Albert. "I know it has been fashionable to express that only men are habitually troubled by sexual feelings, but I believe that to be quite untrue. In nature, the females of the species are often eager to copulate. Especially mammals."

"Dear God, Albert. Do shut up. In a moment I'm going to put my knickers back on."

"Sorry."

For once he looked quite abashed, and Greta seized her advantage.

"Lie back on the bed, Albert. And please don't talk."

"Yes, madam."

He obeyed with enthusiasm.

A little time afterward, when Anna had buttoned Greta into her evening dress and wrapped her fur around her shoulders, Greta thought of the indecent interlude with some satisfaction. Surprisingly, asking Albert to give her pleasure seemed to increase her influence over him rather than lessen it. She had not known that there was power in surrender.

They drifted down the river in a flotilla of gondolas, the lines of flares spilling out into the dusk. It was a small, informal gathering of a mere fifty guests. The kaiser was traveling in a relaxed style without his court. Greta held on to Albert's arm, feeling both unsteady and seasick. The air was laden with the scent of larch, pine and river mud. The family orchestra played on a boat beside them, the slap of the oars and the knock of water against the wooden hull adding an extra note to the percussion. The kaiser waved at a clump of cedar trees that were momentarily obscuring the view back up to Temple Court.

"Those must be felled," he said, in his perfect and unaccented English.

"Alas, Your Imperial and Royal Majesty, we cannot," said Lady Goldbaum. "They were planted by Agatha, my husband's aunt, in the shape of Hebrew letters. It would be sacrilege to cut them."

"I can't see any letters," objected the kaiser.

"No, Your Imperial and Royal Majesty, they can only be seen from above, by God himself."

"Charming but pointless," said the kaiser. "What you need is an airplane, then man can share God's view."

After their trip along the river, they returned to the house. Footmen waited on the steps with trays of champagne and warming brandies. Lord Goldbaum ushered the kaiser into the East Gallery, where the orchestra had hastily reassembled.

"My revered grandmother spoke with admiration of the remarkable collections at Temple Court. Tomorrow let us take this into the sunlight to see it," said the kaiser, holding up an early-nineteenth-century Beauvais tapestry cushion.

Lord Goldbaum coughed. "I regret not, Your Imperial and Royal Majesty. It is frightfully bad for the textiles, as they're extremely fragile."

There was an uneasy pause and the assembled company held its breath, then the kaiser threw back his head and laughed.

"I was simply testing. I remember my grandmother saying the same thing. That she had asked for all the curtains to be opened, and was refused. Your father said, 'Not even for Your Majesty.' Now," he went on, waggling his finger, "if you had opened the curtains for my little cousin King George and not for me, then I might have made a tiny fuss." He grinned broadly. The others did not.

The kaiser was an unsettling presence: when he spoke in English, he appeared almost the perfect country squire. Greta reminded herself that, after all, his mother was English, his summers spent with his royal cousins on the Isle of Wight, not far from Temple Court itself. He alluded to his late grandmother, great Queen Victoria, as often as possible. Yet with his damaged arm concealed Napoléon-style beneath a sumptuous lynx-fur coat, apparently cool despite the intense heat of the East Gallery, and with his extravagant mustache and his sharp, watchful eyes, he was also the epitome of the Prussian prince. Perhaps that was why he was so disconcerting: he was at once perfectly English and German. He switched constantly between the two languages, and the Goldbaums answered effortlessly in whichever language they had been addressed in. He admired the Renaissance jewelry with relish, marveling at the delicacy of the pearls, and pretended to drop a seventeenth-century rock-crystal cup, with great hilarity.

After a time he declared himself bored, and Lady Goldbaum led him through to dinner, to everyone's considerable relief. Greta took the arm of the German ambassador, Prince Karl Max von Lichnowsky, a charming Anglophile. He patted her arm conspiratorially.

"It is going well, Mrs. Goldbaum."

"Is it?" she asked. "I'm glad you told me."

The kaiser was seated at the head of the table, but as his page pulled out the chair, he hesitated before sitting down.

"The ivory throne belonging to the maharaja of Travancore. I should like to sit on that during dinner. It only seems right, after all. A chair fit for a king. And," he added with a look at Lord Goldbaum, "it is nicely dark in here and I shall do my best not to spill my dinner."

Lord Goldbaum nodded at Stanton, and the butler hurried from the room. The assembled guests stood awkwardly, no one able to sit until the kaiser did so. Prince Karl Max chatted amiably and valiantly: the splendid fishing to be had in the river, and his admiration for Lady Goldbaum's rhododendrons.

"I do not wish to hear about flowers. They aren't fun," interrupted the kaiser.

Seamlessly Prince Karl began to discuss the easy and pleasant sail between Temple Court and the Isle of Wight.

"I had enjoyable summers there as a boy," said the kaiser. "I learned my skill as a sailor on the Solent. I am an extremely capable sailor. A wonderful thing, in the chief admiral of an imperial naval fleet."

Everyone smiled weakly at this somewhat tactless allusion to the German and English naval race. Prince Karl opened his mouth as if to steer the conversation into safer waters, but he was too slow. He could not now speak without interrupting the kaiser, who gave an impatient snort.

"You English, you wince when I mention the German fleet. But England is not in the minds of those who are bent on creating a powerful navy. Germany is a young and growing empire, and we have an interest in the most distant seas. There is Japan and the problem of the Pacific. My fleet does not exist to cause a rumpus with the British, but to warn off the Japanese. You do not worry enough about the Yellow Peril."

Greta saw that Prince Karl Max was turning pale in horror. In his frenzy to deny his ambitions against British interests, the kaiser was inciting the Japanese. But the kaiser had not finished, and no one could be so rude as to interrupt the emperor.

"You English," he said, "are mad, mad, mad as March hares."

Lord Goldbaum coughed and reddened at the offense. Glancing between him and the pallor of the ambassador, Greta imagined that all the blood had rushed from the cheeks of one to the other.

Indifferent or oblivious to the cascade of insults that he was spewing forth, the kaiser continued, "What has come over you, that you are so completely given over to suspicions quite unworthy of a great nation? My heart is set upon peace, and it is one of my dearest wishes to live on the best of terms with England. Falsehood and prevarication are alien to my nature. My actions ought to speak for themselves, but you listen not to them, but to those who misinterpret and distort them. That is a personal affront that I feel and resent."

The guests stared at him in silence and shock, but the kaiser had warmed to his topic and could not stop.

"France and Russia appealed to me to join them and humiliate England to the dust. I would not do it! You can read in the archives of Windsor Castle the telegram in which I informed the sovereign of England of my answer. I have no wish to see England fall."

"Of course you are not suggesting, Your Imperial and Royal Majesty, that England's allies plotted against her," said Prince Karl Max, with a tiny and desperate laugh, trying to dismiss the tirade as a bad joke.

The kaiser gave his ambassador a look of absolute contempt. "I am stating it. You English choose to cavort in the gutter with those who despise you."

Prince Karl Max was now so white that Greta wondered if she ought to ring for brandy, but fortunately they were rescued from further diplomatic disaster by the return of Stanton and the maharaja's gold-and-ivory throne, carried in by eleven footmen, all struggling under its vast weight. The kaiser clapped his hands in glee on seeing it. With a little help, he climbed up and sat.

"It's no use," he said. "I cannot reach my glass. Take it away."

When dinner was served, Greta glanced at Otto and Albert across the table, and saw that neither man had much appetite for the truffle dauphinoise.

T he following afternoon, after the kaiser had been safely tucked back in the Rolls and borne off to a castle in Scotland, the Goldbaum men gathered in the library with Prince Karl Max. Stanton brought them a tray of coffee, but Lord Goldbaum took out a bottle of whiskey.

"Something a little stronger is called for, I believe."

"We shall of course be discreet," said Otto. "No one will breathe a word of what was said. No one shall hear of his insults."

Prince Karl said nothing, merely waved away the glass of Scotch and sipped his coffee. Lord Goldbaum studied the ambassador closely and then frowned.

"Perhaps His Excellency does not believe total discretion is desirable?"

Prince Karl stood and said pointedly, "Gentlemen, if you would excuse me, I should very much like to see Lady Goldbaum's remarkable glasshouses."

He left the room. Otto and Albert turned to Lord Goldbaum.

"Why does he want the kaiser's idiocy made public? The British visit is supposed to engender better relations with Germany," said Otto.

"The kaiser is vain, volatile and odd. He is, as we've seen, a danger to international diplomacy. Before the salmon mousse was served he managed to insult the British, anticipate war with Japan and attempt to undermine relations between Britain and her French and Russian allies. If the German Reichstag had some leverage to rein him in . . ."

". . . it would be a good thing for a peaceful Europe," said Albert.

"Prince Karl is a patriot, make no mistake," said Lord Goldbaum. "He wants the very best for Germany and that, as you see, means curbing the influence of the kaiser. Sometimes an unexpected opportunity arrives and one must make the most of it."

Albert picked up the telephone. "Which newspaper?"

"The *Telegraph*," said Lord Goldbaum.

Lord Goldbaum brought the papers to his wife in her room while she was breakfasting in bed. The letters column ran to an entire page of fury, outrage and amusement.

"I'm not sure who he's offended most," said Lord Goldbaum, helping himself to a piece of marmalade toast, and elbowing his wife to make room beneath the covers. "The Japanese, the British, the French or his own people."

"It was a private conversation, Robert. However awful, it was not supposed to be public."

"He's an emperor! His very farts are public."

Seeing his wife wince, Lord Goldbaum leaned forward and kissed her on the nose.

"Apologies, Adelheid. But the man should have more sense. And since he doesn't, it's better that his power is kept in check. The Reichstag is making him sign a statement to acknowledge that he respects the constitution."

Lady Goldbaum sighed. "That's something, I suppose. But don't you think the article also confirmed to the British public their worst fears? That the emperor is a despot and a fool, in pursuit of an empire. And that the German people view the English with contempt." She set down her teacup and looked at her husband. "I think sometimes, my dear, you forget that I was born a German."

"I wouldn't dare." He kissed her cheek.

Hampshire, June

———◦◦◦◦———

Enid Witherick was arrested for breaking the window of the post office during a demonstration by the suffragettes. Greta paid her fine and summoned her to the library immediately upon her release.

"I shan't apologize, madam," said Withers, defiant and more than a little disheveled.

"Very well. But are you going to break any more windows?" inquired Greta. "If you plan on getting arrested with any degree of frequency, it will interrupt our planting schedule. I'm sympathetic to your cause—"

"*Our* cause," interrupted Enid.

"No. It is not my cause. I do not condone violence and the breaking of property. I have written several letters to His Majesty's Government regarding the matter myself. But I have not smashed poor Mr. Manners's shop front. You shall pay for the repair yourself out of your wages. He was terribly upset. He says he always voted exactly as Mrs. Manners told him to, until her untimely demise."

"And now, with Mrs. Manners unable to instruct him?"

"He doesn't vote at all, out of respect for her memory."

Enid Witherick gave a hiss of exasperation like a kettle letting off steam. "And such men have the vote before us."

Greta sat up very straight in her chair and looked the other woman directly in the eye.

"Unjust as it may be, no further acts of vandalism—or you will be free to find another situation. My husband is an MP, Withers. How will it look if the newspapers decide to run a story that his wife employs a suffragette and a vandal?"

Enid Witherick was silent and then nodded. "I shall refrain from any further violence, madam. You have my word."

Greta softened. "Very well. Now, have all the sweet peas been planted out?"

"Yes, madam."

"Good. I shall be out shortly to inspect."

Released, Withers hurried away, while Greta stepped out onto the terrace, wishing for the umpteenth time that she could simply wear breeches like the other women gardeners, but Albert would not approve. She was learning to pick her battles. This one would come, but not yet.

The garden was a blaze of June glory. The sweet-pea seedlings had been planted around a dozen wigwams in the cuttings garden. To the west, Greta was restoring the old kitchen gardens. Rather than relying on glasshouses, she had decreed that they would be planted according to the season. It was nicely sheltered, the repaired Victorian brick wall keeping out the wind, and Greta had it laid out in a vast circle, like a clock face, so that the winter vegetables were positioned in the prime place for winter sun, while strawberries basked at the summer solstice. To her surprise, it was almost her favorite part of the garden. The glossy heads of cabbage in January, the show of leeks with their feathered fronds on a cold morning: who knew you could paint on a landscape with vegetables? The zucchini plants were spreading their dark umbrella-like leaves, the beans twirled around their poles, their tiny curved flowers like black beaks. Pinpricks of virulent orange tomatoes clashed joyously with gleaming strawberries, Crimean red.

Beyond the kitchen garden was a large area of uncleared land, too wet and steep to be sown with crops and not needed for the garden. Greta reached around her waist to where a polished cowbell hung on a leather strap and rang it vigorously, the sound echoing throughout the garden, traveling all the way down to the river and back up toward the house. The cowbell had been a gift from Otto. Greta complained that when she rang a regular silver service bell in the garden, no one could hear its delicate tinkle and she was reduced to sending a boy to hunt for Withers, or else was forced to tramp, exasperated, through the gardens to look herself. Otto had sourced the cowbell from the Alps. The sound could echo gamely from Matterhorn slope to grassed valley, and could easily be heard throughout every acre of the Fontmell gardens. Otto suggested it was not even out of place—after all, the cloisters would have chimed hourly with the pealing of the abbey bell.

A few minutes later Withers appeared.

"You rang, madam."

"Yes. Have you seen those pamphlets that Lord Goldbaum and Mr. Goldbaum have been getting frightfully upset about?"

"The Rowntree ones? Some were dropped in the village."

"I know. The fury over dinner was palpable. 'A Landlord is no more necessary to agriculture than a gold chain to a watch,'" said Greta, doing her best to sound like an outraged Lord Goldbaum. "The pamphlets are full of brimstone and revolution. But the point is, they demand allotments for all who want them. Is there any reason we couldn't give over the land from here to the river?"

"I'm not sure there is a straight line between the lack of allotments and revolution, madam."

"No, of course not, Withers. Don't be facetious. But an allotment might make things a little easier for the workingman. And woman," she added, with a pointed look at her companion.

"I think it's an excellent suggestion, madam."

Lord Goldbaum agreed, providing that the allotments were properly screened from the estate, and the garden walks did not skirt so close that family or guest would be forced to converse with those working on the allotments. The family sat in the dining room at Temple Court, enduring an uneasy dinner. It was Clement's first night home since his exile in Switzerland and everyone was on edge. Albert and Otto tried to distract Lord Goldbaum by reminding him of the success with the kaiser, who was, for the present at least, apparently listening to the advice of his counselors. Lord Goldbaum remained irritable, declaring the burgundy improperly decanted, the fish not sufficiently boned and the smell of the lilies on the table too strong.

"They overpower the fish, Adelheid. I'm eating flowers, not trout."

"I thought you weren't eating the trout in any case."

Scowling, Lord Goldbaum turned to look upon his eldest son with displeasure. Clement had returned several stone lighter and with a smooth tan, like a perfectly browned cake taken out of the oven at the ideal moment. Exile had agreed with him. While he did his best to appear chastened and meek, he exuded good health and contentment, which exasperated his father. Clement basked in the private knowledge that he was loved by a good woman who asked for nothing except the freedom to play chess with whomsoever she liked, and most importantly, he was freed from the ghastliness of his destiny. His father had taken away from him everything he could: money, responsibility, the possibility of power; but it had not been the punishment Lord Goldbaum had intended. Instead, Clement realized it had freed him. He still felt the rebuke, his father's deep and ringing disappointment— now, sitting across the table from him, Lord Goldbaum could barely look at him—but he also experienced a lightness and freedom of possibilities. He had promised Irena that he would not place a single bet, not even a pretend one with a button, and so far his promise had held. His conscience had cleared, with the emptying of the laundry baskets. His only regret was what he had done to his brother. Everything he had been relieved of was now inflicted upon Albert.

The evening was cool and a fire had been lit in the grate. Lord Goldbaum was pink with anger. Greta's garden scheme had reminded him again of the outrage of Rowntree's blasted pamphlet.

"Have you seen the thing?" he asked Clement.

"I have not, sir. It did not reach Switzerland."

"That's something, I suppose. Lloyd George himself wrote the bloody introduction. Where is it, Adelheid?"

"I really have no idea, Robert. I think the best place for it is in the wastepaper basket."

Lord Goldbaum, not to be so easily put off, commanded Stanton the butler to produce it. Stanton reappeared a few minutes later with both the pamphlet and his lordship's reading glasses.

"This is the bit that really gets my goat: 'We are afraid of curtailing our luxuries: it is the curtailment of our ideals we should fear. We are afraid of Germany, we should be afraid of England. We talk about the "yellow peril"—the real yellow peril is nearer home, it is the greed of gold.'" He paused and surveyed his family over the top of his spectacles. "That's us. How dare he single us out? Who is more dedicated to the service of England than us? Surely the business with the kaiser ought to have shown him that."

Lady Goldbaum sighed. "It's a turn of phrase, Robert. The chancellor of the Exchequer does not waste nearly as much thought on you as you do on him."

She rang for coffee. Lord Goldbaum spilled his, in annoyance, and a terrified maid hurried over with a clean saucer.

Suspecting that he was the true source of his father's irascibility, Clement ate half a dozen petits fours out of anxiety. Faced with his family, his promise to Irena not to eat too much was proving difficult to keep. He assured himself that this was a mere temporary lapse. He would absolutely resume his diet in the morning.

When the morning came, all thoughts of diets or anything else were forgotten. In the early hours, Lord Goldbaum had suffered a small stroke. Lady Goldbaum, whatever her private thoughts, reassured her stricken eldest son that it had nothing to do with his homecoming. His father had been pushing himself too hard for months. The finest doctors were rushed in from London, their advice unanimous: total rest and then, in time, he could expect to recover.

Albert was summoned to see his father. He lay propped up in bed on several pillows, his face waxy and pale. Lady Goldbaum sat beside him, while a nurse busied herself in the corner. When he spoke, it was as if he were drunk and he slurred very slightly.

"You must go directly to London. Release a statement. Say—"

"He knows what it should say, Robert. Leave him to it and rest," interrupted Lady Goldbaum, exasperated.

"Say I'll be back on my feet in a jiffy," insisted Lord Goldbaum, his voice indistinct.

"I know what to say, Father. And—"

"Make sure you are seen at the stock exchange."

"To calm the markets. I know, Papa, I know."

Lord Goldbaum appeared briefly to fall asleep. Albert leaned over and kissed him on the cheek. He embraced his mother and caught the train to London.

Albert telephoned his mother each morning to inquire after his father's night, and called Greta every evening. Any immediate danger appeared to have passed and mostly he slept. Lady Goldbaum woke him so that he could eat and drink. Yet an odd pall spread over the house. The maids spoke in whispers—even where they could not possibly be overheard—and Greta found herself trying to reassure Clement of the coincidence of the timing, while also persuading him not to visit his father more than necessary. She instructed Stanton to refrain from putting out the newspapers in the morning room, so that Lady Goldbaum would not read the reports on her husband or see the corresponding wobbles on the stock market. Greta did not have time to venture out in the garden for more than a quick taking of the air before dusk, not wishing to miss Albert's telephone call. One evening it was Otto who telephoned rather than Albert.

"He wants me to talk to you," he said. "Thinks I'll be better able to tell if you're putting a brave face on it. How is his lordship?"

"Put Albert on this instant."

Albert came on the line.

"Don't be absurd, Albert. There is nothing about your father I would tell Otto that I wouldn't tell you."

"I'm sorry. How is he?"

"Same as yesterday. Try not to worry."

"Thank you. And, Greta, I shall be glad to see you on Friday."

When Friday came, Albert found her in the garden as was his wont, and they walked around together discussing his father, and with Greta pointing out the new happenings in the flower beds—the polished heads of the tightly furled peonies, round and smooth as cricket balls, exploding here and there into a tutu of petals.

"What can I do to help?" she asked. "I mean, I'm doing what I can at Temple Court so that your mother can be with him, but I should so like to feel useful."

She ran her fingers through the lavender and rosemary as they passed, inhaling the scent they left on her skin. Albert stopped beside a pool of yellow lilies. Then he turned to Greta, visibly uncomfortable.

"You really want to help?"

"Of course. I said so."

"Then we need to start our family. I want to stop being careful. It's no longer about you and me, Greta. My father worries that, after me, there is no heir. The markets similarly don't like it. The House of Goldbaum needs continuity. It is a family bank, but for that we need a family."

He began to walk away, and after hesitating for a moment, she followed him. He paused to pull a cleaver of goosegrass from his trousers, disposing of it in the undergrowth. He sighed and glanced at her.

"I'm afraid that, with Clement cut out of the partnership, it all falls to me. And, in time, our son."

They reached the butterfly garden, where a horde of tortoiseshell butterflies landed on a purple cloud of verbena, an expanse of pompoms stretching down to the river in streaks of mauve and blue. Half a dozen beehives stamped with the gilded Goldbaum crest were dotted among the nettles and buddleia; two of them were made from blown glass, a present from Greta to Albert so that he could watch the bees inside. She could tell when Albert was troubled, as she would find him out in the butterfly garden, his shooting stick pegged beside one of the glass hives as he leaned against it in silence, hypnotized by the liquid teeming of the bees. Greta knew that many husbands would not have been as patient as Albert and would have insisted upon trying for a son immediately. She was not ungrateful.

"May I think about it?" she said at last.

Albert nodded. She took his arm and they returned to the house.

Vienna, August

———◆◆◆———

Karl had not meant to leave the hostel. While the rules irked him—
for years he'd answered to no one and nothing, except the needs of his
own body—for the most part he considered the petty grievances a
worthwhile sacrifice for the food and warmth. He blamed the summer. In the heat of a restless August night, his body could not remember the pain of a January when even the underground canals froze
solid, the bones and slops and shit and carcasses of birds and rotting
fish heads all suspended together in dirty ice. Instead, he hankered for
a mild evening spent out in the park among the wayward stars and for
the smell of turned earth in the darkness.

Forty boys slept in his dormitory, and the window was small and
barred to prevent them sliding in and out. In the midst of August it was
too hot, and the smell and sweat from too many bodies fetid. Worse, his
bunk was itchy—there was an outbreak of lice again—and his bedmate
snored. Karl appreciated that he was fed and clothed, but somehow he
found that he spent his days waiting: he waited for morning prayers to
end so that he could eat breakfast, and after that he waited for lunch.
There were odd moments of pleasure, when time sped up and rattled
like the trains from the grand central Bahnhof, such as when the young
Rabbi Herzel took their morning lessons and recited Moses's feats of daring with a light in his eye and a fleck of spittle in his beard, sprayed
from his chops in his enthusiasm. The rabbi didn't come every day, and
mostly Karl waited for the day to end, so that he could slide into bed for

another uncomfortable and restless night of heat and scratching and other fellows' moans while he waited for morning to come, so that he could wait for it all over again. He imagined that his life was pegged along a string, with his birth fixed at one end and his death, unknown, at the other, and he had the urge to tug the string, simply to jiggle things a bit, to make something—*anything*—happen.

More out of boredom than any rage, he fought with Rudolf Johannes, blackening his eye, but declined to apologize. Rudolf snored and whimpered in his sleep and Karl was tired of company. The warden gave him until the morning to apologize. Karl left at daybreak.

The freedom was glorious. He walked and walked, returning to his old haunts. Rosy light toasted the city and the Goldbaum Palace was finally awash with gold, its stone radiant in the dawn. He had taken his few possessions with him: his knapsack of treasures and his blanket—lice or not, he would be grateful for it soon. He did not take any books. Those he was most sorry to leave, but to have kept them would have felt like theft. He walked on for hours, listening to the morning howls of the city dogs. It all belonged to him. He sat on a bench and closed his eyes. He did not pray.

By twelve o'clock he was hungry. His stomach growled and he knew he ought to start to knock on doors and ask for pennies in exchange for work, but he could not bring himself to do so. His hunger irritated him. He'd softened, he realized. In the old days, he'd trained himself not to notice the demands of his belly. He could manage entire days without either eating or feeling hungry. The first he would know of it was the cramps and the unreal sensation of light-headedness. Yes, he had grown soft in his months of cosseting in the hostel. He would have to toughen up again before winter. Still, it was difficult to imagine such things now. The warm sun baked the pavements. Smart ladies walked with parasols, less smart ones dabbed their faces with cotton handkerchiefs or with a sleeve. The air was thick with the scent of summer, but already his euphoria at his newfound freedom had dissipated, popping like soap bubbles in the wind.

In the early afternoon he found himself in a synagogue. It was unpleasantly hot outside and he told himself that he simply wanted a drink of water, a break from the sun. He helped himself to a yarmulke from a basket and slid into a chair at the back. It was empty and cool, and tired from the heat and walking, he slept.

When he woke, he was no longer alone. A rabbi busied himself at the side of the synagogue, piling up prayer books and muttering to himself.

"Good, you're awake," he said, looking over toward Karl.

Karl suspected that the banging of books had been deliberate.

"Hungry?" asked the rabbi.

Karl nodded. The rabbi led him to a small room off the main hall. He opened a cupboard and produced a loaf of bread and a packet of cheese, carefully cutting a slice of each and putting them on a plate for Karl. He gestured to a sink in the corner of the room. Obediently, Karl washed his hands, reciting the prayer before meals under his breath, because it was expected and he half-feared that if he did not say it, the rabbi would take the bread and cheese and put them back in the cupboard. The rabbi sat and watched as Karl ate, interrupting only to offer him a drink of water and another piece of bread.

"There's a hostel for unfortunate Jewish boys. I can take you," said the rabbi, when Karl had finished.

"I've tried it," said Karl. "It didn't take."

The rabbi was silent, considering.

"The caretaker here has left. I was about to advertise, but I think you could manage it. Some cleaning. Preparing the *shul* before a service. You'd sleep in the synagogue at night on a camp bed, close enough to the ark and *bimah* to keep away any thieves. The Torah scrolls here are very precious. They were a gift from the Goldbaums."

Karl studied the face of the rabbi. He had only the merest touch of gray in his beard and wore thick spectacles. Each eye looked in a slightly different direction, so that when he smiled, Karl couldn't quite be certain that it was at him.

"It is a very kind offer," he said at last.

"So you accept?" asked the rabbi.

Karl hesitated. "I am not sure if I am a Jew. They say I am. But who can say for sure?"

"God. Or your mother, but I take it we can't rely on her?"

Karl shook his head.

"Then we trust in God." The rabbi smiled, each eye glancing out to the side. "What do you say? Are you a Jew?"

Karl said nothing for a moment. A great deal depended upon his answer. It would be comfortable here and he would be freer than in the hostel. He had learned not to pass up good things. Yet perhaps it was also . . . what was the word they used to describe destiny? *Bashert.* That was it. Perhaps his coming here was *bashert.*

"Yes," he said. "I am a Jew."

Hampshire, September

———⟶⋅✦⋅⟵———

It was a secret as small as a leaf. It belonged only to her. Greta wanted to know exactly how she felt, before telling anyone else. She did not want Albert's dynastic joy, his satisfaction that the family would go on. This tiny thing inside her was not yet a Goldbaum, with all that entailed; it was only an ash leaf or a willow fish, flicking and twisting. The thought of it gave her great pleasure, a warming sense of possibility. She planted seeds and bulbs all through the borders, hundreds upon hundreds of alliums, the hairy bulbs stinking of onions. When they bloomed the following spring in giant lollipops of white and lilac, they would herald the arrival of her baby. She liked to think of it growing inside her like a bulb in the ground, warm and snug, nudging outward.

For the first time since they had moved into Fontmell, she climbed the stairs into the nursery. The rooms were chilled and smelled damply of thatch, and she could hear the scuttle of mice in the rafters, but the views through the windows stretched all the way down to the river. On a clear day from up here it might even be possible to glimpse the sea—such an outlook must be good for a child's soul. There was no outward sign of her new state; her stomach was perfectly flat and she felt neither sick nor tired. Her breasts were sore but no larger, and Anna made no remark when she fastened Greta into her corset, nor did she comment on the lack of soiled napkins for the last weeks.

She barely noticed her reluctance toward motherhood ebb away. It disappeared, slowly and absolutely, melting like frost in the sun. If the child was a girl, she'd give it a flower's name—but which one? Finally, confident of her own happiness, she told Albert. His joy was not abstract or rooted in a sense of family. It was personal and absolute. It lasted three days. On the fourth, Greta began to bleed, only a little at first, then a torrent of pain and black blood.

The doctor came and diagnosed a miscarriage. She could not have been more than three months along was his guess. It was a pity, of course, but she was young and healthy and in time there would be another baby, a stronger one.

"Now, you're a gardener, aren't you, Mrs. Goldbaum?" asked the doctor, after she had been tucked back into bed, pale faced and desolate.

She nodded.

He continued. "A baby is like a seed. Some germinate and flower, but others never do. We don't know why. It is the mystery of life. You can call it God's will, if you like."

Greta did not want to call it God. It was an unnamed sadness. She begged Albert not to tell anyone. It was their shared disappointment. The first thing they had lost together. It had not yet been a baby or a person, but it had been the hope of one, the possibility of a family, and that was gone. At first Greta believed that the fact no one knew, and there had been no outward sign of her pregnancy, would make it easier. But it did not. It was as if she had never been pregnant at all; there was no mark upon her body or the world. Her loss was internal. Nothing had changed except for Greta herself. Before, she had not wanted to be a mother. She had agreed to try for the baby out of obligation and resignation. Now she longed for one with a franticness that took both her and Albert aback. Nothing could fill the hollowness except a baby. She was furious with Albert when he refused to make love to her in the weeks after the miscarriage, worried about hurting her, damaging her womb. She cried and tried to dig up the allium bulbs, insistent that she could not bear to see them flower and reproach her. When she found one, it was starting to germinate, a tiny green shoot like a curved finger pushed out of the bulb, and, suddenly guilty, she buried it again.

All anyone else could speak of was Ireland and the bill for home rule, the whisperings of civil war. Otto found it an odd experience to be an outsider resident in a country in the midst of a national crisis. The Goldbaums were conservatives and unionists, and Otto, as a citizen of the Austro-Hungarian Empire, could not help sympathizing. If countries were permitted to secede from political union according to religion or nationality, then England and Ireland would only be the first. Europe would break apart, the map redrawn like a checkerboard into a series of thumbnail nations. Yet the prospect of war between fellow countrymen was abhorrent. The Ulster Volunteer Force approached the House of Goldbaum for a donation of ten thousand pounds. Albert rejected them out of hand, appalled that they had come to him.

Otto saw the first strands of gray brushing his cousin's temples. He knew that Albert worried about the constant labor strikes, and civil war in England and Ireland, but most of all, he worried about his wife. With Lord Goldbaum in Hampshire and Clement rarely in London, Otto and Albert often found themselves dining alone together at Number One Park Lane. Albert complained that no sooner did he arrive in Parliament to attend a debate on Irish home rule at the House of Commons than he was summoned urgently to the House of Goldbaum, as the price of gold and other safe commodities soared in these uncertain times. Neither Albert nor Greta divulged to Otto the reason for her present unhappiness, and Otto did not like to pry.

Otto and Albert tried to divert Greta with their news, when they returned to Hampshire at weekends, but it was clear that she was distracted and could not attend. All she took in, with apparent relief, was that the Germans had dropped out of the naval race. Otto was among the first to know. The German government requested from the Berlin House no further loans to pay for dreadnoughts. The Berlin cousins confided in Baron Peter, who told his son, who shared the information with Albert and Greta.

"I'm exhausted by all the lazy chatter of Germans as warmongers," said Greta. "All they want is the same as us: peace and sunny afternoons."

A fortnight later, Otto received another report. The Berlin House had received a request for a loan: the German government wished to reequip the army. He shared this information with Albert, but by mutual accord neither man mentioned it to Greta.

By the middle of October, Lord Goldbaum was considered well enough to start receiving the minutes from meetings at the London House. They were returned with scribbled notes in the margins, to which Albert was expected to pay close attention. At the end of the month, when the leaves on the beech trees in the park at Temple Court were burnishing gold, Lord Goldbaum summoned Otto to his rooms. He was sitting in his dressing gown at the bureau, surrounded by neat stacks of correspondence and typed reports. He glanced up and gestured to an upright chair beside the desk.

"I hope you consider your time in England to have been useful, Otto. Your experiences in the London House will serve you in good stead when you leave us. But, even more importantly, your friendship with my sons will strengthen the bonds between the Houses."

"So I take it I'm to be sent back to Vienna, sir?" asked Otto. He and Albert had delayed any suggestion of his return, hoping that Lord Goldbaum's present incapacity was an excellent reason to prolong his stay.

"The cousins have been discussing America again, this time with resolve. We require a presence on Wall Street. Fifty years ago we made a mistake, and every year that there is no House of Goldbaum in New York, we compound it. The decision has finally been made to start a bank there. Each of the European Houses will provide capital. It will take a decade to establish, twenty-five to turn a modest profit. The man who is to go there must determine to make America his home, and his nation, for the rest of his life."

"And the cousins wish that man to be me?"

Lord Goldbaum shifted in his chair, tucking back in the cord of his dressing gown around his ample middle.

"We consider you able, qualified and the most suitable man in the family." He adjusted his spectacles and studied the younger man. "But you must want to go to America, and eventually to become an American. You would represent the interests not only of the Goldbaums, but of America. And, I'm afraid, since we are so late in our arrival in the New World, you will have fearsome rivals—the Fricks, the Rockefellers and the Astors. We are on good terms with them, assisting with their European business. You might not find them quite so accommodating when there is a House of Goldbaum on Wall Street."

Otto was very quiet, considering. Everything that appalled him about Vienna—the decaying empire and emperor, the stultifying society—promised to be transformed in America. If Europe was winter, then America was spring. Poor Jews were pouring out of Russia and arriving in America in a flood. Why shouldn't the wealthy join them?

"May I have a few days to consider?"

"Take a week. This is not a decision that can be undone."

Otto said nothing to anyone. He was being offered an adventure— or the closest a Goldbaum heir could come to one. It might not have been an exploration of the stars, but it did involve new worlds. He resolved privately to accept the offer, his excitement tempered only by the prospect of telling Greta.

Quite unable to sleep, he finally completed his paper on celestial mechanics, sending the article to the journal of the Royal Astronomical Society. On Saturday evening, as they held a dinner for the German ambassador, Prince Karl Max, at Temple Court, Otto found himself discussing his paper. The prince was particularly popular with Greta and Adelheid, who engaged in a constant battle to persuade their guest to converse with them in German. Aware of his diplomatic position, in addition to his penchant for all things British, Prince Karl Max insisted on speaking English, while they—equally intent on demonstrating their warmth toward his nation—answered only in German. It made conversation for the non-bilingual somewhat baffling.

Greta leaned across the table, reaching for Otto's hand.

"I'm so glad you've written another paper. I've been nagging you for months to write something."

"Does this mean you'd like to read it, Mrs. Goldbaum?" asked the ambassador, in his beautiful English.

"Heavens, no!" answered Greta, switching to German. "I'm afraid I lack my brother's starry gifts. My talents are muddier."

"Indeed they are. You have to see my sister's garden," said Otto. "It is the German ideal of an English garden. She has even thatched her house."

"You have not!" said the ambassador, amused. "It must be the largest cottage in England."

"It is indeed thatched. Whether it is a cottage, you must decide for yourself, ambassador," said Greta, still in German. "Now, what size are your feet? We'll need to lend you some boots, if you want to see the gardens. They are particularly filthy at the moment."

The English rain was certainly something he would not miss, decided Otto.

The following morning being Sunday, the Goldbaums politely asked the ambassador whether he would like to attend church. After he had equally politely declined, Otto walked with him to Fontmell to tour the gardens.

"It is good to have an ally like yourself in such a position within the English House of Goldbaum," said Prince Karl Max.

"Not for much longer, I'm afraid," said Otto. "And you must know that while I'm here, my loyalty is toward the British Goldbaums."

"Of course," demurred the ambassador.

"And let us say that I ask this so that I can reassure my sister: the German nation and her government want only peace, despite their investment in the army?"

The prince smiled and bowed. "The army, as you know, is a nineteenth-century relic. It is unequipped for the modern world. As far as I can see and as far as I know, there is no reason to fear war."

"Thank you."

The ambassador raised his bowler hat in acknowledgment. It amused Otto that the German ambassador looked more impeccably English than the average country squire. His suits were cut in Savile Row and his hats were from Lock of St. James's, his mustache oiled and clipped. Since yesterday he had somehow found a pair of English Wellington boots. All he lacked, decided Otto, was a Labrador.

"And the kaiser is so chastened by his humiliation that he's hardly interfering in government at all," said Prince Karl Max.

"And leaving all military decisions to his generals," said Otto with unease.

"For a young man, you worry too much," said the prince with a smile. "The kaiser is presently confining himself to shooting Pomeranian ducks and writing his memoirs. All of us who aren't Pomeranian ducks should be relieved."

"Very well," said Otto, trying to smile at the ambassador's joke.

They found Greta waiting for them on the terrace.

"I'm sorry that you're not seeing the gardens at their best," said Greta. "Summer is color and scent and flash and show, but then autumn is all about texture and sound." She led them down to the wilderness beyond, running her fingers along a feathered bank of pampas grass.

"Listen to the wind in the larches. It sounds like rain."

She plucked a transparent seed head of honesty and pressed it into the prince's hand.

The vista was clear all the way down to the Fontmell River, a fat silver streak gleaming among the wide salt marshes on either side. A murmuration of starlings rose and fell, sweeping through the air in a single movement, each bird a limb of the same colossal being. The flock of starlings joined another, merging as smoothly as two pools of ink on blotting paper, until the murmuration was a vast black arrow rushing across the sky, darkening the clouds, turning and switching.

"I think that, through the wonder of your garden, you have learned to love England, Mrs. Goldbaum," said Prince Karl Max with a small smile.

"Yes, I suppose I have," said Greta. "Still, one inevitably misses home."

"You can always visit," said Otto.

"Yes, perhaps. But it isn't the same."

"A German garden is not so different from an English one," said the prince. "We share the same love of flowers and color and texture. And peace, in which to enjoy it."

Greta had almost convinced herself that she was expecting again. Her monthly had not come and she was almost ready to consult the doctor. To distract herself she supervised the cutting of nearly fifteen thousand small holes for crocuses under the cedar trees on the lawn, to commemorate Albert's election as MP for Fontmell West— one purple crocus for each vote cast for him. The fresh air and planting did not revive her, it only made her tired and sore. She retreated to her bedroom to rest and almost immediately fell asleep.

There was a horrid bang, almost like a gun going off, and she awoke with a start, disoriented. Padding across the room to the window, she saw the imprint of a bird against the glass and, opening it, saw a wood pigeon caught in the ropes of rose thorns beneath the sill. Its neck was twisted at an odd angle and it lay quite still, stunned and unable to flap. The only movement was the slow blinking of its eyes. Greta watched it, disconcerted. It must have been in pain, but unlike a person it could not scream, and with its neck broken, it could not flap or fuss. It stared at her with wet black eyes. She wished it would hurry up and die. If she rang for Anna, the maid would come and wring its neck and put it out of its misery, but somehow she couldn't bear to do that, either.

She closed the curtains and retreated to bed, but all she could think of was the bird dying just outside the window. What had she been doing when Claire and the baby were busy dying? The shot of Claire's gun must have been infinitely louder than a bird flying into a window. She slipped out of bed and opened the curtains. The wood pigeon was still alive, blinking at her. She closed them again. She sat down at her dressing table and realized that she had begun to bleed. There was no baby after all. A heaviness descended over her and she indulged in private tears of frustration and regret. It was the bird. It had brought death with it, she decided wildly. Flinging open the window, she rustled the creeper so that the small body of the wood pigeon tumbled earthward, landing with surprising heaviness on the terrace below. Greta could not bring herself to look.

There was a knock at the door and Anna entered with a note on a silver tray.

Greta took it with impatience. Otto was asking himself to dinner. Usually she would have been glad to see him, but today the prospect of any company filled her with dread.

New York? You are really going?" she asked, incredulous and dismayed.

"You could visit," said Otto.

"Yes. Every few years. How often have Mama and Papa been to see me in England?" she demanded.

Otto did not reply, but tactically spooned his soup. He ought to have waited until the cheese course before telling her. He knew Greta would not be pleased, but the vehemence of her reaction took him aback. She'd turned quite white and abandoned any pretense of eating. Albert signaled to the butler to refill her glass and urged her to drink.

"The packet sails regularly, Greta. And if it would make Otto happy?" Albert said.

"The ship will sink," she said, her face quite drained of all color. "I know it will. The dead bird was a bad omen."

"Greta, you're being quite absurd," said Otto, trying to laugh, but not finding it funny in the least. He'd known her obstinate and argumentative, but never irrational.

"If you must leave us, can you not simply go to Vienna? At least there you are only a few days' journey. A week at most. But America? We'd be lucky to meet half a dozen more times in this lifetime."

"If my ship doesn't sink," said Otto, wryly.

"Yes," said Greta, not smiling.

Usually Fontmell dinners were a delight. The thick elm table was always left bare, the reddish gleam of the grain swirling in the firelight, and the food was excellent, unfussy and decidedly Austrian in flavor: golden-crumbed veal schnitzel with *spätzle* noodles and caramelized onions, crisp apple strudel with thick cream from the Temple Court herd of Jersey cows. But tonight Otto could not even find solace in the clear soup with *Griessnockerl* dumplings. Greta drained her wineglass and an unnatural pink flush appeared on each cheek. He realized she did not look well.

"Greta, what is it? You seemed perfectly all right this afternoon with the ambassador."

"I don't like the thought of my only brother going to America. Isn't that enough?" Her voice was thin and petulant. She rose. "I shall leave you to your port," she said, quitting the room, despite the fact that the first course had not even been cleared.

G reta retreated to the drawing room. A fire had been lit and it was too hot. She drew back the curtains and sat in the window seat, making patterns in the condensation on the glass pane. She knew that she was being snappish and unreasonable. She'd become used to Otto's being here, and had succeeded in forgetting that his presence was not permanent. They'd been companions for most of their lives, so having him in England seemed perfectly ordinary. She opened the window and let the brackish air cool her face. She could smell the river mud. After a little while she heard Otto enter the drawing room. He stood behind her, watching her trace patterns on the pane.

"Albert told me about the baby. Why didn't you?"

Greta shrugged. "Does one usually tell such things? It wasn't even a baby. I'm not supposed to be so upset about such a little thing. A proper English wife would dust herself off and have another."

Otto sat down on the seat beside her. "I wouldn't know how you're supposed to feel."

Greta sighed and closed the curtain, turning to face her brother.

"You have to go to America, Otto, but does it have to be right away?"

Otto looked at her, but said nothing.

"Surely setting up a bank in America takes a good deal of preparation?" she added, pleading a little. "Can't I have a little time to get used to the idea? Tell Lord Goldbaum that yes, you'll go, but not until next year?"

Otto was silent, considering.

"It sounds like a sensible plan to me," said Albert, joining them and sitting beside his wife in the window seat.

Otto rose and placed another log on the fire.

Albert cleared his throat and continued. "You could return to

Vienna in the New Year, and plan on leaving for America in autumn. That way, you would have some months to make arrangements. The capital required is going to be considerable, and the other Houses will be glad to have more time to raise such a sum."

"I suppose I could delay for a few months," said Otto, reluctantly.

"Vienna already in January?" said Greta, only partly mollified.

"Yes, but why don't we visit?" said Albert, placing a hand on her shoulder. "We could go in June and spend the summer in Austria?"

Husband and wife turned to Otto, faces bright with expectation.

He sighed, defeated by their united opposition. "All right."

Greta kissed him on the cheek and rang for champagne.

1914

Does anyone seriously suppose that a great war
could be undertaken by any European State . . .
if the house of [Goldbaum] and its connections
set their face against it?

J. A. Hobson, historian, 1905

Lake Geneva, Switzerland, June

—❦—

Lord Goldbaum could not understand why Albert and Greta needed to be away for quite so long. Surely a month was more than sufficient to visit her family? Albert was adamant. He had promised his wife. They would, of course, return before the baby was born. And, he told his father, she needed a holiday. So long as Greta was near her garden, she was pulling out the aquilegia that had seeded rampantly along the path. The doctor told her to rest, but Greta, while intending to obey his instructions, was seemingly incapable of doing so. One afternoon Albert found her curled up asleep in a wheelbarrow of compost, parked in a sunlit corner. Not wishing to wake her, he trundled it back to the house and placed a blanket over her. He did not mention the wheelbarrow to his father, but he expressed in no uncertain terms that the only way he could ensure that his wife did not exhaust herself in the garden was to take her away from it.

Greta kept busy so that she didn't need to think. This time she had not planted bulbs to flower in time with the baby's arrival, and she would not discuss possible names with Albert. She could not name the small being inside her because that would make it real, and if it was real she couldn't bear to lose it. She gave no orders for the nurseries to be repainted or for furniture to be delivered. Albert spoke quietly to his mother, who made the necessary arrangements. A crib, rocker, baby chair and nursery table were all commissioned in English oak, the paints for the walls chosen, but nothing would be placed in the rooms until after the baby's arrival. In any case, Lady Goldbaum told her son, this was the old way of things. A pregnancy was not mentioned in the ghetto until after the child was born and seen to be healthy. Until then, no one could be sure of God's will, and His wrath ought not be incurred by making assumptions about the gift of life.

Greta's regret at being away from the garden was assuaged by her pleasure at the prospect of reuniting with her family. She and Albert did not travel straight to Vienna, meeting them instead at Lake Geneva. The family villa was undergoing a great refurbishment, but Greta and Albert persuaded the baroness to endure the Grand Hotel Elizabeth Excelsior. They rented the entire first floor, and the owner was thrilled to have the Goldbaums as his guests and accepted reverentially their every request. They brought their own maids and footmen to work alongside the hotel staff; the suites were rehung with artworks from the family's villa; the wine at dinner was from their cellars. The pianist who played at breakfast on the first morning was unobtrusively replaced on the second with a gentleman from the conservatoire in Vienna.

Greta did not notice any such trifling details. She liked the hotel. The splendid gardens belonged to someone else, and she could walk through them with pleasure without seeing everything that needed to be done. The air was fragranced with honeyed mimosa and pink waterfalls of magnolia blossom. In the morning as she sipped coffee in her suite, she gazed across the waters of the lake to Mont Blanc through a haze of scarlet geraniums. She ate rolls thickly spread with butter and runny Swiss cheese, and poured smooth hot chocolate from a silver kettle. Her own happiness on seeing Otto again was increased on realizing the genuine pleasure with which he and Albert greeted one another. In the afternoons while she slept, Otto, Albert and her father drove out into the countryside to shoot or walk or fish.

The baroness offered Greta no advice on motherhood or her confinement, only sympathy, for which Greta was grateful. She nagged her daughter to eat and, realizing how Greta hankered for her childhood foods, recalled the chef from his holiday in the Tyrol and

summoned him to the hotel to cook. Greta was unaware of these ma-
neuverings; she only knew that she sipped beef broth with horseradish
dumplings and spread chopped liver and pickles on slivers of rye
bread—dishes that were precisely as she remembered them, and ones
that she could not replicate in England however often she ordered the
cook to try. As she ate her second helping of Tête de Moine cheese with
figs and honey, she noticed that she was finally growing fat, her belly
swelling comfortably beneath her dress. She relaxed and allowed
herself to luxuriate in her mother's fuss and concern. They sat on the
expansive terrace of the baroness's suite. The baroness ventured downstairs to the gardens and main hotel only in the evenings, concerned
that she might otherwise be forced to converse with other hotel guests,
some of whom she had never even heard of. She lay back in her
chair, shading her eyes from the sun.

"Will you come to England afterward?" Greta asked uncertainly,
knowing how her mother detested all forms of travel.

"Yes," said the baroness, who had just been waiting to be asked.

She poured tea, a special blend of second-flush Darjeeling with
bergamot and scented with lemon. She passed a cup to Greta, who
sipped, closing her eyes in contentment.

"Let us do this every summer, Mama. Otto will simply have to
come back from New York and join us. He'll have to, if we both
tell him."

"Before he leaves, he must marry an Austrian girl. Or an English
one, I suppose," said the baroness. "Then he'll be tied to Europe. His
wife will want to come home from time to time. We mustn't let him
marry an American."

"Heavens, no," agreed Greta.

Days drifted past, then weeks, as easily as the clouds sliding past
the mountaintops. Sometimes Otto and Baron Peter disappeared
to Geneva or Vienna for a few days, returning with news and fresh

gossip. Otto's departure for America remained sufficiently far off that Greta could think of it without alarm. He would sail from Liverpool and would come to Hampshire to meet his niece before he left. Albert was certain that the baby was a girl, and declared himself delighted at the prospect. Greta wished she could hold on to this time with her fingertips, bottle it as they had the fireflies they caught on the lake shores as children. Although, she recalled with disquiet, the fireflies never lasted. In the morning they were always dead and dry at the bottom of the glass, their fire extinguished.

Albert had the suite of rooms beside hers, but he used them only to work, knocking on her door every night and slipping into her bed so regularly that Anna brought his tea and newspaper on a tray each morning. Released from the perpetual scrutiny of his father, Albert appeared more at ease. The couple breakfasted on their terrace in their dressing gowns. Having read the previous day's copy of the *Times* sent from London, he turned next to the German and French editions.

"Your crown prince has been shot by some Serbian rebel group," he said, appalled.

"Let me see," said Greta, taking the paper from him in dismay.

She read, shaking her head. "How absolutely horrid."

"The Austrian government is outraged," said Albert. "Understandably so."

Greta handed him back the paper, unwilling to read any more. "The emperor has never liked him. I think he will probably be relieved he is dead. The poor man. And his poor wife. They married for love, you know."

Albert poured himself another cup of tea. "I should speak to your father. He'll have a good idea whether there will be any consequences from this."

Greta closed her eyes. She didn't want anything to intrude upon these halcyon days. She would not consider death while among the tangled honeysuckle and vines of scarlet bougainvillea.

"Talk to him later. I want to swim after breakfast."

She caught the collar of his dressing gown and tugged him close, kissing him. Albert set his paper aside. "All right."

As long as the Serbians apologize, I can't see that it will come to much," agreed the baron over luncheon. "Greta is right. The emperor always felt his heir was foisted upon him. But it is an outrage against the empire, and the apology must be abject."

"It is a tragedy for Austria," said Otto with a sigh. "The prince was a modernist and a reformer, not like the emperor. Oughtn't we to return to Vienna?" he added with considerable reluctance.

They were dining under a scented canopy of jasmine and vines shading them from the midday sun. The lake shimmered jewel-like in the heat, and here and there small boats swayed on the surface. A distant paddle steamer made slow progress, as brightly colored as a child's toy. An ant marched along a butter knife to reach Otto's bread roll. The baron was quiet for a moment, considering before he spoke.

"Not yet, I think. Greta and Albert leave in a few days for their trip to the mountains, and I would be unhappy to have our time together cut short." The baron smiled at his daughter.

Otto signaled to the footman to pour them more wine. Above the waters of the lake, a mute swan came in to land, the sunlight catching the white of its wing so that it shone iridescent, brushing the surface of the lake like earthed lightning.

Hampshire, Late June

— ⟶•⟵ —

Lady Goldbaum was immensely cross. A freak hailstorm had wreaked havoc on the tender plants in the shrubbery. The *Magnolia grandiflora* was just coming into bud, and they were badly damaged, turning brown and rotting on the tree. The hailstones looked arresting at first, coating the earth in white glass beads for half an hour or so, and she had dispatched Clement with the camera to take photographs. An hour later they had melted, leaving only sludge and chaos. A team of twenty gardeners had replaced the ruined bedding plants in the parterre within a few hours, but the damage sustained to the fruit trees was irreparable. The surviving apples and pears would be pockmarked and spoiled.

To his wife's chagrin, Lord Goldbaum was working too hard again. She was almost relieved when a summer cold forced him to return to Temple Court, where she could keep a closer eye upon him. He sat in the library under a cashmere blanket, sneezing and complaining equally of headaches and the idiocy of government. For years Lord Goldbaum had been trying to persuade the Bank of England of the wisdom of building up their gold reserves. Now, alarmed at the size of the German war chest, it had requested that all the banks pool their gold, to make up for the paucity of their own reserves. Lord Goldbaum was doubly outraged: at the way his advice had been ignored, and at the means with which the government was now attempting to make up for its lack of foresight.

"And the foreign secretary wants us to remind the German and Austrian government of the British commitment to our entente with France. Should they attack France, Britain will come to her defense." Lord Goldbaum sat back in his chair. "He prefers us to talk to our German cousins than go through the official channels."

"I suppose it seems less of a threat and more of a polite reminder," replied his wife. She paused for a moment. "Ought we to tell Albert and Greta to come home?" she added quietly.

Lord Goldbaum was unable to answer, due to a sneezing fit. He reached for his wife's hand.

"Not yet, Adelheid. Don't worry. I won't let them take any chances. If I'm brought any news to cause me the slightest concern, I'll wire them at once."

Outside there was the grind of hooves on gravel. The Goldbaum couriers were busier than usual, bringing constant news from France, Austria, Germany and Ireland. Even at weekends there was no escape, and Lady Goldbaum had learned to dread the sound of the horsemen. They never brought anything good. She coughed in annoyance.

"Stop it, Adelheid," said her husband. "The arrival of the couriers from the Continent is good news in itself. If the horsemen don't come, that's when you need to worry."

Zirl, Innsbruck District, Early July

—◆>•<◆—

It was a pity the whole sorry business had not already been resolved, but they all agreed that there was no need for Greta and Albert to postpone their holiday in the Alps. After a few weeks' holidaying, they would travel on to Vienna before finally returning to England.

The July heat had become unpleasant for Greta, and she was relieved to retreat to the cool of the mountains. They rose late and walked after lunch in the easy warmth of the afternoons. She had always loved the Alps. Even in high summer there was a freshness in the air, and the cows ambled among lush slopes scattered with yellow flowers as liberally as a sky full of stars. The low echo of the cowbells reminded her of her own bell at Fontmell, and each time she heard one, she half-expected to see Withers hurrying out from behind an alpine chalet. Greta was determined to find gentians and edelweiss to dig up and bring back to the garden, and she walked with a trowel and pots in a canvas knapsack. Albert was hunting for native butterflies and brought his net and killing jar. A mule cart carried them high up a dirt road into the folds of an alpine track, and they ambled down together, sharing a bottle of mild, sweet wine and scouring the slopes.

"I wish we could stay until the middle of August," said Greta. "The whole of Austria-Hungary celebrates the emperor's birthday. Even the smallest villages put on a show. You've never seen anything like it." She paused to investigate a bank of springy moss scattered with violets.

"Have you ever met him?"

"Only once, when he presented my father with a ceremonial glove. He looked old even then, but with remarkably blue eyes. He was surrounded by so many people. Guards in imperial uniforms, dragoons and footmen. I don't think he is ever alone, not even for a minute."

"Hold this." Albert handed her the killing jar as he smoothly scooped a butterfly from the grass beside Greta. He slid it into the jar, which she shoved back into his hands.

"I'm not holding the jar while it dies. I hate feeling them thud against the glass," said Greta.

"It doesn't feel pain," said Albert.

"How do you know? You're not a butterfly."

"They don't have pain receptors like people. They can tell when they've been touched, but that's all. A butterfly will fly and eat and try to mate, even if it's missing its abdomen."

Greta studied the dying butterfly. It was white with a mist of gray around the apex of its wings, but on its hind wing it had several scarlet spots, like drops of blood squeezed from a finger onto a handkerchief.

"I'm tired. Let's go back," she said.

Albert packed away his equipment, and they returned slowly down the mountain path.

Later that night Greta dreamed she stood in the Schönbrunn Palace, watching Emperor Franz Joseph playing cards with Death. The emperor wore his imperial uniform and sported his mutton-chop whiskers, while Death had the wings of a vast Apollo butterfly, white with a spray of deep red. They played in companionable silence, two old, old friends.

Vienna, July 23

The House of Goldbaum set itself against war. In the partners' rooms in the banking houses across Europe, the Goldbaum men wrote letters and paid visits to other men who mattered, working to soothe the international crisis. Otto and his father sat in the darkly paneled partners' room in Vienna, listening to the rattle of typewriters below and waiting for couriers to bring news from London, Paris and Berlin.

"So much confusion and posturing," objected the baron. "Everybody speaks and nobody listens." He sat down at his desk and started to draft a telegram to his cousins in Berlin and London. "We must inform the cousinhood that our government is to issue a six-point ultimatum to the Serbians."

"The ultimatum is clearly intended to be inflammatory. I can't understand it. Cousin Edgar was absolutely confident that the German government would rein in ours," complained Otto.

"He was wrong. Besides, who rules in Berlin? The kaiser? The generals? No one seems able to tell us for certain."

"The Serbians might accede to all the conditions," said Otto, still hopeful.

His father pursed his lips. "The Serbians do what the Russians tell them to. If the Russians tell them to concede, then they shall concede; if they tell them to reject the ultimatum, it is because the Russians want a war."

Otto took out his pen. "France is Russia's greatest creditor. Perhaps the French can pressure them to avoid war. I shall write to Henri."

The courier waited just outside the door to receive the letter. Down below the groom prepared a fresh horse.

Further below, beneath the street itself, Karl sat in the dark. Despite the comfort of the synagogue, he always felt like a visitor. He was often alone, but people were constantly dropping by and he found himself on edge, waiting. He liked to be discovered doing something useful—sweeping, studying his Torah portion. On learning that Karl had never had his bar mitzvah, the rabbi had declared he must have one, and that he himself would prepare him. Karl murmured prayers as he worked, out of boredom rather than diligence, feeling that he was acting a part.

When he wanted peace, he disappeared from the synagogue and slipped down one of the many entrances to the tunnels. Unlike Karl the Jew, Karl the Kanalrat was perfectly at ease. He slid into the shadow streets beneath the Ringstrasse and sat in the dark, listening. It stank of rot and death in the heat—Karl noticed the reek, now that he was clean. Yet it was strangely comforting here. He was alone, unwatched.

Somewhere in the streets above, people were making decisions about war. Karl couldn't understand what the murder of a prince had to do with him. If he died, the prince would not avenge him. Perhaps he ought to feel frightened, but to Karl, sitting in the hot dark, listening to the rush and chug of the underground river, war was too distant to contemplate. War and noise and the hurry of men belonged to that other world above.

London, July 27

—◆⟫•⟪◆—

Lord Goldbaum read the markets like a soothsayer interpreted coffee grounds, and the markets themselves reassured him. The Vienna Stock Exchange had slid in the middle of the month, but in London any turbulence remained undetectable. The headlines roared catastrophe and dread, but the markets revealed men's true expectations. In his experience, a man was more honest with his broker than with his rabbi, taking more care with his cash than with his soul.

Then, on July 27, his head clerk knocked on the door to the partners' room to inform him that there was a great deal of movement on the stock exchange. Within an hour, Lord Goldbaum detected that all the Continental banks, most particularly the German and Austrian ones, were taking out a very large amount of money from the stock exchange and that the German government had stopped paying interest on its loans to British banks, including those owing to the House of Goldbaum. Those firms that conducted large amounts of their business with the Continent would soon be in dire straits. He estimated that there were already three hundred million pounds' worth of bills of exchange currently outstanding. If war broke out, they would never be honored. He wired a warning to Paris. Jacques replied with a coded telegram requesting a vast sale of gold for the French government. When it arrived, Lord Goldbaum drew down the blind in the partners' room and ate chicken-and-leek pie without tasting a mouthful.

His French cousins clearly believed that war was imminent and wanted to stock their government's war chest.

He found himself caught in a ghastly moral quandary. It was taken as a matter of faith that communications between the partners of the different Houses of Gold were utterly confidential. But he realized with creeping dread that he now had to put nation before family. Always before, there had been a way to serve his country and the interests of the Goldbaums. He felt something inside him snap, like a tendon. He was unmoored and unhappy. He took a sip of milk to soothe his stomach and sighed. Jacques had been his friend and confidant for many years. Edgar he admired and respected. These men were his cousins as well as his partners, and while he worked in the London office, frustrated by the demands of industry or government, he took solace in the fact that his kin in Vienna and Paris and Berlin toiled in near-identical rooms, feeling much the same.

He pictured the various European Houses of Goldbaum as pearls strung upon a necklace, and he saw war as the anvil strike to smash that chain apart. With a sense of sadness rising in his throat, he understood that in the end it would be his younger son who must navigate the British family through this new and unfortunate age. This was not the legacy he had wished to leave Albert.

Forcing his hand not to shake, Lord Goldbaum composed a reply to Jacques: "Regret no. Treachery to send British gold to Europe with war on knife edge."

He then sent two further telegrams. The first was to the prime minister, breaking the unspoken oath to his family, and warning Asquith that the markets clearly sensed imminent war. The second telegram he sent was to Albert. It said: "Return Home Immediately."

Zirl, July 28

Albert and Greta had left the hotel for a picnic when the telegram arrived. The postmaster placed the message into Anna's hand himself, and on reading it, she was torn between putting on her hat and venturing out to look for her mistress herself, and starting to pack what things she could. She spoke to the innkeeper, seized her hat and started to run.

Exuberantly, Greta had discovered a large clump of edelweiss and, with Albert's help, was spending a cheerful morning digging up a large specimen and packing it into a hatbox, lined with a mackintosh. She sprinkled it meticulously with water from Albert's flask.

"Are you sure it wouldn't like a drop of whiskey from my other flask?" he asked.

Greta was distracted from answering, on seeing a slight figure in a blue dress hurrying toward them.

On reaching them, Anna doubled over, a stitch burning her side. "We must leave at once. Lord Goldbaum wired."

Greta stared at her, aghast.

Albert took the telegram from Anna, read it and then handed it wordlessly to Greta.

"There's a trap waiting at the hotel to take us to the station at Innsbruck," said Anna, impatient to be gone.

"Well done—good girl," said Albert, already gathering up their things.

They hastened down the mountain path in silence and, on reaching the hotel, climbed into the pony and trap. They arrived at the railway station in Innsbruck with no luggage, only the little money that Albert had on his person, and an edelweiss lovingly wrapped up in brown paper.

London, August

Lord Goldbaum's cold did not improve; instead it strayed into his chest. He retired to his bedroom at Number One Park Lane, and Lady Goldbaum quit Hampshire to be by her husband's side. She did her best to repel all visitors. Every day, as they opened the papers, they expected to find that war had been declared. It appeared inevitable. The only question was when.

To Lord Goldbaum's utter dismay, it was also looking increasingly likely that war could end the banking houses. For years European finances had been woven across borders, all the economies braided together, intricately and firmly. German companies borrowed in London, and London banks raised funds in Paris and Naples and Berlin. Now, after decades of cooperation, nations were attempting to separate in an instant. The ties were being yanked apart in the capitals, and the financial markets of Europe looked suddenly flimsy and bare. Stockbrokers, bankers and politicians scrambled to salvage funds, but money and gold poured out of the stock exchange, rushing like water into a drain during a storm. From his bed, propped up among a multitude of pillows, Lord Goldbaum dictated a letter to the chancellor, urging him to close the stock exchange until the crisis had eased, and to suspend the law insisting upon the convertibility of money into gold. If the law was not relaxed, then banks would start to fail, he warned.

As she sat in her husband's room after supper, it occurred to Lady Goldbaum that she had not been disturbed by a single courier all day.

Lord Goldbaum was asleep when the chancellor of the Exchequer was shown into his bedroom and was somewhat startled to find, on wakening, an embarrassed Lloyd George sitting in the armchair. He stretched out his hand and Lloyd George took it, starting to say, "Lord Goldbaum, we have had some political unpleasantness in the past—"

"Mr. Lloyd George, this is no time to remember such things. What can I do to help?"

A loan of one million pounds was agreed upon, in the event of the war that, although undeclared, now appeared a certainty. Yet the chancellor hesitated, still not taking his leave.

"Is there anything else I can help you with, Mr. Lloyd George?" inquired Lord Goldbaum.

"There is a steamer that has started for South America, and although it is supposedly neutral, we have reason to suspect she contains supplies for the Germans, most probably bullion."

"You wish me to stop the ship?"

"I do."

Lord Goldbaum rang the bell and his valet brought him pen and paper. With some difficulty, he scribbled a note, realizing that his hand did not want to grasp the pen properly. When he glanced down at his own handwriting, he saw that it was the shaky inscription of an old man. He passed the note to the valet.

"It is done. An easy thing," he said to Lloyd George.

After he had gone, Lord Goldbaum lay back on his pillow, exhausted from the effort of conversation. He closed his eyes; he wanted to sleep and he wanted his son.

Austrian/Swiss Border, August

———◆∋◆∈◆———

They only had enough money to travel third class. The shared compartment was cramped and hot. Anna vanished to try to find coffee with a little of what was left of Albert's cash. Greta and Albert sat opposite one another, quiet and tense, squeezed in beside a family with their three young boys, who picnicked constantly from an apparently bottomless hamper, the mother offering pâté and crackers and little smoked fish to Greta and Albert, who accepted out of politeness, too anxious to eat.

Greta had never been on a public train before, let alone in third class, and under different circumstances she would have been fascinated by the cacophony of people and noise, and even a stray chicken, sleeping among the boxes in the luggage rack above them. As it was, she hardly noticed her traveling companions and sat still and silent, staring out of the window. They needed to cross the border into Switzerland before war between Austria and England was declared, or they would be trapped. Albert spoke as little as possible and mostly in whispers, concerned that his English accent would be overheard. Greta had never thought she would feel so afraid, surrounded by her own countrymen. She remembered her last train journey through the Jura with Otto before the wedding. Otto, whom she would not see again until after the war. Otto, who ought now to have been safe in New York, if it hadn't been for her. She sat with her hand on her belly and took long, steady breaths to stop herself from crying.

Outside, the valleys were hazy with heat, the green slopes of the mountains indistinct. Narrow rivers threaded their way beside the railway track, the long grass on the banks sprinkled with blurs of pink and purple that Greta knew to be bird vetch and rampion. Albert brushed a stray hair from her cheek.

"At Feldkirch we must change trains again. I shall take one to Bern and then, from Switzerland, travel to Paris."

"Yes," said Greta, not understanding why he was rehearsing the itinerary again. "I know. We should be safe enough, once we get to Switzerland. From Paris we shall travel quickly to London."

"That is what I shall do," Albert said slowly, taking her hand in his and toying absently with her fingers. Her nails were filthy from constant travel and quick sluices in station sinks. He studied her face and, realizing that she did not understand what he was trying to convey, said, "I shall travel to Paris and back to England, but you don't have to come with me. At Feldkirch there is an express train to Vienna. You could be with your family tomorrow night."

She stared at him. He released her hand as though he did not wish to try to sway her, or perhaps he was already letting her go.

"I must go back to England. But whether you come with me is entirely up to you."

Greta was silent, considering the gift he was presenting to her. To spend a war in England, while the country was fighting her motherland, was a grim proposition. She would be regarded with suspicion by most of their acquaintances, an enemy in their midst. She would have to suffer constant gloating reports of Austrian casualties and defeats, and the denigration of her former nation and home. There was no knowing when she would see her parents and Otto again. The connection between the English and French Houses of Goldbaum on the one side, and the German and Austrian Houses on the opposing one, had to be severed. The family was obliged to break apart and she must choose a side.

She tried to imagine returning to Vienna. The baby would be

placed in her old nursery, in her own crib. Nana would embroider little smocks once again beside the nursery fire. The thought was almost too comforting to bear. But no one could know when she and Albert would see one another again, or when he would meet his own child.

"You would do this for me?" she asked, amazed.

"I would," he answered, but he could not look at her.

During the time they had been married, Greta and Albert had never mentioned love. It was not a word that passed between them. Now, as she looked at him, Greta understood that his offer was an act of love. He wanted her happiness more than his own.

She looked out of the window at the vastness of the mountains, their peaks pointing up at the brilliant blue sky. The world was ending on a glorious summer's day of perfect sunshine and clear skies. The train pulled into a station that was baking in the dust. On the platform, all the papers on the newsstand carried a proclamation from Emperor Franz Joseph, which proclaimed: "To my people."

But I am not one of your people anymore, Greta realized. She turned to Albert, her eyes bright.

"I shall come with you to London," she declared.

He said nothing, only squeezed her hand, and just for a moment. She rested her head against his shoulder and, exhausted, fell asleep for a while. When she woke, it was dark. The mountains were vast shadows out of the window. Too tired and frightened to talk, they sat and waited, their knees touching. Inside her, the baby rolled and fluttered, Greta's heartbeat as steady as another train. On and on they rushed, closer and closer to Switzerland.

1917

War is the normal occupation of man—
war and gardening.

Winston Churchill in conversation with Siegfried Sassoon, World War I

————◆•◆————

Otto's servant had discovered a bottle of champagne. Otto could hardly imagine from where, but it was cold—almost too cold—and the bubbles burst upward like the stars of the Milky Way. At midnight there had risen a volley of fire from behind the Russian position, marking the New Year rather than another skirmish. The army lines were stretched thin, pulled taut over a thousand miles until they snapped and soldiers from one side or another trickled in, before they were cut off from their supply routes. A new front was sketched in pencil on the map, not so thick that Otto couldn't rub it out again in a week, a month. That's all this war was: lines on a page moving forward and back like the tide marks on the beach. A rhythmic rise and fall, but with each ebb the earth was rubbed with blood and filth.

Whenever they pushed on to take ground the Russians had given up, they found stricken villages overflowing with dysentery and typhoid, sloppy rivers contaminated with swollen horses and human excrement. In retreat, it was all they could do to put onto oxen carts their own wounded and sick, trouserless and shitting out of the back of the carts. Otto had instructed his junior officers to threaten the men if they broke the directive of the medical corps to drink only boiled water and eat cooked fruit and vegetables. But then orders came from central command that they mustn't light fires to give away their position, and next they ran out of rations. Otto hadn't the heart to flog a man who drank in desperation from a dirty puddle, or ate raw turnips straight from the field. There was no time to dig latrines during the rush of advance or retreat. Besides, in their weakened state, the men suffering from dysentery had to be held above the latrine pit to stop them from falling in and drowning.

Yet from somewhere Gruber had conjured a bottle of champagne. Otto sat in the dark outside his tent and swigged it out of an empty beef tin, making the vintage oddly metallic on his tongue. He realized he must be drunk. It was a melancholy, joyless kind of drunk, not the dizzy euphoria of an earlier life. To his relief, the champagne bubbles dulled the itching of the lice. He wondered vaguely whether the lice were drunk too, asleep propped up beneath a strand of armpit hair. He longed to shave or at least trim his beard, but the best he could manage was to allow Gruber to hack at it with a knife. It was odd, this slow descent from man into creature. His soft gentleman's hands were now cracked and hard, the nails stuck with dirt, but it didn't prevent him from eating with them. They'd lost their cutlery canteen a year ago on the scrambled retreat through the Carpathian Mountains, and after six months had stopped requesting a replacement. The cutlery canteen in its handsome wicker basket, along with the Hapsburg-blue officers' picnicking rugs and their polished brass guns, belonged to another era of civilized warfare. They were abandoned with the saddles that were calculated to give a cavalry officer the perfect seat— designed, presumably, to disarm enemies with their elegance, concluded Otto—but that chafed rider and mount so severely that the horses had to be led into battle.

Otto was almost the only officer in his battalion who remained from the start of the war. The rest had been wounded and sent home, killed or captured. When he awoke each morning, he wondered with casual interest which gun was pointed at him, the one marked "luck" or the one marked "death." The only fellow who had been with him since they arrived in the east was his servant. He'd grown fond of Gruber. He was a constant, the anchored spike in the spinning top of men

coming and going and dying. The battalion and some entire companies within it were now filled out with Germans. Few Austrians remained, and those who did were an assortment of Hungarians, Czechs
and Russian-speaking Ruthenians who tended to desert in the night,
slipping across the lines toward the Russian front and disappearing.
Some of the officers now needed to issue commands in seven languages before all soldiers understood.

Otto no longer thought about the futility of war. Instead, he accepted the futility of everything else. He had longed for freedom from
being a Goldbaum, and here, alone on the frozen Galician marshes
despite the presence of half a million other men, Otto felt the bony
hand of fate in granting his wish. He had joined up in the fervor of
that first August—his father bewildered, but touched by the apparent
patriotism of his son. Otto had known that his regiment would call up
all reserves and preferred to choose his own moment rather than wait,
restless and uneasy. His wish had been granted. Out here his name
could gain him nothing, for he had strayed beyond the tether of its
influence. He felt an odd sort of relief at the liberty. Despite the acute
discomfort, the stink and the cold, he was at last the man he wanted
to be: he was no one. He kept two vestiges of his old life: his father's
watch, as he liked it, and it kept perfect time; and, secreted beside his
skin, he kept his checkbook. He was dubious that a check written out
here would do very much. He did not use it to produce another blanket
or lighter duties, for anonymity was more precious to him than
warmth. And yet he did not toss the checkbook away. He tried to once
or twice, standing beside the brazier or a deep snowdrift, but somehow
it made its way back inside his shirt, carefully stashed beside his heart,
the way other soldiers hid prayers or letters from their lovers.

"Here, Gruber, have a taste," said Otto, passing the beef tin brimming with champagne to the servant.

Karl "Kanalrat" Gruber sipped, the bubbles tickling his tongue. It
was neither pleasant nor unpleasant. For nearly two years Karl had
pretended that his master was an ordinary officer, and an ordinary

Jew. Goldbaum—the name shone in the dark. It was a polished coin from another life. It lay gleaming in Karl's mind, a flare in a cavern. Yet out of respect and affection for his master, he remained complicit in the pretense. Otto Goldbaum had never asked him to treat him like a prince, and sometimes Karl wondered if he himself even remembered who he had been.

"*L'chaim*," said Otto, smiling.

"To life," said Karl, raising the champagne tin.

"You see, Gruber, you're learning," said Otto, amused.

On discovering that his servant was a Jew who was only recently aware of his heritage, Otto had dedicated himself to Gruber's secular education, teaching him snatches of Yiddish and old jokes. The Yiddish Karl liked—but the jokes he rarely understood, laughing only to satisfy Otto.

Karl presently sported an intriguing mixture of German and imperial uniform: the Austrian army was no longer able to resupply kit, and the empire's summer-blue tunic and trousers were silently replaced with kaiser green. To Karl's frustration, his master refused, insisted that he was not fighting for Germany, but for Austria and the ideal of an empire of mixed peoples united under one nation and flag and emperor. Only now the emperor was dead, and Otto's imperial *Rittmeister* uniform had worn almost to rags, however often Karl stitched it back together.

The Russian guns fired, crimson rain fell earthward and then darkness. A moment later there was a scuffle and commotion from the dirt road, a clatter and shouts. Instinctively Karl reached for his rifle. Their camp lay beside a bedraggled, burned-out copse set back from the flat of the endless swamp. This had been a Russian position during the spring, and in retreat they had burned everything: trees, barns, crops and villages. He had watched, half in awe, as fields blazed, blackening the skies, and fountains of earth rose from the ground under the barrage of shells. Now it was mostly hidden beneath a layer of snow, the ruined cottages with their caved-in walls desolate and dark, the windows unlit. The rattle came closer, louder.

Otto stood, seizing his helmet. He turned to Karl. "Come. We must see what it is."

Karl saluted and fastened his coat, apprehension rising in him like heat. He followed Otto out into the snow and down toward the marshes. Shudders of white fire rose up his leg. He'd suffered frostbite last winter and his little toe had turned to blackened jelly—as long as the swelling didn't get so bad that he had to take his boot off; if you had to go without boots, you were done for. He refused to tell Otto. The officer would send him to the field hospital, and then Otto would be allocated another servant who wouldn't take such fine care of him. And afterward, when Karl was sent back, who knew what sort of fellow he would be ordered to serve. The pain wasn't so bad, nothing a little schnapps wouldn't soften.

They crouched at the edge of the marsh, listening. They crept low along the planks, taking care not to look to either side, grateful that the cold masked the stench of bodies. At the far edge of the marsh, Karl made out the flash of Russian guns on top of the hill, too distant to cause alarm.

"Can you hear anything else, Gruber?" asked Otto.

"No, sir, nothing."

The two men slid back across the darkened marsh. The stars lurked behind clouds, so that the frozen faces of the dead stayed hidden in the waters. In the autumn, a Russian officer had approached with a white flag asking for permission to bury the corpses sinking among the reeds, but the German commandant refused: the dead served to remind both sides of the folly of fighting in the swamp.

The rattle started again, louder this time, accompanied by voices. Karl stiffened and then, realizing the voices were German, relaxed. Then, as they turned, they saw several soldiers from another company pushing a piano covered in tarpaulin up the slope toward them. It rattled a discordant tune as they shoved it along, the hammers hitting the strings as it jolted across the ruts.

The men halted, sweaty and triumphant.

"Know anyone who can play?" asked one.

Karl and Otto stared at them in bemusement, Karl half-wondering if Otto was about to issue a reprimand.

"Schwartz, in D Company, used to play the violin at the opera house," said Otto at last.

Karl and Otto lingered apart from the others, reluctant to leave, and curious. A few minutes later, Schwartz was produced and stood staring at the solitary piano in disbelief. The men jollied him to the piano, fashioning a stool out of an ammunition box. He sat, and after a moment's hesitation removed his gloves and started to play. He paused, a blissful childish smile spreading across his face.

"It's not bad! Almost in tune."

He launched into a melody, rippling up and down the keys, and as Karl listened he saw notes drifting upward and spattering the graying snow with color. Through a haze of champagne and pulsing feet, he watched the blackened trees festooned with pink and blue and green and the imaginings of spring. He glanced at Otto and saw that his master listened with his eyes closed, a beatific calm spread across his face.

"'Clair de Lune.' This was one of my sister's favorite pieces," said Otto quietly. He opened his eyes again and recited:

> *"While singing in a minor key*
> *"Of victorious love and an easy life*
> *"They do not seem to believe in their happiness*
> *"And their song mingles with the moonlight."*

When he had joined up, Karl had expected the discomfort, the terror and even the boredom. He had not expected poetry. His reverie was punctured by a patter of distant guns.

"How can they fire on New Year?" grumbled a soldier, wiping his nose with the back of his glove.

"Maybe it's a mutiny," added another, hopefully.

The pianist continued to play, and Karl felt the music roll down across the flat marshes, the sound echoing and carrying out in the distance.

"It isn't gunfire," exclaimed Otto with sudden understanding. "They're clapping."

"Yes," agreed Schwartz serenely, with the recognition of a performer, not stopping his playing, "it's definitely applause."

Karl studied the huddled figure seated at the piano in the open field and understood that he too must once have been something, someone else.

Temple Court, Hampshire, One Minute Past Midnight

———◦❧◦———

Greta had wanted to have the baby in her own house, but the pains came on quickly during coffee with her mother-in-law. Two timorous and elderly footmen carried her upstairs, despite her protestations that they should send round the car and drive her back to Fontmell. They were puffing as they reached Greta's old suite of rooms; at nine months pregnant and resisting furiously, Greta was quite a parcel. Lady Goldbaum followed and then stayed with her daughter-in-law, attempting to comfort her and apply cooling flannels to her forehead while they waited for the midwife. Greta paced the carpet, measuring the distance between tightenings by the number of red suns she could count. Soon, the woven orbs became beacons for the agony—a fire that spread across her pelvis and lodged in the base of her spine. There was a wrongness to the pain that frightened her. It had not felt like this when she had labored with Celia. Her back felt as if it were being stretched and split, gathering into a howl during each contraction and barely easing as it fell away.

Anna, the midwife and Lady Goldbaum took turns to hold Greta's hands, and the more they whispered everything was going to be perfectly all right, the more Greta feared it would not. The hours passed, measured out only in the rush and hurry of hurting. Each time she thought she could not bear it, that she must break apart. She cried and sobbed as Anna and Adelheid rocked her between them and she shuddered and gasped, her belly tight and hard. By the afternoon Greta could no longer speak in English, able only to murmur in her mother tongue. At dusk she could no longer speak at all, but only scream and whimper. The doctor had been summoned, but Greta had not been due for a fortnight and the best physicians were all busy tending to the wounded.

The doctor arrived late in the evening and they laid her back on the bed, so that he could shove his hand deep inside her to rupture her waters with a crochet hook. Greta vomited on his shoes.

"She's exhausted. We must hurry it along before baby tires," he explained, trying to keep the anxiety from his voice.

Greta had thought it couldn't get worse, but the next contraction was so powerful that she fainted for a few seconds. She wanted to stay there, at a distance from the twisting and wrenching in her back. Through a fog of crimson suns she heard herself scream, and the midwife and doctor pleaded with her to push. I don't want to push, I want to die, she thought. I only want this pain to stop.

In her distraction, Lady Goldbaum had quite forgotten that it was New Year's Eve and she had thirty guests for dinner. She sent her apologies downstairs, told her husband to host alone and instructed the pianist in the salon to play the Debussy a little louder and, should the commotion upstairs become audible, to switch to Wagner.

Greta sobbed, hopeless and weary. Between each contraction she fell asleep for a few seconds, only to wake with a start as the pain lit up again, slicing through her spine and the depths of her belly like an open wound.

"Think of the baby. Just a little longer," consoled Adelheid.

"Celia. Remember Celia," whispered Anna.

Through the torment, Greta understood that Anna was reminding her of her duty to her daughter. She could not die, not now when Albert was in France. She did not love this baby yet, but she did love Celia. With an animal cry, she pushed. The sound filled the corridors, feral and fierce. From down below came the strains of Wagner.

The baby arrived quickly, in a rush of blood, while Greta yelled, ignoring the doctor's pleas to be mindful of the guests attempting to enjoy their cognac below. It gave a mournful wail, as if put out at the indignity of its arrival, and then settled against Greta. She lay on the soaked bed and clutched the baby to her breast, resisting Anna's attempts to take it from her. The doctor listened to the noisy chiming of the clocks calling from the East Gallery.

"Time of birth, just after midnight, January the first."

Greta closed her eyes. The clocks continued to ring. The footman who had the knack of winding on all the clocks properly, so that each timepiece rang the hour at approximately the same time, had been called up, and subsequently time in the house had become vague. She did not think it at all clear whether the baby had been born at the last moment of 1916 or the first of 1917.

"May I inspect the infant?" asked the doctor, not wishing to be accused of neglecting his duty.

"Soon," said Greta, not bothering to open her eyes, and holding it closer.

"You have a nasty tear below. Would you like chloroform while I stitch you?" he asked.

Greta shook her head. She did not want to take her eyes off her baby, this wondrous stranger. No discomfort could be worse than what she had endured.

"I'm afraid there is a shortage of surgical silk. And what remains is reserved for military hospitals. I'm going to have to stitch you with fishing wire."

Lady Goldbaum grunted in outrage. "So there is a hierarchy of wounds. Injuries sustained by men maiming one another are ranked above those inflicted upon a woman by nature."

The doctor paused in threading his needle to gaze at Lady Goldbaum with reproach. "Those are injuries sustained by men sacrificing themselves for their country, madam."

"And a woman sacrificing her body for her family is ordinary and second-rate, I suppose, worthy only of fishing wire."

"Is it a boy or a girl, madam?" asked Anna, attempting to defuse the impending row.

Realizing that she hadn't checked, Greta looked.

"A boy," she announced. "Benjamin Howard Eli Goldbaum."

After he had finished stitching, the doctor slipped from the room, gratified to be the first to announce to the party gathered below that the British Goldbaums had a male heir to the dynasty at last.

Half an hour later, Greta and Benjamin had been bathed and dressed in clean clothes. Anna bossed the housemaids as they tidied the room, removing bloodied sheets and stoking the fire. Drowsy and warm, and inhaling the strong animal smell of Benjamin's head, Greta wondered about her husband.

"Has Albert been told?"

"They're sending a wire to Montreuil-sur-Mer, madam," replied Anna.

There was a knock at the door and the nursemaids led in Celia, pink-cheeked with sleep and barefoot.

"Hello, darling," said Greta, holding out her hand. "Would you like to meet your brother?"

"No, thanks," said Celia, lingering in the doorway, half-afraid, her mother transformed into a stranger and tucked up with some unknown creature.

"Come on," said Greta. "Hop in."

The nursemaid lifted Celia onto the bed, where she knelt, staring suspiciously at the red and swollen face of her brother. She gave him a good prod.

"He's your baby, too," said Greta.

Celia stared at him, intrigued and a little revolted.

"No, thanks." Celia scrutinized her mother, apparently weighing the moment. "Don't want brother. Want doggy."

"All right," said Greta. "Benjamin will get you a dog. It will be a present from him."

She closed her eyes, overcome with sudden exhaustion, and seizing the opportunity of her mother's inattention, Celia gave Benjamin another, harder poke. He opened a damp, toothless mouth and gave a sharp, plaintive wail. Celia smiled, satisfied.

Château de Beaurepaire, Montreuil-sur-Mer, France, January 1, One Minute Past Midnight

———◈———

"Isn't this one of yours?" said one of the generals, holding up a bottle of Latour Goldbaum for Albert's inspection. "Not bad."

Dutifully Albert rose and glanced at the label, where a damp stain bloomed. "Yes, sir. The eighty-nine was a good vintage. Solid. The eighty-eight was better. There was very little rain and most of the harvest was spoiled, but the few bottles they made were remarkable."

"A good tip," said the general, tapping his nose and calling for the staff sergeant to inspect the cellars for the fabled vintage.

Albert sighed inwardly, repelled but conscious this was part of the pageantry. The brigadiers and generals had transformed the petite château into a gentlemen's club, a weekend version of those on St. James's or Pall Mall, where chaps could drink excellent wine, play tennis and swim, untroubled by women or war. Some mornings he rode out with General Haig himself, a fine figure on a beautifully groomed white horse flanked by his escort of lancers, all the party sporting their red hatbands, red tabs and the blue-and-red armlet of headquarters. To Albert they looked like the spectacular male of some species of rare beetle, spotted with color. It was all for show. Red was no longer permitted at the front, not since one of the chipper colonels with his scarlet hat and tall head was shot during a tour of the trenches.

Albert was torn between guilt and relief at his posting to Montreuil. He kept a plane at the airfield so that on the occasions he was granted leave he could be back in Hampshire in about an hour. It added to the oddness of the experience: breakfast in France, lunch at home. He had expected to be sent to the front, but the order had come down that Albert Goldbaum, member of Parliament for Fontmell West, with his familial and political influence and superb French, ought not to be sacrificed upon the enemy, but found a role on the British staff. Here at the château Albert understood that he was playing at war, while sixty miles away men were being shot, gassed and mutilated. Tonight in the officers' mess they had dined on partridge and almond soufflé while the band played ragtime. In June he had been awarded a medal for his exemplary service as an aide-de-camp in arranging the triumphant official visit of King George (and sourcing not only partridge, but grouse, pears, walnuts, Roquefort, truffles and champagne), but he was too ashamed to wear the medal upon his breast until, after a month of reminders, he was so ordered by a brigadier.

Two privates from the Royal Highland Fusiliers began to play "Auld Lang Syne" on a pair of bagpipes, the sound maudlin and unpleasant. After a minute the officers joined in. Albert couldn't bear it. The pipers started a slow and melancholic performance of "God Save the King" as everyone scrambled to their feet. He stood and sang obediently with his fellow officers, a mixture of regular soldiers (old career bombardiers, exultant at this stage of life to enjoy one last jolly war) and newly commissioned nonregular officers, seconded from regular life as mild-mannered surveyors and country solicitors. Life at general staff headquarters was a living monument to life before the war. They were woken at six by a servant bearing a tea tray and, after a bath, worked from eight in the morning until retiring to shave again before dinner at eight thirty. The façade of croquet and bracing swims in the frigid waters of the pool, the gin martinis and swirling glasses of burgundy, were echoes of another life, trappings of false continuity.

Albert became aware that the great general himself was seated at a table and eyeing him with interest, while listening to a civvy chap wearing small round glasses and a matching series of circular double chins. The man caught Albert's eye and nodded. General Haig beckoned him over. Albert waited, knowing that three months of regimental training had not been enough to instill in him either soldierly bearing or compliance.

"This is Simon Grenville, from the War Office. Wants a quick word."

Albert held out his hand, but did not move to join them.

"Sit," commanded the general, getting up and leaving the two men alone.

Albert sat.

Grenville coughed and cleaned his glasses with a small silken cloth, even though they were not dirty.

"We were hoping, Captain Goldbaum, that you would speak to your father."

Albert frowned. "If this is business, Mr. Grenville, you'd do better calling in at the office in London."

"Yes, indeed."

Albert waited, but Mr. Grenville made no move to dismiss him or to leave. Instead he licked dry lips with a darting pink tongue.

"Without giving precise figures, the war is expensive," he said at last.

"Five and a half million pounds every day, without precise figures," said Albert.

Grenville glanced at him in surprise.

"It's my business to know what things cost, Mr. Grenville. England is nearly out of money. You want the Goldbaum Bank to make the government further loans, despite the fact my father has told you we have reached the absolute limit of our credit."

Grenville sighed and nodded, reached into his pocket for his spectacle cloth and then lost heart.

"I can only echo what I'm sure Lord Goldbaum has already told you," said Albert. "The House of Goldbaum cannot lend the war fund any more money. If we do, we risk bankruptcy. If banks start to fail, that will not help the war effort."

"I know. But I was sent to ask," said Grenville, with an air of gloom.

"You must borrow from the Americans. They are the only ones with any money," said Albert with resolve.

"We are. Our chap on Wall Street is raising money through the American banks. Nearly two million dollars a day."

At the size of the figure, even Albert was taken aback for a moment.

"It isn't enough," said Grenville with a sigh. "And the terms are crippling. The Yanks won't lend unless the money is guaranteed against British securities or gold. Shipment after shipment of gold is sailing across the Atlantic."

Albert looked at him closely. "How low are the Bank of England's gold reserves?"

Grenville hesitated. "I can't say. It's classified." He signaled to a waiter. "Another glass of brandy."

After it was brought to him, Grenville swirled his glass, the contents a spinning gold in the gaslight. He took a sip. "This glass wasn't as full as it ought to have been in 1914. We didn't think there would be such demand, and we let our stocks run low. And then we drank an awful lot of brandy in 1915, 1916."

"It was a popular drink in America," said Albert, eyeing the glass.

"Quite." Grenville took a large gulp and then another and put it down on the table, the merest drop left in the bottom, just enough to color the glass. "By March or April it will be empty."

"You can't get any more from the Russians or the French?"

"We try. They prevaricate, delay; send some, but a fraction of what we asked for and need."

"Meanwhile the value of the British pound is pegged to gold."

They both glanced at the almost-empty brandy glass.

"There is nothing to be done but turn to the Americans. They must lend us more," said Albert, aware of a shrill desperation in his voice.

"And when we run out of gold to pay them?" Grenville was silent for a moment and then leaned in a little closer. "I'm afraid it's rather worse than that. President Wilson has firmed his position. The American Federal Reserve Board has issued a decree warning banks against making loans to belligerent governments."

Albert snorted. "Wilson's way of exerting pressure to force us into peace negotiations, I suppose. Because he is a moral man, whose Christian conscience dictates that he try everything he can to end the wanton slaughter of men? I believe that is what he said in his reelection campaign."

Grenville gazed at him steadily, his eyes magnified through his spectacles. "I think the president may indeed be a moral man, tormented by the prospect of war. But there are others in America who have noticed that they have done magnificently out of it. While we scrabble in the dirt, money falls on them like rain. We all want their cotton, guns and grain, and we borrow their money on horrible terms to buy it from them. They have won the jackpot, and they want to cash in before the casino goes out of business."

Albert felt a gloom suffuse his being like a cold draft. "I suppose, whether their motives are moral or avarice, it doesn't matter. The Americans are using their formidable financial influence to end the war and the effect will be just the same. We lose."

Grenville nodded miserably. "The British government is in an invidious position—if the loan embargo is maintained, the collapse of the Allies will come in a matter of months."

Albert gestured toward where General Haig held court among lesser generals in the corner. "The next battle is irrelevant. The real war is away from the trenches and in the countinghouses. The great push needs to be not against the Germans, but to push the Americans into the war. That is the only solution I can see. If they fight with us, it is against their interests for us to crash out, defeated and bankrupt."

The man from the War Office nodded unhappily. "The prime minister has been suavely trying to nudge them out of neutrality."

"Any luck?"

"None."

There was nothing Albert could say, no sympathy he could offer. The flow of money was drying up, and like the slowing of blood rushing from a wound as the pressure drops and the heart ceases to beat, the British economy had nearly bled to death. He waved to a servant and ordered more brandy and cigars. They drank and smoked in silence. There was nothing useful to be said, and both men were too preoccupied to engage in small talk. Neither noticed when General Haig rejoined them, and he stood for half a minute before Albert hurried to his feet and saluted. The general grunted in displeasure.

"I thought you were stuck to that chair, Goldbaum."

"My profound apologies, sir."

"Business satisfactorily concluded, I take it?"

"Indeed, General," said Grenville quickly.

Albert understood. The great architect of war should not be distracted with trivialities such as cost. In this instance the general was like a lady diner in a restaurant, presented with a menu without prices.

A second lieutenant appeared at their table, with two telegrams on a polished silver tray. Haig took one and read it, a tiny twitch of his mustache betraying his satisfaction at the contents. He glanced at Albert.

"That's addressed to you, Goldbaum. I can't fathom precisely how your family manages to make use of the GHQ urgent messaging system as if it were their own private postal service."

Albert read his message with almost as much satisfaction as the general had read his. He looked up and smiled. He thought that perhaps he ought not to feel such happiness, considering the world into which his son had just been born, but, he reasoned, joy cannot be contained by logic.

"Well?" demanded the general.

"I have a son," said Albert. "And your telegram, sir? Good news, I hope?"

"The king has sent me a New Year's gift from the nation. I am promoted to field marshal."

There were general shouts for champagne. As it was liberally distributed throughout the company, Albert accepted the congratulations of staff officers, colonels and the odd brigadier, all the time feeling the watchful eye of Field Marshal Haig on his back, as if even now the effect of Haig's great promotion had been outshone: there was more than one field marshal in Britain, but there was only one son and heir to the British Goldbaums.

Villa Gold, Lake Geneva, January 1, One Minute Past Midnight

—⟩•⟨—

Clement lay fast asleep in bed with Irena, their small daughter, Lara, tucked between them, fingers curled in her mother's long hair. The nursemaids and housekeeper murmured their disapproval—who had ever heard of such a thing? Only peasants slept together in one bed, and that was out of necessity. But Clement and Irena couldn't have cared less what the servants or neighbors whispered, and each evening they dismissed the nurse at six and put Lara to bed themselves, reading her stories in Russian and English and every now and again, in deference to Cousin Otto, in German.

Clement knew his happiness was gauche and entirely out of place during such a time, but he couldn't help himself. He lived quietly beside the lake with two women who adored him, beyond the sting of his father's disappointment. The house was too big for them—they did not need the ballroom to entertain, but Lara liked to be pushed on her tricycle from one end to the other, shrieking with joy. The house was known as Villa Gold, in deference both to its owners and to the battalions of dahlias planted along the villa's drive, ten thousand orbs in shades of gold and yellow and saffron. In summer, the villa windows looked past striped lawns and urns of yet more nodding dahlias to the blue waters of the lake, and in winter the vista stretched beyond the starched white of the gardens to the frozen waters and the snow-capped

Alps. Clement wrote his parents brief letters assuring them of his scrupulous caretaking of the villa.

The cuckoo clock in the unused night nursery woke him briefly as it cooed midnight, and Clement climbed out of bed and opened the curtains. The moon was bright and the snow glowed all around like phosphorus. Despite the beauty of the place, and the tender affections of Irena and Lara, Clement missed Albert. He wished his daughter could meet her cousins, but he accepted the impossibility of such a desire. He felt a little uneasy. Tomorrow he would drive away such feelings with a game of chess, and perhaps take Lara skating on the lake. He clambered back into bed, where it was warm and soft. A minute later, he was asleep.

Esther Château, Paris, January 1, One Minute Past Midnight

Henri read his papers with itching frustration, unaware of the old year passing into the new. The government desired the House of Goldbaum in Paris to issue another showing of war bonds, but they wanted the interest rate to be fixed, and with inflation rising like damp, Henri had been forced to warn the finance minister that there would be few investors. He wished that he were in America. While Europe bled flesh and money, American profits from exports in grain and arms grew like Jack's beanstalk. The merchants there must have thought they had discovered the golden goose, Henri decided. He was tired of shitting golden eggs and putting them in a ship and sending them to America.

There was a knock at the door and a footman appeared, hesitating on the threshold. His wig was neither clean nor straight, and he had a slight limp. All the best servants had been swallowed up by the army, minnows into Jonah's whale.

"There's a man and a woman here to see you. They say the professor sent them."

Henri pushed aside his papers. "Well, show them in."

The footman stood back, and an older man in a brown suit and a young woman in a none-too-clean blue dress entered. Their faces were etched with exhaustion. The woman swayed, appearing on the edge of fainting.

"Bring a supper tray and some brandy," ordered Henri, rising.

The footman remained on the spot. "There's none left in the pantry," he said softly.

"Then you must go to the cellar," snapped Henri, irritated.

The footman swallowed and nodded, clearly terrified at the thought of searching the vast and cavernous cellars of the château by candlelight.

"Sit, sit," said Henri, helping the woman to a seat on the sofa.

"I am Voska," said the man. "This is my daughter. We have been traveling for some time."

Henri studied his guests with interest. These occasional furtive visits from the Czech nationalists intrigued and troubled him.

"Where have you traveled from?" asked Henri, out of conversational politeness, and quite forgetting that he was not supposed to ask.

The man paused and licked his lips, a little nervous. "First Vienna. Then Berlin. Many, many trains."

The footman reappeared with a tray of bread, fruit and cheese and the brandy. Henri dismissed him and served his guests himself. They ate with indecent haste.

"May I be of any assistance, other than refreshments?"

"We have documents for you to pass to the British. You have a connection, yes?"

Henri nodded. "My cousin."

"You cannot send it through your courier network; you must take this to Beaurepaire and place it in Monsieur Goldbaum's hands yourself."

Henri smiled and helped himself to a grape. "Monsieur Voska, I'm afraid I'm rather tied up in Paris. I don't get involved in these"—he searched for the right word—"*clandestine* matters myself."

Henri was dubious about the effectiveness of the Bohemian Alliance. They were Austro-Hungarians who had been born as citizens of the empire, but who considered themselves Czech patriots. They wanted the Allies to win the war and the great Austro-Hungarian

Empire to shatter, so that a new Czech nation could be born. Their ardent nationalism and hatred of the Austrian Empire unnerved Henri. The Goldbaum dynasty might have begun in Prussia, but Henri knew himself to be a Frenchman and could as soon imagine betraying his family as his country. In fact he dared not imagine Otto's hurt at his perfidy: this odd couple presently seated on his sofa were citizens of Otto's beloved Austria and they were busily plotting its downfall, while he, Henri—Otto's favorite cousin and childhood companion—was assisting them.

"It is a document of importance," said Voska softly.

"Regarding?" asked Henri, vexed at the position in which he had been placed. He would not be some dupe, passing on information that did not help the cause of France.

Voska looked sheepish, and before he could speak, the girl from the sofa rose to her feet.

"My father and I have traveled for five days through Europe without stopping to eat or change our clothes, always risking discovery to bring you this paper. It is a telegram in code. We do not know what it says, but we know it is written in the German diplomatic code. The British can read it."

"They can?" asked Henri.

"We believe so," said Voska grimly.

"How did you get it?" asked Henri. "I'm sorry, but I must ask. Else how am I to persuade Albert, or his acquaintance at Naval Intelligence, that the document is genuine?"

Again, the girl spoke. "It was sent at night from Berlin to Mexico. We have a telegraph operator in the Alliance who made a copy. But if the British reveal this, they are sentencing him to death."

Henri studied her for a moment, considering. "Yes. Very well. I shall do it. You may give me the document."

The girl smiled, revealing a tiny gap between her front teeth. "You must allow me somewhere to change. The telegram is rolled and hidden in the bones of my corset."

Henri rang the bell and instructed the footman to wake one of the maids to assist the young Czech girl. He was surprised that the commotion had not woken his father, but then Jacques was becoming deaf. Henri remained with Voska. Neither man spoke. Henri hoped they would not meet again. When he glanced once more at the clock, he saw that it was nearly one.

Hampshire, January

—⋖⋗—

"I can't see why you're so put out," said Greta, admiring the sleeping form of baby Benjamin parked among the cabbages. "After all, he's in the perambulator, not a wheelbarrow."

Lady Goldbaum sighed and coughed. Greta had refused to lie in for more than a week, declaring herself bored and too busy to laze in bed. She did not admit to her mother-in-law that, in the stillness of her bedroom, she was tormented by the memory of Benjamin's birth. While it was true that she couldn't physically recall the actual pain, the terror remained, vivid and acute. She could not bear to think about the black stitches in her flesh, and was relieved when the doctor put up a discreet little screen when he removed them at the end of a fortnight.

She instructed Nanny to wrap the baby up in furs and take him out into the garden, as she didn't wish to return to the house to nurse him. She had declined a wet nurse and scoffed at the idea of feeding Benjamin with one of the new bottles. Instead, she wrapped him in a shawl and plucked out a nipple and fed him while seated among the flowerpots and compost.

"I wish you wouldn't, dearest," said Lady Goldbaum, limiting her remarks with a struggle.

Greta smiled and adjusted the blanket around Benjamin's head.

"I know, Adelheid, but no one is in the least bit interested."

. . .

Greta rarely ventured up to town anymore; technically, as a friendly enemy alien, she was supposed to notify the police in Fontmell town—even though Albert assured her they would overlook such a formality for the wife of a member of Parliament. But Greta found herself acutely aware of her foreignness in a way that she had not been before, even as a new bride fresh from the Continent. She tried not to speak—whether it was to the ticket clerk at the railway station or the waiter at a charitable luncheon. The ladies at the luncheons already knew her shame before she opened her mouth, and they eyed her with pert interest, whispering to one another behind their auction cards. They either avoided speaking to her at all or offered vicious consolation on the vast German losses—never quite remembering that her family was Austrian. She minded less for herself than for her children. A friend of Celia, the nice little daughter of the vicar of Fontmell, was suddenly indisposed when she had been supposed to come to a dolls' tea party. Celia had wept with disappointment, while Greta knew in her heart that the real sickness wasn't German measles, but a German mother. She understood that she wore the stain of her motherland like a crimson birthmark, but it was too much to have it inflicted upon the children. Celia couldn't even find Austria in the atlas.

To Albert's weary resignation, Greta had transformed Fontmell Abbey into a lying-in and convalescent home for some of London's most unfortunate souls. To her dismay, she'd learned that now that the London labor wards were given over to the wounded from the front, women were starting to die in childbirth with horrible frequency. Since unmarried mothers were unable to gain admittance to a general hospital, and were forbidden from collecting the thirty-shillings maternity benefit given to married women, they could not afford a midwife's fee.

Greta had the barns converted into a ward, rebuilt with corrugated iron and paneled with reused wood from old packing crates. There were eighteen beds—nine for those still confined, and nine for those who had already delivered.

Several local handywomen offered their services, but Greta was insistent: only qualified midwives with good character who had registered with the Central Midwives Board would be engaged. She wanted even the poorest women to be tended to using the best of modern medicine and science, not soothed with folk remedies. She had used all her influence to try to procure a resident doctor, but even with his lordship's assistance, she had failed. All the doctors were required at military hospitals. The best they could manage was to send a car to Southampton for a surgeon during emergencies. Mostly it was sufficient, but sometimes it was not. The first mother to have her baby stillborn asked to have it buried at Fontmell. The ground at the abbey chapel was still consecrated, so Greta asked the vicar to commit the tiny coffin into the earth. The vicar apologized: the baby had not drawn breath; it had not been baptized. Greta experienced an anger in her veins that fizzed like electricity. They buried the baby outside the walls of the abbey churchyard. During the night, Greta instructed that the wall be moved and rebuilt around the tiny grave. In that first winter, two more small headstones bloomed among the grass.

Only one mother died. It had happened on Christmas Eve. Helen had been working in a munitions factory right up until her nine months, but after she began to bleed, she'd been put on a train to Hampshire to rest. Helen was bright yellow, from her daffodil hair to her lemon-peel skin and flaking nails. To their relief, her delivery had been quick and easy enough, although the baby girl was born as yellow as a canary. Greta had called a few hours afterward to present the new mother with a blanket stitched with pink and a few hothouse roses in a jam jar. Then, suddenly, Helen had started to bleed. Greta had watched in horror as a waterfall of red soaked through the bedcovers and poured onto the floor, drenching the frantic nurses' shoes.

The wet noise of their feet. The poor woman's face drew back tightly over her skull, as though she were aging decades in a few minutes; her hands became the thin, bony hands of an old woman. And then she was dead. Greta had stared at the hothouse roses on the bedside, their petals flecked with blood. At the yellow baby wailing in its crib.

The doctor assured Greta that a single maternal death was a triumph. It did not feel like one. Greta made herself watch as an old woman appeared to collect her infant granddaughter bundled up in blankets, five pounds slipped in an envelope along with useless expressions of regret. The mother's coffin was sent up to London on the milk train, the body unstitched, for there was not suture thread to waste.

Greta found herself thinking: what if Helen had lived? Then, like scores of other mothers who had left Fontmell, she would have been forced to return to the factory and nurse her baby with yellow, glowing milk. Greta wanted the women to have a way of supporting their children without risking their own health. She observed how much the women seemed to enjoy walking among the allotments, admiring the vegetables and, when they were sufficiently recovered, helping the gardeners bring inside the cabbages and parsnips.

Greta and Withers took tea with Miss Winifred Hathaway and Miss Ursula Ogden in the glasshouse beside the kitchen garden. As they nibbled seedcake and cookies from Fortnum's, they watched a pair of heavily pregnant women walk uncomfortably among the rows of glossy chard. Despite the vast protrusions of their bellies, the women looked thin and pinched. Miss Hathaway and Miss Ogden complimented Greta and Withers on the beauty and profusion of their parsnips and the luxuriance of the snowdrops, but made no remark about the women. Greta waved to them, and the women nodded in acknowledgment.

"The women who have had their babies stay here for a week or two, but then we send them back. What happens to them then?" said Greta.

"What indeed?" said Ursula, putting down her teacup.

"They need an occupation. A skill," said Greta. "And Withers and I have seen how much they enjoy helping in the garden."

"A healthful pursuit," agreed Miss Hathaway.

"And with so many of the nation's gardeners away at war, we thought it would be jolly useful to train up a few more," said Greta.

"Oh dear," said Ursula, sensing what was coming and lowering her garibaldi cookie in discomfort.

"Yes," said Greta, ruthlessly. "We wish to open a Hathaway gardening school here at Fontmell for the poor and unfortunate mothers."

Miss Hathaway stared at Greta and Withers in shock. "But Miss Hathaway's Gardening and Finishing School is for *ladies*."

Greta fixed Miss Hathaway with a look. "The delphiniums won't blush."

"It's a wonderful opportunity to spread the Hathaway natural gardening method throughout the nation, like a rich and glorious compost," said Withers.

"Well, I suppose if you put it like that, it sounds quite nice," agreed Ursula softly.

All three women turned to study Winifred Hathaway, knowing that it was her opinion that mattered.

"Gardening is an elegant pursuit," said Miss Hathaway at last.

"And so is a mother's desire to support her family," said Greta with conviction.

"Some have no choice but to prostitute themselves," said Withers, never one to flinch from simple facts.

Greta watched as the two good lady gardeners flinched. She realized with some embarrassment that she was leaking milk through the bodice of her dress, and rearranged the lace of her shawl. After Celia's birth, Greta had lived through the first six months in a blue haze of dislocation and melancholy, too tired to venture further than the house or garden, but never quite able to sleep. Yet from the morning after Benjamin's arrival she'd been filled with sympathy for the other mothers—expectant or delivered—who paced the walkways. She was adamant that these mothers must not spend these precious days at Fontmell in fear of a dreadful future. The answer lay in the soil. She closed her eyes and conjured up the smell of Benjamin's silky head, the milky dampness of his skin, the blurred blue of his eyes and the perfect rosy curve of his upturned lip. When she opened her eyes again, she realized the other women were watching her with some anxiety.

"We must do this," said Greta. She met Miss Hathaway's sharp gaze.

Miss Hathaway sighed, knowing when she'd been beaten. "Very well."

Château de Beaurepaire, January

———◦›•‹◦———

Henri arrived late in the afternoon. He'd hoped to arrive earlier, but the checkpoints had been interminable. He wished he'd brought a novel to while away the hours. When he finally arrived at the château, tired, cross and extremely hungry, it was to discover that luncheon was over, and worse than that, Albert was nowhere to be found. The general staff had vanished to attend to their duties, and a fire burned cozily in the deserted mess. A lone orderly tidied up the newspapers and rearranged the cushions on an ottoman.

"I think he's on leave, sir," said a staff sergeant manning the desk. "He went to visit his son."

"He has a son?" asked Henri, delighted.

A captain with the privilege of being Albert's tennis partner appeared and shook his head. "He's not gone to visit his son. He was ordered to the front. Left this morning."

Henri cursed under his breath. "Do you know when he will return?"

The captain shrugged. "Perhaps tonight. Maybe not for a week. He's been sent to division headquarters. You can catch up with him there. But you'll need a permit to travel to the British section of the front line, old chap."

Henri smiled. "Do you know to whom I must speak to obtain such a thing?"

The captain frowned, twitched his mustache. "I might. May I ask your name, monsieur? And the nature of your business?"

Henri turned and smiled charmingly at the young captain, who felt for a moment that the sun had appeared on an overcast day.

"My name is Henri Louis David Goldbaum. I'm afraid I cannot state my business to anyone but Monsieur Albert Goldbaum. But if you assist me in obtaining this permit to travel, I shall be in your debt. I am a good man to have in your debt, Captain."

He smiled again, and the captain quite forgot what he'd been busily doing before Monsieur Goldbaum required his help.

Western Front, Flanders, January

———◁•▷———

Albert loathed journeying to the front line—he was a day-tripper to hell. All through the motorcar ride the sense of guilt and shirking hypocrisy rose in his gut like heartburn. Back from the lines, it was bitterly cold and a hoarfrost clung thickly to the trees. A robin jealously guarded its scarlet hoard of holly berries. In the distance came the constant boom of the guns, disconnected and as bodiless as thunder. They passed troops walking the other way, returning for a fortnight's rest—a weary trudge, mud covered and spent, their faces blank, more surprised than relieved to still be alive. They were blasted in soil and muck, the glowing ends of their cigarettes and the pinkish whites of their eyes the only notes of color. The sergeant yelled at the men to salute the car from GHQ, and Albert cringed as they obeyed, slack-jawed and half-asleep.

They paused a mile back from the front line, where the support trenches began to furrow onward, and climbed out from the motor. Every half minute a lorry rattled up behind them and men hurried forward to unload supplies. Albert suspected his driver was lost. The roads were routinely destroyed in the bombardments and hastily rebuilt, but not necessarily in the same place. He didn't recognize anything in the obliterated landscape. Any remaining trees were burned and twisted, while a blackened ball of mistletoe swung like the disembodied head of a gorgon. Shells shrieked, and Albert cast about in surprise that they were so close. Then he realized they were starlings returning with the troops from the thick of it, having learned the song of war.

"Wait," Albert instructed the driver, and disappeared around the side of a ruined cottage to relieve himself.

As he fastened his fly, he observed the neat channels of the support trenches, each about the proportion of the allotments in the fields behind Fontmell. He strode a little closer, and to his surprise noted that at the rear some had been turned into little gardens. He saw tufts of winter parsnips and a vast white head of cauliflower. A company of infantrymen marched by the trench, and to his amusement they each saluted the cauliflower as they passed. In this decimated countryside, a massive cauliflower was the closest thing to a landmark. It seemed appropriate to Albert; after all, it was an army of gardeners and allotment keepers who had been sent to war.

A minute later they were off, the car bouncing around shell holes. They swerved to miss the corpse of a horse, too large for anyone to bury in the January ground. It had been left on the side of the track to rot, but remained preserved in the cold, its black coat gray with frost, its eyes pecked clean by crows.

They reached Cassel hill at dusk. Cassel was a pretty French town, unspoiled and cobbled with painted houses and cafés, which, in summer, must have spilled out onto the square. The army headquarters were in a modern building that had been a large casino before the war. The car drew up and Albert hurried in, almost at a run, aware of the papers in his pocket and the fact that he was late. The sergeant-at-arms pointed him toward a glasshouse in the grounds. Albert rushed along in the semidarkness, cursing the casino architect who had specified the slippery paving slabs. No one looked up as he entered; he drew an envelope out of his pocket and slid it across to the general, trying to listen to the conversation, but distracted by the darkening views across Flanders and the sweep to the Ypres salient and the southern country below. The sun was sinking below the horizon, and whether it was the last rays igniting the clouds or shellfire that he could see, Albert couldn't tell.

Trestle tables were spread with maps, and fog began to sneak in through the cracks between the windowpanes. They were listening to a meteorologist give a gloomy prognosis of the next week's weather—cold surrendering to rain and churning the ground into mud. As if to underscore his point, rain began to fall on the glass roof with a fearful clatter. Albert thought of the poor souls huddled below, cold and soggy, boots and toes moldering. You plant vegetables and seedlings underground, not men, he decided.

There was a flash of gunfire and then another, silent as lightning. He glanced along the grim faces of the generals; these were the gods, deciding the fate of the wretched mortals beneath. They shall decree the red lights in the sky, the rivers of horses and bloody men, the slick corpses in the muck, the ridges of Flanders that are to be captured. From up here the cost is great and small, spread out so far below. No wonder the drama of a single human life is the snapping of a matchstick. They are too high up to hear the bones break, to see the guts spill out, the grimy backwash of battle.

"Goldbaum," snapped General Harrison, "do you have something to add?"

"No, sir."

Albert longed to sit, but remained standing, half-listening and watching the cold fingers of fog reach their way inside. There was a knock at the door, and an uneasy sergeant cleared his throat.

"There's a Frenchman here to see Captain Goldbaum. Says it's urgent war business."

General Harrison glanced up in displeasure. "Bloody better be war business. Go!"

Albert followed the sergeant, slipping again on the wet path, feeling the raindrops slide beneath his collar. There, standing in the former gaming salon of the casino, was Henri. He lounged against a pillar, smoking a cigarette and looking as if he might be about to place a bet on blackjack or spin the roulette wheel. On seeing Albert, his face lit up with joy, and he took both his hands and embraced him.

"A son! What felicity among such madness." He conjured a pair of cigars and bottle of cognac from his pocket. "Here, let us sit."

Quickly he confided to Albert all he knew about the telegram, and deftly placed it into Albert's coat pocket.

"I am not fond of the Czech nationalists. Their Bohemian Alliance makes me uneasy, but so far their information has been good."

Albert nodded in agreement, touching his jacket pocket absently. The war had turned him into a courier of other men's secrets.

"You have a contact in Naval Intelligence?" asked Henri.

"I do. In London."

Henri groaned. "You must be due leave? When will they allow you to see your son?"

Albert sighed. "When they choose."

Henri sucked on his cigar, considering, while Albert drained his glass. After a moment Albert stood, resolved.

"Wait here," he told Henri.

Albert hurried back out to the glasshouse in the rain. The meeting had finished and he nearly collided with General Harrison.

"Slow down, Goldbaum!"

"My apologies, sir."

"Important war business resolved?"

"It wasn't war business, sir."

The general muttered an expletive. "You blasted Goldbaums! You use our communication lines like a mothers' gossip circle. Next time I'll make sure that permission to headquarters is refused for all your bloody relations."

"Yes, sir. I am sorry, sir, but my cousin came to tell me that my wife is poorly. She's not yet recovered from the birth of my son. I should very much like to see her, sir."

The general studied Albert, exasperated, but not without sympathy.

"I want you back here in a week or I'll have you court-martialed— Goldbaum or not."

"Yes, sir. I'm most grateful." He pressed the remains of the cognac into the general's hand. "In gratitude, sir."

Albert found Henri where he had left him. He seized his arm and steered him out of army headquarters.

"Henri, do you have a car?"

"Yes. My driver is waiting in the café on the square."

"Fetch him."

Ten minutes later Henri called to him from the back of a Delaunay-Belleville motorcar.

Albert climbed in beside him. "There's an airfield close to the front line," he said, barking out instructions in French to the driver, who raced through the dark streets at nearly twenty miles an hour. "Slow down!" called Albert. "We don't need an accident."

The tires made an awful noise against the cobbles and Albert's head began to throb. The driver took a corner too fast, and Albert slammed into Henri. He eased himself away and tried to look out of the window. Most of the villages were huddled in darkness. Here and there lights shone in a farmhouse, mostly ones taken over by the army.

Henri hummed and tried to make conversation. "How is your family? Your brother?"

"At Lake Geneva, with his mistress and daughter. The arrangement suits everyone. He can pretend to us that they don't exist, and we can pretend that we don't know that they do."

"One day such things won't matter," said Henri softly.

"But until then, we are grateful for Switzerland," said Albert. He did not waste time on days like these imagining beyond next week.

"Kiss Greta for me when you see her," said Henri.

"I shall do no such thing," said Albert. "I don't trust you in the least."

Henri laughed.

Lulled by the rhythm of the road, Albert fell asleep, waking only as they drew up outside the airfield. He opened his window and showed his papers to the guard on duty. It was dark, the stillness broken only by the far-off rattle of the guns. The guard returned after a few minutes and opened the barrier, waving them through. After he stopped the car, the driver raced round to open the doors for his two passengers. Albert and Henri stood on the silent airfield, glancing round at the half-dozen or so planes. A small shed stood at one end. Henri shivered. Albert drew his coat under his ears and walked quickly to the shed, Henri behind him. Albert opened the door and the smell of sweat, engine oil and sleeping bodies spilled out into the night air.

"Hello," called Albert. "I need *Goldfinch* made ready." He turned to Henri. "There's no need for you to wait."

Henri grinned. "Wouldn't miss it. I want to see you fly."

Albert shrugged. They sat for some time, finishing the brandy and watching as a pair of engineers pushed to the start of the little runway the airplane, a Sopwith Camel painted dark blue instead of army green, with small wooden struts separating the wings of the biplane, and a soaring goldfinch painted on the tip of each wing.

They waited until a watery dawn light began to seep along the edge of the sky. Albert stood and an engineer approached with Albert's leathers, hat and flying goggles. The two men shook hands and exchanged a few words. Henri watched as Albert climbed into the Sopwith and the engineers cranked the propellers.

"Don't fly too close to the sun," shouted Henri. Albert waved back cheerily, unable to hear over the din. It made an awful clatter and, Henri considered, it looked faintly comical as it trundled along the runway, like a novice bird fresh from the nest on a maiden flight. Then it was up and scrabbling toward the clouds, the orange light of dawn catching the gilding of the goldfinch on its wing and briefly transforming it into a blazing phoenix. He was relieved to have the telegram in his possession no longer and felt unimaginably lighter.

"Monsieur?" said an engineer, calling to him from the bunk shed.

Henri turned.

"We have a pilot returning to Paris in a two-seater. Would you like to join him?"

Henri smiled and then shrugged. "Why not," he said.

He glanced back up at the sky, but Albert's plane had gone. The sky was empty except for the tidal drift of the clouds.

Hampshire, January

⸺◈⸺

They quietly dropped the word "Finishing" from the Fontmell branch of Miss Hathaway's Gardening School for Women. Greta instructed that one of the potting sheds be transformed into a makeshift classroom, where they set up half a dozen chairs, and while Ursula or Winifred spoke about acidity and soil types or the effect of sea air there was rapt attention, accompanied by the rhythmic suckling of several babies. Greta wanted the classes to be practical and for the mothers to bring their babies along—to the kitchen gardens or the glasshouses for demonstrations on planting out seed potatoes or the propagation of sweet peas.

The take-up for the school was not what Greta had hoped for—they did not have space for whole families, and those women with other children vanished back to London as soon as they were declared fit, or very often before. She fretted about the fate of those who left, but there was little she could do. Often it seemed that no sooner had she learned their names than they had gone.

Greta watched in admiration as Joan and Bertha, a pair of young mothers from the East End, strapped their babies to their fronts, each using a shawl; she longed to try the same technique herself. She paused to admire the infants.

"A girl or boy?" she asked Joan.

"Girl," answered Joan.

"Your first?" asked Greta.

"The first to live," answered Joan.

Greta murmured her sympathies and retreated to sit on a bench in the cool January sunshine. She decided not to ask such casual questions again. Nanny brought her Benjamin for his midmorning feed, and Greta unbuttoned her blouse with creeping weariness. Her nipple was sore and chafed. She searched Benjamin's face for his father's, but she couldn't see it. Benjamin still had the coiled, unfinished look of a new infant. Nearly three weeks old and he still had not met his father. "Leave not granted" was all the telegrams stated. Albert was scrupulous about not calling in favors. "Busyness is better than loneliness," Greta rehearsed.

A rogue bramble wound its way along the struts of the bench, its prickles tiny and sharp, its leaves sugared with frost. From across the garden she spied Celia being led out by a nursery maid for her morning walk. She hesitated for a moment before calling out, too tired to play and longing to sit for a moment longer in the peace of the winter sunshine. Celia stopped to peer beneath a snowdrop, looking carefully under its petticoat, prodding at it with a stubby finger.

"Can you see the snowdrop's bloomers?" Greta called, and Celia jumped and, on seeing her mother, skipped over, chattering and hopping from foot to foot. To the nursemaid's dismay, she sneezed and wiped her nose along the back of her sheepskin mitten, leaving a shining trail of snot.

"Let's do watering, Mama."

"It's January, my darling. The plants aren't thirsty."

Celia eyed her mother contemptuously. "That's silly. Celia get water can."

She trotted off, returning a minute later with her painted watering can.

"You'll get frightfully wet," objected Greta.

Celia blinked up at her, indifferent to such irrelevant observations. She wanted to do watering at this very moment; there was no room for any other thought. Greta sighed and, handing Benjamin back to Nanny, accompanied Celia into one of the glasshouses.

"Let us check on the edelweiss."

Celia obediently dawdled beside her, dribbling a line of water from the spout of her watering can behind them and splashing it all over her button boots. She paused only to smash a snail with her heel.

"Bad snail," she said to the grisly remains, with considerable satisfaction.

"When did I teach you to be such a brute?" asked Greta.

Celia smiled. "Withers hates snails. Little bastards eat lettuce."

Greta made a note to discuss appropriate language with the garden staff, although she did have some sympathy with them. Celia had a remarkable talent for hearing and remembering things she ought not to. Greta led her daughter over to a bench where trays of edelweiss had been propagated from her single alpine specimen. She'd planted out some in the limestone rockery beside the terrace, but remained anxious in case it should be damaged by drought or pest, and kept some in the glasshouse to be nurtured, the seeds carefully collected and stored.

"Here," she instructed Celia, "sprinkle on a few drops of water. Not too many."

"Can I eat it?" asked Celia.

Greta shook her head, and Celia retired to hunt for wood lice among the flowerpots.

"Nancy said they is choppin' off a bit of Benjimmy's finger," said Celia.

Greta winced. Poor language overheard by the garden staff was one thing, gossip about Jewish customs by the nursery staff quite another.

"No one is chopping off Benjamin's finger," said Greta.

Celia looked disappointed. "But they is choppin' off something?" she asked hopefully.

"A rabbi will come and give Benjamin a tiny cut, and then we will have a little party."

Celia beamed. Greta hoped it was at the prospect of a party rather than at her brother's misfortune.

Lord and Lady Goldbaum's disapproval at the delay of Benjamin's *bris* had reached such heights of sighs and unhappiness that Greta felt she could not delay any longer. While planning the new season's herbaceous borders, Withers observed to her that shepherds trimmed lambs' tails when they were as young as possible, so that they felt less pain and quickly forgot. Greta wondered if perhaps it would be worse for poor Benjamin if they waited, so she reluctantly agreed to Lady Goldbaum's suggestion that the *mohel* attend later in the afternoon.

Celia was carefully tucking in the wood lice on a bed of straw, complaining as they scuttled out from under their covers, refusing to stay put for a story. She flicked one in angry retribution.

"Stay a-bed, lous-ey. Do what you're bloomin' told."

"That's not very kind, Celia."

Celia blinked at her, eyes round with distaste.

"Wood lice aren't really insects at all," said Greta half to herself. "Daddy would tell you that they're land shrimps. A miniature marvel."

The edelweiss safely watered, and the surviving wood lice tucked in, Greta steered Celia up to the nursery for her rest before the festivities. A little later she stood in her dressing room, with Anna lacing her into a tea dress, trying to conceal her soft stomach. Greta felt a shiver of dread crawl up her spine like a draft of cold air. This was supposed to be a celebration of Benjamin's covenant with God, but did it have to be marked with a tiny act of barbarism and blood? This, she realized, was why the baby's father was supposed to be here. A father would not suffer from such nervous sentimentality. The cut was nothing, a mere pruning of dead wood—no worse than the snipping of last year's withered hydrangea heads or the browning petals of a rose.

She wore a dark dress, so that if her breasts leaked when Benjamin cried, it could not be seen. From habit, she sprayed herself with scent— gardenia—and selected a shawl. She had never dressed so miserably for a party. She felt a cramp deep inside her belly, like the clenching of a fist, and then a rush of blood between her legs, soaking through her underclothes as her womb contracted.

Lord and Lady Goldbaum greeted their guests with warmth and enthusiasm. Among the family and friends were scattered a dozen wounded officers who were staying at Temple Court during their recuperation. They understood that an invitation to such an event showed great attention, and they wore their dress uniforms along with uneasy expressions, uncertain what to expect. Greta drifted among them, Benjamin clutched tightly in her arms. From across the room she eyed the *mohel* with distaste. He spoke with earnest dignity to the family rabbi and smiled at Greta with warmth. She nodded, but did not move to speak with him. She felt sick and had nothing to say.

"He's going to be quite all right, dearest," said Lady Goldbaum, appearing at her side. "I went through it with both my boys. The mother suffers more than the child, I promise you."

"How do you know?" asked Greta.

"I remember. They don't."

"Have you asked them whether they've suffered since?"

"Well, no," agreed Lady Goldbaum, coloring at the outlandish suggestion. "But it doesn't seem likely. And, my dear, I should have thought you'd be more able to answer that question than me."

Albert had certainly never voiced a complaint, and she had noticed nothing untoward. Not that she had any point of comparison.

"Benjamin will cry for a moment, and then it will be over," continued Lady Goldbaum.

"Let's get it over with, then," said Greta.

Lady Goldbaum signaled to her husband, who crossed the room and, with great tenderness, took his grandson in his arms.

"I'll take excellent care of him," he said gently.

Greta did not reply. There was a lump in her throat and she could not speak. Lady Goldbaum took her by the arm and led her away into the Blue Drawing Room. Ladies were not present for the circumcision itself. Greta perched on the sofa, then stood and circled the room, picking up priceless knickknacks and putting them down again. She held an exquisitely jeweled box that she had not seen before and then shoved it back.

"It's a reliquary box, supposedly containing a shard of the Cross. It was sent by the Pope for Benjamin. It's the traditional gift sent at the birth of a king," said Lady Goldbaum.

"An interesting choice for a Jew," said Greta archly, trying to smile and failing.

Lady Goldbaum glided over to the drinks trolley and poured her a brandy. Greta took it, swallowed it in one gulp and handed her glass back to Lady Goldbaum. Outside the window, rain began to fall, a fine misting that gave way to fog, blowing in from the Solent and concealing the white cyclamens and low hedges of the parterre. A filmy towel of fog hid a naked Aphrodite bathing in one of the fountains, so that it appeared as if she were coyly drying herself.

A footman appeared at the door.

"It is done, madam," he announced.

Greta pushed past him and ran along the East Gallery to the saloon where the deed had been performed, hearing Benjamin's howl. She snatched her son from Lord Goldbaum and clutched him to her, noting the tiny spot of crimson on his gown.

"It's all right, my darling," she said.

She plucked uselessly at her clothing, unable to reach her bosom through the complicated pleats of her tea dress. Nanny appeared with a bottle, but Benjamin was red faced and furious, outraged and wriggling and quite unable to eat.

"Let me take him," said Nanny, perfectly calm and matter-of-fact.

Greta held him away from her. "No, thank you."

She rested him against her shoulder, rubbing his back and whispering to him as he trembled and sobbed. The guests toasted and drank champagne, looking with sympathy toward poor Benjamin.

"Adelheid, I'm going to take him somewhere quiet for a minute," said Greta.

The footman opened the door and Greta hastened out. She jiggled the baby, smoothing her face against his hot cheek, aware of a figure at the other end of the gallery. It took her a moment to realize who it was.

"Albert," she said, helpless with joy, sweat patches and roses of leaking milk blooming on her dress.

He walked swiftly toward her, stopping at her side to examine the small and furious baby. He reached out and stroked his cheek, and Benjamin bucked and screamed, red from his toes to his scalp.

"He's such a good boy," she said defensively. "He never cries."

She hadn't wanted Albert to meet his son like this. She felt like crying herself. But, perfectly calm and unperturbed, Albert lifted him out of her arms. Benjamin was promptly and thoroughly sick on his shoulder and then, exhausted, went to sleep.

In the Clouds Above Ypres, January

—⋙•⋘—

Henri had imagined that being up in the Bristol would be more like the flight of a bird, the noiseless drift of a gull or kite, but in front of him was the engine, and its roar and clatter made his ears hurt. He felt the rattle in his teeth and throat like the dentist's drill. Beyond the battle, Henri observed the flatness of the land and then the shimmering marshes and the narrow roads like pencil lines, the glow of the sun on the reddish roof tiles. The plane turned again—the pilot taking a winding path, for safety—back toward the front. There was an awesome magnificence to war from this height, the jewel-like flames glittering against the charcoal wasteland.

Henri noticed a squadron of half a dozen other machines approaching, and he waved and felt a childish stab of glee when one of the gunners in the other craft waved back. He looked again and saw a pair of German Fokkers rising skyward, the friendly Nieuports maneuvering into position to fire upon them. The pilot of his own plane banked sharply and turned away from the looming scuffle, but, craning round, Henri saw an arc of flame from a Nieuport's tracer round, and then, to his horror, he saw the other Fokker close behind, in his own pilot's blind spot. He yelled and yelled, but the pilot couldn't hear. He craned forward to hammer on his shoulder but, fastened into his seat, couldn't reach him. The pilot glanced round and, seeing the enemy plane, banked sharply again, so that Henri was initially forced back into his seat and then, a moment later, nearly hurled out of it. He clung on, gripping the belt and screaming, his voice lost among the howl of the engine and the racket of the surrounding machine guns.

He saw the moment his pilot was hit. Blood flowered instantly like a red rose on his cheek, streaming down and soaking his jacket. Yet, somehow, he managed to carry on flying. The plane zigzagged like a blackbird stunned from colliding with a windowpane, aiming for behind the French lines. For a moment it seemed they would make it. Then, as Henri watched, the pilot leaned forward, lower and lower over the controls. The nose of the plane sank, and then, with an explosion of earth and a plume of flames and mud, they crashed.

Hands were yanking him from the wreckage, dragging him out of the fire. He heard German voices. "Leave the pilot. He's dead. This one isn't a soldier. If he's a spy, we shoot him."

"Please don't," said Henri, aiming for German, but feeling dazed and uncertain whether he spoke French or even English. "I'm not a spy. I'm a civilian."

"British?"

"French."

They pulled him away from the plane and he felt himself being passed from one set of arms to another, and then fumbled down and down into what, he realized, was a dugout. Hands unceremoniously grabbed and shoved at him, and shakily he tried to stand, but his legs gave way and he slumped down next to an ammunition box. A Prussian officer scrutinized him.

"Name? Rank? Occupation?"

Henri coughed, hoping to gain a little time to think, and dissolved into a choking fit, signaling for water. He was roughly passed a canteen. He sipped, shaking and spilling some.

"Henri. Goldbaum," he said at last.

He fixed his gaze upon the Prussian officer who appeared to be in charge of the ragged band of men. He wore a field-gray uniform, the collar of his greatcoat pulled up against the cold. Between straight white teeth he clenched a pipe. The airplane crash had clearly taken them by surprise, because glancing about, Henri saw a makeshift table laid with breakfast and, to his intrigue, a copy of the *Daily Mail*. He studied the pips on the officer's cap.

"Leutnant—" Henri began.

"Oberleutnant," the officer corrected.

"*Oberleutnant*," said Henri, hoping wildly, "I wonder whether you have heard of my cousins. Edgar Goldbaum? Otto Goldbaum?" He cursed under his breath, realizing he must be slightly concussed, for Otto was far away, on another front.

The officer stared at him with dubious hostility. "I know nothing of French prisoners."

Henri shook his head, and regretted it. His vision was blurred, and bloody rain drifted in the corner of his left eye. "No, German officers." He wished he could recall which division.

The Oberleutnant studied Henri with more interest.

He had doubtless been told where his cousins were serving—Baron Jacques sent the German family messages via Clement in Switzerland. Henri tried to remember something about them, anything. Edgar was moral and clever. He was a chess player to rival Clement, lacking only his cousin's fanaticism. Such a mind must be useful to the German staff.

"Edgar Goldbaum is a staff officer. At Spa," he added, feeling that it was likely to be true.

The Oberleutnant summoned a soldier. "Gefreiter, send a message up to division headquarters that we have a French prisoner. Henri Goldbaum. Possibly a spy."

Henri closed his eyes. He wondered if they would shoot him.

The Oberleutnant, apparently sensing his thoughts, cleared his throat and said, "We don't shoot spies. We hang them."

He offered Henri a cigarette. Although he rarely smoked, Henri accepted it and, as the Oberleutnant struck a match, wondered whether his driver had reached Paris. The cook at the Esther Château would be preparing a light luncheon of venison and endive salad for Henri and the finance minister. He had ordered a chocolate-and-clementine mousse for dessert—the minister's favorite—to soften unhappy tidings regarding the latest offering of government bonds, along with a twenty-year-old bottle of muscat, a glorious honeyed amber. He wondered when the minister would realize that his host was not coming, and whether he would still open the muscat.

For the first few days they watched him with hostile suspicion, but Henri was polite and solicitous and had a seemingly endless supply of increasingly filthy jokes. And after all, he pointed out, where could he run? The only question, if he attempted an escape across no-man's-land, was who would shoot him first: the Germans or the British. Deciding that he posed little risk, the company relaxed, mostly ignoring him.

The Gunners liked to play cards or gamble—on anything and everything: flea bites on a right leg; the number of corpses they could count from a vantage point; who would be next to join them, and by what injury. Henri helped to calculate the odds, and kept the pool. "We can trust him," said Helmut, the leader of the Gunners. "After all, if he cheats, we shoot him." Henri agreed that this indeed was a worthy incentive.

It was the incessant noise that he couldn't bear. His ears rang even during the brief times the bombardment stopped. He heard it in his dreams and suspected that, should he ever be freed, he would hear it always, as though his very thoughts had been bombed.

Every day, at least twice, he asked Stefan, the Oberleutnant, or Frank, another junior officer, "When am I to be sent to the prisoner-of-war camp?" But there was never an answer, only a shrug. Henri realized that by this stage of the war a lone Frenchman lost in a German trench was of very little interest to anyone.

On the eighth day of his capture, Stefan and Helmut yelled at

Henri to get moving. They were taking him to battalion headquarters in the valley. Henri scrambled upright and helplessly combed his fingers through his hair. He caught a glimpse of himself on the mirrored base of a mess tin and, wincing, realized that he looked like exactly what he was: a disheveled, hungry prisoner of war, red eyed and unshaven. Although Helmut and Stefan had donned their helmets with some care, no one thought to lend him one. But then, Henri supposed, a stray sniper bullet through his skull would save the Germans some inconvenience.

They walked quickly and low, aware that the British front line was less than a hundred yards from their own. Helmut swore that sometimes at night, during a lull, he could hear the snores of the British Tommies. The reserve section was six hundred yards behind the front through the skeleton of a wood, the pine trees white and blasted, while here and there bodies of the fallen lay among the shell holes. Revolted, Henri did his best not to look. He tried not to think of Claire. Bodies are alike in death; they slouch back into the dirt and earth, wet and squalid. He blinked and for a moment saw her lying in her pale nightdress propped against a tree, her belly swollen.

The wood was in a valley, and beyond the ruins of the trees, where the heaviest of the fighting had been, soldiers had constructed a garden. They had dragged the tops of blasted pines and replaced them in the soil. Primroses had been dug up and replanted in clusters of buttered yellow, the smooth glow against the gray startling in its beauty. There were drifts of snowdrops and here and there a hawthorn, the first hints of blossoms starting to unfurl like tiny hands. A small stream wound its way through the middle and someone had built a series of wooden dams and toy watermills, so that it appeared as if a child's miniature pleasure garden had been conjured amid the chaos a hundred yards beyond. Even in war, it seemed, men needed a garden.

They continued for half a mile to battalion headquarters in the ruins of a château. Stefan gave their names to the sentry on duty. The sentry returned with another officer, this time with the scarlet pips of general staff, who led them into the principal salon of the manor, where half a dozen officers sat around tables in their coats and scarfs, drinking coffee and conducting earnest discussions in low tones. A fire burned feebly in the grate. Henri saw that the glass in the windows had all been blown out and had been boarded up to keep out the draft. He wondered if he was here to be tried and shot and, if so, how his father would discover the news.

"Henri?"

He turned and, with a maelstrom of relief, saw Edgar Goldbaum. His cousin looked grayer and drawn. If he still wore his yarmulke, it was hidden beneath his Leutnant's hat. Henri stepped forward to embrace him, but, observing Edgar give a tiny shake of his head, faltered and stopped short.

"Edgar! You truly are a sight for sore eyes," he said in French.

"You have been treated well?" said Edgar, loudly and in German.

"With great kindness," said Henri, changing to German, with a glance at Stefan, who relaxed a little.

"Come," said Edgar, "sit. Have coffee. They told me you had been captured."

"Yes. It was unfortunate. Next time I'm offered a ride in a plane, I shall refuse and take the car. Even a bicycle."

"A bicycle to Paris would take some time."

"Yes, but at least I'd get there. Well, whatever happens one way or another, I suppose the Goldbaums will be on the winning side," he said.

"And the losing one," replied Edgar, his voice sharp.

They perched opposite one another on a pair of dilapidated sofas, matching in stripes and rosettes of vivid mold. Henri accepted the weak and bitter coffee with a gratitude he would not have recognized little more than a week ago. They stirred their coffee and sipped, grateful for something to do with their hands, awkward and uncertain what to say, aware that everyone in the room was listening avidly while pretending not to. The two men studied one another surreptitiously, conscious of the absurdity of their position.

Henri couldn't help thinking of the last time they had met, at the Esther Château, for what had turned out to be the last gathering of the family. He hardly remembered speaking with Edgar. He found him tedious and mercurial and he did not drink—a grave black mark with Henri in those days. And then Claire had died and he remembered little else about the gathering. He realized Edgar was surveying him with concern.

"I am sorry that there is so little I can do for you," said Edgar. "I am not sure that we will even be permitted to meet again. It took some pulling of strings to arrange even this. I'm only a Leutnant, after all."

Henri leaned forward and said quietly, "You are the partner of one of the largest banks in Berlin. Why are you only a Leutnant? Surely you ought to be a captain or an Oberleutnant at the least?"

Edgar gave a rueful smile. "I'm a Jew. I'm considered lucky to be an officer at all." He gave an anxious glance around the room, checking that he had not been overheard.

Henri gave a sad laugh. "Every Tuesday, as a boy, I would take tea with my grandmother, who gave me macaroons and taught me the conversational niceties of every social occasion I might encounter. Alas, this once I find myself unprepared."

Edgar nodded but said nothing. Henri smiled inwardly; his cousin was notoriously parsimonious and did not like even to waste words.

"Will you tell my father I am alive? And let him know if anything happens?"

"It is still so cold. Almost as cold as Switzerland," said Edgar.

Henri understood. Edgar would send a message to Clement, and Clement would pass it to Jacques. Let it simply be that he had been captured, and nothing worse.

They said good-bye with an affection and regret that previously neither would have thought possible.

Hampshire, February

———⬥⭕⬥———

Greta had longed for Albert for months, imagining ghastly deaths and worrying that he'd never meet his son. He insisted on flying himself home in his wretched plane—he claimed for convenience, but Greta suspected it was to even up the odds of dying. Albert didn't like to feel he was shirking risk, however pointless. Yet from the moment he returned home again, this time for a fortnight's leave, and she had the joy of him in her arms, he irritated her. Since the start of the war he had been away so long and so often that they had rebuilt the family without him, like a house losing a wall in a storm and repaired in a different shape.

But Albert expected everything to alter with his arrival, to revert to how it used to be. He wanted Greta to take coffee with him in the snug, as had been their habit, and he did not wish to discover her among the women in the servants' hall, her grimy gardening apron still fastened about her waist, Benjamin asleep on her lap with a confetti of cookie crumbs in his hair, while the room rang with unruly laughter. To make the outrage worse, all the women turned round to stare at him when he entered, as though it was he who was the intruder. He wished the world to have paused, waited for his return like statues in a children's game of grandmother's footsteps. But they had crept forward when he wasn't looking. He found himself irrationally put out that Celia had grown; he longed to take her into his arms and chide her for not staying as she was, for having lost the marshmallow pudge around her wrists and cheeks. War had torn from him lumps of her childhood and he resented it.

Albert was pleased with his son, spending whole half hours with Benjamin on his knee in his study, reading him aloud columns from the *Times* with the news from France, but found himself perfectly content to hand him back to Greta, confessing that until Benjamin could bring him ladybirds and Red Admirals from the garden like his clever Celia, he didn't have much use for him.

"But he's so beautiful," objected Greta.

"Yes," agreed Albert, not looking up from his paper. "A finer fellow never existed. But he's not interesting. Not yet."

Greta, while knowing intellectually that Albert was correct, nonetheless took offense on Benjamin's behalf.

"I don't want to go to London," said Greta stubbornly.

"It will do you good," said Albert.

She had repeatedly remonstrated against traveling, but Albert insisted. The London house had been given over to a hospital for the wounded, so they were to take a suite at the Savoy, while Benjamin and Celia remained at home in the nursery. Greta fretted over leaving Benjamin, but Nanny assured her that he would be perfectly well. A wet nurse would walk up from the village—Albert refused to believe that the new artificial milk formula was an improvement on nature. Greta, however, refused to believe that a hired nipple belonging to a village drudge would be as nourishing as a mother's own milk, but here again Albert objected. He remembered a time in the county when redheaded wet nurses could not find work, their milk being feared as pap of the devil. He was impatient with such superstition and would not tolerate it in his wife. Greta tried to explain that her reluctance was not superstition (she objected to fair, dark and redheaded wet nurses equally), but simply due to her desire to nurse her baby herself. The thought of Benjamin attached to another woman's breast filled her with a kind of revulsion, and a surge of jealousy so sharp that she felt it inside her as a physical pain.

For his part, as he watched his wife slice open an invitation card with a silver knife using considerably more force than the task required, Albert was glad he had returned home on leave. It was clear to him that his parents were quite unable to govern his wife. He adored Greta, and mostly her Continental eccentricities amused and endeared her to him, but in such times as these, limits must be set. He was gratified that Greta took such an interest in the children, but the interest had to be moderated by her obligations to her other duties. A few nights in town would remind her of her role as a wife. Her protests bewildered him. She could not remain tied to the infant for six months or a year—she was a Goldbaum, not a milking cow. She would nurse Benjamin when she was at home and when it was convenient to her. He did not acknowledge that it was rather when it was convenient to him.

The suite at the Savoy was the one Greta had stayed in for the days before her wedding, and she half-wondered whether her old resentment had seeped into the fabric of the room and now released itself into the air like ether, because she prickled with cold fury toward her husband. She wanted to be in her own home with her children, the hospital and the Hathaway gardening women—those were her true concerns, not the interests that Albert demanded of her. Anna had laid out her evening dress, and when Greta saw the butterfly choker gleaming in its box on the dresser, she shoved it under a pillow. She would not wear it. She took a hot lavender bath, expressing milk into the water, wondering if Cleopatra's biographers had it all wrong, and it was not asses' milk in which she had bathed, but her own.

After she had dressed, Albert came to collect her from her room, watching her from the doorway. She continued the theater of her toilet, spraying perfume and adjusting the rubies in her ears, each as small and round as a drop of blood. She saw him behind her in the mirror, in his splendid dress uniform sporting the red tabs of the general staff. It might have been tailored to the perfect fit, but to Greta it seemed that he was playing dress-up. Albert was not a soldier, despite appearances to the contrary.

"You have roses in your cheeks. Shall I fasten your necklace?" he asked.

Greta gestured to a box on the dresser. Albert opened it.

"Where is the butterfly?"

"It's too much for a Tuesday night," she said roughly, meaning to wound him. "I wouldn't want to seem vulgar."

"Perhaps you're right," he said with a note of regret, as though something he'd longed for had not come to pass, and instantly she felt guilty. It was not Albert's fault that he had disrupted things, and she was glad to see him. For an awful moment she thought she might cry, a muddled rush of tears and gloom that pounced on her most days. She turned to him, her eyes wide with love and unfallen tears, and smiled.

"I really am glad you're home."

He leaned forward and, brushing a strand of hair from her neck, kissed a line from her ear to her throat, tickling her. He fastened the necklace, the diamonds as clear and smooth as raindrops.

"Come on, darling, it will be pleasant to be in town and to have nothing to do for a few days but amuse ourselves," said Albert. "Benjamin will be just as content with Nanny. He won't even know the difference."

Her anger returned in an instant like the lighting of a lamp.

"We mustn't be late," she said, and stood abruptly.

"Very well," said Albert, a little surprised. Greta rarely cared about punctuality. He offered her his arm, but she did not take it.

The palm-filled dining room of the Savoy Grill was brimming with officers on leave, desperate to listen to the band play ragtime and drink gin cocktails till they were drunk. Sailing alongside them, like dreadnoughts among fishing boats, were the regular patrons of the Savoy, generals and brigadiers with the red pips of the general staff, denoting both seniority and safety. These, Albert whispered to Greta, were the old chaps who retired after the Boer War and who couldn't quite believe their luck in enjoying one last jolly war, even if they were missing out on all the fun at the front and the chance to bag a few Boches.

Greta and Albert sat at their table sipping champagne, while every few minutes—or so it seemed to Greta—Albert rose to his feet to salute one man or another.

"Goodness, it's rather ridiculous, isn't it? Can't we go somewhere else tomorrow, where you'll be less of a jack-in-the-box?" she complained.

Albert shrugged. "It's all right. It's the poor buggers back from the front that I feel sorry for. Every time one of them salutes me, I feel more of a fraud than ever."

Struck by his confidence, Greta put out her hand to take Albert's and then, deciding she was still too cross, started to withdraw without touching him.

"No you don't," he said, seizing her hand and holding it fast and stroking her knuckles through her glove.

"You despise public affection, Albert."

"Haven't you heard there's a war on?"

Greta relented and gave a small smile. The chandeliers were reflected into infinity in the silvered mirrors, and cigarette smoke hung like a veil of evening mist. Waiters in long white aprons hurried between tables bedecked with towering vases of bird-of-paradise, squeezing between the palm fronds. The noise of the dining room was like a parrot's cage, and the whirling women in their feathers and finery were reminiscent of the preening birds. Greta saw many faces that she recognized, but no one came to speak to them.

"Isn't that Lady Dorchester?" asked Albert.

Greta looked. "Yes, I think so."

"She's been to stay with us more than half a dozen times, but she doesn't come over?"

"She will in a minute, when she realizes you're with me."

Sure enough, a thin middle-aged lady with a headdress formed from a waterfall of ostrich feathers glanced in their direction, her expression rigid as her eye passed over Greta, but on seeing Albert, she smiled and sashayed over.

"Here she comes. She'll want a donation to one of her charities," said Greta.

"Greta, Albert, what a delight!"

They greeted her politely and spoke for a few minutes, asking with trepidation about one another's family, unwilling to hear more bad news. As Lady Dorchester sauntered to another table, Albert turned to his wife. "No one comes over when you lunch alone?"

Greta gave a little sigh of exasperation. "No, darling. No one. I'm one of the enemy, you see."

"I quite forgot."

"I'm afraid I can't. Now do you see why London holds little charm for me?"

He stared gloomily into his glass and did not answer. When he spoke, it was half to himself. "By now, what will winning mean? Whoever does so will win a broken world."

He looked so desolate that, despite her annoyance, Greta reached out and brushed his cheek with her fingertips. He smiled at her, but it was the tight, forlorn smile given once hope has gone.

Later that night Greta hadn't the heart to lock her door. She listened with pleasure and dread for the sound of Albert entering her room. A little after midnight, she felt him slide into her bed.

"Are you asleep?" he whispered.

It would have been easier to pretend that she was, but Greta whispered back, "No."

He reached out for her and, tentative, unsure of his reception, eased closer and kissed her. He tasted of brandy and there was familiarity in his warmth and the solidity of his body. For months she had lain awake, alone and trying to picture his narrow room in France with its camp bed and small, high window. She was grateful of course that he was not serving at the front—*she* had no qualms about that—but the effect of the separation was similar. Their easy intimacy had been lost, one of the small but not insignificant bodiless things sacrificed in the pursuit of victory. Albert had metamorphosed into a temporary stranger. She found she was unsure of him. The smell of his skin was both the same and different. He stroked the soft down on her thigh with the pad of his thumb and then, moving firmly and gently upward, he started to lift her nightgown. Greta flinched.

"No, darling. I'm sorry."

"Oh, is it one in three?" he asked.

Greta had confided, to his great amusement, her mother's advice as to how to manage husbands in bedroom negotiations.

"No, it's too soon after Benjamin. I'm sore. I need more time to heal," she said.

"Of course. How thoughtless of me," he said, turning away.

"Soon, darling, soon," she lied, clasping his hand, glad he could not see her in the dark.

Greta did not want another child. The prospect of giving birth again filled her with cold dread. She thought of the tiny new graves in the ancient churchyard. She had survived twice, and so had both her children. She would not risk her luck running out. Making love with Albert was a blissful indulgence, a pleasure she had not known to anticipate, but she would not risk orphaning her children because she took great enjoyment in lying with her husband. She would not, she could not. Albert assured her that his position in the army was safe, but it was war—no soldier was safe. He was compelled to risk his life; she did not have to risk hers. At present she considered the prospect of intimate relations an act of absolute selfishness.

She glanced across at him and saw he was wide-awake, too restless and aroused to sleep. Greta sighed. When they had first started lying together, Albert had tried his best to avoid planting his seed inside her, but she suspected that it had been mostly luck that she hadn't fallen pregnant. She knew of only one absolutely effective method to prevent making a baby: to abstain from all marital relations. Albert would be hurt and appalled. Troubled, she lay awake, feeling him hot and sleepless in the dark, turning over and over beside her.

When she woke the next morning, she was alone. After breakfast, she declined the car and sauntered along Piccadilly to her appointment at Lock of St. James's. Greta's interest in fashion was moderate. The kind of dresses she longed to wear were out of the question, and everything else was a dreary second best, which she chose quickly and with little interest. But she was fond of hats. She didn't want swaths of palm leaves, or to look as if she'd emerged from a jungle with part of it still attached, like Lady Goldbaum. She wanted the milliner to use her favorite plants as inspiration.

When she arrived at the shop, she saw that her dicentra hat had been placed in the center of the window. It had a broad brim trimmed in white, with a slash of cherry painted geometrically across the crown, and was adorned with velvet blooms of split dicentra hearts, with pale tongues fashioned in silk. It was elegant, striking and playful. It was the perfect hat.

"I adore it, Mrs. Paulson. You're a genius," she said as she pushed open the door.

"Oh, I'm so pleased, Mrs. Goldbaum," said a plump and pretty woman, coming out from behind the counter. She wore her hair in a neat bun, the exact size and shape of the pincushion beside her order book. "I hoped you wouldn't mind, my putting it in the window, but it's quite the nicest hat I've ever made."

"I don't mind. Such beauty must be shared, especially now."

"Of course everyone wanted one. But I wouldn't make another the same. The other hats only pay 'omage, as it were."

"Oh dear," said Greta.

Mrs. Paulson's pleasant face creased into anxiety. "Have I done something wrong, Mrs. Goldbaum? You always said, before, that imitation was flattery or some such."

"Yes, but they didn't know who they were imitating?"

Mrs. Paulson shook her head. "And I've had three ladies each day asking about it."

"I'm afraid I'm not very popular at the present," said Greta with a little shake of her head.

She spent the next half hour very pleasantly inspecting all the new creations, particularly pleased with Celia's cloche hat, which had been dyed to look like a cloudy sky and had tiny swifts stenciled on top. As she was preparing to leave, the bell jangled and another customer entered. A tall and elegant woman wearing a heavy brown hat, which reminded Greta of a field mushroom, ignored Greta and sailed straight up to the counter.

"The Duchess of Grosvenor said that everyone is talking about a hat with fuchsias on it."

"Dicentra. They're not part of the Fuchsia family. They belong to the Fumariaceae family," said Greta, smiling.

The woman turned to look at Greta and frowned, disapproving, on hearing Greta's accent. "The Fumariaceae family. Never heard of them. Are they from Scotland?"

Mrs. Paulson saved Greta from a reply. "I'm afraid I've had to pack up the hat, Mrs. Jarvis. The lady who ordered it is come to collect."

Mrs. Jarvis looked again at Greta, who smiled once more. It took Mrs. Jarvis a moment, and then, finally recognizing Greta and her understanding dawning, she flinched.

"Mrs. Goldbaum has kindly said that she doesn't mind if I make something similar for other customers. She's inspired half the hats in London for next season," said Mrs. Paulson with a hint of pride.

Mrs. Jarvis shook her head vigorously, the mushroom puff wobbling. "No, thank you. I shall have something quite different."

Greta studied the other woman, knowing that she was silently thanking her lucky stars for her escape, tingling for the moment she could gleefully inform the Duchess of Grosvenor and a dozen others that they had gleaned their style from the infamous Greta Goldbaum, a Jew and a *German*. They never did remember that she was born in Austria. Greta rather worried that poor Mrs. Paulson would be busy until Michaelmas, picking apart hats and remaking them.

"Tell them not to worry," said Greta serenely to Mrs. Jarvis. "I'm rarely invited to anything anymore."

Mrs. Jarvis departed on a hastily remembered errand, leaving Greta and an embarrassed Mrs. Paulson alone in the shop. After instructing Mrs. Paulson to wrap all her purchases ready for the car to collect them, Greta decided to walk back to the hotel along Piccadilly. She passed streams of soldiers at home on leave, officers and men, all with the same dazed expression, many of them younger than herself. How could anyone imagine that she—a mother—whether born in Austria or not, would wish harm on these poor fellows? True, she longed for similar protection for Austrian and German soldiers. She could never quite manage to call them "the enemy," even in her own mind. Here in town, her loneliness wrapped itself close about her until she couldn't breathe. She imagined that everyone looked at her with dislike and suspicion, even strangers.

Glancing into a mews off the street, she saw a pair of elderly kitchen porters sharing a cigarette. She turned and hastened over to them.

"Would you mind?" she asked.

Stupefied, one of them passed her a cigarette.

"And a light, if you would," said Greta, placing it between her lips.

Slack-jawed, he lit it. Calling her thanks over her shoulder, Greta strolled back onto Piccadilly. Smoking a cigarette in the street, Greta didn't think she had ever done anything so lewd, so gauche. She wanted to laugh. She wanted someone to see her. There was no pleasure in performing such an act if one wasn't caught. All that could make it worse would be if she were hatless. With a flick, she removed her hat—last season's Ascot—and tossed it away. To her great satisfaction, she noticed Lord Parnicott driving past in a cab. She waved. At least when they whisper about me now, they will have something to say, she decided. She took another pull on her cigarette.

Albert walked to his appointment along the Thames, inhaling the cold air. Soon, Greta had said, soon. Knowing that he couldn't lie with her made him want her even more. The dampness of her skin, the curve of her back. It was unbearable—he was tormented by desire for his wife. He hummed with frustration. He longed to kiss her, lips soft and slightly chapped, the slight dimples like matching commas at the base of her spine, her full and rounded bottom. He pictured licking the creases in the arch of her instep while she laughed, complaining that he was tickling her. Twists of smoke daubed the clouds, dirtying them. The river was busy with boatmen, the surface of the water threaded with mist. Frost glinted on the stonework along the embankment, and in the bare chestnut trees along the pavement, someone had written names of the dead upon scraps of paper and threaded them from the branches so that they hung there, spiraling in the light.

To his surprise, Albert was shown into the dusty, unremarkable office of Admiral Sir William Reginald Hall himself. The admiral was small and ruddy-cheeked and he blinked steadily at Albert, in no hurry at all, with the shining self-confidence and authority of a man with a gold stripe on the arm of his uniform. He sat comfortably in his leather chair, but left Albert standing.

"Some weeks ago, Captain Goldbaum, you delivered a telegram in code to one of my colleagues."

"Yes, sir. I gave it to Nigel de Gray. He's an old friend from school."

The admiral continued to watch him, his blue eyes blinking, tufts of white hair around his bald head like the fluff of a dandelion-seed clock.

"And what do you know of the telegram, Captain?"

"What do you know, sir?"

The admiral chuckled. "We'll come to that." He sat and opened a box of cigars, first offering one to Albert, who declined, and then helping himself. "We had hoped that the German declaration of unrestricted submarine warfare would bring in America."

"It might," said Albert. "They've cut off diplomatic relations with Berlin. I've heard the German ambassador is to be sent packing."

"Yes, but that is all they will do. Wilson thinks that's enough. He's shown the Germans that he disapproves. The pride of the American people is satisfied."

"And he still won't allow the American banks to extend our credit," said Albert, frowning. "My father tells me that the pound teeters on the brink. The moment the Americans stop accepting government credit, we shan't be able to pay our soldiers, or the Americans themselves for grain or cotton. The ultimate weapon isn't the machine gun or barbed wire or the new tank, but money. And the Americans appear to have it all," he added, with an arch look.

Admiral Hall sucked on his cigar. Although Albert was a captain supplicant before an admiral, a minnow flicking its tail before a pike, there was nothing submissive about him. He met the admiral's eye like a captain of finance, not of the general staff.

"There are those on our side in America," said the admiral. "The moral chaps who want to join the fight for honor and justice, but also those chaps at the Federal Reserve who worry that they've lent us a staggering amount of money, and that the only way to make sure *they* get it back is to make sure *we* win."

"I like both those sorts of chaps. Anything we can do to give them a helpful nudge?"

"We're rather hoping that the contents of your telegram might just do it. Bring 'em in at last. If it's real, of course," said Admiral Hall.

"And is it?" asked Albert, interested.

"Perhaps. But we'd like you to furnish us with a few more details."

The admiral listened as Albert repeated what little he knew: that it had been given to Henri by members of the Bohemian Alliance.

"You can verify all this from Henri, of course. Wire him in Paris," Albert suggested.

"I fear that won't do any good. He's missing, I'm afraid. Plane was shot down. Dead, most likely. Very sorry, thought you knew."

From his tone, it was clear that the admiral had not expected Albert to know any such thing. Albert sat down on a low wooden chair unthinkingly, even though he had not been given permission. He stared at the admiral. He had to return to the hotel and tell Greta at once. The thought made him feel sick.

"Was there anything else I could help with, sir?"

The admiral scrutinized him and said nothing for half a minute, only blinked with those blue eyes.

"You are not returning to France. I've seconded you from GHQ. You are now part of Naval Intelligence."

"Thank you, sir," said Albert, bewildered rather than grateful.

"We have decoded most of the telegram. It matches a copy we intercepted ourselves. It's from Zimmermann."

"The German foreign minister?"

Admiral Hall nodded and slid a typed sheet across the table to Albert, who read:

We intend to begin unrestricted submarine warfare on the first of February. We shall endeavor in spite of this to keep the United States neutral. In the event of this not succeeding, we make Mexico a proposal of alliance on the following basis: make war together, make peace together, generous financial support and an understanding on our part that Mexico is to reconquer the lost territory in Texas, New Mexico and Arizona. You will inform the

president of Mexico of the above most secretly as soon as the
outbreak of war with the United States is certain.

Zimmermann

Albert read it twice and then looked up at Admiral Hall.

"To whom was this sent, sir?"

"The German ambassador in Washington. Von Bernstorff."

"And have the Americans seen it yet, sir?"

Admiral Hall held up his hand. "You are asking good questions, Captain. They will see it, of course. But it must be done in the right way. The Americans will be understandably angry and will go straight to the Germans."

"And the Germans can't know that we can read their code."

The admiral chuckled. "You see? You have the right bent of mind for this sort of thing." He paused. "We hope it will bring the Americans into the war, because we need men, munitions and, most of all, money. In a week we want you to go to Washington and be ready to negotiate for that money."

Albert sat in silence for a moment, considering. The admiral smoothed the cotton-wool tufts of his hair. Albert did not ask why they had settled upon him. He was indeed an astute choice: a money man, a member of Parliament, and the Americans at least were not averse to Jews.

"I have just a week, sir?"

"Yes. Then you sail to America. We want you there in time for when they declare war on Germany."

"And if they don't?"

The admiral smiled without humor. "It is for us here in Room Forty to see that they do."

Albert considered for a moment. "Very well. To whom do I report?"

"Myself, and the Cabinet Office."

Albert stood and, saluting, took his leave. As he opened the door, the admiral said, "You can inform your wife that you're going to America, but not why. The Zimmermann telegram is classified. As, I'm afraid, is the fact that Monsieur Henri Goldbaum is missing. Until your wife discovers the news through ordinary channels, you can say nothing to her."

"Yes, sir."

Albert walked back along Whitehall in the drizzle. Henri's probable death weighed upon him. It was ghastly, to hold in his breast news that would devastate his wife and yet be forced to conceal it from her. She deserved to know. It was her right to worry or to grieve. The drizzle turned to rain, and with a huff of irritation, Albert realized he had left his umbrella in the admiral's office. He would not return and fetch it. He turned up his collar and hurried faster, sloshing through puddles that were quickly forming on the pavement.

Hampshire, February

———◆◇◆———

Greta was relieved to be at home again. To her surprise, Albert had
agreed that they could return to Fontmell for the weekend. They arrived in time for Shabbat dinner, held with pomp and festivity at Temple Court. Hands were washed, candles lit and a glossy loaf of plaited
challah blessed. Celia had been allowed to stay up, and sat on a throne
of cushions with great solemnity between two officers, recuperating
guests of Lady Goldbaum. One cut up Celia's chicken with his good
arm, while the other regaled her with stories of battling tigers in his
years before the war. Greta considered this unlikely, knowing that
he'd been a solicitor in Bournemouth, but Celia sat agape until Lady
Goldbaum inquired as to whether her granddaughter was catching
many flies in her open mouth.

Greta looked at Albert through the glimmer of the candles, and he
met her eye and forced a smile. At the end of their London trip he
seemed to have caught her ill temper like a cold, but now that she had
had the satisfaction of passing on her crossness, she regretted it. He
alluded to having to leave England soon, but became evasive when
pressed. Perhaps Greta could simply avoid the subject of the boudoir
until he left, and then write it in a letter. No, she was many things, but
she was not a coward. It was an unhappy topic and must be confronted
directly, with tact and fortitude. She reached for her wineglass and
realized that Albert was gazing at her with a look of such melancholy
and desire that she wanted to reach across the table for him. She

fidgeted in her seat, paying no attention at all to the earnest conversation of the officer on her left.

The fish course was carried in, borne aloft on two vast serving platters: on one, a turbot in a white sauce with moss-green dill, and on the other, chilled trout with slivers of baked almonds, translucent as mother-of-pearl. To her amusement, Greta watched as one of the officers asked for both hot and cold fish, not realizing he was supposed to choose only one. Her mother-in-law winced, conscious that his extra plate would take time to consume and would throw off all the precise timings for the rest of the meal. Sure enough, by the time the lamb rolled in pistachios and chicken in aspic were served, Celia had fallen asleep in her chair. Greta signaled to a footman.

"Fetch Nanny, and carry Miss Celia to the car."

Albert stood, waving away the footman. "No, I'll take her."

Between them, Greta and Albert wrapped Celia in a blanket, and then Albert carried her, bundled, to the car where Nanny waited, ready to bear her charge safely back to the nursery. The parents watched side by side as the Wolseley drove away at a steady speed of no more than five miles an hour, as insisted upon by Nanny, who considered traveling faster than was natural dangerous for a child's constitution.

Albert turned to return to the house, but Greta caught his arm.

"Walk with me."

Gladly he followed her. They walked in the cold night air, their footsteps uncannily loud on the gravel paths. The white of the cyclamen petals shone like parings of bone in the darkness. Behind them the great house loomed, a vast paper lantern buoyed upon the night. Greta turned to face her husband, her skin pale, her eyes black and big with worry.

"I don't want another baby," she said.

"All right," said Albert, half-amused by her sincerity.

"Celia's a doll, and now there is Benjamin, we needn't have any more."

"We needn't," agreed Albert, taking her arm and pulling her close and trying to kiss her. She wriggled away like a fish unwilling to be hooked.

"I mean it, Albert. I am very sorry, but I have thought about it a good deal and I simply can't. I can't."

"Can't what?" he asked slowly, the horrid realization now dawning upon him. "Say precisely what you mean. You know I can't stand obfuscation."

"I can't make love with you again, Albert," said Greta, angry in her shame. "I'm so very sorry, but I can't."

Albert stared at her in horror and disbelief. "You're sorry? You can't?" He gave a short laugh, but it was hard and without humor. "Am I to have no choice in this?"

Greta bit her lip to stop herself from crying. "I won't risk it, Albert. I've seen what happens to women in labor. There is more than one kind of battlefield."

"That wretched bloody hospital. I agreed to your having it here. It's taken over my home, and it's taken my wife."

Greta shook her head; she heard his frustration and anger, but she would not be swayed.

"So what are we to be? Friends? Cousins? I'm a man, not some milksop, Greta."

Glancing up at him, she saw his lips were thin and set firm with disappointment. Inside her belly, she felt her guts crawl and scuttle like a nest of insects. He took a step back and continued to stare at her with abject distaste.

"This is the stupidest idea I ever heard. We had such a wretched beginning. Then somehow we stumbled into happiness. It matters to me. I thought it mattered to you."

"It does, of course it does. But the children? If something should happen to us? I won't be that selfish, Albert."

"So I'm selfish then. I want to sleep with my wife."

He turned and walked away, leaving her standing cold and alone in the dark.

T he next morning Albert had gone back up to town and had not asked her to accompany him. There had been no argument over wet nurses or her leaving the children. He had made it quite clear that her company was neither necessary nor desired. "I do not want a sister. I want a wife" had been his only remark.

For several days Miss Hathaway and Miss Ogden had observed Greta's unhappiness in silence. Anna confided to Withers that Albert did not telephone his wife. This, she informed Withers, who clearly knew nothing about such matters, was unusual. Withers was too discreet to ask, but Anna confessed that the fight was over children, and Greta not wanting any more. Withers considered this very sensible. She had grown extremely fond of Celia, who was shrewd and already, at three, demonstrated a keen horticultural interest, but while Ursula adored the babies, neither she nor Miss Hathaway really understood the appeal of the small, mewling creatures who accompanied their mothers to the lectures in the potting shed and kitchen garden. In fact Miss Hathaway had quietly remarked to her, while fishing a stray leaf from between the gaping lobes of a Venus flytrap, that it reminded her extremely of a baby's mouth. Both women privately resolved that they preferred the flytrap.

T he little maternity ward was filled with the smell of cigarette smoke and the sound of gossip. Half a dozen women, sentenced to bed rest, laughed as they considered their exile to Hampshire.

"Never been to the country before."

"Boring as shit."

"I know. I'm loving every minute."

They hadn't realized Greta had entered, and seeing her standing in the doorway, schoolmarmish and trying to pretend that she hadn't overheard the coarse language, caused them all to laugh harder.

"Don't! When I laugh, I pee a bit," said one, wiping tears from her eyes.

Greta smiled awkwardly. "Is there anything you need? A pack of cards?"

"Don't mind us. We're just not used to a holiday," said a woman with a shock of unbrushed red hair.

Greta introduced herself and described the gardening school that was available, should she wish to stay in Hampshire, to more squeals of laughter.

The red-haired woman grinned, showing a mouth of strong yellow teeth. "That's very kind. But I can make more money by other means."

Greta had learned not to comment, and quietly withdrew.

"Thank you. I'm sorry. We must seem dreadful rude. I'm Hetty Cohen," called the redhead.

Greta hesitated in the doorway to the cowshed. She knew it was an uncharitable thought, and that all people must be considered equal, but the Jewish prostitutes upset her the most. She had been taught that all Jews were her brethren, but while the rabbi had explained that some of her kin were peasants or oppressed in Russia, he had not explicitly stated that others were redheaded harlots forced by circumstance to earn their livings on their backs.

But all thoughts of Hetty Cohen were soon driven away, because shortly after luncheon, Lady Goldbaum arrived with a telegram from Clement in Switzerland.

After she had read it, Greta sat quietly in her bedroom and looked out over the garden. The wind lifted the whips of the willows and the wisteria rapped gently against the glass. She had not seen Henri since her visit to Paris before the war, and yet at that moment she missed him intensely. She hoped, if the Germans shot him, that it would be quick and he would not suffer. She found that she did not want to cry. He wasn't dead yet, and she would not grieve. She glanced behind her at the wedding present Henri had sent—the Rossetti painting of one of his flame-haired women, her eyes green and her skin the color of milk. Greta looked again. It could have been a portrait of Hetty Cohen. For a moment, it seemed that the woman in the picture grinned, her lips paring back to reveal a mouth full of square yellow teeth.

They waited for more news regarding Henri, but nothing came. Greta took Benjamin with her to visit Hetty, who had delivered a little girl in the night. She found Hetty sitting up in bed, cradling the baby attached to a large bosom as veiny as a ripe blue cheese, while reading a copy of the *Daily Mail*. Greta glanced at the headline—"Send Them All Home"—and looked away, revolted.

Hetty laughed. "That's all you Krauts. My ma. You."

"I don't think it's funny. I find it awful," said Greta, sounding sanctimonious, even to herself.

Hetty prized the baby off her nipple with her finger, attached it to the other breast and set down the paper. "There's nothing much we can do. They'll round 'em up and send 'em off, or they won't. Can't imagine 'em packing you off though, madam." Hetty laughed again, and this time Greta didn't reprimand her.

She saw the glint in Hetty's eye—one she recognized from Celia—and knew that a challenge had been issued.

"So who is you cheerin' for, then? The British or the Boches?"

Greta recoiled and said with as much dignity as she could summon, "My children are British, Hetty."

Hetty rolled her eyes and removed the baby from her nipple with a loud popping sound. It continued to root for her. "Yes, but you must have an old beau fighting away in them other trenches."

She mimed a sword fight with her rolled newspaper, jabbing away. Greta stood, affronted despite her silent resolution.

"My brother, Hetty. There are no winners. Only death."

She started to leave, but Hetty caught her hand and squeezed it hard.

"Don't go. I'm awful sorry, Mrs. Goldbaum. I don't know what's wrong with me. These terrible things come into my head and I say 'em. It's like my own thoughts is what's egging me on. I know it's horrid. Can't blame Frank for not puttin' up with it."

Greta saw Hetty's green eyes fill with tears, and beneath the bravado and the halo of red hair, she looked terribly young.

"Don't you dare! Don't you bloody pity me," snapped Hetty, her complexion clashing magnificently with her hair. "I never said you could do that."

"You really ought to take a walk around the gardens. Have some fresh air. Take baby Ruth."

Hetty shook her head vigorously. "I can't. Don't you see? If I start prancing about the flowers, going for bloody walks, how much harder it'll be to go back?"

"You could stay awhile."

"Just stop with the bloody gardening school. My pink lily is a work of art. The only flower we need." Hetty spoke with bravado, but her eyes were bright with tears.

Admiral Hall not only gave permission for Albert to discuss his American mission with his father but encouraged him. Albert agreed it would be in the national interest, he insisted, to take advice from the principal banker in England, and more than that, the simplest way of raising the money was to have the House of Goldbaum act as banker. He must obtain the approval of the head of the bank, which was still Lord Goldbaum—even if he was now too frail to sail to America himself.

It was a relief to be sitting beside a pleasant coal fire in the partners' room at the office in the city, and to be thinking of something other than Greta. His father listened in silence, waiting until Albert had finished. Lord Goldbaum studied him for a moment before speaking.

"It is a great honor and privilege that they are sending you—a Goldbaum and a Jew—to manage this vast undertaking. England's hopes, and the Goldbaum reputation, rest on your success."

Albert laughed. "Thank you for putting me at ease, Father."

Lord Goldbaum smiled. "My apologies, Albert. Of course you understand. How large a loan is the government seeking?"

"One billion dollars."

The number hung in the air, vast and awful. Albert imagined he could see it like a film of poison gas. Even Lord Goldbaum was taken aback.

"That is almost twice the amount raised in taxation last year," he said.

Albert nodded.

"It's too big for Wall Street alone," said Lord Goldbaum, considering. "The bonds must be offered to the American people as well. Now is the chance to tempt Americans from across the nation to invest in Europe."

Albert saw in his father's eye a glint of the old excitement. He wished he could feel it himself.

"The House of Goldbaum cannot underwrite such a large offering by itself," said Albert. "We will need at least two or three partners— more if we can."

"Marcus Ullman will arrange it. I'll wire him. You can stay with him in New York."

Lord Goldbaum surveyed Albert for a moment with a mixture of pleasure and pride. "My son," he said. "My son, banker and diplomat. This is what old Moses Salomon Goldbaum dreamed of, when he sent his sons out from the ghetto with their letter of credit and their sycamore seed."

"But I have no letter of credit, Father. I don't even have a sycamore seed."

"You have the weight of the British government behind you, Albert."

"The only weight that investors are interested in, Father, is the weight of gold."

Albert looked at his father and for a moment saw in him a shadow of the jolly generals, their unwavering belief in empire and a good war, and their unshakable belief that somehow or other, despite the carnage of the flesh and of finance, all would be well.

"We need to agree on a limit to our exposure, Father. I want to help the government, but not at the risk of ruin."

His father dismissed his anxiety with a wave.

There was flush on the great banker's cheeks. Albert understood that for decades his father had worked tirelessly, granting favor after favor to successive governments, perpetually demonstrating his loyalty to nation and empire and yet, to his disappointment, always remaining on the outside of the circle, set apart. Now Albert worried that his father was so exercised at the thought that at last his family had been accepted that he was not making sound financial decisions. With a moment of horrid cynicism, Albert wondered if the chaps in the Treasury knew how much his father longed for assimilation and were relying on this to push the House of Goldbaum to underwrite the loan.

Although it was only a little after half past nine in the morning, Lord Goldbaum reached for the brandy decanter, pouring each of them a large measure. Albert vowed privately to try to protect his father, even if it was against his own wishes.

A lbert returned to Fontmell to see his children and say good-bye. He found that he was too angry to speak to Greta beyond the barest civilities. He did not want to fight with her on his last evening at home, so he pretended to be buried in his papers during dinner. He had not loved her at first. He had married a stranger out of duty. He'd grown to accept that joy was to be discovered at the edge of existence, fluttering in the corner of one's eye, glimpsed only in those moments of serenity at dawn before one was fully awake. Happiness, when it came to Albert, was an explosion of sunlight. He walked out into the garden to discover he was bathed in summer and was replete, having not known that he was hungry. He hadn't expected to love his wife, but he did. He felt love unspool from him. And now she was telling him to gather it back into himself, as though the miracle of it—the surprise of it—were nothing. He turned the paper before him, with its list of figures, even though they passed as rain before his eyes.

After dinner, they sat in the drawing room watching the great yews sway like dancers in the wind. He expressed regrets and sympathy regarding Henri, but had few words of comfort to offer.

"I won't tell you that it will be all right. I have never lied to you, Greta."

He fidgeted, jiggling his leg, and then stood up and poked the fire, sending up a spray of sparks. He leaned against the mantelpiece, staring into the flames as though some wisdom or comfort could be found lurking in the depths of the coals. He observed Greta by the window, her eyes ringed from crying, her cheeks painted with the glow from the fire. There was still a postnatal plumpness to her figure, a pleasant fullness around her belly. She had never looked prettier. And yet you are willing to squander all that we are, he mused. He thought of the two small creatures sleeping upstairs. Was the risk of another child really a danger to be feared?

A maid brought in a tray with tea and withdrew. Greta carefully poured Albert a cup and carried it over to him. She stood before him for a moment, offering it up to him.

"I don't want you to leave." She set the cup down on the table. "I love you."

He wondered whether she'd ever actually said that before. She twisted her wedding ring round and round her finger. They'd never needed the words before. It was an incantation, a prayer for hope that, with these words, all would be well.

Albert took her hand. "Love isn't the problem," he said.

She leaned against him, and he rested his chin on the top of her head.

"We managed before," he said. "We were careful."

"We were lucky. We might be lucky again, for a while. But then we wouldn't," she said.

She hesitated, for once shy. She wished they could discuss the specific geography of bedroom maneuvers with the same ease and precision with which they examined the planting of the crocuses or the positioning of the beehives.

"There are other things we can do," she whispered, looking up to meet his eye.

Turning, she walked to the door and locked it. Albert watched with interest as she sauntered back toward him. She pressed him down onto an armchair, sat on his lap and kissed him, her fingers edging up his thigh. After a minute, Albert gave a little groan and pushed her back in the chair, but Greta cried out in pain.

"My corset," she said.

Unless she sat very upright, the hard edge of the corset protruding between her legs cut sharply into her flesh. Albert started to fumble with the buttons on her blouse and attempted to loosen the undergarments beneath, but Greta flinched, reluctant to reveal the spongy softness of her stomach, the slack, unhealed muscles. The corset had to be pulled so tight nowadays that it left red welts upon her flesh. She supposed it wouldn't look so ugly in the candlelight. She realized that she was almost as anxious as the very first time Albert and she had attempted the marital act, and far more self-conscious.

She was vaguely aware that Albert was either oblivious or indifferent to her unease as, after unfastening her, he tugged her down to the floor, lying her on her back. He kissed her neck and progressed down toward her bosom. From her vantage point on the rug, she noticed blackened smut lodged up the chimney like hardened mucus in a nostril. She must order the chimneys to be swept again.

"Are you with me?" said Albert, pausing to look down at her, his expression hurt and indignant.

"I'm sorry, darling. I'm out of practice," she replied guiltily.

She pulled him toward her and kissed him again, feeling the tickle of his mustache against her lip, and the hardness of the floor beneath her. Deep inside her, she felt the first tingle of desire; there was something comfortable and satisfying about the heaviness of his weight upon her, and with more enthusiasm, she began to touch him through his trousers. The fire spat and crackled. Albert moved against her, shoving aside her skirts, pressing into her. A moment later she realized that he was trying to push inside her and she wriggled away, whispering, "Not that, darling. Not that."

He swore, but before he could further object, she touched him again, carefully maneuvering herself beyond his reach. She unpeeled her glove and brushed him with bare fingertips. In a few moments he gave in to her, silently and without delight.

A little later, while she turned away so that he could tidy himself, she regretted the awkwardness of their encounter. Attempting anything of the sort in the drawing room had been a mistake. It was not a room shaped for comfortable enjoyment of such a thing. Before, their acts of intimacy had always brought them closer. They laughed and took pleasure in one another. This interlude had not been an act of intimacy. Instead, it had served to make her feel more alone.

"We'll get better at it," she said, hoping this to be true.

Albert did not reply. As he climbed the stairs to bed, aware of a damp stain on his trousers, he felt revolted and annoyed. He was married. He loved his wife and wanted her. Yet he had been reduced to grubby fumblings. Away from Greta for months at a time, he had imagined and longed for her. During excursions to the front he had glimpsed blackened death everywhere, inhaled its stink. It made him want her even more. He desired sex as an affirmation of life, a declaration of love and his eagerness to cling to the world. He needed to lose himself inside her. That encounter, in the drawing room, whatever it had been, was wholly inadequate. It was not what he had pictured, alone in his narrow bunk.

Unable to sleep, Albert rose before dawn. He dressed without the assistance of his valet, and walked through the gardens as the first light pushed its way through the trees. Crocuses were beginning to shove tiny green snouts through the ground beneath the willows. He wouldn't return until long after they had flowered. He rambled down to the wilderness, passing beneath a copse of sycamore trees. He stooped and saw buried beneath the leaf litter a seedpod, curved like a wishbone. Perhaps it would bring him luck. He pocketed it. The air was cold and the grass heavy with dew, while mist puffed in from the river like steam. The bees huddled in their hives. Albert found the glass hive that Greta had commissioned for him, and watched as the bees clustered around the queen for warmth, those nearest the center a blur of wings, those at the edge feasting on honey. They emitted a low thrum, which he felt in his chest, a throb of animal contentment, and felt oddly envious. The sun had nearly risen, and with a pang, he turned for home.

He kissed his children while they slept in their cribs. He could not bear to say good-bye to Greta. He stroked her cheek and slipped from the room and out to the waiting motorcar without waking her.

As she heard the door slam, the grind of the gravel, Greta touched her hand to her cheek. It was still warm from his fingers. She kept her eyes tightly shut; so long as she kept them closed, she could pretend he was still there.

P&O's Wentworth, *Liverpool Docks, February*

⟡

Albert and Simon Grenville from the War Office observed the stowing of the kegs of gold in the ship's specie room, concealed at the bottom of the vessel. They stood alongside the purser in the second-class baggage room above, watching as a team of seamen slung bars of gold into the hold using wire treasure nets.

"It's really safe here?" asked Albert, intrigued.

"As a baby," replied the purser. "This specie room is right at the bottom of a trunk hatch, and after all the specie is on board, we'll fill the hatch with the baggage not wanted on voyage. It's quite impossible to get at the treasure without hoisting out the entire cargo. Unless there's a U-boat, of course. Nothing sinks faster than gold," he added cheerfully.

They watched in silence, Albert considering that although he spent most of his adult life trading in money backed by gold, and even in gold as a commodity, it was only figures in a column, marks on a page. He had not glimpsed gold like this, in great shining bars, stamped and embossed with the Bank of England coat of arms. He stared at the glittering cargo, aware that he was mesmerized. He knew the adage about the desire for gold driving men mad, but until now he'd considered it a figurative expression about ambition.

Mr. Grenville watched in silence, his round eyes rounder still.

"This is the last of England's gold?" asked Albert.

"More or less," said Mr. Grenville, rousing himself. "The Americans have us now."

Albert stifled a shiver, conscious of all that was riding on the Zimmermann telegram.

"What if the Americans haven't entered the war by the time I arrive? What do I do then? There won't be any loans to negotiate."

Mr. Grenville snorted. "I should stay there. There won't be any point coming home. We'll be overrun with Germans."

They set sail that night, and as the steam liner pushed out into dark waters, her lights shrouded and her engines muffled, Albert thought of the haul far below, stashed beneath the waterline, shining in the gloom.

Pinsk, February

———◆❯•❮◆———

Otto crouched over a paraffin burner in the makeshift barracks. Behind him in the hut, Gruber attempted to assemble dinner. The wind thundered against the tin walls. Snow had silenced the guns. Men on both sides shivered over guttering fires and cursed their lot. Otto had salvaged a fur coat from the corpse of a dead Russian officer, and instructed Gruber to stitch his Austrian Leutnant's insignia onto the lapel. From time to time Otto had been forced to go for three days without eating, forced to lick the dew from the grass, and at those times he sensed himself retreat from civility into instinct. He liked the bear coat. It fitted him like his rightful skin and felt better than any of his exquisitely tailored suits had ever done. He liked the wariness with which others eyed him when he wore it, as though he had donned not simply the fur of the bear, but its essence. He supposed that war had driven him slightly mad. He didn't care. He almost threw away the checkbook.

In his hands he held an order that he surveyed with contempt.

"Last month it was paranoia over deserters—watch the Czechs, watch the Italians. Don't let them patrol alone. Shoot without trial. Now it's the Jews again. What happens if I refuse to answer this?" he asked, tugging his hat further down his forehead.

He read it once more, with anger and distaste. It had arrived more than a week ago and he had ignored it, shoving it into his pocket, where it seemed to burn a hole.

"Read it again, sir," said Karl.

Otto removed the creased and grease-stained document from his jacket: "'The War Ministry is continually receiving complaints from the population that large numbers of men of the Israelite faith who are fit for military service are either exempt from military duties or evading their obligation to serve under every conceivable pretext.'" Otto coughed in profound annoyance. "I ought to burn it."

Karl shrugged, knowing better than to argue with Otto in one of these moods.

"I'm required to fill in a questionnaire tallying the precise number of men of Jewish faith stationed at the front," said Otto.

"Well, you can put me down," said Karl cheerfully. "And with you, sir, that's two. Could always add a couple more. I don't really see them coming down here to check," he added, stirring the brown slop that was cooking on the burner.

"I shan't prove that we're not cowards by lying, Soldat."

Otto scrutinized the paper again, reading, "'Jew count. Number of Jewish officers. Number of enlisted Jews killed. How many Jews in your company have been decorated for bravery?'"

He balled it up, shoved it into the paraffin burner. They watched the paper flare and then quickly blacken.

"Can we do that with all our orders, sir? Save an awful lot of trouble and effort," said Karl, wafting away the smoke.

Otto shifted and flicked the ash dust from the burned paper. He blew and it fluttered like gray snow.

"It wasn't an Austrian command. I'm only being told to fill in their wretched questionnaire as the battalion is now mostly Germans."

"Two surviving Austrians. Can't be many of us left. They should pull us all out and put us in a museum," said Karl, spooning the hash into a mess tin and handing it to Otto, who swallowed each spoonful with a shudder. Karl wasn't permitted to eat in the presence of an officer; his role was to linger in case something was needed—a napkin, some more pepper. For the first few months Otto had ignored him, or rather hadn't noticed he was there, but now when they were alone in the hut with no other officers present, he was tolerant of Karl, permitting him to ask the odd question.

"Leutnant Goldbaum—all the men are talking about how the Russkis have had enough. Apparently, the tsar's had it."

Otto shook his head. "We're a long way from St. Petersburg, Gruber. We fight until they surrender." He sighed. "The Russians will charge when the snow clears, but the ground is still hard enough for their horses."

"What is it with the Russians and their bloody horses? Apparently they're using metal tanks on the Western Front," said Karl, taking Otto's empty tin.

"I'd rather have horses coming at me," said Otto.

"It's afterward I can't stand. The horses take so long to die. I can hear them there all night, screaming in the marshes."

Otto checked his watch. "It's nearly nine. It's time to send out a patrol."

Karl saluted. "Yes, sir. I'll find Muller."

Otto shook his head. "It's all right. I need the air."

Unthinkingly Karl reached for his own helmet. It did not occur to him that Otto could go alone.

They ambled down a dirt track leading to the open ground. It had been a village once, filled mostly with Jews, but the Russians had driven them out—they hadn't wanted Jews so close to enemy territory, convinced of their treachery. All that remained of the huts was rubble. Otto picked out a *mezuzah*, forgotten, half-crushed, so that the paper Hebrew prayer hidden inside like a golden egg yolk had spilled out and spoiled. The tiny synagogue had been shelled, while the army used the remains of the women's *mikvah* bath as a useful coop for the balding chickens they found pecking disconsolately among the wreckage. As they picked their way across the ruins, Otto felt he couldn't move for ghosts. They clung to his coat and skin like cleavers and burrs. Dislike of the Jews was something both sides shared, he thought miserably. Peace comes out of common ground—perhaps they could begin with that. Otto wondered if he was sickening for something. His thoughts were restless, his heart beat light and fast, and beneath his coat he began to sweat. It wasn't as bitterly cold as it had been, but the ground was still hard, and as they approached the sentry points, he knew that the corpses in the marsh beyond lay suspended in the ice, set like pieces of salmon in aspic.

He inspected the soldiers stationed at the sentry posts along the marsh. Everyone was waiting for the start of the thaw.

"Nothing much happening," said one.

Otto glanced down and saw that the soldier's feet were wrapped in layers of sackcloth.

"Where are your boots?"

The soldier opened his jacket to reveal them strung around his neck. "Won't fit. Feet too swollen from frostbite."

Otto grimaced. "Go to army medical when you come off watch, soldier. That's an order."

The soldier shrugged. "If you say so, sir. But won't do any good. It was them what gave me the brown paper and sacks."

It was futile. The medical corps would have nothing with which to treat him. Otto dismissed the soldiers, and by midnight he and Gruber had nearly finished their rounds. They turned back toward the weather station. Frost glinted like gunmetal. The night was clear and the sky bursting with stars. Otto couldn't help pausing to look. Even surrounded by cruelty and ugliness, there was beauty above. As long as he could see the stars, he enjoyed both companionship and occupation. He was like a rabbi who had memorized the Torah and the commentaries and held them cheerfully in his breast, always busy in his own mind. He took a breath of clean, damp air and held it deep in his lungs, before letting it out with a sigh. This was a moment of pleasure, however fleeting. He picked out the constellations like the faces of loved ones from a photograph. The jewels on Orion's Belt. The coiled tail of Scorpio. As a child, he'd been told that this was the curving Goldbaum sycamore branch, and the five stars forming the pincers of the scorpion were instead the five Goldbaum brothers. He'd been awed and frightened that the fortune of his family was preordained in the heavens, and whenever he looked at the night sky they were the first constellation he searched for, like a soldier looking for his name on the list of those being sent up to the line. Now, his family's recasting of the myth of the stars both amused him with its audacity and alarmed him with its hubris. As he watched, a star sailed across Pisces, a shuttlecock of light.

"Look, Gruber. A meteor." He laid his arm round his servant's shoulders and laughed. "Dust and ice from the outer cosmos. There are still marvels in this world, Gruber, even now."

The meteor burned white, a luminous smear of light chalking the sky, and then, before it was quite gone, there was a whine and snap, and Otto fell to his knees in a spurt of blood. He clutched his throat, choking, drowning. Karl stared at him aghast, too surprised for a moment to move. Otto saw the horror on the other man's face and understood he must be dying. He was drowning in air; when he tried to breathe there was only wetness. He put his hand over his throat and managed to take a squelching gasp of air. The pain was everywhere. It burned in his throat, his lungs, his eyes. He screamed, but no sound came. Then he lost consciousness.

He woke to see a black face staring at him, only it wasn't black at all; it was Karl Gruber painted with blood, clear paths of skin beneath his eyes cleaned by tears. Otto closed his eyes again.

Karl knelt in the snow, trying to stop the fount of blood with his hand, but it oozed around his fingers, warm and sticky, and splashed his face. He screamed for help, but then realized he was screaming wordlessly. No one came. With every ounce of strength, Karl lifted Otto in his arms. The fur of Otto's bear coat stuck in his mouth. Otto wasn't a big man, but Karl was slight and underfed. He buckled under Otto's weight, sinking to his knees in the snow. With a howl of effort and hurt, he hoisted him onto his shoulders like a *babushka* lugging firewood.

When Otto came to once more, he was in a church, watching while two aproned priests sliced at a body lying on the altar, fingers glossy and red as they pushed them inside its throat, a tray of mirrored instruments spread out before them. An ornate crucifix carved with the Tree of Life hung above, the figure of Jesus seeming to gaze at the body on the altar with shared sympathy. Vaguely Otto realized he was looking down at himself from the ceiling of the church. I don't want to die in a church, he thought, my mother wouldn't like it. I'll die if I must, but not here.

Karl screamed so much that at first they thought he too had been shot. He watched in shock as they sluiced down the makeshift operating table, then hauled Otto onto it and drew across a screen. A nurse hustled him outside, hushing him. "You did all that you could, bringing him here. Go back to your company."

Karl shook his head. He wouldn't leave. The nurse gave him a little shove. "You must go. Fetch his things. Come back in a little while."

Nodding dumbly, Karl trailed back toward the hut. Hungry birds called overhead. No fresh snow had fallen. With exactitude, he forced himself to pass the spot where Otto had been hit, and saw the disaster sprayed out in red across the snow. Here Otto had been shot. Crimson blood fountained and lay feathered brightly against the white, with callous beauty. Here he had fallen to his knees, and there he had lain, bleeding into that thick, viscous pool. There Karl saw his own footsteps, deeply set and edged with red. Otto might live to reach Vienna, he told himself. They would look after him there—the best doctors, the best care. He knew that their friendship was one born of the oddest circumstance. A *Kanaltrotter* and a prince of the Jews forced into companionship at the end of the world, and one way or another, Otto was leaving this godforsaken place. If Otto lived, if Karl survived the war, if the war ever ended and Karl called at the Goldbaum Palace in Vienna, Otto would receive him. He was that sort of fellow. But after a few minutes it would be clear to them both that this was a charade. They were not comrades in the civilized, ordinary world. Karl understood that whether Otto lived or died, their friendship was at an end. And, he realized, friendship was what it had been. Their association went beyond master and servant, the obligation of one and the duty of the other. He looked down again at the snow, and saw the whole sorry tale of himself and Otto transcribed in blood. He wept, whether for his friend or for the friendship, he did not know.

O tto woke at dawn to find he was alive but could not speak. Out of habit, he looked around for Karl, realizing with a pang that he was not there. They had taken the bullet out of his throat, but it had torn through his windpipe. They had stitched it as best they could, but the swelling had closed his airway and the surgeon had put a little rubber tube in his throat for him to breathe through.

"When you feel a bit better, you will be able to whisper by putting your finger over the hole," explained the nurse.

Otto touched his hand to his throat and gasped at the agony.

"No, no, not yet. It must heal first. Try again in a week or two," said the nurse. "You must stay here for a few weeks until you are well enough to travel, and then you are going home."

Otto tried to turn his face away so that she could not see him cry, but it hurt too much and he lay on his back as tears rolled down onto his pillow. Tactfully the nurse withdrew. He'd thought he'd relinquished all thoughts of home. He'd hidden himself inside his bearskin and eaten with his hands and learned to think of little beyond the next few hours—days at the most. And yet, and yet. He allowed himself the briefest glimpse of his mother. The baroness in her sitting room, stirring liqueur into horrid, over-sweet coffee, unsmiling as she pushed the cup toward him. To Otto, it was a demonstration of great tenderness. She expressed love with solemnity over the stirring of coffee, not with quick smiles and laughter. And Greta. Vienna would still be bereft of Greta. My sister, my enemy. What lies they make us tell.

Karl sat on the floor of the hut, having packed Otto's few possessions hastily into his officer's valise. A couple of corporals from the platoon lingered, dismally sharing a cigarette.

"It was rotten luck," said one. "You surprised a band of Russians who were trying to surrender."

Karl shrugged. He considered it bad luck to be shot in the throat, whether the Russian who fired the gun was surrendering or not.

Shouldering the valise, he trudged painfully back toward the church, his foot throbbing. The church had been chosen as a field hospital since the enemy viewed the displaying of a red cross as a target invitation, but the Russians proved superstitious and reluctant to bomb a church, apparently more concerned about divine retribution than Austrian revenge.

Karl pushed his way inside, dumping the valise on the floor and demanding, "Where is Leutnant Goldbaum? I want to see him. Is he dead?"

The nurse tried to quiet him. "Sit down, Soldat, and mind the other fellows resting. See? He's sleeping. They're finding him a bed now."

Two orderlies carried an unconscious figure along the transept on a stretcher. Hardly knowing what he was doing, Karl stood, shouting, "Leutnant Goldbaum. Wake up, Goldbaum."

The nurse tried to subdue him again, reminding him helplessly of the other injured and dying men. Karl wouldn't be budged, and finally exasperated, the nurse allowed him to wait. An orderly brought him a ration of beef tea and black bread. Karl chewed it slowly, with little hunger. His teeth felt loose in his head. Across the church, the nave had been portioned off with a grubby curtain to demarcate the officers' ward. Even here, the niceties of social order had to be maintained. A nurse made up a bed for Otto. A pair of stout German *Füsiliers* sat on either side of Karl, waiting their turn for triage. They had waterproof boots and sturdy gloves and gas masks. As he struggled to stay awake, Karl heard them muttering about their lot—they were here only because of the incompetence of the Austrians, whom they considered an unpalatable blend of peasants and useless aristocrats, fighting with heirloom pistols.

Too exhausted to take offense, Karl dozed off, the mug of beef tea still clasped in his hand.

On waking, the pain in Otto's throat choked him. He coughed and thought he would faint from the agony; the cough dislodged the tube in his windpipe and he hammered on the bedside, unable to scream. He tried to call for help. But no sound came out. He began to suffocate.

Across the church, Karl slept. Beef tea, cold now, trickled onto his leg, soaking his thigh, and he woke with a start, panicked that he had urinated on himself. He set down the cup, glancing anxiously from side to side, hoping that no one had noticed. He observed that the nurse had not properly closed the curtain on the officers' side. He looked along the beds for Otto. A man in one bed was twisting, having some sort of fit. Karl sat up. He realized it was Otto, silently turning blue.

"Nurse!" he yelled, pointing.

She saw where he signaled and, with a call to the doctor, ran to Otto's bed. Karl watched as they laid Otto back down and reinserted the tube in his neck. The nurse noticed Karl's gaze and, with a deft flick, drew the curtain. Vaguely aware that he was risking a court-martial for insubordination, he hastened across the aisle and, pushing aside the curtain, sat on Otto's bed. Karl reached for his hand.

"I won't let them send me away again, sir," he said quietly. "It's my job to take care of you."

Otto stared up at him, his eyes huge and frightened.

Out of pity, the nurse allowed Karl to sit with Otto. She was run off her feet, and he could keep an eye on the naughty tube. Karl knew the reprieve was only temporary. He considered what he could do to stay in the hospital. It would have been easier if he too had been shot. Briefly he considered shooting himself—a flesh wound in the arm or leg. That was certain to earn a court-martial, and probably a death sentence for cowardice. He glanced around the dressing station. At least half the cases were frostbite rather than wounds. He remembered the first winter in Galicia, when their toes had been warmed by woolen socks knitted by women across the empire. It had seemed then that the diligence of the women could save them, but then they ran out of wool and the supply trains didn't come as often as they should have, and when they did arrive, they brought shells instead of socks. Socks, Karl thought grimly, were as necessary as shells and bullets in winning a war.

The pain in his left foot pulsed like a heartbeat. He hadn't taken off his boot for some weeks, worried that if he did, he'd never get it back on again. He started to unfasten it and, with some trepidation, peeled off his sock. His toe was jellied and black. The stench was foul. He waved to the nurse. She ignored him. He waved again, pointing to his foot. Half an hour later she finally came over, breathed in the awful smell and summoned the doctor.

"You soldiers—I can't understand why you didn't come here sooner," exclaimed the doctor, exasperated. "Now your foot is putrefying from frostbite. No one survives amputations here at the field station anymore. We've no chloroform, or dressings, or antiseptic." The doctor turned to the nurse. "I want him out of the officers' section.

Find him a bed." He looked at Karl and shook his head. "We'll have to send you back to Vienna. You might very well lose the foot."

All Karl heard was "Vienna." He and Otto were going back to Vienna. The thought that, once there, their paths would immediately and irrevocably diverge was unwelcome and he pushed it away.

O tto lay in the cool afternoon light, trying to swallow soup. It seeped out of the hole in his throat. Only his raging thirst forced him to try again. "Vienna," he mouthed. He must gain strength to survive the journey home. Two orderlies wrapped a body in a sheet and carried it out on a stretcher. Otto looked away and concentrated on his soup. Exhausted from the sheer effort of swallowing three mouthfuls without choking, he set down his spoon. He glanced across the nave to Gruber's bed. If the boy lost his foot, he must see to it that work could be found for him in the house on Heugasse. He realized that Gruber was looking at him, and he raised a hand in recognition.

Dusk fell. The church was lit by a single hurricane lamp. A nervousness hung in the air of the dressing station like electricity that needed to discharge. It was very quiet outside, an uneasy stillness. Nurses muttered. An orderly hurried out. The silence broke apart.

Shots echoed, not just rifle fire but cannon, and with an intensity Otto had not heard since the start of winter. In a minute, all the patients were awake. They glanced at one another with big eyes. Quietly, surreptitiously, one or two began to pull on trousers and shirts as best they could. Otto succeeded only in sitting up. If he moved his head too fast, the hole in his throat seeped blood and he felt light-headed. There were no clothes beside his bed for him to put on, even if he had been able to.

The orderly returned at a run.

"Orders are to evacuate the wounded! We're under attack!"

A pair of stretcher bearers lifted the officer from the bed next to Otto's, while all those men who could stand shuffled toward the church doors, half of them without any boots. Otto struggled to the edge of his bed. He tried to ask the orderly when they would be coming back for him, but no sound came out. A single nurse remained, tending those few patients unable to leave their beds without a stretcher. Otto waved at her, and she turned to him with a tight, worried smile.

"They'll be back, just as soon as they can. Don't worry about a thing, Leutnant."

Otto sat back and listened, alert as a rabbit sensing a fox. There was no sound but the guns. Karl padded across the room, limping horribly. Otto wondered how he'd not noticed before. Everyone was too busy to notice the trespass, and Karl sat, silent and unrebuked, on the edge of Otto's bed. Dusk gave way to an uneasy, light-filled night. If a second were a bullet, then this battle would already have lasted a hundred years, thought Otto. A shell landed close to the church and there was a cascade of roof tiles, like the furious peals of a xylophone at a concert. It was odd to be in the midst of a bombardment, unable to fire back. Otto felt perfectly useless, able to do nothing but listen. He tried to hear the different notes of the guns; the Austrian rifles had a hollower sound and came from farther west, while those of the Russians snapped from across the marshes. It seemed to Otto as if they were creeping closer, but it could have been the amplifying effect of the marsh. Karl went very still, his boots and knapsack resting on his knee. Then, rising in the distance, there came the sound of horses, a waterfall of feet on hard ground and harsh, guttural shouts, louder and louder. A glass window above them shattered, the glass raining down onto the floor. Otto signaled for a pen and paper. Karl rummaged in his rucksack. Otto wrote a single word on the paper.

"Run."

Karl stared at him, his face pale with fear, appalled at the suggestion. Otto jabbed at the paper, hoping with that one word he could convey to him the futility of staying. He would be captured as a prisoner of war—and for what purpose? Otto glanced around at the lumpen shapes of men in the beds surrounding him. Still Karl did not move. Otto scribbled another word. *"Please."* He squeezed Karl's hand. Karl looked at him, considering, and then stood. He hobbled across the room and then, hesitating only for a moment, quitted the church.

Karl lingered on the porch, outraged. How dare Otto order him away, as if he were nothing? He contemplated going after the others; there was a column of soldiers retreating, but now that his foot was free of his boot and had been poked and dressed in rags, the pain was excruciating. He doubted he could run, even if he wanted to. His belly rolled, and he realized that he urgently needed to shit. Cursing at the pain in his foot, he hobbled to the latrine erected outside the church. He lowered his trousers and groaned as his guts gave way beneath him.

O tto leaned back against the wall behind his bed and waited. He wasn't sure whether the other men left in the church were conscious of what was happening. Clearly no one was coming back for them. The air was filled with groans and cries like the constant croaking of frogs. A surge of fear pulsed around his body, dulling the pain in his throat. The door opened, and Otto braced himself for the Russians.

Karl stood shivering in the doorway. Otto looked at him with a wash of relief, ashamed at how glad he was to see him. He wanted to shout at him for his idiocy in not leaving, but he could not speak. Karl looked around the deserted church in desperation, observing the chaos. At last his eye fixed on Otto, who held up an arm in greeting. Karl limped over, hesitating at his bedside.

Otto tapped the space beside him; after a moment Karl sat and then, apparently unable to hold himself upright any longer, slid in beside him. Then, despite the looming disaster, the gunfire and the screams, he fell asleep, his head resting on Otto's shoulder. He was warm, his skin clammy with sweat, but his breath was even and quiet; apparently he was comforted by Otto's proximity. Otto knew that as soon as the Russians arrived, they would be taken prisoner and probably shot, yet at this moment, with the sleeping boy beside him, he was filled with an odd calm and a simple pleasure at human contact and warmth.

They were not shot. There were seven men left behind. Three died that first day without anyone's knowing their names. Two more were given morphine and told to march, until only Otto and Karl remained. They stayed side by side, allies, reluctant to be separated even for an instant. A Russian doctor examined them both; he spoke to them brusquely in German, but he was not unkind, except that he would not lie.

"Your risk is infection," he said to Otto, peering at the tube in his throat. "If you were at a good hospital in Vienna or St. Petersburg, with clean sheets and efficient nurses, then you might live to heal. But here, my friend, the odds are against you. Not impossible. I've seen men with the will to live overcome worse things through sheer force of personality, but you? I don't know."

Otto didn't know, either.

The doctor robbed them unapologetically. He discovered Otto's few remaining possessions in the small stand beside his bed.

"The soldiers will rob you in any case, my friend. You may as well give them to a fellow who will appreciate such things," said the doctor, fingering Otto's gold watch. "This is a thing of beauty and should be in the pocket of a man who will take joy from it." He smiled at Otto with sorrow and benevolence. "Who were you, to have such a watch? The tsar himself need not be ashamed of a watch such as this."

For once, Otto was glad he could not answer. He saw the watch that his father had given him on his first day at the bank go into the fat doctor's waistcoat with something like regret. The doctor went through the papers with little interest.

"The army will take a note of your name and rank and, if you're lucky, tell the Red Cross. Your family might even find out that you were here."

He started to examine Karl, who sat slackly, avoiding eye contact, reluctant to be noticed by any figure of authority.

"That foot doesn't smell too good. I think we should send you to one of the hospitals further back and have it amputated. Sooner is better than later."

Karl gripped Otto's hand.

"I don't want to go alone," he murmured. "Make him send you, too."

Otto hesitated. He had resisted using it through the war, but that was to help himself. This was to help the boy. Karl was his servant, and he had an obligation toward him. He pointed to the pile of papers resting on his valise. Karl, grasping what he wanted, pushed them over. Otto sorted through them and then, with a silent snort of relief, found what he wanted. He tugged the doctor's sleeve and gestured to the pamphlet in his hand. The doctor snatched back his arm, irritated at being pawed by a prisoner, but Otto was insistent, holding out the pamphlet. The doctor took it and peered at the small book.

"A checkbook?" asked the doctor.

Otto nodded, wincing at the pain. He pointed to the name printed at the bottom: OTTO MOSES ABRAHAM GOLDBAUM.

"You?" asked the doctor.

"Yes," mouthed Otto.

"What's to stop me from taking this and writing my own checks, if that's what they are?"

Otto signaled for paper and, when it was given to him, began to write, hoping that the doctor believed that what he was writing was true, even if Otto harbored his own doubts:

The checks will travel to the Goldbaum Bank in Switzerland. Money knows no sides, Herr Doktor, even in war. Switzerland will send money to England, to Germany, to Russia. But the signature on the check must match the one held on file with the bank. You need not look disappointed, for I shall write you a check larger than you would dare to steal.

The doctor's eyes widened with interest and greed. "And in return you want . . . ?"

Otto began to write:

My friend and I are not to be separated. We are not to be beaten or starved. If he is sent to the hospital, then I am sent there too.

"You may not survive the trip," said the doctor.

Otto shrugged, indicating that this was his choice. He picked up the pen, turning the paper over:

You give the check into a bank, they cash it like any other, for a commission of course, and they will undertake to send it on to Switzerland. Money has no passport and every passport, Herr Doktor. It has little respect for borders. Money, like water, finds a way.

The doctor gave a nod and passed the checkbook to Otto, who filled out a page, signed it, and passed it back. The doctor read the numbers, his eyes widening. He threw his head back and laughed.

"You are crazy. Or crazy rich. I don't know which."

Still chuckling to himself, the doctor slid the check into his waistcoat pocket and signaled to a pair of soldiers smoking in the corner. "These two are for the hospital in Pinsk. Take care of them. I don't want to hear of injuries along the way."

Otto and Karl found themselves lifted onto stretchers and, with a thin blanket flung over their legs, loaded onto the back of an old cattle truck with a dozen wounded Russians, who eyed them with equal sympathy and suspicion. Although neither man voiced it, each was filled with a belief as fervent as any superstition that, so long as they remained together, somehow all would be well.

Lake Geneva, March

On the slopes edging the lake the snow receded, revealing hoards of golden primulas like thousands of scattered coins hidden among the browning grass.

Clement stood on the loggia of the villa in his rabbit-fur slippers and stared, unable to take all of it in at once. He knew that on the other side of the mountain range men fought and froze, and died of frostbite and starvation, but from the terrace of the Villa Gold the mountains were a white backdrop, a stage set to better show off the concert of primulas and the first pots of sentinel tulips in grenadier red.

At parties, the hosts were careful not to invite Germans and Austrians to dine on the same night as the English, French and Russians, although sometimes at the grand hotels or boating clubs they glimpsed each other, greeting each other with a cool nod. It was a different kind of war on this side of the mountains, one where the difficulties lay in tactful seating arrangements and invitational etiquette. Yet Clement knew that if he left Switzerland he might not be able to return, and sometimes he felt as if the entire country were a prison, however gilded. Mostly he endured a pleasant exile, admiring the varying effect of light on the lake while drinking French brandy and eating German ham.

One evening he was obliged to attend a champagne reception at the American embassy in Geneva. It was the night for the Allies. They knew perfectly well that the German ministers holidaying beside the lake had been invited the night before. Clement found himself collared by a bright-eyed young diplomat, full of his position and oozing optimism. He pressed a glass into Clement's hand and asked him in confidential tones what could be done to persuade the British government to agree to peace talks.

"The Germans consider Chancellor von Bethmann to be such a drip that if he enters into negotiations with the British, the folks at home would consider themselves lucky to hang on to Berlin," said the young American.

He smiled, flashing his white teeth like a debutante her legs, but watched Clement closely. Clement understood that this was an anecdote supposed to find its way back to Britain, to hint of favorable terms in any deal. The American was well fed and had sumptuous hair, and Clement felt conscious of his own thinning locks. He said with a sigh, "I'm afraid that however much President Wilson might wish the Europeans to behave and see sense, Wilson is not in fact a headmaster, and nations—like children—won't do what they are told, even if it is for the best."

Privately Clement knew that the British couldn't consider peace. Their position was far too poor to negotiate, and now there was even talk that the Russians were seeking a separate peace. All hope remained pinned on America's entering the war.

The young diplomat frowned, his effervescence momentarily flattened.

"You fellows are all the same: 'The stalemate's irrevocable. Nothing's ever gonna change.'"

"Except the weather," corrected Clement. "The snow is coming off the mountains. I heard the first boom today of a spring avalanche."

"And Zimmermann!" exclaimed the diplomat, pressing on regardless. "The German foreign minister. He's new. He's not one of the old guard. He's a self-made man, and not a von or a count."

"No," agreed Clement, wishing he could return to discussing the weather. "But sometimes those who have fought their way upstream then have to show that they belong. I fear that Herr Zimmermann isn't quite the radical you're hoping for in Washington."

"All you Europeans are as cynical as each other. It's one thing you and the Germans share."

"We share many things. Borders. People. Ambition. I'm afraid that is the problem."

"Well, I like Zimmermann," insisted the young man.

"So do I," replied Clement. "I hear he always drinks at least two quarts of Moselle with luncheon every day, and that is a quality to be admired in any man, regardless of his politics."

The following morning Zimmermann interrupted Clement's breakfast. Clement sat down to kaiser rolls (a delicacy that he relished, while worrying that his enjoyment was unpatriotic) with unsalted butter and apricot jam, marmalade being impossible to procure—a rare and irritating failure of the Goldbaums' capabilities under trying circumstances. He unfolded his newspaper. Zimmermann greeted him in the headlines of the *New York Times*, the *Times* and the *World*:

GERMANY SEEKS ALLIANCE AGAINST U.S.,
ASKS MEXICO TO JOIN.
SECRETARY ZIMMERMANN EMBROILED IN PLOT
TO GIVE AWAY TEXAS, ARIZONA AND NEW MEXICO.

In amazement, Clement read the details of the telegram. He wondered if it was true and, if it was, whether the Americans would believe it. He trotted upstairs to where Irena and Lara were breakfasting in bed, and showed Irena the newspaper. She read it in silence, then handed it back to him with a frown.

"Do you think it's true?" he asked softly, sitting on the edge of the bed.

Irena shrugged. "It doesn't matter. The American people won't believe it. They don't want it to be true. Whether he sent it or not, all Zimmermann has to do is deny it."

Clement dined out. He rarely lunched at his club, but he wanted to hear the chatter. The Americans were evenly spread between the Colony Club and the Mansion House. They preferred the bar at the Colony, but the steaks were better at the Mansion. He sat at the bar and ordered port and oysters for every American who came in. It was a forgery, said a prosperous gentleman with a monocle and a sense of entitlement. A preposterous document, obviously faked and planted by British agents. No such thing, refuted another, sucking on his cigar. Of course it's real! The whole country will demand war, and at last Mr. Wilson is in a position where he will have to give it to them. Pondering it all, Clement thanked them for their company, paid the bill and took a cab back to the villa.

In the evening, after Lara was tucked up into the double bed, Clement and Irena sipped brandies by the library fire.

"I think you're right," he said at last. He usually deferred to her in matters concerning human nature. As a superlative chess player, Irena had an instinct for motive. "The telegram is not the simple touch paper to make the Americans declare war, however much we might wish it so." He swirled his brandy so that it caught in the firelight, and for a moment it looked as if he held a glass of swooshing rubies. He continued, "In the modern world, the public is cynical. Convinced that everything is a conspiracy and that their government is out to dupe and manipulate its own people. They must be convinced it is authentic. No easy task."

Irena shrugged. "And, again, I tell you that all Zimmermann need do is say it isn't true."

And yet the following morning, when Zimmermann once more greeted Clement at breakfast, it was with not a denial but an admission.

"I cannot deny it. It is true," declared Zimmermann from the front pages of half a dozen newspapers.

Clement read the *New York Times* twice and, folding it carefully under his arm, retrieved a bottle of Krug '89 Private Cuvée, then carried them both upstairs to where Irena and Lara still slept. He kissed Irena awake, passed her the newspaper and opened the champagne, rousing Lara with a start. Irena poured a few drops into her milk.

"Three is a good age to learn to drink champagne," she said. "And this is the day to start."

Every pot, urn, vase and border brimmed with tulips—yellow, scarlet, hoary white and dipped in pink. In the afternoon, Lara padded through the gardens with Irena, picking up blooms battered by the wind, spearing bruised petals with a stick and gathering the fallen heads into a basket like dozens of smooth, oval eggs in every color. Behind the banks of tulips and the vivid expanse of green lawn, Lake Geneva glinted cold and blue, while behind it loomed the Alps, still spread with snow and piercing white. Clement watched as Lara squatted on plump haunches to inspect a bristled caterpillar.

A car glided up the driveway. Clement strolled over to intercept, sweating slightly, aware that he had put on weight. He must be thinner again for summer or the heat would be intolerable. He hesitated on the steps of the villa as the driver slid out and raced round to open the passenger door. He wondered briefly whether he ought to hurry inside to hide, and deny he was home—he had a profound dislike of visitors disturbing his little idyll.

He watched as Monsieur Abelard, the manager of the Swiss branch of the Goldbaum Bank, climbed out and stood, blinking, on the gravel. Clement considered him with dissatisfaction. He stepped forward and offered the older man his hand.

"Monsieur, what a delight. What can it be that lures you away from the bank? The pleasures of a bright afternoon, perhaps?"

Monsieur Abelard reached into his pocket and drew out a crumpled piece of paper and passed it to Clement, who looked at it, uncomprehending.

"What is it, monsieur?"

"A check, Mr. Goldbaum. From Russia."

Hampshire, April

———◆◇◆———

It seemed to Greta that the whole of England was waiting. The nation lay parched and brown, exhausted and withered as if from endless drought, but when President Wilson at last went before Congress with a message of war, it did not bring immediate respite, like the coming of rain. America might have joined the conflict, but her soldiers would first have to be trained and then be put onto ships to sail through the perilous Atlantic, where the monstrous U-boats lurked. The first expeditionary force was not expected in France until June.

In the summer before the war she had planted half an acre of milk parsley on the riverbanks, and as she walked out one morning, Greta was gladdened by the sight of several large swallowtail butterflies wheeling powerfully in the air, their wing tips curved like those of a real swallow, their intricate black-and-white coloring like miniature leaded church windows. Albert would have been ecstatic to witness such a display. Greta tried to put it into a letter, but then Celia cut open her head, jumping off a flowerpot onto the stone terrace, and the ward laundry had again run out of linen. The letter remained unwritten.

Lady Goldbaum visited most afternoons to read improving works to the mothers recovering from their lying-in. From time to time she gave lectures at the gardening school on the cultivation of orchids, but she complained to Greta that her talks were not nearly as well attended as those on the propagation of radishes and the planting of potato tubers. Tactfully, Greta explained that the women sought practical knowledge, and that they had little hope of obtaining employment in the sort of households with glasshouses stocked with rare plants. She suggested that Lady Goldbaum might prefer to spend her afternoons with the children, assisting Celia with her bug hotel.

Lady Goldbaum took the task seriously and had one of the estate carpenters build Celia a bug hotel that was a scale replica of the Ritz, complete with gilded fretwork and lights above the awning that flashed when Celia cranked a handle—to attract moths, or so Lady Goldbaum said. Each window of the hotel was a tiny burrow or hole for a bug, and the famous swing doors opened to reveal a box stuffed with hay. Lady Goldbaum liked to stroll through the Fontmell gardens with a walking stick, using it to point out any stray weeds and instructing Celia to pluck them out. She had a pair of small gardening gloves made for her granddaughter in the softest kid. Each week they were rubbed with beeswax to keep them supple. Celia thought her grandmother was a marvel. She admired the way that when Lady Goldbaum shouted, every gardener within earshot came running. She knew the name and history of every plant, and told of its journey to England like one of Robinson Crusoe's adventures. Celia liked it that everyone was a tiny bit frightened of her grandmother—everyone except her.

Greta watched her mother-in-law and daughter's relationship with equal pleasure and anguish. She knew how much her own mother longed to see Celia. The war had cheated the baroness of her granddaughter's childhood—she had not held her as a baby, or kissed the round bagels on her wrists. In the terms of war, it was one of the smaller crimes, but it was a theft nonetheless, and even when the war ended, those years could not be returned. She had sent via the Red Cross a single photograph of Celia holding Benjamin, but did not know whether the baroness had even received it. As for Otto—Greta tried not to think of him. She did not even know where to picture him—had he been sent east or west? Her only solace was that if he was dead, she must have heard.

Greta slipped into bed, exhausted from another day supervising the garden school and hospital, but found herself, as usual, unable to sleep. The fire in the room was too hot and the moon too bright. She opened the curtains and let the cold light flood the room. The cedar trees on the lawn cast moon shadows, the beaks of the crocuses black and gray like baby crows. She waited for sleep, trying not to think. There was a list of names to be pushed away. From the nursery above, she heard Benjamin mewing for a bottle, the soft opening of the door as one of the nursery maids hurried to him. She considered what it must be like for the mothers at the little Fontmell hospital when they returned home. They would have no maids to help with the nights, keep their houses or prepare their meals. If they had older children, they might help with the baby and the chores. Greta tried to picture Celia usefully tending to Benjamin, rather than surreptitiously pinching him in his pram. The thought was so unlikely that she laughed.

She was newly awakened to the rare privilege of her position and yet, however selfish and ungrateful it might have made her, she was not happy. She was lonely and discontented. It was different from the way she had felt in the first years of her marriage—then she had not known what happiness was possible, or the quiet satisfaction of true companionship. She and Albert had enjoyed it just long enough for Greta to understand what she had now lost. She was awake until dawn, watching as the moon retreated across the sky and then as dawn stretched rose-red fingers behind the river. She slid out of bed; tugged on her dress—buttoning it with difficulty herself—padded downstairs, pulling on her boots; and ventured out into the garden.

The moss gatherers waited in the kitchen gardens. They looked surprised to see her. Half a dozen women had assembled, before Withers and Miss Hathaway joined them. Miss Hathaway glanced at Greta, making no remark on her presence.

"Shall we?"

The women took a large basket in each hand and proceeded to follow Withers and Miss Hathaway out of the gardens into the estate beyond. They walked for half an hour until they reached the salt marshes. The air thrummed with birds; Greta observed the early-morning tussle of a pair of little terns over an elver, while all around them rose the cries of black-headed gulls, cormorants, redshanks and oystercatchers. The water lay in mirrored pools, untroubled by the tide, and everywhere there was the reek of sandy mud. Worm casings lay spooled in the shallows, while the light caught sea asters and a stray poppy wedged in the shingle. Greta licked her lips and tasted salt. The wind worked her hair free and it struck against her cheeks, knotting in her mouth and eyes. The birds fell silent for a moment as they passed by, and then started up again immediately. Across the salt marsh lay the expanse of the Solent, smooth from this distance, but there was the snap and wash of the waves. Through the early-morning haze she could just make out a smear of land that was the Isle of Wight.

All around her the women stooped and knelt, unfastening blunt knives from their pockets, and started to roll up lines of sphagnum moss. Greta watched for a moment and then copied them. Her dress and knees were soaked in an instant and she cut her finger on the knife, but she didn't mind. She placed the moss reverently in the basket, brushing away a furrowing insect. They were running out of cotton with the German blockade, and sphagnum moss was as absorbent as any sponge or swab. They collected more than they needed for the hospital, combing it free of insects and steaming it to clean it. The spare moss would be taken by train to the front for use as dressings. Greta thought that if she were injured, she would like to have her wounds packed with moss, earthy and green and sprayed with sea-water, a scrap of England's wild place strapped to her flesh.

The tide licked closer, and baskets full now, the women walked slowly back to Fontmell. Mostly they were tired and busy with their own thoughts, and Greta was grateful for their silence. They reached the edge of the gardens, and as they ambled back toward the driveway where the horse and trap waited to take the moss to the station, Greta noticed a telegraph boy waiting by the front steps. A sick feeling rose in her belly. He stepped forward.

"Mrs. Goldbaum?" he asked.

Greta nodded and took the envelope from him. The other women carefully averted their eyes as she tore it open. She read it twice and then looked up, half-dazed.

"My cousin Henri," she said. "He's escaped. The British have him. He's safe."

G reta wanted to share the good news. She raced up to the nursery and swept up into her arms a bewildered Celia, still pink with sleep and barefoot in her nightdress. Greta realized that she must have appeared like an apparition, with her dirty and damp-stained dress and mud-smeared cheeks. Nanny busied herself with the breakfast things and pretended to ignore the disruption to the sovereign routine. Greta confided the tidings about Henri in a flood of joyful tears and kisses.

"Is Cousin Henri real?" asked Celia, who was trying to establish things that were real (God, the tooth fairy, the kaiser) and those that were simply made up to frighten her and make her good (Old Nick, ghosts, the kaiser). She was undecided about fairies, and angels outside of the Torah. Angels, she concluded, were real only in the olden days, having been hunted to extinction like dodos, woolly mammoths and narwhals. For a week or two, she'd half-expected to see an angel stuffed and mounted among the stags and tiger skins at her grandparents' house.

"Yes, Henri is real," said Greta, half-amused, half-disappointed.

"I've never *sawed* him," said Celia with a shrug. "So I don't know."

She stared at her mother, absorbing the dirty dress, the lack of a hat, the snag of moss behind one ear.

"You been on a picnic without me," she reproached.

"No, darling, I went for a walk," said Greta quickly.

"Hmm," said Celia, eyeing her narrowly.

Nanny coughed, and Greta saw that she held Benjamin in her arms.

"Are you going to nurse him, madam, or shall I give him a little porridge for his breakfast?"

Greta settled in the nursing chair and fed Benjamin, stroking the fluffy down on his head. To her shame, she was relieved when he was finished and, after kissing him, handed him back to Nanny and hurried downstairs to dress. She needed to confide her news to someone who would share in her relief.

A quarter of an hour later Greta was walking up to Temple Court, too impatient even to wait for the car to be brought round. It was not yet nine, but as she cut across the rhododendron walks, the gardeners were already tending their charges. Cool, damp air swaddled the shrubs, and there were flowers popping from their buds in a spangled display of pink, crimson, orange and white. The gardeners were all either aged or terribly young. Come June, Lady Goldbaum had agreed to take on half a dozen of Greta's women gardeners, on the proviso that they did not wear trousers, but skirts of a proper length. Greta realized that only desperation must have driven Lady Goldbaum to consider such a drastic step; the estate and its gardens were a glorious tapestry that was starting to fray around the edges. As she strode along the paths, she glimpsed trails of cleavers knotting their way around the waxy leaves of the camellia, bindweed reaching up an unwashed statue of Aphrodite as if to stroke a nipple, while a profusion of the red spidery hearts of herb Robert were like an insect infestation along the gravel. Women gardeners, it appeared, were preferable to weeds.

She hurried up the steps, the great front doors opening to receive her before she had reached the top. The hall was swathed in its usual darkness, the curtains shrouding the treasures against the light. Two maids were busily arranging extravagant floral displays of palms and exotic lilies and forced roses. They bowed to Greta as she passed.

"I'm afraid Lady Goldbaum isn't yet receiving visitors," said the butler, with regret.

"Goodness, is Adelheid still in bed?" said Greta. "My father-in-law must be up."

"Indeed, Lord Goldbaum is at breakfast. Would you like me to lay you a place, madam?" asked Stanton.

Greta realized that she'd been busy all morning without so much as a slice of toast and was, as a consequence, extremely hungry. "Yes, please, Stanton. If you would. And some coffee."

A footman, the shortest and oldest Greta had ever seen at Temple Court, opened the door to the breakfast room.

"Mrs. Albert Goldbaum," he announced.

Lord Goldbaum looked up as she entered, crossing the room, his hands raised in welcome and distress.

"My dear, I am so sorry. I had hoped to tell you the news myself. I had not realized Clement had written to you also."

Greta stared at him in confusion. Lord Goldbaum held both her hands, and apparently uncertain of what to do, he kissed one and then the other.

"Your poor brother. He did the best thing he could, by writing a check. We at least know where he is, or where he was. The check was cashed at a bank near Rovno."

Greta took a step back and stared at her father-in-law with growing dread.

"I do not follow, Lord Goldbaum. I came here to talk to you about Henri."

Lord Goldbaum frowned and shook his head. "I don't know anything about Henri. No, my dear. Clement wrote to me with news about your brother." He hesitated.

"And? What does he say?"

"Otto has been captured by the Russians. He wrote a check out to a Russian doctor, so we gather that he is injured, but how badly—or anything else—we do not know."

Greta stood quite still, her joy curdling to horror. Lord Goldbaum surveyed her with watery blue eyes. He polished his spectacles on a silken cloth in his waistcoat pocket.

"But Otto isn't dead," she said, clutching at the shred of good news.

Lord Goldbaum spoke carefully. "He was certainly alive when he wrote the check in February. The signature matches the one held at the bank in Switzerland. There is no reason to think that anything . . ."—he reached for the right word—"*unfortunate* has happened since."

Greta felt sick and realized she was starting to sweat. Her heart beat in her ears. When she spoke, her voice sounded tight and strange, not quite hers.

"We must hope for more checks. It is our only way to know if he is alive," she said.

"Yes. It is the peculiar circumstance of war that people and goods are subject to borders, but money somehow finds its way through. We will watch for the money."

The door opened and Stanton entered, bearing a tray with a pot of fresh coffee. He set it on the sideboard and poured Greta a cup, placing it on the table beside her, along with jugs of milk and cream and bowls of sugar, one of cubed white, one of fine brown. She stared at them in confusion, momentarily unsure what she was supposed to do—what did it matter whether she had coffee with milk or cream or sugar? She closed her eyes and wished she could put out the lights across Europe, plunge the Continent into darkness.

There was nothing she could do. Everyone agreed there was nothing to be done, but Greta couldn't bear it. She paced the garden walks, deadheading living flowers, or read to the women recovering in their hospital beds, losing her place halfway through a paragraph.

Miss Hathaway took pity on her, suggesting that she prepare a box to be sent to Otto via the Red Cross.

"Will it reach him?" Greta asked helplessly.

Miss Hathaway blinked. "It won't if you don't send it."

Relieved to have a task, Greta set about ordering a hamper. Fortnum's prepared several especially to be sent to the trenches. Most of those were no good—designed to be preserved for only a day or two until reaching France, they contained sides of smoked salmon, apples and fruitcakes. She chose one with tins of foie gras, lobster bisque and caviar; jars of marmalade; half a pound of tea; half a pound of cocoa; and a box of shortbread cookies. When it arrived at Fontmell a few days later, Greta looked at it helplessly. She summoned Miss Hathaway.

"What am I allowed to put in a Red Cross parcel? What if it's all stolen?"

Miss Hathaway was silent for a minute, considering.

"Select a few tins, some tea. And let us include a few seeds. Books are permitted. We can slip a packet into the binding. If he's lucky, he'll be able to grow his own medicine box. Meadowsweet is an excellent painkiller and easy to grow. Lavender is an antiseptic; we'll include a little dried. He can use what there is, or try to grow some more. Arnica is good for swelling, and chamomile flowers will soothe his nerves."

Greta flushed with enthusiasm. "I shall write him a letter explaining carefully how to grow and dry each of them."

The two women sat in the library, with their packets of seeds spread on the table before them, while Greta wrote in English—hoping it would be viewed by the Russians with less hostility than German—instructions for tending and drying each plant. She knew as she wrote that it was a fantasy, but somehow as her hand moved across the page it became a shared game, like those of summers long ago, when for as long as they pretended, it was real. She did not know what else to write—she could not bear to write of her fears: that she worried he would die and the war would never end, but go on forever and swallow up the lives of both her children; that she would not see him again and he would never meet Benjamin or Celia. It was easier to write that feverfew grows best in the shade and must not be overwatered, that the chamomile flowers should be brewed in water that was not quite boiling.

Just before the parcel was sealed and given to the Red Cross, Greta slipped in one last packet of seeds—taken from the edelweiss she had been gathering in the Alps when war was declared. It was a tiny kernel of home—perhaps Otto could grow a seedling and it would comfort him.

New York, May

———◆⊰•⊱◆———

Albert hadn't realized how exhausted and dreary London had become until he walked through New York. He visited all the sites that his acquaintance said he had to: He toured the marvel of Grand Central Terminal, a cathedral dedicated to the new gods of modernity and engineering. He paid his respects to the Statue of Liberty, and dutifully admired the Brooklyn Bridge. Yet what he preferred to do was to walk the streets, anonymous and unregarded: a rare treat. The city was a garden of cherry blossoms. It sashayed on every branch, in every shade of pink. He dined with acquaintances and went to the theater when it would be rude to refuse, but he never quite understood the ribald exuberance of Broadway, and declined all invitations to meet the lady stars—he was wary of actresses, after what happened with Claire. He preferred to walk beneath the cherry-blossom trees. They reminded him of those in the vast glasshouses at Temple Court, forced to flower in winter so that his father could have cherries out of season. Here the trees bloomed in spring, and Albert felt an odd sense of relief at the rightness of it.

For the first month he stayed with Marcus Ullman at his mansion on the banks of the Hudson. It was a sprawling seventy-two-room palace of pink granite and white limestone, stuffed like a doll's house with paintings by Botticelli and Velázquez, and planted in the middle of a vast park. Ullman, charmed by Temple Court on a visit to England, had employed the Goldbaum family architect to create a similar French confection. Surveying it, Albert considered that the brief must have been very simple: in the style of the Goldbaum houses, but bigger, much bigger. Albert swam in the indoor pool each morning, waiting for the English valet to pass him a towel and a lemonade. All Ullman's staff were British; Marcus insisted upon it. He liked to be waited on by the former masters of empire. Sometimes Albert felt he was another of Ullman's staff—intended to amuse and to remind the millionaire that here was the scion of one of the richest families in Europe, but he, Marcus Ullman, was richer still.

Used to the relative simplicity of life at general staff headquarters, where it was comfortable rather than opulent, and to Greta's more modest mode of living at Fontmell, Albert realized he found Riverview oppressive. The priceless paintings were hung closely together to impress the viewer with their quantity, rather than allow one to admire a single picture. And, most disconcerting of all, Marcus had commissioned a dozen of the rooms to be copies of those he admired elsewhere. He slept in a perfect replica of the Sun King's bedchamber at Versailles, while the dining room was a facsimile of Albert's parents' dining salon at Temple Court. He had even obtained a series of original paintings by Watteau, and the walnut table was a precise replica of the one in their home. The sole difference was that the table, like the room itself, was larger. Marcus was unmarried, but Albert almost expected to find a clockwork version of his mother presiding over it all—the same but taller, louder.

With apologies, and hoping fervently not to cause offense, Albert withdrew to the relative anonymity and parsimony of the newly opened Plaza Hotel. While he missed the pleasure of his morning swim, he took solace in the privacy and simplicity of his new residence. He enjoyed early-morning walks through the park and along the city streets, admiring the American ingenuity that he glimpsed everywhere—from the road sweepers rigged with water sprinklers, to the advertisements on the back of the *New York Tribune* for a jaw contraption to prevent off-putting "mouth-breathing" and "drooping-chins." Albert was confident that he suffered from neither, but was nevertheless tempted. While in England they were struggling to import enough cotton, here in America every store window was stuffed with mannequins dressed in a haberdashery of outfits. Quite clearly, Americans needed to find new and inventive ways to spend the money that the British lavished upon them.

Some evenings Albert attended lectures at the American Museum of Natural History, which provided the only diversion from his task. He sat in the cool of the theater and listened with great attention to the "Creation of the Maned Wolves" diorama and "The Symbiotic Relationship Between Milkweed and the Monarch Butterfly." He preferred lectures upon nature to those upon man, feeling at present disillusioned with his own species, but to avoid a dinner party he attended the memorial lecture given in honor of a lady scientist, Mary Putnam Jacobi, on female fertility. In the cedar-paneled hall, Albert began to listen with the interest of a husband rather than a scientist. Mrs. Jacobi had been an expert on female ovulation, one of the first to insist that women were not like dogs and, unlike canines, were not fertile during menstruation. The present lecturer was not a woman (whether to Albert's regret or relief, he wasn't sure), but he quoted Mrs. Jacobi at length, and Albert found himself writing copious notes in his pocket diary:

"The woman buds as surely and incessantly as the plant."
And Mrs. Jacobi observes that ovulation is linked to raised
blood pressure, increased temperature and pulse.

Albert began to speculate whether he could persuade Greta to use science for a practical purpose. If she would allow him to take her temperature each morning and record her pulse, they could consider marital relations only on those days signaling ovulation was improbable. He sighed. He could not guarantee its accuracy and he thought it unlikely she would agree.

. . .

Marcus and Albert met every morning at the offices of the Ullman Bank to prepare for the offering of the loan. Albert recognized the same excitement in Marcus that he sensed in his father—Marcus was exhilarated to be involved in the floating of the biggest loan on Wall Street. Yet Albert sensed trouble almost immediately when, despite Marcus's assurances, they struggled to find other banks to partner with them and underwrite the loan.

"I expected the difficulties to be great, but not stupendous," said Albert, reaching in his pocket for the papery sycamore pod gathered on his last morning at home, and brushing it with his fingers like a charm.

Marcus Ullman grinned. "That's the fun! The more obstacles, the greater the challenge."

Seeing Albert was not reassured, Marcus reached an arm around his shoulders.

"I'll find another partner, my friend. You're blue. Homesick. You're coming with me to a party. That'll soon set you up."

Albert dared not refuse. Later that evening he found himself in a cab driving to Union Square. The driver pulled up several blocks away, unable to get any closer due to the volume of the crowd. Albert climbed out and walked the rest of the way, jostled by a ribald and enthusiastic throng. At the edge of Union Square he stopped. There, in the center of the park, stood a full-size battleship, dominating the entire square and surrounding blocks as though it had run aground, stranded amid the towering offices and apartment buildings. Its massive hull was painted gray and it was fitted out with all the equipment of a modern dreadnought: two cage masts, a conning tower and a funnel. Albert counted six wooden replicas of fourteen-inch guns housed in three twin turrets, and five anti-torpedo boat guns. At that moment the one-pound saluting guns fired, echoing around the square and reverberating off the surrounding buildings. The crowd cheered. Albert gazed up at the dreadnought, wedged between the city blocks. It lurked like the Ark, poised and ready for the Flood.

He pushed his way through the mass of people until he reached the low fence enclosing the ship. Two men stood beside the gate, keeping back the hordes. On seeing Albert in full evening dress, they opened it and ushered him in. Albert followed a new, beautifully attired crowd up the gangway and out onto the upper deck of the battleship. Her masts had been festooned with lights, and a military band played while sailors in blue and white carried trays of canapés, champagne and rum cocktails. Albert stood back from the throng. It was rare for him to be at a party knowing almost no one. The sailors in white moved like specters among guests awash with jewels. A pair of young women, speckled with diamonds, were entreating a sailor to teach them how to salute.

"That's a miserable face for a party," said Marcus Ullman, appearing at Albert's side and pressing a glass of whiskey into his hand. "Smile. Tell everyone the war's going swell, and let's see if we can't find ourselves another partner by the end of the night."

Albert sipped his whiskey and nodded. Marcus was right. All the money in New York was on the deck of the ship, cheering the launch of the USS *Recruit* and her mission to find a new navy. It was his duty as an Englishman to raise as much money as he could. Steeling himself, he allowed Marcus to steer him through the crowd, introducing him to men of industry: fishing and finance, steel and shipping, rubber and timber.

"Captain Goldbaum of the general staff of His Majesty's army," declared Marcus to everyone in earshot.

To his embarrassment, Albert found himself thanked vociferously by the men, and petted with great sympathy by the women, who all assumed that since he was no longer serving at the front he must have suffered some grotesque, hidden injury. He longed to admit that the most strenuous part of his war so far had been obtaining partridge and Brie for His Majesty's visit to headquarters in France. However, he was presently engaged in his most vital mission, and that required accepting with deferential reluctance the approbation of America's finest.

"No one wants to say no to a hero," whispered Marcus, after chiding him for dismissing the gratitude of one of the directors of the House of Morgan with too much vigor.

A headache born of humiliation began to pulse in Albert's left temple. Yet his pallor and the way he was forced to rub his head seemed only to reaffirm to his fellow guests that here before them was one of England's famed officers, his very soul damaged by the catastrophe of war. The ladies confided to Marcus that when the fund floated, they would of course buy stock and persuade their husbands likewise.

"Magnificent," whispered Marcus, guiding Albert to the next guests. "But they're small fry. We need a big fish."

He cast his eye about the room, his face flushed with the thrill of the chase. Looking at him, Albert saw that Marcus was experiencing the same pleasure of pursuit that he himself felt when striding through the fields with his butterfly net after some rare species of moth. Marcus touched Albert's elbow.

"Let me introduce you to Senator Morris. He has considerable influence with the Federal Reserve."

The senator, a large tanned man from New Mexico, greeted Marcus with exquisite politeness, if not warmth, and held out his hand to Albert. They shook. Albert and the senator eyed one another: the tall self-contained English Jew and the broad-shouldered senator, who was equally at ease in Congress as on his five-thousand-acre ranch; the two men belonged to the same species, but a different breed.

"Come, Senator, can't you persuade the fellows on the Federal Reserve Board to relax the regulations on foreign loans? Make all our lives a little easier. I mean, now that we're all on the same side, it's in all of our interests," said Marcus with a nudge and a smile full of bonhomie.

The senator grimaced as though his drink had turned sour. He looked at Albert as he answered, not Marcus. "I'd be perfectly content to relax 'em, friend. But it's in American interests, not the British. I want the American Federal Reserve to take the place of the Bank of England as the kingpin of finance."

Albert winced. "I appreciate your honesty, if not your sentiments, Senator."

The senator acknowledged him with a nod. "I have more honesty, which I think you'll like about as much." He turned to Marcus. "Leave me to talk to your friend for a minute, Marcus."

Marcus smiled and walked away, immediately greeting fellow guests.

Albert gestured for Senator Morris to continue.

"Marcus Ullman is kidding himself. Americans aren't gonna invest one billion of their hard-earned dollars into a foreign fund. They don't trust foreigners, or their money. You won't raise a billion dollars. Hell, I don't know if you'll do half a billion."

Albert felt his color rising. "Everyone has listened to us with the greatest sympathy."

The senator snorted. "Sympathy makes the door easy to open, but once inside, finance looks to hard facts. We don't like war bonds. They're risky. My sympathy means I'll gladly pour you a drink, but it doesn't mean I'm giving you my money."

The senator drained his glass and signaled to a sailor to bring him another.

"That's not true. I like you, Captain Goldbaum, and I appreciate your service. I will give you two thousand dollars for your fund, but that's charity, not investment. When I give to charity, I don't expect that money back; on an investment I want a return. If I lend you more than a few thousand dollars, I sure as hell want it back. America has lent you a tidy sum. We're going to want it back, and we're going to make damn sure that you pay your debts."

Albert started to run through the terms of the loan, but the senator held out his hand, halting him midflow.

"No, Captain Goldbaum. You are not listening. I'm telling you that America has entered your war because we have lent you so much money, we can't afford for you to lose and fail to repay us."

Albert shook his head in disbelief. "You had to declare war because of Zimmermann. The man offered your own state to Mexico as a spoil."

"That was quite something," said the senator, clenching his fists. "But make no mistake, Zimmermann was an excuse. Many of my colleagues disagree with me, but our decision to enter the war wasn't a moral one. It wasn't because of Zimmermann, or German U-boats murdering Americans, it was because of money. The object in having war, and preparing for war, is to make money."

Albert looked at him with profound distaste, but the senator shrugged.

"I am not saying it is a good or decent thing, only stating how it is. Human suffering and the sacrifice of human life are necessary, but Wall Street considers only the dollars and cents. We are going into war upon the command of gold."

Albert disagreed fervently with the senator, as did most Americans he knew. They were appalled by the senator's belief, and were adamant that this was a moral war, and yet the senator was certainly correct about one thing. The American public did not want to buy their foreign bonds. Marcus used all his influence to persuade the House of Morgan to come in as a partner, but beyond Wall Street the American people would not invest.

Albert and Marcus abandoned hope of raising one billion dollars. Marcus's ebullience began to ebb. Albert wired Simon Grenville and Admiral Hall and, with regret, informed them that the House of Goldbaum, together with its partners at the House of Morgan and the Bank of Ullman, would be willing to underwrite a loan for only half a billion dollars; they could not hope to sell any more to the American public. Lord Goldbaum wired Albert, urging him to contract an equal share of the profit and risk as the two great American banks, but for the first time in his life Albert ignored his father's instruction. He would protect his father's legacy and his family, even against Lord Goldbaum's orders. Humbled and with an unpleasant realization that he was a supplicant, one morning in the Bank of Ullman's palatial boardroom on Fifth Avenue he explained to Marcus and the directors of the House of Morgan that the House of Goldbaum could not underwrite a third share of the half billion dollars. If the bond was not fully subscribed, the House of Goldbaum would sink under the debt. Even in better times they could not contemplate such an amount. Albert did not look at the men's faces, but out of the window, where he glimpsed the last of the cherry blossoms like scrunched-up lace.

"So the House of Gold is made only of brass," said Marcus, a little cruelly.

Albert met his eye. "I will not risk more than the House can afford to lose."

He was newly awakened to humility. His bank was a force in England, a gale that trembled the golden leaves in the City of London, but here in America it produced barely a squall. We were kings of the castle, thought Albert, but we didn't notice that the island on which our castle sat was very small.

"Our power in Europe came from the alliance of the Houses across the Continent, but war has broken the union, and unable to draw on Berlin or Vienna, the London House's capacity is severely limited," said Albert.

The others listened with polite interest, but the facts were irrefutable. The House of Goldbaum could not afford its share.

Even if the war ended, Albert began to doubt whether the House of Goldbaum could rise to its former position. And even if it could, it would be dwarfed by the reach of the American banks, swollen larger still with British gold. Albert found himself wishing they had opened a New York House fifty years ago, but back then they had believed in both the eternal God and the everlasting dominance of Europe and the Old World. They had sealed their fate two generations ago.

The issue was presented during a sixty-day offering. Six large munitions manufacturers bought two hundred million dollars, but by the end of the summer nearly a hundred and fifty million dollars remained unsubscribed. Albert stopped sleeping at night, no longer tormented by visions of Greta's rejection but by the prospect of the vast liabilities to which the House of Goldbaum would still be exposed. Marcus invited him to dinner at the Riverview mansion, and Albert went on a hot August night, churning with self-disgust—he should have limited the family liability even further. They dined on foie gras and lemon sole stuffed with lobster, paired with a chilled pre-revolutionary Dom Pérignon, but Albert tasted nothing. It was as hot and airless as the dining room at home. He glanced around, dreading the moment when he would have to return to the original, smaller room in Temple Court and consider the disaster of the loan with his father. The disappointment was not merely personal; it spread outward, cancerous. Albert had failed the House of Goldbaum, which had failed the Bank of England and, in turn, England herself.

Albert looked up to see that Marcus was waiting for him to answer a question to which he had not listened.

"I'm terribly sorry, Marcus. Would you mind saying that again?"

"I asked how much of a loss can the Goldbaum Bank absorb at present?"

Albert sighed and considered. "Not more than two million. If we sell the unsubscribed bonds now at a discount, I am not entirely sure how the bank will manage the loss."

Albert was aware that Marcus was watching him closely.

"The Bank of Ullman will take upon itself the balance for future distribution," said Marcus levelly.

Albert's instinct was to decline the offer. He was too embarrassed to accept. It was to admit to his rival that they were beaten. Yet the

Bank of Ullman could absorb a temporary loss, and offer the bond again at a time when the market was more favorable. The House of Goldbaum could not.

"Thank you, I accept," said Albert.

Marcus raised a glass of champagne, and Albert joined him. As he drank, Albert tasted only defeat.

Rovno, Ukraine, September

—◆❯•❮◆—

Otto ran out of checks, so he started writing them on any scraps of paper he could find: envelopes, pages from his notepad, the wrapper of a tin of pilchards. Every two weeks he wrote out another and handed it to Dr. Pytor Makarovich, who placed it reverently inside his jacket pocket. Otto was taken aback at the efficiency with which the checks were cashed, although he did not admit to Karl that he had ever harbored doubts.

"It doesn't matter what I write it on," he explained to Karl. "A check isn't a particular piece of paper, but an agreement between the writer and his bank that it will pay the amount stated from his account, when the check is presented. I could inscribe it on the side of a cow and it would still be valid, as long as the Goldbaum Bank accepts it is my intention that the money be paid."

Otto spoke in a mixture of croaking whispers, signs and scribbled remarks. He wrote the increasingly expensive checks partly to secure notebooks to communicate, Karl being the only person who could decipher the hiss that Otto produced when he placed his hand over the hole in his throat. The bullet and scar tissue had quite destroyed his vocal cords. The rest of the money purchased more digestible food— most of the prisoners dined on Russian cabbage soup and black bread—and, most important of all, Karl's presence in the officers' ward. Otto argued as best he could that Karl was an officer, a junior ensign, no mere soldier to be put on the *teplushka* train to Siberia.

Since the overthrow of the tsar, the number of transportations had increased. The fact that they had been captured together helped Karl's case, but Dr. Pytor Makarovich made it quite clear to Otto that he understood they were lying. He, personally, didn't mind in the least, but his silence had a price. Otto added it to the fortnightly bill.

As officers, Otto and Karl were given the freedom to leave the ward and stroll around the gardens. The afternoons were pleasantly warm and the two men liked to sit on a bench beside the curve of the river and watch the gnats swirl above the surface of the water. They knew that if they followed the river, soon it would lead them to the front, which lurked upstream like some foul, despicable monster, its teeth snagged with blood and death. Friendships during war were as intense and fragile as eggshell, destroyed in a single moment. Otto's memories of so many things belonged peculiarly to him. For so long he had not met anyone who knew Greta, or who had walked through the orangery in the great house on Heugasse. He clung to Karl, the boy from Vienna.

Yet now the autumn colors were starting, and the leaves on the trees were turning to shades of crimson and honey. Russia might have been in the midst of a revolution, but this was something they knew rather than experienced. The portraits of the tsar had been ripped down from the hospital walls, and each evening the prisoners were no longer cajoled into reciting a prayer for the good health of the royal family, but only for the brilliant success of the Russian Empire. The hospital was an unlikely refuge. It might have lacked bandages, dressings, medicines and food, and had a paucity of doctors (Pytor Makarovich was one of the very few, and his greatest skill was in extracting money, not shrapnel), but here at least one was left in peace. But each day, as men improved, they were loaded onto the snaking *teplushka* trains and sent into Mother Russia. None came back. There were only whispers—hundreds of thousands of men, dressed solely in rags, dying in the snow as they built railway tracks; feverish heat in summer, and swarms of mosquitoes spreading malaria among the winter's survivors. The hospital was an island. War crackled on one side of the river, while the malevolent trains were always waiting at the platform on the opposite bank.

Otto and Karl understood this was stolen time. Sometimes each man wondered privately whether any of it was real. It was too serene, the days warm and the evenings mild. The rain came softly, stirring the branches of the trees so that the leaves shuddered and rustled like paper, while the birds woke them at dawn with melodious, unfamiliar song. They had found a private scrap of paradise. But there was another intrusion into the idyll that Otto could not ignore. He suspected he was dying. He refused to tell Karl, because if spoken aloud, it would spoil everything. Knowledge in this case was a rotten apple that would infect all the others.

Karl took pleasure in each moment. He did not worry that it could not last. He had lived for years as the Kanalrat, when he snatched each joy as he found it—he was good at living in the present tense. He guessed that Otto was dying, but he would not risk distressing his friend by telling him. He recognized the signs from earlier days—the suppurating wound, the slow shrinking of flesh; already Otto reached for Karl's arm when they walked together. In time, Otto would start to shuffle, and his skin would stretch tight and yellow across his skull. Or perhaps not; Karl held out hope. Otto was not like the men he had known before. He commanded all of them unthinkingly—Austrian, German, even the Russian guards did not insult him. Perhaps Otto Goldbaum could command death himself.

For now, the two men savored the afternoon sunlight cascading yellow and gold through the leaves, and watched as a fish, lithe and liquid, pierced the water's surface and jumped in a smooth arc, the light making its silver skin glint like metal.

"Let's pretend we're just two men fishing," said Karl.

"I could attempt to get us a rod and line," mouthed Otto, uncertain, but willing to try anything to please his friend.

Karl shook his head. "No. I couldn't face bludgeoning anything. I've had quite enough of death. Even that of a fish."

Otto laughed without making a sound. Karl was from another Vienna, but Vienna nonetheless. It was an inversion of his own city, one glimpsed in a blackened mirror.

"I told everyone in the hostels that my address was the Goldbaum Palace, or just beneath."

Otto smiled, having heard this before. "If only I'd known," he mouthed.

Karl gave a snort. "And what then? What would you have done? Invited me up for brandy and cigars?"

Otto did not reply. It was perfectly true; the Otto from before would have done nothing. War had raised Karl up and pulled Otto down, not quite to the sewer tunnels, but almost. It was only Otto's checkbook that kept them out.

"The palace always gave away the best food. Better than any of the soup kitchens. Especially after parties," added Karl, grinning with satisfaction at the recollection.

Otto nodded, gesturing for Karl to go on. He loved to hear anything about home, especially when their Viennas overlapped. It was such a relief to be stranded in the middle of White Russia with a fellow who had stepped through the golden gates to his house, even if it was to queue for bread rather than to dance.

"The last time I went, there was some fancy party in the palace. A wedding or some such. There were flaming torches and music. And I got a double portion. A pretty girl with plaits gave it to me."

Otto thought for a moment and then clapped his hands with sudden exuberance. "My sister's wedding party," he said, forgetting in his excitement to put his hand over the hole in his throat. "How remarkable that you were there! You remember it, too."

In that moment it did not matter that Karl remembered only standing in a line of hungry men and being handed two wedges of bread by a girl with plaits in her hair; he had been there. For Otto, it solidified his mirage of home. On that night, her last in Vienna, Greta had paddled in one of the ponds, and she had cajoled him into joining her. Perhaps at that very moment, just around the corner, Karl had been accepting his soup. It felt almost as if they were old friends who had known each other a long time, without somehow being aware of it. Otto was immensely comforted.

He was growing tired, but the warmth on his face was drowsy and pleasant. "And what would you like to learn today?" he signed.

Each afternoon he asked Karl the same question. He'd explained on their first trip to the bench that he knew only two subjects: astronomy and finance.

"Money," said Karl, as always. "What use are the stars to me? I used to live underground. I can manage just fine without them."

"Very well," mouthed Otto, amused. Taking out his notebook, he began to sketch diagrams to show the rise and fall of stocks, the right time to buy and sell. Karl listened with fierce acuity. Starting to tire, Otto wrote:

You have a head for figures. You're like me. Numbers make sense to you. It's a shame you won't try astronomy.

"I told you. Stars can't make me rich." Karl stretched out his legs and yawned. With rest and food, amazingly, his foot was healing. Otto had paid Pytor Makarovich to delay the amputation. They kept it bandaged, and Karl remembered to limp and groan, so no one suggested he was well enough to be loaded aboard the *teplushka* train and sent to Siberia and the lower depths of hell.

Otto glanced at Karl. The boy was starting to tan. In the sunshine the rough brown of his hair shone with a hint of gold. There were freckles across his nose and cheeks. Otto reached out and traced them with his finger.

"The Goldbaum constellation," he whispered. "The five sons sent out across Europe to find their fortunes."

"Does that grant me entry to the family?" asked Karl. "If I've got their stars on my face?"

Otto chuckled and shook his head.

"I keep telling you. Stars are bloody pointless."

Otto was exhausted and suddenly fell asleep, leaning heavily on Karl's shoulder. Karl remained quite still, listening to the whistle as Otto breathed. In an hour they would have to return for the daily meal. Karl dreaded mealtimes with a horror he hadn't thought possible. He had to watch while Otto soaked tiny pieces of bread in milk or gravy and attempted to swallow them without choking. Frequently they lodged in his throat and would come up on a sea of mucus and vomit. It was a triumph when Otto succeeded in eating an entire slice of soggy bread.

Karl looked at the sheet of figures and rehearsed Otto's lesson in his mind. He did like numbers, he decided. Numbers didn't give a shit who you were or who you had been. Much like Otto. Otto was his first great friend. Karl had had army pals and, before that, pals in the hostels and sewers, but those had been more like allegiances. Boys ganged up together for a few days or weeks to see if they could find better food, a better place to scavenge as a crew. One didn't talk beyond planning where to try for a meal in the morning, or who had seen the most ferocious, fattest rats. Otto wanted to know what he thought and felt about all sorts of things. Often Karl had no opinion. He made them up on the spot, not wanting to disappoint. In whispers, between gasps and coughs, Otto told him about his own world, a different Austria. It sounded nice. Maybe even nice enough to fight for. Maybe. Karl liked it best when Otto told him about his family, his sister, Greta. She sounded all right. She sounded as if she would have managed as a *Kanaltrotter*, and that remained the highest compliment Karl could bestow.

A little while later the dinner bell sounded. Otto didn't stir and

Karl had to wake him. They walked inside slowly, Otto leaning on his arm. Karl helped him to sit up in his bed, before climbing onto his own next to it. They watched as the nurses pushed a trolley around the ward. It held a bucket filled with thick soup and another with bread. Each man was given a bowl and two slices of bread. There would be nothing else, before coffee and bread in the morning. At Otto's bed the nurse paused, and pulled out a parcel from under the trolley.

"This came for you," she said in French.

"Thank you," answered Otto in Russian. His voice was barely a whisper, but the nurse understood the intent and smiled.

Otto ignored his bowl of soup and turned his attention to the Red Cross parcel. Karl came and sat on his bed, spooning his soup quickly, and carefully cleaning the bowl with the coarse rye bread.

"I've had worse meals in the archduke's army," he observed. "What's in it? Who sent it?"

Otto turned it over and saw, with a pang fierce enough to bring on a choking fit, his sister's handwriting. "*Sender: Mrs. Albert Goldbaum, Fontmell Abbey, Hampshire, England.*"

"I suppose it only got here because it's from England. They're the Russkis' allies, after all," said Karl.

The parcel had been opened already and thoroughly searched, the contents hastily repacked. The box was large, but mostly empty.

"They bloody steal everything," complained Karl. "Is there any-thing left?"

Otto pulled out a tin of Fortnum & Mason fish soup—clearly no one had fancied it enough to filch it. The gold-embossed label looked oddly out of place.

"Anything else?" asked Karl.

Otto searched the box and found, wedged at the bottom, a slim vol-ume of Anna Barbauld's poems. He glanced at it in confusion. He had no interest in poetry, and hadn't known Greta had, either. He felt a shiver of childish disappointment—what a careless choice to send. Then, as he examined it, he realized that beneath the binding was a letter and a packet. Greta had selected a book that she considered no one would bother to steal. He prized out the envelopes and opened them with fearful tenderness. Seeds spilled onto the white sheet, along with a handful of faded flowers. He sniffed them and inhaled the dry, herbal scent of an English summer. Otto held the letter to his breast. He couldn't bear to read it. There was nothing she could have written that wouldn't cut through him: he did not want a glimpse of Greta's life, for it had diverged so distinctly and painfully from his. He willed himself to look down:

Brew the chamomile flowers in water that is not quite boiling.

He laughed. It was perfect, of course it was. She had written him the only letter he could read and reread.

"What are those?" asked Karl, prodding the tiny brown seeds.

Otto glanced at the letter. "Edelweiss," he mouthed.

"Let's plant them by the bench," said Karl.

Otto shook his head, and reached for his pencil:

They need three months of frost to trigger germination. They want a Russian winter.

Otto looked at his friend and, for the first time in weeks, hoped he would live long enough to see Greta's edelweiss flower. He pictured the hospital wreathed in snow, transformed. There would still be soup. A winter here, with walls and a roof, would be better than one on the front. It might be cold, but as he lay shivering beneath his blanket he would think of the edelweiss seeds on the windowsill, slowly stratifying, poised for spring and white flowers.

The next morning Otto waited for Dr. Pytor Makarovich to collect his check. A little would need to be added, for the safe arrival of the Red Cross parcel. Otto guessed the doctor had checked the contents and helped himself to a few packages, but he would still expect payment for the soup and book. At midmorning another doctor appeared; he was thin with an untrimmed beard, more Cossack than surgeon. Otto had not seen him before. The doctor went first to Karl's bed, tore off the sheet and ordered a nurse to take off the bandage from his foot.

"It's healing. He's well enough to travel." He turned to Karl. "Get dressed, soldier."

"He's an officer," said Otto, but no sound came out. He put his finger over the hole in his throat.

"I'm an ensign," said Karl, remembering the lie.

The doctor hit him across the jaw and Karl fell back onto his pillow.

"You address me as 'sir,'" said the doctor evenly.

"I'm an ensign, sir, and Dr. Pytor Makarovich ordered rest. I am not to travel." There was a tremor in Karl's voice.

"Dr. Pytor Makarovich is gone," said the new doctor. "You prefer to have your foot amputated? I thought it was healing, but we can cut it off, if you like. Then you can stay."

Otto reached out and yanked the hem of the doctor's coat. He spun around, outraged at the impudence, and drew back his arm to slap the culprit, but on seeing Otto's yellow, stretched skin and the seeping, undressed wound on his throat, he hesitated.

"You can stay. I doubt you'll inconvenience us for long."

Otto reached for his pad. He began to scribble:

We had an arrangement with Pytor Makarovich. I am Otto
Goldbaum of the House of Goldbaum and I shall write you,
Herr Doktor, a large check. Large enough to keep your
children and wife in comfort for some time.

The doctor turned to Otto, his face creased with distaste.

"You bourgeoisie fucks think you can buy your way out of everything. Let's see this check, then."

Otto wrote out a sum on a piece of paper. His heart beat wildly, his thoughts swam indistinctly, dull with panic. His hand shook as he held the pen, and his signature was wobbly. It did not matter, he told himself; the bank would send the money—they would be much more concerned about his not receiving funds than about the risk of an imposter writing checks for trifling sums. He tapped the space he had left for the doctor's name. The doctor took the pen from him and filled it in. Otto felt a rush of relief, like a cool drink of water.

The doctor held up the paper for Otto to read. Instead of his name he had scrawled the word "Idiot." He tore the sheet into pieces and thrust them in Otto's face.

"Take this one, too," he snapped to an orderly. "He wants to stay with his friend."

The two men started to pull on clothes. Otto stumbled, exhausted from the effort of fastening his buttons. Karl, naked, caught him. The doctor turned and eyed Karl with disgust.

"A Jew. A dirty Jew," he exclaimed, pointing to Karl's exposed genitals.

He tugged Otto's trousers to his ankles and, seeing his circumcision, muttered an expletive.

"These are Jews, not officers," he said, swearing and spitting on the floor. "They get no privileges."

With trepidation, Otto remembered the Russian ambassador's words to Henri, on refusing him a visa. "We have Jews enough of our own."

Finally, dressed in tattered and mismatched uniforms salvaged from other prisoners, the two men stood to attention beside their beds. Karl's lip was stained with blood and had started to swell. They had already guessed where they were going. The *teplushka* train. But beyond that, no one could say.

North Atlantic, November

—◦◦◦—

Albert sailed for England, once again aboard P&O's *Wentworth*. They traveled in a convoy of nearly forty ships—merchant, passenger and two huge American troopships—escorted by a cruiser, six destroyers, five armed trawlers and a pair of torpedo boats. It was a tense voyage, but the passengers on board the *Wentworth* all displayed a false gaiety, as though by sipping gin cocktails and swaying unsteadily to swing, hammered out upon a baby grand, they could ward off disaster. Albert wanted none of it.

In the midst of the North Atlantic two of the passengers fell sick with typhoid. The bursar quickly had them quarantined. But to be safe, the captain banned dances and the piano. There was to be no unnecessary socializing, and meals were served in shifts to reduce the number of people gathering. Passengers were told the hours they could be out on deck, no more than ten or fifteen together at once. The rest of the time they were restricted to their cabins. Everyone except Albert complained vociferously. He was relieved.

The captain invited him to dine at his table most nights, but Albert couldn't fathom why. He had little conversation. Mostly he sipped a glass of burgundy and wondered silently how he would face his father. Finally, he asked why he was invited and the captain replied, "You are the quietest and most restful dinner companion about this ship. The only one not to complain."

Afterward, they became friends of a sort and the captain allowed him up onto the bridge most evenings after dinner. Albert liked the peace. The second officer rarely spoke, but sat reviewing the ship's log, while the steady tap of the wireless operator merged with the hypnotic rise and swell of the waves in the darkness. There was no other human sound, only the churning of the engines and the crack and splash of water against the metal hull. The ship's windows below were covered at night in heavy blackout material, and the bridge itself was lit with a single dim bulb, painted red, so it would not be seen out at sea. Albert could barely make out the other ships in the convoy; he knew only that they were there, hidden in the blackness. He stood and watched the sea, oddly soothed by the bloody glow from the lamp.

One of the typhoid sufferers recovered and was glimpsed in the dining room sipping beef broth. Albert watched as the other was quietly and unobtrusively tipped over the gunwale as the ship's chaplain murmured a prayer. The body slipped into the water, the splash of its entry lost in the churn of the wake. Albert observed it float for a moment, the linen wrappings pale against the black waves, and then it sank.

"A sad business for the family, for him to be buried at sea. But the risk of infection . . . ," said the captain, watching alongside him.

Albert struggled to feel sympathy for anyone else. He was too busy with his own melancholy thoughts. He longed for Greta. She had sent him the design for a special life jacket and urged him to wear it beneath his shirt. He'd had it made, but it chafed and hung, unworn, in his cabin. She wrote to him about the children, his parents and the fact that the bees were suffering from a sickness brought from the Isle of Wight, but she did not say that she had experienced a change of heart. She told him of her love, but did not say that she wanted him inside her. Albert began to wonder whether seeing her and being unable to touch her would be worse than not seeing her at all.

The specie room far beneath was empty on the return voyage, its glittering hoard safely deposited in American banks, drawing steady interest. Money is a magnet, and gathers more money to it, thought Albert. All the gold is in America and it calls all other gold to it, slowly, inexorably, across the Atlantic. He found himself thinking more and more of that empty room at the heart of the ship. The war would end, but what of the Old World would remain?

After dinner one evening Albert joined the captain on the bridge as usual. The captain pointed to a tiny bobbing shape before them. He handed Albert binoculars.

"HMS *Mimosa*. A Flower-class minesweeper. She's clearing our way." The captain glanced down at his hands and frowned, displeased. "I must fetch a clean pair of gloves from my room. You can stay and watch, if you like."

The captain left and Albert searched the sea for the ship. He blinked and rubbed his eyes and then, picking the binoculars up, once more focused on a small shadow, several hundred yards ahead, at the precise moment she exploded in a massive whorl of light. For a few moments he saw every ship in the convoy, silhouetted like shadows. Meteors of flame shot up into the sky before crashing into the sea, setting it ablaze in small pools of fire. A moment later another explosion rocked the *Wentworth*. Albert fell, tossed to the floor like a bag of rice, striking his head against the leg of a chair. Glass from the window rained down upon his back and covered the ground like hail pellets. He struggled to his feet, unsteady as a drunk, feeling the ship list horribly.

There was a mechanical scream from the engine room and a volley of flaming stars whizzed up into the sky like a macabre firework display. The second officer yelled to the wireless operator to signal SOS, but Albert saw that his cheeks had been sliced open by broken glass. The apparatus was smashed and perfectly useless. The captain returned, pointlessly clutching spotless white gloves. He reached for the voice tube to give verbal orders to the engine room, only to discover it was also broken. Albert watched with horror as the starboard propeller turned clear of the water. The ship was sinking, the captain could not communicate with the engine room and, with her propellers still turning, she was steadily forcing herself under the water.

Not waiting to hear the order to abandon ship, Albert lurched out of the bridge. His life jacket hung in his first-class cabin below. There was little chance of getting to a lifeboat. From a deck nearby came a scream, and Albert turned to see one of the nursemaids from the ship's nursery yelling for help. He ran. Babies had fallen from their cots and lay crying on the floor, surrounded by a smashed rocking horse and glowing coals from the nursery fire. Albert picked up a pair of infants and tucked them into a wicker Moses basket, already strapped with floats. Clutching the basket, he struggled back out onto the deck.

The ship now listed at a grotesque angle. The air was full of fire and shrieks. Steadily *Wentworth* cruised deeper and deeper under the waves, her engines dragging her to the bottom of the Atlantic. Black water rushed in roaring torrents over the sides. Albert clutched the edge of the bulwark, terrified that he would tip the babies out of their basket and into the sea. The waters licked closer. He unfastened a life ring and, sliding it over his head, slipped over the gunwale, the basket in his hand. The water was so cold it took his breath away; he gasped and blinked.

He kicked in panic, furious and rapid, unable to tell whether the thundering was his heart or the chop of the waves smacking against them. He forced himself to take long, slow breaths. He gave short, powerful kicks as he tried to propel himself, and the basket, further from the sinking ship. They must not be dragged under as it finally went down. Spray soaked the babies. At a little distance he paused, treading water. There was no sign of the ship. He could make out bundles in the dark. He called out desperately to a man nearby, only to realize as they drifted closer that he had been beseeching a suitcase for help. He could not tell how much time had passed, minutes or hours. He glanced at his watch, but it had misted up, stopped at the moment he had entered the water at a little after half past ten. The sky was dark and full of clouds, obscuring the stars and the light of the moon. There was no hint of dawn along the horizon. He tried talking to the babies to soothe them, but, breathless, he stopped. He could help them best by conserving his own strength. A nurse could comfort them later. If only it weren't so cold. If only their blankets weren't quite so wet. The infants wailed and then grew quiet. Albert's teeth chattered violently.

One of the babies whimpered and cried again, but the other stayed so quiet, Albert feared it had fallen out. He peered into the floating basket and saw, to his relief, that it was fast asleep, apparently soothed by the motion of the waves. He brushed his hand across its cold cheek. It did not stir, and Albert marveled at how an infant could sleep so peacefully at such a time.

He felt the tide begin to turn. For the first time he glimpsed a lifeboat and then another, but they drifted out of reach, never close enough to see him. He trod water, urging himself not to fall asleep. He understood it was terribly important that he stay awake. He started to recite his name and those of his family, a prayer against the dark and the cold, and the sumptuous pull of closing his eyes: *My name is Albert Haim Moses Goldbaum. My wife is Greta Margot Esther Goldbaum.* A shoal of fish floated past, bumping them, only for him to realize that they weren't fish, but the shoes of drowned passengers. At least he had an answer to his question. Even if Greta wouldn't let him kiss so much as her elbow, he knew beyond any doubt that he wanted to see her again.

He was so very cold and so very tired, and the story was all wrong. The Ark didn't sink in the Atlantic, and Moses was cast adrift upon the Nile. He stopped shivering and vaguely realized he was no longer cold. It took great effort to think. *I am Albert. My wife is Greta. I have two children. Celia is three and Benjamin is a baby.* It was terribly important that he remember. He gave a little kick, but his legs wouldn't move. *I am Albert. My wife is Greta. I have two children. Celia and a baby boy. His name is* ... Albert had been trying very hard to keep his chin above the water, but he couldn't remember why. He was so very tired. No one could blame him if he had a little sleep. *I am Albert. My wife is. I am. I am. I am.*

His eyes closed and he slid ever so gently beneath the surface.

Hampshire, November

❦

Greta sowed hundreds and hundreds of seeds in trays of compost. She could neither sleep nor eat. Nanny refused to let her walk Benjamin in his perambulator, objecting that she pushed it at such a frantic speed that she had broken off a wheel on a rut and, according to Nanny, caused him to suffer indigestion. But Greta couldn't walk slowly. She couldn't read or write letters or settle to anything. All she could do was rake out the sweetly rotting compost and push seed after seed into the pliant earth with her thumb.

Otto had not written a check since September, or certainly none had arrived. Before then, one had appeared at the bank in Switzerland every two weeks, reliable as a rabbi on his way to Friday prayers. If only Albert were here to share in her anxiety, but his ship was not expected to dock for another fortnight. She felt alone and untethered in her misery. Her earliest memory was of Otto, peering at her through the bars of her cot. Sometimes he would fetch slices of toast and poke them through to her, while she roared, obediently playing the lion. Otto who had quietly, unobtrusively devoted himself to rescuing her from muddles of her own creation.

Lord Goldbaum ventured out to the greenhouse in his attempt to console her. He talked while she placed tray after tray of smooth black earth on racks.

"There are a hundred reasons why the checks might have stopped," he said. "He might be too far from a bank for the recipient to cash them. The transport that took them might have been halted. The local bank may have decided no longer to cash them—despite our best efforts, it's possible the money did not always arrive."

"Or he might be dead," said Greta, not stopping her work.

"That is a possibility," Lord Goldbaum was forced to admit. "But it is only one of many possibilities."

She took his hand, vaguely aware that she was dirtying his pristine cuffs with soil. "It is kind to give me hope, but not false hope."

And then, a few days later, Albert was gone, too. No one said officially that he was dead, only missing with his ship. The *Wentworth* had been hit by a U-boat lurking close to an Atlantic minefield and the passenger list was published in the *Times*. How could both men be missing at once? How was she to bear such a thing? Greta kissed her children, instructing the nurses with some ferocity not to tell them or to treat them with extra kindness or pity.

She took turns to worry over each man. First Albert, then Otto. Then Albert again. She walked through her garden in the rain. She wore only a thin coat and in minutes she was soaked to the skin, but the cold was a relief. When she had arrived in England she was lonely, but she had always been so. She dutifully loved her parents, and of course there was Otto, but beyond these familial threads, there had been little that bound her. Now there was Albert, and her children. Her love for them was not a thread but a rope, muscular and visceral.

She knew Albert adored Celia. His daughter amused and exasperated him with her willfulness and cleverness. If he really was dead, would Celia remember him? At least Greta could tell her how her father felt about her, and Celia would know what she had lost. Greta tried to imagine telling Benjamin about Albert. Your father loved you, she would say, because that's what one does. But the love Albert felt for Benjamin was a reflex, an obligatory parental attachment. He hadn't had an opportunity for deeper love to unfurl.

"How am I to raise a boy alone?" Greta wondered aloud.

Benjamin was the heir to the bank and the dynasty, and it would fall to her to teach him all that meant. Benjamin would not understand for years, and soon grief and loss would become part of their childhood, an inhabitant of the nursery as familiar as the spinning globe.

There were tactful columns written about Lord Goldbaum's missing son, a scion lost at sea. The convoy remained in the Atlantic. He might yet be found. Greta sought out Lord Goldbaum. They nurtured each other's anxiety. She took him seedlings, which she lined up on his windowsills, squeezed in between eighteenth-century Kändler porcelain figurines. She picked up one of the parrots and hurled it to the floor and watched it shatter. He uttered no rebuke. What did it matter? It was a mere thing. A beautiful object that money could buy.

Lady Goldbaum refused to discuss it. Her son was not dead, merely missing. He had been lost before. He had often disappeared for hours as a child, walking for miles in his pursuit of a moth or beetle and not coming back until long after dark, when half the house had turned out to search for him. This was the same. He would come back. She'd learned not to worry.

Greta and Lord Goldbaum would not argue with her. Perhaps she was right. There was no knowing, and if not, then they were glad not to face her fears as well as their own. A mother grieving for her dead son—to look at such a loss straight on was like staring into the sun.

There was no more space in the potting sheds. Every shelf and workbench was covered in seed trays. Greta had not thought where they would all be planted out in spring. She could not think beyond this minute, this hour. The very thought that spring would come was an affront. Yet, indifferent and unyielding, the seasons turned. Gales blew down the last of the browning leaves and brought down one of Albert's oaks in the park. It lay upended like a great wounded thing, its filthy muddy roots reaching up into the sky and its branches splintered and smashed on the ground, the world topsy-turvy. She refused to have it cut down and sawn up for firewood. In her mind it was

Albert or Otto lying there. To remove the corpse was to admit, finally, that they were dead.

The endless uncertainty exhausted her, while the ache of missing Albert was a physical pain. She felt constantly as if she were about to get the flu, but it never came. Her joints ached and she sweated through the night. Sometimes in her dreams he was in her bed, both of them naked. She kissed him, pulling him toward her and whispering little pleas in his ear that he make love to her, but, laughing, he'd refuse and tease her with his fingertips, blow warm breath across her belly or slide down her body with the lightest ghost of a touch, until she thought she couldn't bear it any longer. Still, sometimes it was enough, and she'd wake up flooded with pleasure and pierced with sudden joy—he might be alive. Then, as the pleasure ebbed, she lay alone in her bed, filled with self-loathing for surrendering to hope. She told herself it would be kinder to give up, that hope only tormented her, but she could not. She knew she ought to cry. It was expected. Everyone watched her, waiting for her tears, but they would not come. She did not want to cry, but to scream until her throat hurt.

At dusk she walked down to the river and watched rain dimple the surface. The tide was low, and the river slunk through its channel, unable to fill the muddy banks. She picked up a pebble and cast it into the water, watching the ripples spill outward. We leave pebbles beside a grave, thought Greta, but these disappear and sink, because you are not dead yet. Neither of you is dead until I believe it, and I don't. She tried to utter a prayer, but it stuck in her throat like a fishbone. Besides, was it enough simply to ask God, to beseech him with wails and supplications that he listen? She did not need one prayer granted, but two. She wanted both Albert and Otto to come back to her. A tiny voice inside her head whispered, *If you could choose only one man to live, who would you save?*

Albert, came her answer, swiftly and unforced. She had children and they needed their father. It was not her choice, but theirs. She recognized this was a lie. *The truth is that I love Albert more.*

Greta's heart began to beat frantically. She had made an accidental deal with God: if Albert lived, and Otto died, then she had killed her brother with this bargain. She knew her thinking was half-mad, the ravings of dread and loss, but at that moment beside the gray river it seemed more real than anything else.

The sky was dark and bright at once, the moon rising amid the last rays of the sun. She longed for Albert, but remained unsure if she was tormented by desire for a dead man.

Teplushka *Train, Russia, November*

Otto lay on his bunk and looked out at the snow. It was a colorless beauty, infinite and cold. He would never leave this train; he was resigned to that. It ran day and night, rattling his dreams. Sometimes other carriages were attached, ones just like this—wooden boxcars with wooden bunks against the walls and a single metal stove in the middle. The men mostly crouched around the stove, greedy for heat, and fought for a bunk furthest from the unglazed windows. Not Otto. He no longer noticed the cold and he liked to see Russia, the acres of unbroken white, the smudged forests of black trees. Once, when the train stopped at night, he woke to see a wolf just outside the window, watching him unblinking with yellow eyes.

He wanted just to slide away into the darkness with the wolf, to disappear across the snow, and for a few days he refused to eat. But Karl was so upset that he relented. Now he ate, allowing the boy to spoon-feed him mouthfuls from the communal soup pot that was presented to them twice each day.

"We'll be at the camp soon," Karl whispered, trying to console himself more than Otto.

Otto nodded. They would never reach a camp. The train was the destination. It took the prisoners from place to place, from nowhere to nowhere, never stopping longer than was necessary to collect coal or wood or soup, or more prisoners. Some had been in a camp before, working in the fields in the summer, and they listened with reverence to their stories, but all ended the same way. Winter came and then snow. There was no grass to scythe, no seeds to sow, and they were loaded back onto the *teplushka* train.

Otto secreted his edelweiss seeds in a crack inside the window frame, where they were safe from the winds but wrapped in a cocoon of ice. Sometimes he dreamed it was him smothered in ice, but he could still hear them talking about him. "Can't understand how he's not dead yet. They won't notice. Let him stay frozen in his bunk, they'll still send soup for twelve." It always finished with Karl offering to fight any man who wouldn't shut up.

Karl climbed into the bunk beside him. They all had to share, and no one else wanted to be near Otto. His whistling throat unnerved them, and the hole in his neck was swelling shut. Sometimes his skin was so blue that even Otto thought he must be dead. Karl lay against him, his body as warm as bread from the oven.

"It's my fault. It's all my fault we're here," whispered Karl. "They hadn't noticed we were Jews."

Otto tutted in disagreement. Sooner or later they would have had to leave the hospital in any case.

"It's all right. I have a plan," said Karl. "Haven't you noticed that there are fewer guards now? No one seems to know who is in charge."

Otto shrugged. He had not noticed.

"We've been all the way north to Siberia, but we're heading south again now, toward European Russia. At one of the stations when we stop, we'll just disappear. No one will notice. I don't think they'll even care."

"What then?" signed Otto.

"We're going home."

Otto wanted to laugh, but Karl's expression was so serious that he dared not.

"We are. We're going home, even if we have to walk the whole way."

The carriages were usually kept locked, but the bolts were weak and not always drawn; mostly the guards relied on the fact that the prisoners had no desire to escape. They were surrounded by miles upon miles of frozen tundra.

There was a bang and the train door opened. Two men ventured out, returning with the bucket of soup.

"Cabbage," said one.

"And maggots," complained another, pointing to a wriggling creature.

"Nonsense," said the first. "They're *spätzle* noodles."

"See?" said Karl. "It'll be easy. We just go to get soup and don't come back."

Otto nodded. Sure, why not. It was a safe promise.

O ver the next few days, even Otto noticed that there were fewer and fewer guards. There were whispers of another revolution, but all that the men on the *teplushka* train knew was that it made longer and longer stops, sometimes at stations and sometimes simply halting on the line, with empty snowfields or forests stretching out forever. Then, on the third day, the soup arrived only once, instead of twice, and on the fourth, the stove ran out of wood. The train stopped in the middle of a vast boreal forest of larch, pine and spruce. And a guard came and opened the door, ordering them out.

"Go and fetch wood for your stoves. Find enough that you don't freeze your balls off tonight."

"What's to stop us escaping?" asked Karl.

The guard laughed. "Nothing. Be my guest. Sure, the wolves will get you. Or you'll die of hunger and cold. Either way, it saves me a good deal of trouble."

The men jumped down from the car, pulling thin jackets around their ears and stamping to keep warm. Otto lay on his bunk, too weak to get up. Karl slid his arm around him and, ignoring Otto's protestations, half-dragged him off the train. Snow lay in drifts, making tide marks high up the trunks of the trees. The train ruptured the stillness of the forest. The tracks stretched in both directions as far as Otto could see. Karl dragged him from the line of carriages, pulling him through the snow until they were a little distance away. He propped him against a spruce tree. It smelled pleasantly medicinal, and Otto rubbed the needles between his fingers. The needles were oily and almost blue in the cold light.

"This is our moment," said Karl, his eyes gleaming, a sheen of sweat on his top lip.

Otto smiled, still hoping that he was joking.

Karl reached into his pocket and placed something in Otto's hand. "Your edelweiss seeds," he said, taking them back again. "I'll only give them to you if you come with me."

Otto studied Karl. He still had the face of a boy, but thin and hardened. His eyes were the blue-green of the spruce. He reached out and took Karl's hand, placing his fingers over the hole in his throat, so that he could whisper.

"If you go, you will probably die. If I come with you, you certainly shall."

Karl tried to take back his hand, but Otto gripped it with surprising strength.

"Don't go home. Go to England. Take the edelweiss seeds. Plant them in spring, and when you reach England, give them to my sister. Lie to her. Tell her I didn't suffer."

Karl shook his head. "I won't go without you."

"This is a good place to die." Otto looked about him, admiring the snowcaps on the trees. Here and there the trunks were speckled with bright green moss. Above, the sky was a clear, unbroken blue. The train was hidden by the forest, and they could almost be alone. "Yes, I would very much like to die here with you," he whispered. "Please."

He took Karl's hands and placed one over his mouth and nose and the other over the hole in his throat. For a minute, Karl did not resist, and Otto felt the soft warmth of his skin. And then, revolted, Karl wrenched them away.

"I'm not going to murder you."

"It would be the kindest murder in the world."

Karl started to sob. Furious tears streaked his cheeks, and he shook his head, his hands clenched in fists by his sides.

"Then go," said Otto, exhausted. "Always look for Jews. They will help you."

Not bothering to wipe away his tears, Karl leaned forward and kissed his friend. Then, steeling himself with a shudder, he once again placed his hands over Otto's mouth, his nose and the wound on his throat. Otto closed his eyes and found himself struggling against Karl, flailing with all his strength against the death he wanted. Karl released him with a cry and sat back in the snow.

"I can't," he said. "I'm sorry, Otto, but I can't."

Otto patted his shoulders, unable to speak. His throat burned and he could hardly breathe through the swelling hole. He raised a hand and pointed to the wood. Karl stood, still hesitating, and then with one last look at Otto, he turned and ran.

Otto felt sweat trickle from his forehead and sting his eyes. He prayed the boy would live. He offered God his own life in exchange for that of the boy. He looked up at the sky, pierced by the trees. He smelled pine and spruce. Somewhere a bird sang. The train lurked behind the trees, waiting to swallow him back up. He would not let it. He picked up a spruce needle and placed it in the tear in his throat, then another and another, until the hole was sealed up. He coughed and kicked out, his legs scrabbling in the snow. Falling back, he looked up at the cloudless sky.

Hampshire, November

——◆>•<◆——

Watching the flakes drift lazily past the window of the East Gallery after luncheon, Greta was reminded viscerally of home. She remembered those afternoons as a child with Otto, sitting at the nursery window watching for the first flakes—the sheer thrill of knowing that in the morning when they woke the world would be transformed. Vienna was a city always waiting for winter. It managed it with such panache: the streets rang with the bells from horse-drawn sleighs, the lamps lit in the afternoon. With melancholy settling in her chest like a cough, Greta pulled on her coat and went outside for a walk, declining all offers of company. Everyone meant well, but she wanted only to be alone.

The low hedges of the parterre were dusted with snow, the leaves on the cyclamen curled and frosted. The statues in the fountains mimed their bathing rituals without water, the mechanisms seized with ice. She tramped her way out into the arboretum, walking between the vast conifer specimens, the branches dipped in snow. She looked up through the green of the trees at the heavy gray of the sky. She paused; the house was hidden behind the trees, and in the muffled hush, she could almost imagine herself in a forest somewhere far from here. Yet rising through the pines was the familiar ooze of Solent mud, the two worlds of snow-covered forest and the Fontmell River jammed up against each other. She had read how, in Japan, mourners are often haunted by their dead, but casting about among the blue-green of the spruce, Greta was aware only that she was alone.

"Why won't you haunt me?" she called. "Why did you both leave me?"

She was furious with them both. They had left her so thoroughly alone, bereft even of ghosts. She closed her eyes and took a breath, feeling the unhappiness swell in her chest. It lodged there like a solid bead. My grief is ordinary and commonplace, she reasoned. Half the women on the estate are red eyed from weeping, the streets are thick with widows. Yet the ubiquity of grief did nothing to lessen hers. It seemed crueler that the world did not stop to acknowledge the unfairness and horror of her double loss. Greta had to force herself to say their names: *Otto. Albert.* She always paused for a fraction of a second before saying them, like hesitating before popping a blister, anticipating the sharp prick of pain.

The snow was falling more thickly now, and she blinked it from her eyelashes. She left the cluster of trees and walked down to Lady Goldbaum's hothouses, illuminated among the snow like a fleet of glass ships in a storm. Palm trees and velvet orchids bloomed contentedly, oblivious to the weather outside. She passed the kitchen glasshouses, filled with fruit trees, and for a moment thought the roof must have broken, as the trees were tossed with snow. Then she realized that the cherry trees were covered not with snow, but with blossoms. Unable to resist, she opened the door and let herself inside. The air was thick with bees, their hum loud and insistent. Inside it was a warm spring day, and she felt like Persephone released from the Underworld. She unbuttoned her coat and paced the walkways between the trees. On the bark of a wild cherry presided a fat stag beetle. She bent down to examine its polished shell, the black feathered horns. The beetle's glossy case cracked open and Greta had an obscene glimpse of the lips of its wings beneath. For once she understood Albert's fascination—the creature did possess a repellent magnificence.

She pressed her forehead against the window, inhaling the floral scent of spring and watching the snow fall. Her reflection was pale in the glass. She looked thin and unhappy, hardly here at all. It took her a moment to realize that there was another face looking back at her. Had he heard her plea and, in tenderness, agreed to haunt her? Longing for someone is a hunger never sated, she supposed. It makes one imagine things that aren't there. I see Albert because I want to. Or he's dead, and I'm seeing a ghost that I don't believe in. She blinked, and sure enough, the face had gone.

She did not hear the door of the glasshouse open. The hand she felt on her arm a moment later did not seem ghostlike at all, but warm and solid and damp from the snow.

"Greta?"

Albert stood before her among the cherry trees. Thinner, his beard a little gray, but it was Albert. They stood for a minute, neither daring to touch the other in case this glorious phantasm disappeared. What did he say? Everything and nothing at all. He apologized for not sending a wire, but he wanted to tell her himself. He told her of the infant he had saved. He did not mention the one who was lost.

Greta tried to speak, but found she could not. She reached for his hand, and it was warm, the skin rough and chapped. She rubbed her fingertips across his knuckles.

She shook her head. He pulled her close, and she breathed in the smell of damp wool and journeys.

She pushed free from his arms and stepped back so that she could scrutinize him against the image she'd held in her imagination. The real flesh-and-blood Albert quickly painted over the other, ephemeral one. He was gray with fatigue, and now that she looked, she could see a deep cut beneath one eye. He looked older, sadder, but then so was she.

Her head was giddy, whether with relief or the damp heat of the glasshouse, she couldn't tell. She slipped her hand in his, and he squeezed it so hard she felt the bones in her fingers crack. They walked together among the orchard, listening to the purr of the bees and the steady patter of snow against the glass. Greta felt as if they were figurines inside the bubble of a child's snow globe.

She stood up on tiptoe to kiss him. His cheeks were rough and

unevenly shaven and grazed her skin. It made him more real. Eventually, reluctantly, she pulled away. Taking his hand, she rubbed it
against her cheek. She felt as if she had had a limb amputated, and
now awoke to find it stitched back on. "If I close my eyes, will you
disappear?"

Albert shook his head. Greta bit her lip to stop herself from crying.
If she started, she wasn't sure she would ever stop. They sat down on
the damp earth beneath a tree, the bruised and browning blossoms
catching like spoiled confetti in her hair. The ground itself was warm,
heated by a labyrinth of hot-water pipes. One day she would relearn
how to feel happiness. This was too raw, the relief reflexive and over-
whelming. She needed to learn to take Albert for granted again.

They lay back, hand in hand, and Greta gazed upward through the
lacework of blossoms and spinning flakes.

"We must go back to the house. Tell the others you're home," she
said.

"Not yet," said Albert. "Not yet."

In an hour, they would return, so that the relief at Albert's homecoming could be shared, champagne uncorked and tears of joy shed. A
quarter hour after that, the Goldbaum couriers would be dispatched,
telegrams sent, so that the message of Albert's survival could be spread
to the Houses across Europe: the son and heir to the British House of
Goldbaum lives. But for a little while at least, a man and a woman lay
in silence under the cherry trees. The Goldbaums lacked the power to
bring the war to an end, but they could still conjure spring amid the
snow.

Acknowledgments

There is an adage that it takes a village to raise a child, but I have also discovered that it takes a village to research a book when the author has two small children. Thanks to my mother, Carol, for both babysitting and being willing to come on research trips up and down the UK with baby in tow—armed with earplugs when all three generations were squeezed into a single room. My father, Clive, for his help on British history, and my father-in-law, Bernard, for reading many vintage financial articles so that we could discuss them together. My sister, Dr. Jo Garstang, for her knowledge on maternal and child mortality. Thanks to garden historian Christine Stones, who gave me both advice on the imaginary planning of Greta's garden schemes and access to her library. Thanks as always to my agent, Stan, and also to Catherine Oldfield at Tall Story Pictures.

The bibliography for this book is too long to list, but I must particularly thank Niall Ferguson for his remarkable books on banking and the financial history of the Rothschilds in his two-volume *The House of Rothschild*. Norman Stone's *The Eastern Front*, Miriam Rothschild's beautifully illustrated book, *The Rothschild Gardens*, and Richard J. Evans's *The Pursuit of Power: Europe 1815–1914* were also especially helpful.

I wouldn't have written this book without my editor and friend, Jocasta Hamilton. Her confidence and enthusiasm that I not only could, but should, write this book never wavered. She always knows when to wield the big red pen and when to send sugared almonds or to apply gin. I am hugely indebted to both Jocasta and to the lovely Tara Singh Carlson for all their patience and kindness while editing this novel—together they have undoubtedly helped me make this a much better book and for that I am incredibly grateful.

And almost last, but definitely not least, thanks to my husband and collaborator, David, who during the writing of this novel decided that he'd had enough of sharing a studio and wanted his own. I blame Greta. And lastly, thanks to my children—as far as they're concerned, I've been writing this book their whole lives. The tiny baby who was asleep in a Moses basket at my feet when I began is now running around with a dinosaur in each hand shouting, "Have you finished yet?" And yes, darling, now I have.